THE PROMISE OF LIGHTNING

JENNA WEATHERWAX

GW00645317

SMASH BEAR
·PUBLISHING·

First published in Great Britain in 2022 by SMASHBEAR PUBLISHING.

Office 6945, London, W1A 6US, United Kingdom

www.smashbearpublishing.com

Available as paperback and ebook.

ISBN: 978-1-8382561-8-0

To my mother,
Who never stopped believing in me.

1

MEETING APHRODITE

When I was a little girl, daydreaming of the moment I would find my soulmate, I imagined it would be like a fairytale. A prince or princess Charming would meet me in the bursting cherry orchards of my childhood home, fall madly in love with me and kiss me beneath a multicolored sunset. When *The End* approached, our souls would come back together, just as the gods intended. It would be the envy of every storybook. Nothing short of *Happily Ever After*.

My day was finally here, the moment that would inspire a hundred stories and memories, and it looked… awkward. The Ceremonial Building stood stark against the rainy fuzziness of a Michigan fall. The off-white marble columns sat like braces on stained teeth, marking the architecture as wincingly modern – though at least they had tried to create something ancient-inspired to honor the gods. The sun peeked through the mist of the sprinkling rain, and I could just make out the parking lot, empty aside from Ronan's car and a handful of others.

I rushed towards the front door, ignoring the rain attempting to slosh over my shoes and into my socks. In my mind's eye, I pictured the doors swinging open, accepting me into the warmth as the Priestesses gathered to ready me for what came next. Instead, I skidded to an abrupt stop, my face just inches away from smacking into the glass as the doors remained firmly closed. Jogging behind me to catch up, Ronan, my platonic soulmate, snorted out a laugh, and I sent him a mild glare over my shoulder. His soulmate, Sam, had been the one to initiate their Ceremony at this very same building almost two years ago now, so he was experiencing it all for the first time through me. Ronan grinned back at my soft glare.

"Someone's excited," he teased, covering his perfectly gelled hair with one hand to protect it from the rain that was still pelting us. Late summer had arrived with scattered showers almost every night, streams of gray rainwater snaked between the marble blocks on the path beneath my feet and the hydrangeas, sparsely growing next to the door, bowed their heads with the weight of the storm. Their edges were browning, in part from the terrible heat of the last month and now from the biting night chill. Ronan waved his free hand in front of the motion detector. He would be working with his own soulmate later today and was worried the rain would ruin his hair and leave him looking young. I smiled at how normal his thoughts were despite the enormity of the day.

The doors remained shut, and Ronan frowned as he began to wave a little more aggressively at the sensor with no change. He stared at it for a second, his confusion filtering through me and intertwining with my own as the worry continued to mount.

"What time is it?"

I pulled my phone out of my pocket and glanced at the screen, ignoring the sinking feeling beginning in my chest. "7:03."

"They're late," he sighed.

I had imagined this day a million times, but the reality was already proving itself to be a challenge. I had made a perfect breakfast and promptly spilled it all over the outfit I had so carefully laid out the night before. We had left early and still got caught in morning traffic, hitting every red light on the way and getting stuck behind a broken-down bus. By the time we had pulled up to the building, we were nearly late. And now, after all of that, we were stuck waiting outside.

Somewhere nearby, songbirds sang in the trees, oblivious to my world beginning to crumble around me. The sound of the highway around the corner was not a fitting soundtrack to one of the most important moments of my life. My lip wobbled, and I bit it harshly. Maybe it had been foolish to expect this to be like the movies. I pushed through my panic with a forced smile and said with fake cheer, "I'm sure they're just busy this morning! It's a great day to find your soulmate, after all."

Ronan knocked on the door with three firm motions, choosing to politely ignore the panic he must have felt swirling around inside my head. The glass bounced the sound back at us, but no one came. The rain picked up and a sharp wind began to pull at my hair. I pulled my backpack off and clutched it to my chest, hoping it protected the papers inside. The roof barely jutted out to allow for the ionic columns and did little to shelter us.

Still knocking, I finally took a deep breath and called loudly, "Hello? Anyone in there?"

There was no response. I took another breath, slightly shakier than the last, and prepared to speak again when a voice called out an apology. The doors slid open, and I caught my first glimpse of the interior. Warm brown walls, simple, elegant furniture and framed paintings of Aphrodite on every surface. She looked beautiful in every one – powerful with sharp, blue eyes. A simple wooden table stood in the entryway covered in pamphlets reading: *What Happens After Your Soulmate Ceremony?* and *Wear Your Bracelet! It's the law!* and *Consider a Career in the*

Department of Aphrodite! Application Inside. The sight of the goddess' image, of even her name, sent tingles down to my fingers and adrenaline coursed through my veins as I realized that this was really happening. It was finally my turn.

I had to stop myself from skipping over to the front desk. I forced myself to take in every detail; the flickering lights created graceful shadows, the warmth of the room was a comfort after the rain, and the rows of chairs to my right in the waiting area stood empty, waiting for their next occupant. I'd waited *years* for this day. All my life. All of my lives, probably.

The Priestess was young with a square jaw and dark eyebrows and was dressed in the official chiton of the Cult of Aphrodite. It was made of the lightest pink, like the inside of a seashell or the sandy beaches of Crete. Her hair curled in elaborate designs, but she wore only one piece of jewelry: a dove pendant on a leather chain – the mark of her patron goddess.

"Good morning." Her eyes sparkled, and her smile was big as she greeted us, and I felt any remaining tension leave my body. This was more like it. "Walk-in or appointment?"

"Appointment," I answered immediately and set my soggy backpack on the counter to unzip it. My hands shook with the nerves that had started to catch up to me, but I smiled brightly at her. The noise of the zipper was loud in the silent room, and a nervous flush swept through me as I pulled out my slightly damp, but still legible, paperwork. "It should be under Vanessa Reyes."

The Priestess picked up a clipboard and after a few seconds of searching, nodded and checked my name. "Sounds great, Vanessa. Let me just look at your paperwork – oh." Her face pulled into a small frown as she took in the rain-smudged forms. The expression was strange on her face. Cult of Aphrodite members were usually pretty smiley. "I'm not sure I can accept those. The gods might not—"

"Oh," I echoed, pulling them closer to me. My heart thudded, and my entire body stiffened. I felt my face tighten with the effort to hold back tears. After everything it took to get here, years of wanting and wishing and watching others get the soulmate love story of their dreams, my soul shook with the devastation of watching my own vanish into smoke. Shakily, I tried, "If you have another copy, I could—"

She shook her head. "I'm sorry, it'd take too long. You'll have to reschedule—"

"They're only wet because the doors didn't open on time," Ronan pointed out, holding eye contact with the Priestess. He reached out a hand and stopped me from putting the packet back into my backpack. "It's not her fault. Can we just see if the gods accept them and then, if not, we can go from there?"

A swell of relief washed over me as Ronan's hand rested comfortingly on mine. *I'm not alone. Everything will be fine.* I looked up at him gratefully as he stared down the Priestess, who looked vaguely startled like she wasn't used to being challenged so politely. Eventually, she nodded, and I placed the papers in her hands. I held my breath at the frown that crossed her face when she touched them, but my brow softened when the papers instantly disappeared from the outgoing mail shelf she'd placed them in. Godly magic.

"See?" Ronan said, bumping his shoulder into mine. "It'll all be okay."

I swallowed back the lingering panic, reaching out to squeeze his hand in thanks. Ronan nodded in acknowledgement, used to swooping in to save me. Though I was sure he'd rather have spent the early morning with his own soulmate, he was still at my side, protecting me. Regret filled me, followed quickly by a familiar longing. I wasn't sure I'd have the strength to leave my soulmate for my plat as often as he did. My desire for belonging felt like starvation in my stomach, growing hungrier the closer I came to finding my soulmate. The literal other half of my soul. My heart pounded, and the ghost of electricity sparked in my chest.

"Everything seems to be in order," the Priestess said, moving around the desk toward the door on the other side. "Vanessa, please follow me. Your platonic soulmate will have to stay out here."

I clasped Ronan's hands sharply at the Priestess' words, the reality of the moment hitting me. His soul, wrapped around my own and pulsing with comfort, stability, and love, was as familiar to me as my own. Platonic soulmates often met young, but we'd been at each other's sides since kindergarten, basically living at each other's houses when we were kids before moving in together for college. He was a part of every important moment of my life. With this Ceremony, everything would change. I'd have a new person, a new soul, to intertwine my own with. I was excited, beyond excited, but Ronan had been with me through every milestone in my life, and I wasn't sure how he would fit into this next stage.

A family with two crying children came through the front door and Ronan grimaced. "You're lucky I love you. Go and find your soulmate, Ness."

I squeezed his hand again, afraid to let go.

"I'm nervous," I admitted, shifting on my feet.

His blue eyes softened as he squeezed back and pulled away. "Go. You'll be fine."

The Priestess held the door open for me, and I tried not to shake as I stepped through. Cracks spun through the marble flooring and wallpaper. They blended with the faded design of elegant swooping doves and gold flowers to create a dizzying display that I could barely focus on as we moved towards the ritual room. Rosemary and sweet roses perfumed the air, and I knew it would linger in my hair and clothes long after I left, a tangible reminder of the next phase of my life. Aphrodite, even when she wasn't present, filled my head with headiness.

We stopped in front of a wide door, framed by olive wood with Ancient Greek carved into it, polished and nearly reflective with the shine of oil. I couldn't resist reaching out and touching it, and the words glowed gold as I heard them in my head: *Enter to Find Your Soul.*

The Priestess walked into the room before me, and my skin buzzed with the power she exuded, granted to her by Aphrodite herself as she prepared to act as a conduit for the gods. The door slipped shut behind us, untouched. Magic filled the air, a strange ozone smell, and the hair on the back of my neck pricked up. This was as close to a god as I'd ever come and my knees shook, instinct urging me to fall to my knees, to worship.

Other than the door, every inch of the room was marble, pearly white and cut with storm gray, with an elaborate altar set up on the far side. Almost as tall as me, the center of it was hollowed for a roaring fire, hot enough to feel even from the door. Above it was a small window on the ceiling where the gods could accept their tribute. An intricately carved olive-wood table sat with a handful of items: a miniature bottle of wine, something wrapped in plastic that I knew from my research to be a needle, and a box of tissues. Nothing unexpected.

An ancient bowl sat on the altar, just above the fire. Images decorated the side of the red clay – a goddess emerging from the waves of the Aegean, a god speaking from the clouds, announcing the Return of Soulmates and three strange, vaguely-human creatures.

A new image, one that I'd never seen before in all the lore, flickered between the familiar images: a goddess with sharp teeth, grinning at me. It disappeared so quickly, I wasn't sure if I had imagined it.

The Priestess settled now that all the items were gathered and began to recite the story that was already achingly familiar to me. I had thought of it every day of my life, dreaming and hoping and wishing that the soulmates in the storybooks were my own. The sparkling eyes, the lingering, electric touches, the love that eclipsed any pain or strife...

My mother had read me picture books of the Return of Soulmates as bedtime stories, romantic movies whispered its origins in loving songs and the gift from the gods was remembered in all wedding vows.

"At the beginning of time," she said and the air around her voice seemed to go quiet. Power built with each word, humming through the air until my heart began to pound. *Finally*, I thought, *finally.* "The original humans walked the earth. They were strange creatures – two heads, four legs, four arms – and Zeus feared their power. He split them with lightning, separating not only their bodies but their souls as well. When humanity's faith in the gods began to waver, he offered them a deal: if they promised to worship the Greek gods forever, he'd reunite each human with their original half, their soulmate. The humans accepted, and now it is your turn, Vanessa Reyes, to be reunited in this life with the rest of your soul."

The altar began to hum and the paintings on the bowl began to move through their cycles like a flipbook. The goddess emerged and drowned. The god spoke and was moved to silence. And the creatures, the original humans, Children of the Sun, Moon, and Earth, were split and reconnected.

"Led by the power and grace of Aphrodite and Lord Zeus, are you ready to begin?"

"I am."

The Priestess plucked something off the table – the bottle of wine, about the size of my palm. She broke the seal as she offered it to me.

"Drink," she commanded, "and praise Dionysus, who brings

joy to all mortals. Mix your blood with the wine, then pour the rest into the bowl and repeat after me."

Accepting the bottle from her hands, I crossed the room in only four steps and double-checked over my shoulder to make sure this was right. The Priestess nodded encouragingly, and I sipped from the bottle before pouring the sweet liquid into the bowl. The paintings paused their cycles, blinking up at me.

"I, Vanessa Reyes." She paused, waiting for me to repeat and smiled softly when I did. "Daughter of Demetria and Rafael Reyes, loyal servant of..." Like many college students, I had yet to choose a patron god to dedicate my life and career. My mother, as was the tradition for women in my family, chose Demeter to help with the fertility of the soil in the orchard. My father ran the marketing and financial side of the family business and so chose Hermes. He had been thrilled to help initiate Ronan last year. My platonic soulmate had chosen the clever god a few months ago after deciding he wanted to help more with the financial aspects of running the Laurel Leaf – the tattoo shop his soulmate Sam owned.

By default, all men and women were sorted into the Cult of Zeus and Hera, respectively, with anybody who didn't belong to those categories finding solace in the Cult of Dionysus.

"I, Vanessa Reyes, daughter of Demetria and Rafael Reyes, loyal servant of Hera, Queen of Olympus and Raiser of the Gods, offer a libation to smiling Aphrodite to find my romantic soulmate." Their website had an outline of the entire script, and I had read it so many times I could probably have recited it in my sleep.

The Priestess blinked, surprised. "Are you willing to offer your blood as well, to find the heart that pumps the same in its veins?"

"I am."

She pulled the small, plastic package from the table. Like I'd predicted, it contained a small hypodermic needle. I steeled my nerves. Of course, like any excited soulmate-seeker, I had looked up the process online before I arrived, but there was something about the blood that made my stomach roil.

She held out a hand for me to take. I gave it to her, discreetly wiping my palm on the skirt of my dress. Her hands were quick to take it, but there was tension in her shoulders, sweat collecting on her hairline and her eyes looked distant. Instinctively, my mouth opened to ask her if she was okay, then hesitated. What if I messed up the ritual by speaking out of turn? Before I could decide, she shook off whatever it was and pressed the needle into my thumb.

I gasped and my muscles jerked, trying to pull my hand back. The Priestess paid me little attention. My blood welled into a circle, and she dropped the needle into a trash can below the table, grabbing a napkin and pressing it to my skin. The stark red of my blood stained the corner of the napkin, and she made a little *hm* of satisfaction when she pulled it away.

"Oh, Great Goddess," she called into the room, throwing the bloodied material onto the altar. The light above us flickered, and the magic in the air crept across my skin once more, tightening it to somewhere between pleasure and pain. "If you accept the blood offering of Vanessa, burn it with the power of your divinity. Reunite her with her other heart and allow them to beat together. For our blood is all the blood of Great Zeus, King and Father of All."

We both stared at the napkin in silence.

Sleep hadn't come easily last night. With a curdled mix of excitement and nervousness churning through me, I had attempted to distract myself with more research. I had been awake until the fragile morning hours, scouring the internet for more details of the Ceremony. Of course, the gods had different plans for everyone, but some people reported jumping from how fast and high the flames had blazed for them. A sign of an easy relationship, it was said.

I blinked at the bowl containing all of my fragile hopes and dreams and waited. It certainly seemed to be taking a long time... maybe the people online had exaggerated. I glanced towards the Priestess and worry began to pull at me from the frown on her face.

The napkin didn't burn. Five seconds, ten, and then thirty passed. The Priestess' eyebrows were now fully scrunched together. She clenched her jaw and her eyes took on that distant look again. Another ten seconds passed, and I counted them with each of my inhalations. Nothing. I sent a panicked look towards the Priestess, but she still stared at the napkin as if she could make it burn through willpower alone.

"I don't..." she started, shaking her head and touching the pendant at her throat. "I don't know why it isn't— I've never seen— Vanessa, I'm *so* sorry."

Everything, my entire life up to this point, was supposed to lead me to this moment. To my soulmate. But the goddess had abandoned me. The air in the room grew heavier, pushing down on my shoulders until I felt like Atlas. Doomed and tragic. Alone.

I fell to my knees, ignoring the sharp pain of the marble cracking into my skin.

Please, Aphrodite, I prayed, worry constricting my throat until all I could do was plead internally. *This means – this means everything to me.* I felt as if I was standing at the precipice of a crossroads, like standing on a ledge and waiting to fall or be pushed. I closed my eyes and prayed to every god and goddess on Olympus and below. *I need the other half of my soul. I need to know what it's like to not be alone. To never be alone again. Please. I'll do anything.*

The Priestess' eyes rolled back in her head and her mouth opened a fraction as if on queue. Her body contorted, spine bent and mouth open to the sky as if something gripped her with such force her body could not contain it. Words poured from her, alien and strange, the sound harsh against my ears, and I flinched at the unexpected break in the silence. Rapid Ancient Greek, much too fast for me to translate or understand, cut the air. The smell of spices burning grew stronger amidst the cutting tang of magic, and I gagged as it coated my tongue and throat. The dove pendant around the Priestess' neck began to glow, her skin sizzling. My senses were full as one horror after another fought for my attention, the smell of burning flesh, the lingering taste of smoke on my tongue, the sight of my blood, unburned and unwelcome to the goddess.

Please, I prayed again. *What can I give?*

When the Priestess' body slumped to the ground at last, her eyes fluttered open to stare in confusion at the ceiling until she gasped, sitting bolt upright. Her dove necklace still glowed a bright silver in the darkness, fading fast. In front of us, the napkin caught alight, blazing brightly for a second before turning to dust an instant later. The magic still permeating the air seemed to laugh, as though it had been merely waiting for me to ask, to beg. The light flickered again and darkness fell as the magic slowly retreated.

"What did I say?" the Priestess demanded suddenly, her voice coming from within the shadows and making me jolt. Perhaps this was the closest she'd ever gotten to the goddess, to the magic that she'd dedicated her life to.

"I don't know," I admitted, running my mind back over the words she had spouted. Like all students, I had taken Ancient Greek and Latin throughout middle and elementary school, but it had been a year since I had even looked up vocab for Ancient Greek. The words *defender* and *gift* had been the only words I could catch. But even then I wasn't wholly sure I was remembering them correctly. The lights finally clicked back on and I scanned the Priestess' face anxiously. "Did it work? Did the goddess accept my offering?"

The Priestess smiled without conviction, clutching her

woven-leather belt to stop the shaking of her hands. Her shoulders straightened as she took a deep breath and it was as if she turned to marble in front of me, expressionless. "As far as I know, yes. She only burns what she wants." She glanced at the clock and pulled the door open for me with more force than necessary. "That is all that I and the goddess need from you. You should have your results in five to seven business days."

2

FORTUNE SMILES

y hands shook. The stench of burning flesh still clung to my skin as I exited the ritual room. I attempted a smile, but it withered quickly as I caught sight of my plat still sitting in the waiting room. The Priestess practically pushed me into Ronan's arms as she rushed away, murmuring errantly to herself. I watched her go, and Ronan watched me in turn. Clearing my throat, I called out, "Thank you!"

My only response was the slamming of a distant door.

"Hey," Ronan greeted me, smiling faintly. His concern brushed against my temples as he looked at me, no doubt noting my pale, sweaty face. His hands clasped my shoulders and I felt instantly grounded. "What happened in there? Are you okay?"

The napkin had burned. Aphrodite had accepted my offer. But nothing had happened how it was supposed to. The image in my mind of a perfect ceremony followed a week later by a perfect soulmate who would fulfill every fantasy of Prince or Princess Charming was fraying at the edges. Frustration built in the back of my throat. I leaned into Ronan and shook my head.

Still, his curiosity spread gentle and genuine against my mind, butting up against my worry and winning out, I had to answer truthfully. He would be able to tell if I didn't.

"I have no fucking idea."

The buzzing of the tattoo machine from the next room made me feel like I was coming out of my skin. I had one headphone in my left ear to help block out the noise, but the other had to remain clear in case the phone rang. I would have made a pretty lousy receptionist for the Laurel Leaf Tattoo Shop otherwise.

It had been a slow day, especially compared to the morning's excitement. The early fall rain had slowed the spur-of-the-moment customers somewhat. Everyone who had come in so far today had been pre-booked – two nose piercings and a few small Cult tattoos. Sam was finishing up with the last of those while Ronan was in the back office, working on the books and making sure that all the tips had been properly reported to the Cult of Hermes.

I sat with my favorite pink notebook open, the lined paper staring up at me, partly judgemental, partly apologetic. The only words written in my measured, even handwriting were: *Possible Volunteers For Society for Ethical Sacrifice Event.* Only Ronan's name was listed, followed by two question marks.

The Society for Ethical Sacrifice, abbreviated by almost every member as SES, was a multi-Cult student organization dedicated to reducing the number of blood sacrifices at Golden Valley State University, which sat in middle-of-nowhere Michigan, tucked amongst cornfields and apple orchards. A single bus route made the closest city, Golden Rapids, accessible for students, especially those who jumped between the bigger campus in the country and the smaller one in the middle of the city.

When the bells above the door chimed, I quickly checked the time to see it was just before three. I swiftly pulled up the appointment log before closing my notebook.

"Hi!" I greeted the guy walking in. My enthusiasm must have surprised him because his eyes grew wide as he approached the desk. He was beautiful, like a Renaissance painting or a statue of an ancient Anatolian king, with interesting features – sharp cheekbones, a full bottom lip, a pronounced nose, skin like bronze. Licking my dry lips, I called, "Welcome to Laurel Leaf Tattoo. How can I help you?"

"Uh, hi. Theodore Patras," he told me, nodding towards the computer on the desk, his dark curls falling into his eyes. His hair was long and tied back with a single piece of dark leather, save a few curls around his temples that were wet from the rain. His strong jaw looked sharp with the dark hair framing it, something between a beard and a shadow. There was a care to his features as if he was crafted by the gods to be the perfect gift for someone. I gave myself a stern mental shake. Beautiful people were common in this world blessed by the gods, but it made no sense to flirt with just anyone when my soulmate results were on the way.

He brushed his damp curls back from his face and tapped the edge of the desk, a quick rhythm that immediately told me he was in the Cult of Apollo. "Theo. I have a consultation. With Sam. At 3:00?"

I confirmed the appointment. "Okay, cool. Sam will be ready in a moment, so you can have a seat over there if you want. Can I get you anything? Water? Coffee?"

A look of relief crossed his face. "Coffee, please."

I laughed quietly. I didn't drink the stuff, but after Ronan met Sam, he was practically addicted to the strong-smelling drink. "You got it. Cream? Sugar?" He shook his head, and I filled the compostable cup to the brim. Our hands brushed lightly as I handed it to him and the touch sent a hum through me, oddly like the buzzing of the tattoo machine. He frowned as if he felt it too, but he accepted the drink without saying anything and sat back on the black leather couches in the waiting area.

I went back to my notebook, finishing what I had been writing before he came in. As a new member of the SES, I was expected to be at the event, but getting people from outside the club to attend had been a Herculean task. We'd been killing bulls for the gods since the Bronze Age and no one wanted to change. Traditions were hard to break. Changing your mind about something you thought you knew was almost impossible.

From the waiting area couch, Theo's voice rang out, "Hey, do I know you?"

I blinked at him for a few seconds. "Er, do you?"

"I think you're in my Soulmate 101 class," he explained with a tilt to his head like I was a puzzle he was trying to figure out. My cheeks reddened at the intensity of his gaze. "Professor Lux on Mondays and Wednesdays? You sit by the guy with the red backpack?"

He was talking about Ronan. That very backpack was sitting by my feet under the desk. "Yeah, I'm in her class." I tried to picture the layout of the room, but the semester had only just started, and frankly, I didn't recognize him. I smiled at him anyway. "Funny running into you here. How do you like the class so far?"

Theo rolled his eyes, swallowing his sip of coffee. "I think it's kind of pointless to make us take a class on something we already know everything about. They've been cramming soulmates down our throats since kindergarten."

"Oh, I don't mind. I love learning about it." I shrugged as if it wasn't the very thing I'd been obsessed over since I was old enough to learn about soulmates. He wasn't wearing a gold bracelet, so I assumed he was part of the group that didn't believe in how powerful soulmate bonds were. An ever-increasing percentage of people waited until they were twenty-four to find out who their soulmate was, which was the legal maximum age. After that point, the cupids would drag you, kicking and screaming, to the nearest Ceremonial Building.

And Theo, apparently, was going to wait until he absolutely had to. No point in arguing. He'd know different eventually. I glanced back at my notebook. Try as I might, the names on the list weren't multiplying through divine intervention, despite how much I'd prayed to Hera.

Ronan always teased me for having a face incapable of lying. He said every emotion I felt was telegraphed in the pout of my lip, the scrunching of my eyebrows and the crinkling of my nose. And whatever I was feeling now – my disagreement with Theo's anti-soulmate ideas, the dismissal of his critique of the class – must have shown because Theo frowned. "I just mean that everything in the world talks about romantic soul-mates. Movies, songs, books, it's all about finding them. I just don't see why we have to pay for a class to teach us what we see around us every day."

Because they're lovely, I wanted to say. *Because they're filled with pretty people and happy endings and sweet music and shades of pink. Because what's the harm in something that makes me feel good? Because I've been ready to meet my soulmate since the day I learned about them; since the day I looked across my dining room table and saw my parents smile at each other with a devotion that could only be magic.*

But he was my classmate and, more importantly, Sam's customer, so I tried to even out my expression and said, "That's true."

Three lines appeared between his eyebrows as he frowned and we fell back into a lengthy period of silence, broken only

18

when Sam, Ronan and the "Dionysus Bro" came out of the back room.

The plastic wrap covering the tattoo peeked out from under the guy's collar and he looked a little green. I told him the price and, with a shaking hand, he paid me. He tipped decently though and left with a wink in my direction after a quick reminder from Sam to buy healing cream. He'd be back, for sure.

Putting the money away, I said to Sam, "This is Theo. Your three o'clock."

Theo stood and Sam offered him a tattooed hand. "Hey, man. Come on back."

Ronan plunked down on the chair beside me and leaned against me for a second. Establishing contact was important for plats, especially ones that relied so much on emotional support like Ronan and me. It helped to be reminded that we could ask for physical comfort, too.

"Hey, kid," he greeted me, butting me softly on the shoulder with his forehead. He was a few weeks younger than me, a fact he often conveniently forgot. For years, I was a few inches taller than Ronan, and then, sometime in high school, he shot up seven inches and now towered over my small frame. Sam was even taller and the top of my head was often his favorite place to rest his elbow. I liked to huff and complain, but I didn't mind. Not really.

"Hey," I said, leaning my head against his for a second. "How was that session?"

"I thought he was going to barf, for sure," he said, reaching to grab a candy from the bowl for customers. He unwrapped it with deft fingers, popping it into his mouth. "But Dionysus must've had his back because he held it in. Anything interesting happen out here?"

We dissolved into chatter, and when Sam and Theo came back out, I realized again how fast time could move with a platonic soulmate. My list looked up at me, empty and sad, and I closed my notebook with a small huff.

"How'd it go?" I asked them, smiling at Sam. He winked at me, walking around the desk to place a kiss on Ronan's cheek. He kissed the top of my head too, and I got a closer view of the beautifully written tattoo on his forearm. It was the Latin translation of the Return of Soulmates speech that Zeus gave thousands of years ago. Next to it was Ronan's full name, inked in the same blue as his eyes. Sam's own plat claimed a tattoo on his other arm, and his bicep was covered in an image of Artemis dragging the moon into the sky. I'd never met Sam's plat. Apparently, they were off traveling the world with their soulmate in search of inner peace or something, but I knew from Ronan that they spoke often.

"Good," Sam answered. "I think we're set to make another consultation appointment. I'll have a few sketches ready to go using the drawings you brought, Theo, and then we can agree on a final design."

Theo stood on the other side, his face neutral as he looked down at me. His shoulders were broad under his dark brown leather jacket. He stuffed his hands into the pockets as my gaze lifted to meet his. "Would this time next week work? I'm pretty busy, but I can take more time off from work if I need to."

I looked at the schedule and nodded. "Yeah, that should be fine. If you need to reschedule, let us know as soon as possible, okay?" I smiled up at him, clicking the pen in my hand. "Can I get anything else for you?"

There was a pause again as he seemed to consider the question with more depth than it really warranted, his head tilted once more. Ronan raised one eyebrow at him, and in my head, his emotions flickered from bored-happy to curious-protective. I continued to smile up at Theo, and finally, he released a breath.

"Your phone number?" he asked, his face just as neutral before, but his eyes softer.

I was too taken aback to say anything at first, and next to me, Ronan froze. I could feel his protectiveness swelling; the emotion brushed against my mind, asking me if I wanted him to get involved. I pushed a calming wave at him. "Um, sorry, but I'm waiting for my soulmate results to come in."

Theo swallowed and smiled a little. It was crooked, revealing imperfect, white teeth and laugh-lines around his eyes. It immediately made him more beautiful. He rubbed the stubble on his square jaw. "Worth a try, right? Thanks. I'll see you guys in class tomorrow. Thanks, Sam."

The doorbell chimed as he left and Sam laughed. "What was that about?"

Ronan answered for me, "I don't know, but he was certainly something to look at, huh?"

Sam, who was well over six feet tall with impressive muscles covering his entire body, snorted, not jealous in the least. He bumped his shoulder into mine. "So is Vanessa, apparently."

It was pointless to feel proud of that. My soulmate would love me regardless of how I looked, but it was nice to know that someone found me pretty. I smoothed down my skirt and adjusted the tall socks I was wearing, sitting up straighter. I'd give myself a few moments of pride, I decided. Time to admire my own brown eyes and long, curly hair and the way my eyeliner flicked out into perfect wings. It wasn't vanity to admire the craftsmanship of the gods.

"But class is going to be awkward now." Ronan laughed and I deflated.

"Hey, what are the chances you actually have to interact with him again?" Sam asked, laughing as the next customer came in from the rain. "The Fates can't be that cruel."

Outside, lightning struck the sky.

3

A GROUP PROJECT

"Today's class," Professor Lux said, standing at the podium in six-inch heels and the sleekest blazer I had ever seen, "will be concentrating on the Return of Soulmates, as it's written by the Romans. Now, according to the reading, how did the world find out about the gods?"

The guy in front of me raised his hand. This was only the third class for our Soulmate 101 course, and I was only eighty percent sure his name was Alexander. He was easily the best-looking man in our class with his golden hair, straight nose and classically high cheekbones... with the possible exception of Theo, who sat silently in the corner with his hood up. Alexander never failed to answer a single question Lux asked, and I was pretty sure he thought himself the local expert on soulmates. His left wrist was bare, and I couldn't help but wonder what kind of person would end up as his soulmate. Would they be dark and brooding, like how opposites attract? Or would they be someone as excitable and genuine as he was? Or somewhere in between?

"Humanity was messing everything up," Alexander

answered, prompting Ronan to roll his eyes beside me. I tried not to snort. He was so overeager and blond that he reminded me of a Golden Retriever. I mean, I *loved* learning about soulmates, but he was too much even for me. "They threatened to stop worshiping the gods, so the gods came out of retirement and announced their presence to us. They were worried about humanity's reaction, though, so they gave us our soulmates back."

Lux reminded me of a fox with her ginger hair and clever, sharp eyes. She was young for a tenured professor, somewhere in her mid-thirties, if I had to guess, looking like she belonged in a boardroom more than a classroom. She nodded and asked, "And when was this?"

"About 5,000 years ago," he answered, not even bothering to look at his notes. I could see he was grinning – excited or arrogant, I wasn't sure – and the childish part of my brain begged me to kick the back of his chair to see if that unfaltering smile ever left his face. I was almost always the one who answered questions in class, especially about soulmates, but I couldn't seem to even open my mouth before Alexander was blurting things out eagerly.

"And why do you think the gods feared humanity's reaction?" Lux prompted, aiming the question at the class as a whole. A few more people raised their hands and a smattering of chatter broke out as people began to discuss the gods' potential intentions. I listened eagerly, jotting down all their arguments, even Alexander's – though he'd taken twice as long to voice his opinion than everyone else and likely would have carried on for longer if Lux hadn't called on someone else.

Lux clapped her hands and the chatter died away. "Alright, that's enough discussion. If you could all please stand, I'm going to assign you to a group."

I darted a nervous look Ronan's way. Assigned groups were

hell. I hated not being able to choose, though I was often too hesitant to speak up anyway. I just knew I would inevitably get stuck with people who wouldn't do the work, and I'd end up picking up their slack. Lux separated the platonic soulmates into different groups, causing a few people to groan and my hands to break out in a clammy sweat.

"Come now," Lux urged us, dragging a desk over to a group of three. "I know you're all here to fulfill your gen-ed requirements, but think of this as a chance to meet new people. Who knows? Maybe you'll make a new friend. Okay, Ronan, you can join Eliza and Tori and Vanessa…? Ah, yes, Alexander and—"

She paused and looked about to see who had yet to be grouped. The chatter rose high again as people began to settle into their new groups but – there! I let a quiet groan slide out. Theo sat at the back of the classroom, looking like he wished Gaea would swallow him whole before he had to participate in whatever we were about to do. I remembered what he said about the class at the Laurel Leaf, and I knew before Lux spoke what was about to happen.

"—Theo, too. Come on, everyone, put your desks together."

Fucking called it.

We moved the desks, and just like that, I was wedged between Alexander and Theo. Lux clicked her way back to the podium, looking satisfied as she peered out over us. "Okay, so these are going to be your groups for the semester. Each of the groups is responsible for a presentation about how a god is involved with the soulmate process. Twelve groups, twelve gods, got it? Here, pass these papers around. These outline what's expected of you."

Someone handed Alexander the stack of papers, and he dealt them to us like cards before passing them to the next group. I looked it over, ignoring the dread curdling in my stomach. In the description of the project at the top of the paper, the words *"80% OF FINAL GRADE"* were in bold, and I barely stopped myself from smacking my head against the desk.

Theo seemed to be in the same frame of mind, reading it over. His neutral face went from mildly displeased to genuinely offended by how much work this gen-ed class was going to require. He sighed and pushed his hair from his forehead. My eyes lingered on the pale purple shadows under his eyes before falling back to his bare wrist. He hadn't seemed so tired at the Laurel Leaf. Whatever was troubling him would likely fade away once he found his own soulmate. A burden shared was a burden halved, after all. His obvious fatigue still did little to distract from the dark beauty of his face; he was a mosaic of cutting angles and dark hair with a softness to his mouth and eyes that filled me with an inexplicable warmth. My fingers tingled with the desire to touch him, to see if his dark bronze skin felt as soft as it looked.

Alexander, on the other hand, was grinning and already circling things with his red pen. His blond hair seemed to produce its own light, and the wide grin on his face shone with sincerity and eagerness.

"Okay, one person from the group is going to pick the name of a god out of the bucket," Lux announced, her voice cutting into the horrifying stare-a-thon I had been engaged in. But honestly, who could have blamed me? As annoying as he was, Alexander was like a work of art.

His bone structure was ridiculously sculpted, and the sleeves pushed up to his elbows afforded me a horrifically long look at his gorgeous forearms. Part of me wanted to bite the taut tendons there, but I was half afraid that alarms would go off if I touched him. You're not supposed to touch master-pieces, and Alexander's long arms, broad shoulders and small waist had the power to make any sculptor quit his craft. Like, Michaelangelo *wishes*.

If Theo was Patroclus' reluctant hero, then Alexander was

Achilles, born, bred and trained for his task. Even if that task was just classwork on a dreary afternoon.

Lux made her way around the room, offering a bucket full of names to each group, and I silently thanked the gods that we were near the back of the room and I had some time to pull my head out of the gutter and *focus*. The first group picked Hera and the second pulled Artemis. Ronan's group claimed Poseidon and his partners looked less than pleased.

Professor Lux made her way to us and offered the bucket to Alexander. With the huge grin still adorning his face, he bit his lip and declared, "I hope we get Aphrodite." He pulled out a slip of paper and pumped his fist into the air.

"I guess she was listening." Lux smiled.

"Oh, you have no idea," Alexander laughed.

Theo and I shared a mutual glance of disdain. There was a lot we could say about Aphrodite and her role with soulmates, but there was almost too much to go through in just a semester. From Ronan's group, one of his partners, Tori, actually rolled her eyes at Alexander, and I had to stop myself from doing the same. Ronan winked at me, and gods, Sam was becoming a bad influence – maybe if I could wink, then I wouldn't mind so much.

"Now, I recommend you all meet outside of class soon," Lux said when all of the gods had been assigned, and the clock on the wall told us there were only a few minutes left of class. "Talk about the different parts of the assignment and how you want to structure it. Spend the last couple of minutes exchanging emails or phone numbers to contact each other, and then you can go. Email me if you have any questions."

The other groups began to chatter, but we all looked at each other for a few awkward moments without saying anything. If his face was any indication, Theo was trying to express his thoughts by glaring at our group project partner. I hesitated to open my mouth, not wanting that glare to be turned in my direction. But as the silence stretched on, I knew I had to be the one to break it.

"Texting probably works best," I suggested eventually, pulling my phone out.

Theo snorted, leaning back in his chair. His dark eyes flickered with amusement, and for the first time all class period, a slight smile graced his lips as he looked at me. "I guess I get your phone number, after all."

He said it with just enough humor and self-deprecation that I could tell he meant it as a joke. It was a peace offering. A way to brush aside the possible awkwardness of our exchange at Laurel Leaf. I laughed lightly, accepting the olive branch.

"You asked her out?" Alexander's smile dimmed as he looked at Theo. His eyes were the color of the Mediterranean, somewhere between blue and green, and just as temperamental. "I mean, you asked out someone who wasn't your soulmate? In a class about soulmates?"

Theo's smile faded. "That's not really any of your business."

Alexander frowned. "It is if it makes the project awkward or Vanessa feel uncomfortable. I'm not going to let your poor attempts at flirting hurt my grade or hers. It's still early enough that Lux might switch the groups around—"

I wasn't sure which part offended Theo the most, but he bared his teeth and snarled, "It's not any of your fucking—"

"It's not uncomfortable for me," I interrupted, the quick escalation making my heart pound. I wasn't good at conflict, but I flicked a quick glance to Theo. "Is it awkward for you?"

"Nope," he snapped, turning to Alexander. "Any other issues?"

Alexander looked at me for a moment as if to make sure I was being sincere. It was sort of sweet that he was so worried. He didn't even know me. His eyes scanned my face and then nodded. Protective but not overbearing. Interesting.

"Okay," he agreed, stretching the word out. "Wanna meet Wednesday before class?"

"Can't," Theo said immediately.

"Why?" Alexander sighed.

"Because I can't."

"How about Friday afternoon—"

"Can't."

"Why?"

"Because I *can't*," Theo said, gritting his teeth. "How about Sunday morning?"

"I have swim practice until the evening," Alexander said, shaking his head. That certainly explained his varsity jacket and all the medals decorating its lapels. He looked like he'd be a strong swimmer – lean but not overly muscled. More Apollo than Ares. "Monday before class?"

"Can't."

They glared at each other for another long breath. They reminded me of two lions using a zebra carcass as a tug-of-war toy. Except the zebra was my grade, and I was just a poor gazelle, looking on in horror.

"Listen, I can meet Wednesday before class" – I nodded at Alexander – "and I can meet Sunday morning. I'll meet with you both and exchange notes for you. We'll figure out a time for all of us to meet another week. In the meantime, we can just text if we have any problems. Cool?"

They both turned to look at me, and I shrank back at their sharp stares. People started to get up around us and leave the classroom, their errant chatter broke through the tension hanging over our table. They both gave in at the same time, agreeing to my negotiation.

"Okay," Alexander murmured, softer than anything else he'd said today. "I'll text you tonight to pick a meeting place."

I nodded. "See you Wednesday."

He offered me a small smile, less brilliant than his huge

grin, but it softened him in a pleasant way. It wasn't the sun at midday, bleaching the world white, but the soft light of rosy-fingered dawn. When he stood and walked from the room, Eliza from Ronan's group fell into step beside him, linking their arms together. She murmured something to him, mouth twisted into a smug smirk as he ruffled her hair.

"Gods above, he's a douche," Tori drawled, brushing a hand over Theo's shoulder. He leaned into the touch with a familiarity that surprised me. My fingers ached with the urge to reach out myself. To run my hand through his hair or push aside the fabric of his shirt to see the full tattoo that was peeking out from under his collar.

Your soulmate results are on the way, I thought and kept my hands to myself.

Theo snorted again. "You're telling me."

Ronan came over to stand by me as I got my stuff together, mindlessly grabbing one of my hands to hold in his own. Good. A distraction. He nodded at Theo, who nodded back. It was a silent acceptance that we'd all moved on from the moment in the Laurel Leaf.

I couldn't tell if Tori touched him like a plat or like a lover. It shouldn't have mattered to me. It didn't matter to me. I was only curious. Her wrist was also bare.

"I'll text you tonight, yeah?" Theo offered as he stood with a long stretch. Ronan's eyes hardened, and Theo's face went slightly pink. "For, uh, the project."

"For the project," I agreed with a bland smile.

He stared at me for a moment before turning to the door with Tori at his side. Her hand smoothed down his arm to hold his, and I still couldn't tell. *Eros or Philia?* Did it matter? My soulmate was out there, waiting for me somewhere.

"How'd that go?" Ronan asked. Groaning, I smacked my forehead on his shoulder. He wrapped his arm around me and sent a tendril of warm understanding through the bond, wrapping around my temples to soothe me. "That bad, huh?"

"I'm trying to think of a way to be positive," I mumbled into him. I could feel a migraine building, but Ronan was warm and smelled like sandalwood, and it was almost enough to stop the swelling pain. Almost. "But I don't think it could've gone any worse."

4

AND THE RESULTS ARE IN

Alexander: I was thinking we could meet at the library's coffee shop at 1:30?
Alexander: I've looked over the assignment and have a good idea where I think we should start.
Alexander: I'm excited to hear your thoughts! (: (:
Theo: 9 Sunday? library?

The texts had come in as I waited for the first Society for Ethical Sacrifice meeting of this semester to start. It was a decent-sized group already, even with fifteen minutes before the clock struck noon, and we were all packed into a small room with not nearly enough chairs. This year, a few of the professors were giving extra credit for attending our meetings and the event toward the end of the semester. More people were here, but most of them had bored expressions on their faces as they sat texting their friends.

The group had historically been mostly members of the Cult of Demeter, but I noticed some followers of Artemis and Dionysus here, too, recognizing the symbols of the gods on their backpacks and jackets – a moon or a deer here, a bunch of grapes or a theater mask there. The longer we waited for the meeting to begin, the antsier the Dionysus followers became, and the Artemis girls grew more agitated too. I started to tap my pen, but an Artemis girl with brass knuckles on her keychain glared at me, and I quickly set it down.

The president of the club, Melissa, and the vice president, Olympia, walked in together, already arguing. Melissa slammed her backpack down on the table with enough force to knock over my water bottle.

"I don't care how many times you say it to me," she snapped at her VP, who curled her lip in the usual barely-suppressed rage of a Cult of Dionysus member. "I am not letting the Cult of Dionysus do the opening speech. Last time, they showed up high off their asses—"

"Oh, let me guess," Olympia snapped back. "You want your precious Cult of Demeter to do it. Well, I'm putting my foot down. They do it every year and it's boring as hell. They only ever talk about grain—"

"Better than talking about their dicks for the entire time!" Melissa shrieked and everyone stared at her. She was a senior, which explained why she got the role of president, and how she remembered a more exciting event than I did. "And, of course, they do it every year! Tradition is important—"

"The tradition of animal sacrifice is what we're protesting," Olympia shot back, gesturing theatrically to the name of the club, which I had written on the board when I got here before everyone else. "A tradition the Cult of Demeter continues to support on a governmental level, by the way!"

"Oh, and the Cult of Dionysus is so perfect, huh? What do you have to say about—"

I rubbed my temples while the new members went back to texting. It was going to be a long meeting.

The library was busy in the middle of the week, and it took me a few minutes to find Alexander's blond head amongst all the busy tables. When I finally spotted him, he had his head thrown back in laughter, chatting with Eliza. She had a sly grin on her face, and that same smug energy as before radiated from her. It was like watching a Sphinx and Cerberus get along.

"Oh, hey, Vanessa!" Alexander called, eyes still laughing. He pushed out one of the chairs with a foot and offered me a smile. "Is it okay if Eliza joins us at the table? It's busier than we thought it would be. She's promised to put on headphones and not steal any great ideas we may have for our presentation."

"Yeah, no problem," I answered, smiling at the blonde girl. "Hey, nice to formally meet you."

"Hey." She offered me a hand to shake like we were business associates meeting for the first time. "It's lovely to meet you, as well. I'm Eliza, Alexander's platonic soulmate and probably his only friend – ow! Don't kick me!" Alexander feigned innocence and I snickered. "You're Ronan's, right? He seems sweet."

The way she complimented my platonic soulmate as a compliment to me showed her good breeding. Even the way she enunciated her words, clipped but with just enough emphasis, practically screamed upper-class Cult of Athena. I accepted the compliment for what it was. "Yeah, he's the best. He makes both our souls look good."

"Oh, I don't think you need any help with that." She laughed and nudged her plat with a perfectly manicured hand. Alexander rolled his eyes without looking up from his textbook, and she held her hands up in surrender. "Fine, fine, I'll stop teasing you. I'm putting my headphones on now. Tell your brain to chill out. Your feelings are giving me a headache."

"I feel bad that she has to feel every emotion I have." Alexander winced mockingly when his plat finished listening, but his face was just as amused as hers. "She says I react personally to everything. Our bond is mostly her calming me down."

"Ronan does the same for me. He's the steady one, he says, and I'm the emotional one," I admitted, sitting down and pulling my notebook out. The still mostly-empty list of volunteers for the Society of Ethical Sacrifice taunted me before I flipped to a fresh page. "So, what are these ideas you have?"

"You know the part that requires some kind of field trip?" he asked and I nodded, remembering the syllabus. "Well, Aphrodite is holding a Q&A in Detroit at the end of the semester, and I... know someone who could get us tickets. I figured we could go and see if she'll answer the questions directly."

I nodded with a small smile and quickly scribbled it down in my notebook. "That sounds great. Do you know when it is? We'll have to arrange travel and make sure we can all go, but it sounds like a start. Anything else? Have you thought about the presentation part? We have to decide between a video or an in-person, right?"

We went back and forth for a while. For the first time, I thought Alexander's enthusiasm might be a good thing. One-on-one, he was much easier to handle and our conversation had gone on so long that it was only when Eliza leaned over to ask, "Don't we have class?" that we realized we needed to rush to be on time.

The rain was hitting the ground with the fury of Zeus as we stumbled our way across campus, Alexander grinning over his shoulder at me as I slipped on the wet cement of the sidewalk. He offered me a steadying hand and the rain made the static electricity between us more powerful. We landed in our seats just as the clock turned three, turning to each other and laughing at the way our wet clothes made us slip in our seats. Eliza somehow managed to perch elegantly.

Ronan turned around in his chair and blew me a kiss,

bouncing my happy emotions back to me so that I felt them twice over. A tingle ran down the back of my neck, and I turned to find Theo sitting at the back of the classroom. When I caught his eye, he raised his eyebrows, but I found myself instead distracted by the dark shoulders of his sweatshirt, spotted with rain. Blinking myself free of my stare, I sent him a thumbs-up and a smile, and his face went slack with surprise.

"Okay, rearrange the desks into your presentation groups," Lux announced, coming into the classroom and closing her umbrella with a quick shake. "Some of you emailed to tell me that meeting outside class might be difficult, so we'll start doing fifteen minutes of group work at the beginning of class too."

Alexander started moving the desks right away, helping me push mine and then Eliza's. I shifted into my seat with a shiver, the cool air making my wet clothes feel heavier, and I looked up to find both Alexander and Theo's eyes on me. Oh gods, had I made myself the accidental leader of our group? I was usually more of a mediator, though it was clear from the animosity sparking between the two boys that I would have my work cut out for me there too. I was able to explain, with minimal stutters, Alexander's ideas to Theo, who nodded along whilst tapping out a frantic beat on his paper with his fingers.

It only really started to go wrong when Lux called out for us to talk about the articles we read for class and how they related to the god we were assigned. I guessed we were staying in this seating for the rest of class then. *Joy.* The article was about the connection between wine and its purpose in the soulmate ritual, and the discussion from the Dionysus group grew loud almost immediately.

"Maybe," Alexander raised his own clear, deep voice over their buzzing, "the wine is used to dissolve the barriers between people. That way, love is easier to experience and easier to let in."

Theo shrugged. "Or it's just the libation."

"What do you mean?" Alexander asked, his brows scrunching together.

"The Gods like wine," Theo said slowly and deliberately. I braced myself as they both leaned forward as if preparing for a fight. "So we give them wine. *Do ut des.* You'd think someone with your overpriced education could understand that."

"You don't think that's too obvious?" Alexander fired back. "Maybe *you're* too simple."

Theo's lip curled. He looked extra tired today; dark bags under his eyes and red paint under his fingernails. His silence filled the space with more disdain for Alexander than any words could have put across.

"Did you even do the reading?" Alexander snapped when he didn't get a response. His beautiful face looked as if it were carved from ice, sharp and cold. "Because what I said was in the article—"

"So *glad* to see you're thinking creatively, then," Theo snarked back, rolling his eyes. "No, I didn't read it. Didn't have time. Some of us work outside of class. We can't all rely on daddy's money."

Alexander spluttered, looking surprised, then angry as small pink spots appeared on the apples of his cheeks. "Are you going to be an asshole for the whole project because I'll—"

"You'll what?" Theo leaned forward in his chair, eyes glittering. Cult of Apollo had a violent streak a mile long and rage was, of course, a plague of its own. I wasn't sure which Cult Alexander belonged to, but I could have cut the tension between them with a knife. If they started fighting, it would get bloody fast.

I reluctantly opened my mouth to interrupt them and attempt to diffuse the situation when Lux appeared from almost nowhere. Her blue eyes were bright, and I had no doubt her timely appearance was deliberate. "Everything okay here?"

I looked at her with no small measure of relief and smiled. "Yes! Everything is fine!"

Alexander and Theo still hadn't lifted their gazes from one another and my smile began to wither.

"Because I didn't pick these groups alone," Lux continued casually, looking down at her fingernails which were painted a deep green. "The Fates aided my decisions. So, if you don't work together, it could be seen as a slight on them—"

The words were ominous, and I felt the already-nervous energy in my stomach begin to swirl harder. People who offended the Fates, even during something as simple as a school project, were known to get runs of bad luck like colds or food poisoning after they rejected their duties. And now that Lux had spoken their name, they'd be listening to our responses even closer.

Alexander was the first to break the staring contest, looking towards Lux with a fake smile. For an instant, I could see the typical jock personality begin to leak from his pores. "Yeah, everything is fine. We were just talking about the article that we read. Or, at least, that some of us read."

"Oh my gods, are you five years old?" Theo snapped at him.

"Mr. Patras, did you forget to read for class?" Lux asked, but there was no real heat in her words. Theo shrugged, but there was something apologetic about it. "That's fine. Just send me an email when you've read it to let me know that you did get around to it."

She moved to the next group, and I sighed in relief before turning to my group members and giving them my best approximation of a glare. I was embarrassed that she'd had to come over and convince them to behave like adults. "Seriously? I don't know what your problem is with each other but sort it out. Because I am not doing this for a whole semester."

Neither of them responded, so I flipped to my notes about the article and started reading them aloud. Alexander continued to glare at Theo, who wrote down everything I said. He stopped me occasionally to ask a question, and Alexander frowned every time I answered.

The class moved onto a new topic, and the two became too absorbed in their notes to glare at each other anymore. Ronan sent me a concerned wave of feeling, and I sent one right back, a heady mixture of anger and frustration. I pouted at him from across the classroom, and he shook his head. Of course, *his* group got along just fine.

I gathered my things quickly as soon as class ended, and Ronan followed, matching my pace. I wanted to get out of there before either of my teammates tried to talk to me, not sure if I'd be able to bite my tongue about their ridiculous antics.

Ronan was less than two steps behind me as I quickly swept out of the classroom. I was near the end of the hallway leading to the main doors when someone called my name. I recognised Alexander's voice and walked faster, but his legs were much longer than mine and quickly breached the distance. Eliza's heels clicked slowly and then faster as she kept up with her plat.

A hand reached out to stop me, and a wave of warmth passed through everywhere that our skin connected.

"Hey, wait a second, okay?" Alexander said softly, not out of breath but a little desperate. I looked around nervously. We were right in front of the doors to the building and people muttered as they pushed around us. Ronan and Eliza moved off to the side of the corridor, and I wished I could do the same. "I'm sorry, I didn't mean to make class…" Unbearable? Awkward? Humiliating? Alexander didn't finish the thought. "It's just he's just such an asshole—"

"—he's a *what now*?" a feminine voice called from behind us, and we both looked over, me, nervously and Alexander with irritation. Tori had stopped halfway through pushing the door open, her dark hair swinging with the force of her abrupt stop and her hand intertwined with Theo's, who looked like he was just barely stopping her from lunging at Alexander. "Who are you to talk about him like that, you spoiled dickwad—"

Eliza stepped in front of Alexander, face bored but words sharp. "How dare you—"

Ronan tried to step between them, and I almost wanted to laugh. Our group was so dysfunctional that his group was now fucked, too. "Come on, let's not fight here—"

The girls threw him a glare and I stepped in front of him, just as protective as they were.

"Your plat needs to watch his mouth," Tori snapped at Eliza, and Theo's jaw clenched like he was preparing for a long argument. His hand was still in hers, and he tugged on it lightly as if attempting to draw her away. "It's not Theo's fault that your plat is such a controlling douchebag that he won't even let someone else have an opinion."

"Oh, please," Eliza laughed with a roll of her eyes. She reminded me of a wicked prom queen, dismissive and just as righteous. Tori's eyes sparked with barely-restrained rage. Cult of Dionysus, for sure. "He's so busy making eyes at Vanessa here—"

"Listen, Theo isn't the one that has to prove that he can slum it with the regular people at a public school," Tori shot back, and Alexander flinched from the words. Ronan and I shared a look of mutual agreement – escaping out of the door while they duked it out sounded more than good right about now. Tori continued, apparently not content yet, "Just because his dad owns half the fucking lake—"

Invisible chimes sounded, filling the hallway. Everyone stopped talking, stopped breathing. It was the sound that indicated the presence of divinity; it precluded every announcement from the Olympians. I looked at Ronan, my eyes wide, as we all waited in awe.

My heart quickened. *It's been about seven business days.*

A Cupid appeared suddenly before us in a cloud of rose-scented magic, popping in from Olympus with the blessing of Aphrodite and looking like every drawing I'd ever seen. His hair was the same shade as Alexander's, like woven gold in perfect ringlets, and his face could have been lifted from any holiday card – round with red-apple cheeks.

Most important, however, was the paper in his hand.

"Soulmate results for Vanessa Reyes!" he announced, his voice the same pitch as the chimes that had announced him. The paper was tri-folded and bore the official stamp of Olympus on it. He looked down at us from where he hovered, and surprise washed over his face as he caught sight of Alexander. "Brother?"

"Uh, hey, Eros," Alexander greeted, his own voice surprised, and he glanced around awkwardly. "Nice to see you."

They blinked at each other for a few seconds before the Cupid shook his head and called again, "Vanessa Reyes?"

Ronan gave me a small push forward. "She's Vanessa."

The Cupid handed me the paper as his eyes became completely white. His voice was empty of intonation and feeling, reminding me eerily of the Priestess at the Ceremonial Building. He sounded like a robot, like the information on my paper was pre-programmed into his brain. "Soulmate results for Vanessa Reyes, loyal servant of Hera, Goddess of Women, Raiser of Gods, Wife to Zeus Almighty: *On behalf of the Blessed Gods who Reside on Olympus, I congratulate you on the announcement of your soulmate, Alexander Crest, loyal servant of Aphrodite, Goddess of Love and Soulmates, Born of the Sea and the Seed of the Heavens.* As you are the first of your bond to confirm these results, he will receive contact information for you and, by law, is required to contact you within twenty-four hours."

My eyes locked onto Alexander's as the Cupid carried on about laws and regulations, but nothing else mattered right then. Alexander sucked in a harsh breath, and his jaw trembled. A sound escaped him, something like a whimper, and Eliza made a cooing noise as she grabbed his hand and squeezed it tightly. Ronan's smile slowly spread over his face as he grinned at me in excitement.

"Similarly," the Cupid carried on, ignorant of our reactions, "your Hephaestus-crafted gold bracelet will arrive in that same window. You are legally required to wear them. Congratulations again, and may your minds be as pleased as your souls!"

With another cloud of perfume the Cupid vanished, leaving all six of us to stare at the now-empty space with disbelief. My hands shook so badly that Ronan took the paper from me, obviously afraid I would drop it on the wet floor or accidentally rip it.

"We're soulmates?" Alexander breathed, mouth breaking out into one of those brilliant grins. His whole face turned the sweetest shade of pink as I nodded, my throat too dry for words. Eliza moved to the side as Alexander took a step towards me, and gods, he was so much taller than I'd realized. Taller than Ronan, taller than Sam, even. Cult of Aphrodite? Yeah, that made sense. I'd never seen anyone as beautiful as Alexander... my soulmate.

"You didn't apply to find me?" I asked, the worry bursting from my lips before I could stop it. If he was one of those people that didn't want to know or if he would have preferred that I hadn't applied…

He shook his head vehemently, his blond waves moving like the sea as he reached out and grabbed my hands in his. He was warm and his fingers dwarfed mine, but we fit together. Of course, we did.

My whole body vibrated with his touch, and he cleared his throat lightly. "I don't turn twenty-one until later this year, so I couldn't…" His voice trailed off but there were tears glistening in his sea-blue eyes. I heard the rustle of paper as Ronan opened up my letter behind me. "But I wanted to know, of course, I wanted to know. You have no idea how much I— How long I—"

"I know," I told him, finally pulling him closer to me. This was *Alexander*, the only person I knew more excited about Soulmates than I was. "I've waited for you just as long."

He was everything I'd been waiting for, the perfect Prince Charming from my childhood daydreams. Every movie with teen heartthrobs cast in the role of soulmate, every cheap, silly romance book with overdramatic covers in the one-drachma store. Every story my mom had told me over raspberry tea about meeting my father as a teenager, years before their results came in, about how she knew in her very soul that there was something special about the brown-eyed boy from her English class.

They'd all led to this moment, to this beautiful, kind, smart man—

"Oh, fuck," Ronan said, his voice harsh in contrast to Alexander's honey-sweet words, and the perhaps ridiculous visions of wedding dresses dancing in my head. Everyone looked at him in surprise, and he paled, eyes wide. For the first time since the Cupid said Alexander's name, I paid attention to my surroundings and my eyes caught on Theo's face. Some sort of emotion simmered just under the surface of his skin, but his eyes wouldn't meet mine. My soul jolted in my chest, twisting uncomfortably at whatever emotion Theo was projecting. "Uh, guys, we have a problem. A really, really, big problem. Oh, fuck…"

"Ronan?" I asked, my voice soft and trembling. This was my moment. Everything should be *perfect*. Ready for Alexander and I to ride off into the proverbial sunset.

"Oh, Ness, I'm so sorry—"

"What is it?" Eliza asked, her green eyes worried as she glanced at Alexander. "What's wrong?"

Ronan's eyes met mine, and my stomach dropped as I read the shock in his. He held up the paper slowly, and I squinted, moving closer before I snatched it with a dizzy gasp. *This can't be happening. There's been a mistake.*

The paper trembled in my hand, blurring the name on the page as my eyes filled, but there was no mistaking it. *Impossible.* The Cupid had made a mistake. *Aphrodite* had made a mistake. There was no way the name printed on the bottom of the letter could be right.

Theodore Patras.

5

INTERTWINED IN THE CHAOS

Everyone's eyes swung towards Theo, who stood staring at the paper like the world had just dropped out from under his feet, revealing Tartarus below. I dropped Alexander's hand, feeling a stab of confusion as he tightened his grip before letting me go. I stared down at the small slip of paper that had just changed *everything* and not in a good way. It had the same name on it from the class roster, the same name I had checked into the Laurel Leaf, rippling through my mind in time with the thrumming of my heart. *Theo. Theo. Theo.*

I gulped, my throat dry and tongue heavy, needing to say something – anything, to Alexander, to Theo, to the Gods in the heavens. Theo's hands shook, and his dark eyes were wide, the gold in them completely hidden beneath his blown-out pupils. Alexander looked pale, but Theo looked moments away from hyperventilating. Tori had a white-knuckled grip on his hand at her side, but I could see his fingers were limp in hers.

"This is a mistake," he said with so much conviction that my breath caught, hurt coiling through my chest. "I can't be your soulmate, Vanessa—" He cut himself off, shaking his head as if to clear it, making his curls coil and uncoil. "Hades damn it all. I have to go."

He spun quickly, pushing the doors open so hard they smacked against the walls, leaving black marks against the white stones. Tori looked at me wide-eyed but something about her softened, and I could tell she was moments away from dashing after him, so I grabbed her wrist and hoped she couldn't feel the dampness of my fingers. This was not the way that any of this should have happened.

"Wait," I begged, watching Theo's form disappear into the mist of the rainstorm outside.

"I'm sorry," she said and the look on her face was so sincere, I believed her. Her rage had vanished, leaving only pity in her eyes as she looked at me. "There's been a mistake. I have to go."

She followed Theo out the doors and let them slam behind her with finality, and I jumped in the sudden silence.

I felt the trembling in my hands worsen, despair reaching out to encompass my whole body, and Ronan pulled me to him in a protective embrace that lessened the pain and confusion swirling through me. Eliza's hands were firm on Alexander's waist as if stopping him from toppling over. When Alexander's eyes met mine once more, grief had overwhelmed the joy they had previously contained.

I understood. It bubbled in my own chest, burning – it felt like I had somehow lost not one, but two soulmates in the space of a few minutes. What could I possibly have done to have angered the gods enough to torture me this way? My soul felt adrift in the Chaos with nothing to anchor me down. Not even Ronan, whose mind was reeling just as much as my own but was trying to comfort me. His soul brushing against mine helped, but it couldn't heal this.

Eliza and Ronan started talking, their quiet murmurs mostly passing me by. My stomach lurched as I considered the future before me – one soulmate who might not be mine and another who didn't want me. I turned instinctively to run to the bathroom, my skin breaking out in a cold sweat just as Alexander moved closer, reaching out. My hands moved as though magnetized to his, and I couldn't refrain from touching him. My skin tingled at every point of contact between us, and my nausea calmed. This was good, right? If I was having this reaction, it had to mean he was mine? Or was I just so desperate for it to be true that I was imagining things?

"We'll figure it out," Alexander said quietly as though he'd heard my thoughts. The words sounded dry, scraping his throat on their way out. I wanted to believe him, but the look in his eyes betrayed him even as he rubbed my palm with his thumb. "We'll – *I'll* figure this out for us, okay? I'll take care of this, I – you're my soulmate."

But the words sounded unsure and I pulled away, offering up only a sad smile in response.

He sent a desperate look to Eliza, who immediately pulled out her phone. "I'm calling a cab," she said to him. "The Ceremonial Building should still be open for another hour. I promise, Alexander, we'll get to the bottom of this. Oh, hello, I need a cab as soon as possible. Yes, it's an emergency. I'll pay double if you can... Okay, five minutes."

As she rattled off the address, Ronan turned to me, pressing a cool kiss to my forehead as he said, "Do you have your phone? Can you pull up the emails from your first appointment? We may need the paperwork."

I let out a breath of relief. They were right, we could fix this, and then I'd get my Happily Ever After. I just had to slay a few bureaucratic dragons first. Desperate to take action, my hands shook, and by the time I found the documents on my phone, the cab had arrived outside. The car was painted a vibrant gold and the name of the company – Golden Chariot Services – would have made me laugh any other time. The slogan proudly proclaimed they were the fastest, safest way to complete your journey with the magic of Hermes blessing every ride. On the bumper, two wings fluttered in the wind. It was a little overkill, but I'd take any godly intervention at this point. I prayed Hermes was watching over us all now.

We all piled in, Ronan placing me on his lap so Alexander could reach his hand forward to the front of the cab where Eliza held it as we drove. He closed his eyes with a sigh and another stab of guilt flared through me. It felt like I had somehow put him through this with my botched ceremony and cursed luck.

None of this was right. This wasn't how any of this was supposed to happen. It was supposed to be magical, romantic. Soft and lovely, like a movie. My soulmate – Alexander? Theo? – was supposed to pull me into his arms and kiss me, and then our bond would cement, and we'd... I didn't know, live happy, long lives together.

Instead, Alexander had tears welling in his eyes, and Theo wasn't even here. Didn't want me, or care – or both.

We got out of the cab, and Eliza threw a couple hundred drachmae at the driver. Any other time I would have balked at the money, but right then, all I could focus on was getting inside the building and sorting this mess out. The doors opened promptly this time as we made our way in, and I wanted to both laugh and cry. The woman at the desk stood up at the sight of us, all intertwined and with panic clearly written on our faces.

There were people in the waiting area, but Ronan didn't bother looking at them as he dragged us all to the desk, demanding the complete attention of the Priestess on duty. Most people didn't even seem put out, our distress was that obvious, but a man near the desk glared at us as we cut in line. Alexander murmured an apology, and my heart gave a little squeeze. It wasn't the same Priestess as from my ritual. This one was older with broad shoulders and wrinkles near her eyes.

"We need a private consultation," Ronan said without hesitation. He leaned against the counter, and his gold bracelet made a ringing noise. I winced at the reminder of my own bare wrist, worried it might stay that way forever. "This is an emergency."

The Priestess' eyes ran over us before nodding. "All of you?"

"All of us," Ronan confirmed, and she led us through the door behind the desk without another word. We entered the consultation room in a messy pile of tangled limbs, a long couch took up one side of the room that we all fell into, and a single chair sat facing us. The walls were painted a cheerful pink that grated on my nerves. The Priestess settled in the chair, and I tried to release some of my worries. My shoulders were so tense that I knew they would be sore tomorrow.

Ronan took the lead, explaining the situation as quickly as possible with him and Eliza answering the simple questions as they came up – our ages, our Cults. Next to me, Alexander's eyes were closed, and he was taking deep breaths that hitched in his chest. I didn't take my eyes off of the Priestess, but let one of my hands take his and briefly squeezed. His breaths settled a little in response.

"Do your hands tingle when you touch?" the Priestess asked, directing the question at Alexander.

"Yes." He stared at our intertwined hands like they held the answers of the universe.

"And you?" She pointed to me.

"Yes? Maybe?" My whole body trembled, and I bit my lip.

"And with the other man – with Theodore?"

I forced myself to focus. To think back to when I had handed him the coffee at Laurel Leaf, the way my hand had buzzed with energy at the contact. "Maybe?"

Alexander flinched. Like he had hoped my answer would be a straight no and that the alternative was unbearable.

The Priestess continued, her gaze and words clipped, "Have you kissed either of them yet? After the first kiss, your abilities will manifest. Telepathy, aura reading, deep emotional connection—"

"No," I said, and it was hollow. She nodded in understanding, but my words kept spilling out. "I don't know either of them very well. I was waiting to have my first kiss—"

With my soulmate, I thought but didn't say. Alexander swallowed and nodded in agreement, a hint of a blush ghosting across his cheeks.

"Look," the Priestess said, reminding me of my grandmother, her words blunt but not unkind. "You have a few options. The first is to kiss them both and see which kiss results in the appearance of the psychic abilities that soulmates have."

"No," Eliza interjected as pain flashed over Alexander's face. He looked as if he would vomit from the very thought, his rose-gold skin turning a shade of green like jade. I likely looked the same. Somewhere, deep below my panic and worry, I was grateful she was speaking for Alexander. I would want Ronan to do the same for me. "Not if we have other options."

"The second thing you could do is to re-apply for your results and make a bigger sacrifice to the gods. That'll take between six to eight weeks to get a response because it's not, technically, a priority in the system because there is no protocol for this. I'd advise you not to take this step. If anything, I'd suggest that you wait until Alexander can apply in a month's time. You'll get the results faster."

A whole month of not knowing? The pit in my stomach doubled in size, and my hand tightened involuntarily around Alexander's.

"No," Ronan said, stepping in and pulling me closer. "That's not going to work."

"Well, the first step is to wait to see who receives your contact information and matching bracelet within the next day."

Relief flooded through me. Of course, just a little more patience and this would all be sorted out in a matter of hours without me compromising my first kiss.

"The clock is already close to twenty-three hours now, and you both look like you could collapse. Rest. Sleep will take another eight hours off the timer."

"Okay." I nodded a few times in succession, looking at Ronan for reassurance, and he nodded back. "We can do that."

"And child," the Priestess said, leaning forward in her chair and losing her professional edge as she looked at me steadily. "Pray to your goddess. Pray to the Fates. Pray to every god you can think of. There must be a reason this happened, even if it is a clerical mistake. Nothing happens without a reason, not with the gods. Appeal to their kindness. Pledge further sacrifices if you can afford it. If there's any way to contact them more directly—"

"I can call my mom," Alexander murmured, and Eliza patted his hand soothingly. I couldn't help but wonder how that would help anything. "I mean, at the very least, we'll see her in Detroit at the end of the semester, so we could figure this out then."

His mom. His mother. *The Goddess of Love*. My soulmate was the actual, literal child of Aphrodite, and we were still in this mess. In a perfect world, it would make things as easy as breathing, but of course not. It was never that simple.

"Then do that. You may want to call this Theo, too, if you can and tell him what you plan to do. It's his right to know."

He ran away, I thought as Alexander stiffened again. *He*

thinks I'm a mistake. Instead of voicing those thoughts, I nodded. "Thank you."

The Priestess stood, and we followed suit, exiting the room with slightly less tension than we'd had going in. I was exhausted. I leaned against Ronan as he guided me past the long line of people waiting, and he bore my weight without difficulty. *Whatever he's been doing at the gym with Sam is working*, I thought blearily, blinking twice to push the sleep out of my eyes.

"We'll let you know if we receive anything tonight," Eliza said, pulling out her phone to call another cab and supporting Alexander in the same way Ronan was me. Her nails poked little dimples into the soft fabric of his jacket, and I found myself focusing inordinately on that detail as the day caught up to me in one go and left me swaying on my feet. "I'll try to contact Theo or Tori as well. Does Vanessa have classes tomorrow?"

Ronan answered for me as I buried my face into his shoulder. "No, just work at my soulmate's tattoo parlor. He lives nearby, so we'll crash at his apartment tonight. Call as soon as you hear anything."

I didn't remember the journey back to Sam's, though, I was vaguely aware of Ronan lifting and carrying me the few blocks to Sam's apartment. I was almost completely numb, barely able to recognise my surroundings. Thousands of years ago, my soul had been split by Zeus' lightning, but it wasn't until tonight that I felt like I was burning. Was this the soul trauma I'd read about in my research on soulmates? Sometimes being linked to another person was exhausting, especially in the early stages when it was hard to understand what the fuck you were feeling.

It wasn't even that late, but it was like my soul was tired, reaching out for something unrequited and leaving me empty and exhausted the longer it went without. I mumbled a sleepy *thank you* as Ronan laid me down on the couch and covered me with a blanket.

When I was awake and thinking, my soul was an abstract thing to me. I was aware of it randomly, like when Ronan comforted me, but it wasn't usually so tangible. Sometimes, when I closed my eyes, I liked to think I could picture it. A string of light, of hopes and emotions dancing behind my eyelids, humming and vibrating with every wave of emotion that passed through me. But it existed somewhere *else* within the Chaos of my mind, heart, and body, binding all three together. Alone and waiting for its missing piece, the inter-twining thread.

In the darkness of sleep, I'd always felt closer to my soul. Tonight more so than ever. It pounded against my chest, against the back of my eyelids as another soul reached out. My soulmate, just as anxious, just as worried, sent out a few tentative touches against my soul within the Chaos. I could feel them but just barely. Like a phantom caress, there but imper-manent without anything firm to hold onto. I let out a sleepy sigh of longing. Only the kiss could connect two souls like that.

Even in sleep, as Hypnos touched his warm fingertips to my temples, the humming of my soul filled my head and my chest. I wondered when it would be my turn for love. Real love, not this mess I'd fallen into. First kisses meant a lot, even to people who didn't put much stock in the idea of soulmates. You remembered your first, everyone said.

But for people like me? Like Alexander? Us, the hopeless romantics?

A kiss was the start of forever. The most important moment in any fairytale – waking the maiden, sealing a promise. Yet, my first kiss seemed as far away and complicated as the politics of Olympus.

ἹΣΤΟΡΊΑ - ΘΕΩΡΊΑ

A VISION

Sun-stained grass and yellow-stemmed wildflowers colored the field golden. Their petals spotted the world with purple-blue and white amidst the remaining green trees and bushes circling the edges of the open space. Some were strong enough to still grow oranges – though the juices were sharp and bitter instead of sweet and refreshing.

The air smelled of sea salt. If she were to take her eyes off the ewe in front of her and cast her gaze toward Attica's rocky coast and inevitable navies, she knew the cresting waves of the sea would obscure her view. She had lived her entire life on the island, never wanting to leave for fear of her mortal feet impeding on the territory of more pernicious gods.

"Vanessa," the prince called, standing at the gates of the animal enclosure. She kept her head down, concentrating on milking the ewe, hands steady. She'd watched her mother do the same thing every summer, and the movements were now second nature.

He murmured a metered line of poetry to himself as she finished filling the bucket and patted the gentle creature on her flank, giving the ewe permission to join the rest of the flock. Finally, she turned to him, saying nothing but raising her eyebrows. He was beautiful, and the other women said he was fond of her. They had each warned her during the nights spent working together, for a prince could take what he wanted.

"Vanessa," he said again, the word airy and affectionate. She lifted the bucket and made her way back to the living structures. His tunic, dyed nearly the color of the wine at his father's extravagant parties, hung from his side, exposing strong, golden shoulders. She smiled as she took him in. His hair, much like the embroidery on the tunic, was gold. Both likely gifts from his mother.

She brushed by him, and he chased, as he always did. She gave him a small smile, saying nothing yet, and continued her work. She was barefoot – the strap of her right sandal had snapped last night while the women had run and giggled through the darkness of the night – and so her footfalls were silent. His own sandals snapped against the soft skin of his feet, the leather new and taut.

She didn't stop until they were under the shade of the roof's overhang and then turned to face him, back against the wall but invulnerable. Glancing up at his tall frame, she asked, "Prince Alexandros, what can I help you with?"

He smiled, and she wondered if it was blasphemy to think Apollo could easily grow jealous of his brilliance. After all, he was his blood-relation. Perhaps the god would take it as a compliment. She nearly snorted aloud at that – the gods were not gentle, forgiving creatures. But, sometimes, they could give birth to them.

"My father asked for your help with dinner tonight," he explained, his skin flushed pink high on his cheeks as he rubbed the back of his neck. A nervous gesture. A sincere one. "The kitchen staff is not sufficient—"

"A messenger could not have relayed that?" she interrupted, knowing well that if he had his father's temperament, she'd be reprimanded and punished for speaking out of turn. She had asked for the express purpose of watching that flush darken and disappear under the hemline at his neck.

Still, there was no clever or cunning deception, no coy manipulation, when he answered, "One could have, but I volunteered to bring it. I wanted to see you." He spoke the words with inherent softness, and they brushed against her breast with the sensation of animal fur, soft and expensive. "I know you'll be at the party, serving the guests, but I wanted to speak to you before we were relegated to our titles."

"What about?"

"Anything," he said, eyes wide, leaning closer. She leaned back against the side of the building, crushing the climbing vines with her shoulders. He moved a half-step closer. His eyes fixed on hers. Maybe he was boxing her in, but neither of them were under the impression that he was the one in control here. "I could hear you talk about nothing, and I would still find you the most interesting, most beautiful—"

"My prince," a new voice said, colder, breaking his words off at the sweetest moment. Alexandros stepped back, eyes blurry from their previous closeness, and addressed the source of the new voice. Like the waves, he obscured her view, but Vanessa knew who had spoken. She knew his voice like she knew the hidden paths of the wilderness around the palace. It was almost as familiar to her as her own. "The lady's mother requires her help in preparing the King's dinner."

"Theodoros." Her cheeks flushed a lighter shade of pink. She doubted either would notice the color on her face. Hours under the sun, tending the animals had bronzed her skin. "Surely my mother can wait a few minutes."

He shrugged, his wary eyes still fixed on Alexandros. If her skin was bronze, Theodoros had taken on the color of rich spices from the Near East. His father hailed from Anatolia, or perhaps Lydia. It was hard to tell for he rarely spoke of himself. From the moment they had met in his father's workshop, Theodoros had protected her with religious devotion, watching to make sure that the golden-haired prince never came too close. That liberties were never taken with the soft, dark-haired daughter of the noble family.

But when he had traveled to Attica last summer to learn his father's trade, the suitors had emerged from seemingly every snake hole and sandbar of the sea. The King had turned them away with a *flick of his hand but had done nothing to discourage his own heir. She did not mind the attention, and a part of her desired him, his goodness. Other parts of her, however, gravitated toward something darker.*

"That is for her to decide, my Lady. I am but her messenger."

Alexandros cleared his throat and took one step backwards, then two, nodding. "I will let my father know that you will come along as soon as you're done with your mother." A pause. He looked to Theodoros, his gaze sweeping from head to toe, taking in his thin clothes and strong shoulders and artist's hands. "Theodoros, you look good."

Theodoros bowed his head, mouth firm. "Thank you, my prince."

Alexandros' face appeared sunburnt as he turned and walked back to the palace. The girl and Theodoros stared at each other, refusing to watch the prince walk away until he disappeared. Theodoros offered her his arm to escort her back to her mother.

He said nothing as he walked her the short distance to the front door of her mother's house. His words hit like a club that a giant or a cyclopes would prefer. "Don't trust him. He's not what you want him to be."

Kind? She thought. Beautiful?

"I know," she said instead. She squeezed his arm. He didn't smile – he hardly ever smiled, making them a rare treasure – but his face softened at her touch, just as it had done since childhood. "But you are here to protect me."

"Yes," he said. "Always."

6

GOLDEN HANDCUFFS

S am woke me up in the morning with a cup of green tea and a bowl of peach slices, my favorite breakfast outside of cherry season. I smiled at him in thanks. I loved Sam. He was a dear friend, and he made the Ronan-shaped part of my soul happier than I could have asked for. I only wished I was having this morning with my own soulmate. My face crumpled as everything that happened yesterday rose up and threatened to drown me.

"Oh, *hey*, honey," Sam said, scooping me up and wrapping me in his tattooed arms. He was warm and soft and I started to cry harder, wondering if I would ever have my own soulmate holding me. If I could only figure out who he was. *Hopefully, the one who actually wants you.*

"Do you want to skip work today?" Sam offered, rubbing my back.

I shook my head and wiped away the tears lingering on my cheeks. "No, I think I need something to do."

He agreed with a quick nod, and twenty minutes later, we all left for the Laurel Leaf. When 3:00 rolled around, the doors chiming at almost the same moment the computer notified me

57

that Sam had an appointment, I realized I had made a mistake by coming in.

Because there was Theo, black circles under his eyes and pink paint under his nails, hesitating in the doorway like he too had forgotten that showing up might have been a bad idea.

"Hello," I forced out, trying desperately to channel my customer service voice. He startled like he'd expected me to ignore him – honest-to-gods shocked I'd spoken to him. "Welcome to Laurel Leaf Tattoo Shop. How can I help you?"

He hesitated for a second but eventually just said, "I have an appointment."

I knew that. *Of course* I knew that, but I avoided his gaze by looking through the times on the computer nonetheless before nodding. His eyes ran over the decorations at my desk almost like he was avoiding me too until he opened his mouth with his gaze still fixed on the cherry-themed mug holding my pens and pencils.

"Cherries, huh?" he wondered, filling the awkward silence. I had to smile a little. He was braver than I was to be attempting small-talk.

"Ronan got it for me back home in Traverse City," I answered. "Cherries are my favorite."

"Cool."

More silence. I found his name on the calendar and checked him in.

"Okay. You can have a seat. I'll go get Sam. Coffee?"

He swallowed, hand dancing on the edge of my desk in a complicated rhythm. "Sure."

I made the coffee quickly and handed it over to him, ready to hurry back behind my desk when he stopped me with a soft touch to my sleeved wrist. I hadn't received my bracelet yet and though I was required by law to wear it when I did, I wasn't sure I wanted to. Not if I didn't know who the matching one belonged to or what it all meant.

"I'm sorry," he said with a sigh that sounded heavy. "I wish I could tell you it was me, but it's not."

"You dislike me that much?" I blurted out before I could lose the nerve. My cheeks heated, and I looked away from him again. I'd been checking my phone almost religiously, waiting for any updates, but Alexander obviously hadn't received my contact information yet, otherwise, he would have let me know.

Theo set down his coffee cup a little too hard and droplets splashed onto the desk. I wiped at the mess absentmindedly with my sleeve until he pushed my arm gently aside and moved in with a tissue.

He winced as he cleaned. "It's not like that at all. Sam didn't say?"

What did Sam have to do with anything? "Sam?"

Theo took a large gulp of the remaining bitter coffee and strode towards the couch, leaning back with a sigh. I moved cautiously and gingerly sat next to him, folding my legs under me as I watched him struggle to get his words out. Eventually, he spoke, "I had a romantic soulmate. She died. A year ago. That's why I know I can't be yours, I already had my chance at love and I lost it."

A small stab hit me in the heart, tasting strangely of disappointment. I opened my mouth, wanting to say something that would get across how much that fucking sucked, but what could I really say? I didn't know anyone who'd lost a soulmate. People usually grew old with the other half of their heart, only dying when they were gray and satisfied with the lives they'd lived. Most deaths happened with two soulmates deciding they were ready to go together and asking the gods to deliver them to their afterlives or next lives.

"Why does Sam know?" I shifted away from him slightly to avoid doing something awkward like hold his hand. That stupid yearning sensation still coiled unsettlingly within me despite what he'd revealed.

He pulled out a notebook from the paint-spattered backpack sitting beside him on the couch. It was covered in patches and buttons, everything from bands to artists to simple funny quotes. They looked old, as if nothing new had been added for quite some time. He flipped to a simple but elegant sketch of a bracelet. From the shading of the gray pencil, I assumed it would be silver – the color for a mourning soul.

"I petitioned the gods to get a tattoo instead of a bracelet," he explained quietly, licking his cracked lips. "Margot, my soulmate, she would've been a tattoo artist if she—" He cleared his throat before trying again. "That's why Sam knows. He helped with the design."

My chest still felt hollow. "Thank you for telling me."

He nodded vaguely. "You deserved to know. Listen, Vanessa, I think you're great, and I really would like to be your friend." He tried to smile, a small, forced thing that made my heart ache. "I think, for this project, we'll have to be. But that's all we *can* be. Anything *more* would be too much for me right now."

"I'd like that too." I thought briefly about our group project and the way our last class had gone. "But please try to get along better with Alexander? If he really is – well, I suppose he definitely is... then your fighting isn't going to be good for me."

There were major side effects to having a soulmate in distress, including, but not limited to, headaches, stomachaches, and if they were really upset, even fainting spells. If the last fight the boys had was anything to go off, I had a feeling I would be passing out left, right and center.

"Of course," he said, dark eyes wide with concern. "I would never put you at risk. I think he's an asshole, but petty fights aren't worth you getting hurt."

I nodded with a small smile. We'd see how long they'd last. I couldn't see them being able to avoid clashing. But I appreciated the effort.

"Thank you." I stood up, smoothing my skirt down again. "I should probably go let Sam know you're here."

I hurried over to the back room and stopped short after walking in. Sam's back was to the door and he had Ronan in his arms as he rubbed his back soothingly.

"Sorry," I said quietly as Ronan glanced up at me, likely sensing my presence through the bond. He was undoubtedly dealing with my emotional spill-over. I sighed. It felt like there wasn't a single relationship in my life right now that I wasn't in the process of fucking up. I hoped my mom wasn't due a visit. With the way things were going, it would only end in disaster. Ronan gave a light shrug but couldn't meet my eyes.

I winced and turned back to Sam. "Theo's ready."

"Send him in," he answered, sending me a sympathetic look. The moment Theo shut the door, I dropped my shoulders and took in a breath that I held to push back my tears.

"Please, gods," I murmured, closing my eyes for a moment. "No more surprises."

The gods, as usual, were silent.

I walked through the drizzle of rain to my apartment from the bus stop. The place I shared with Ronan was dark and quiet as I hung my damp coat up by the front door. I half wished that I had asked Ronan to come back with me instead of insisting I was okay.

The apartment was small, just on the edge of campus and surrounded by a hundred identical buildings. We had moved in a year ago, just after Sam came into our lives, and it had once felt like a new home. Nothing quite compared to my family's orchard or Ronan's family lake house, but it had photos of us covering the walls and enough good memories to make up for the stained carpet and dingy appliances.

Ronan rarely came home now. Sam's apartment was just down the street from the Laurel Leaf and all of Ronan's classes were downtown. He had to go out of his way to stay with me here, and more and more these days, he didn't. It was harder to look at the pictures of us on the walls when he wasn't here, so I focussed instead on the carpet as I walked in.

I toed my shoes off with my hands braced against the wall and froze as I spotted a package on the floor with the official Stamp of Hermes emblazoned across it. I nudged it with my foot as if it might bite. Tension curled in my stomach, making me feel nauseous. If I had mine then surely Alexander had received his too? I checked my phone and disappointment rose inside me – no new messages.

I had been hungry but now my stomach continued to roll. I settled instead for filling my water bottle and downing the cool liquid, then filling it up again until my stomach began to settle. Food still sounded too heavy at that moment and I lacked the energy to make anything, regardless. The last couple of days had drained me in a way I had never felt before. Like my very soul was weary. It all played out in my head like an episode of a bad Hallmark movie as I collapsed onto my bed. I felt like the stupid, dramatic main character in an overly complicated love triangle, but movies had happy endings, and I wasn't so sure I was going to get mine anymore.

I hadn't even realized I'd fallen asleep until I was startled awake by my phone ringing. I scrambled to answer it and Eliza's name flashed up on the screen as it started to ring again. For a few seconds, I thought I could remember the dream I'd been having, the gleam of gold, the warmth of an embrace... I shook it off, trying to focus on the present as I hit the green button.

"Hello?" I croaked, pushing myself up into a sitting position. I rubbed a hand over my face and grimaced at the creases the pillow had made in my skin. My mascara had probably smudged into little raccoon circles under my eyes, and I attempted to smear some of it away before giving up and slumping back down into the covers. The nights were getting colder now, and I couldn't sleep without a pile of soft blankets and my childhood stuffed animals next to me – even though it meant fighting through the jungle of them every morning.

"Alexander received your bracelet," Eliza answered, her words blunt and without so much as a hello. I appreciated it. I didn't have the patience for niceties right now. I let loose a sigh of relief but she continued before I could relax completely, "but... the package contained more than one."

"More than one bracelet?" I repeated dumbly, my brain still fogged with sleep as I fought my way to coherency. "That doesn't make sense," I murmured. Fuck, nothing about this whole situation made any sense.

"Check your mail, Vanessa," Eliza said, the command gentle but unavoidable, and I muttered an agreement. She liked me, or at least, she felt bad about my situation – but her priority was Alexander. I couldn't hold it against her. I was sure Ronan felt the same about me. A frown pulled at my mouth as I found myself wishing he was here again.

I stumbled out of bed, back towards the front door where the cardboard package was still waiting, looking for all the world like the contents weren't about to change my life. I couldn't bring myself to open it when I had come in, but now, I couldn't stop my hands from ripping into it, barely taking the time to put the phone on speaker.

Eliza waited silently, but I could hear murmuring in the background that I assumed was Alexander. I was glad that Eliza was there to separate us and could only hope I wasn't on speaker as I opened the package and a strangled sound tore from my throat. There was only one bracelet and no paper-work with any semblance of an explanation.

"There's only one," I told Eliza once my voice was back under control. I pulled it out of the box and shuddered, it was so warm against my skin that it almost burned. I dropped it back in the box. "But none of the paperwork is here – no certificate or instructions. Nothing."

"Maybe you should come over—" Eliza started, but my phone interrupted, ringing with another call.

My stomach dropped. Theo.

"I'll call you back," I said breathlessly as I accepted the call and cut off Eliza as she began to argue. "Theo?"

"I got a package in the mail." His voice was calm, soothing me in a way I didn't want to think about even as my stomach tilted at his words. "It had a bracelet in it. I thought it would be silver, that the gods had decided that a tattoo wouldn't suffice" – he cleared his throat lightly – "but it's gold."

"Just one?"

"Why would there be more than one?"

"Just double-check for me, okay?"

Silence fell for a few seconds, and then a hitched breath sounded through the phone. "How the fuck did you know there'd be two?"

I wanted to slam my head against the floor and scream, but I settled for clenching my hands into fists. "Because Alexander got the same package. I think it's time for us to meet up again. Whatever's going on, it involves all three of us."

7

A KISS WITH FATE

I'd had almost no sleep last night. I laid in bed, worrying, anxiety beating a ferocious drum in my chest and I half-wished we hadn't waited until class today to meet.

Ronan was one of the first into the classroom. Hardly taking a moment to close the door behind him, he rushed towards me and almost lifted me from my desk with his hug. The exertion of running across campus and the seasonal chill of the fall had kissed his cheeks a soft pink. I attempted a smile as I patted one absentmindedly.

"You doing okay?" he asked, letting go of me briefly as his eyes landed on the nondescript box next to me. The one that held only one gold bracelet. I wasn't really sure how to answer him and I knew he could tell as he started to pull me into another hug. I peered over his shoulder at the doorway and my breath hitched when I spotted a familiar blond head.

Eliza led Alexander in by his hand, his own box tucked under her arm. He had a phone pressed tightly to his ear and was speaking in clipped tones but his voice faded as he looked up and our eyes met. He hung up abruptly without looking away from me.

The row of desks between us felt insurmountable as a slight tug pulled in my stomach, like something in my soul was reaching out towards him. Like Ronan, his cheeks were slightly pink but it only served to make him look sweeter, more innocent, and highlighted the gleam of his eyes. His small attempt at a smile made my stomach flutter and I cleared my throat before hesitantly smiling back. Eliza glanced between us, opening her mouth like she wanted to step in but stopped when Tori and Theo shuffled in. Even from across the room, I could see the tension in the set of his shoulders, the clenched fists at his sides.

"Look, man," Alexander said, his face open and his blue eyes wide. He took half a step forward, extending his hand. Theo raised his gaze from the floor and looked at Alexander's hand like it could bite. His hands stayed deep in his pockets. If the situation were different, I might have laughed. These boys were polar opposites. "Just for now, maybe we could have a truce—"

The familiar clicking of heels against tile interrupted him as Lux swayed into the room. She observed us with barely any surprise before nodding and setting her purse on the podium at the front of the room. She pulled out one dry erase marker, her movements almost robotic with the tension in her muscles. I bit the inside of my cheek as I took in the tangible change in her demeanor. It was so different from her usual joking, sarcastic teaching style. Dread slid through me and I let out a resigned sigh. I wasn't sure how she knew we were meeting here, but I knew she couldn't be a harbinger of good news.

"Sit," she said curtly, waving her hand in the direction of the seats.

"We were just going to study," Theo said, the lie surprisingly believable on his lips as he plopped down into the seat next to me, Tori on his other side.

"It's okay. We don't have to pretend." Alexander smiled, dropping into his usual seat from class. Eliza sat next to him and placed a hand on his leg to still its bouncing. "I called her. She thinks she can help."

Theo's face was as dark as Zeus' thunder clouds as he sat up straight from his sprawl next to me and dragged his hands down his cheeks. His teeth were pressed together so tightly that I braced, waiting to hear a crack. "You told someone about this?"

"We obviously have no idea what's going on," Alexander replied, raising one eyebrow at Theo cooly, "and Lux is an expert."

"It's a clerical error," Theo snapped and Tori pressed a comforting hand on his shoulder, though I suspected she was also holding him back. "We didn't need to tell anyone else."

"If you really believed that I don't think you'd be here," Eliza sneered and Tori's upper lip curled. "Why else would you have rushed here, dragging your plat with you? Something weird is happening and there's nothing wrong with calling in reinforcements."

"Easy to say when you're the one calling them," Tori muttered. Her nails were long, sharp and painted dark purple but her fingertips were gentle as she rubbed Theo's arm.

"Now that I have your permission," Lux began, turning back towards the whiteboard. In a triangle, she wrote our names with blocky letters. It was strange to see them together, connected with dashed lines of dry erase marker. "I've read about something like this happening before. I would call it a rare occurrence, but I don't tend to embrace under-exaggeration."

"What have you read?" Eliza asked, flipping a pink notebook open. Tori leaned forward, taking in everything with rapt attention, and Ronan was staring at the board. His own worry increased my own until my hands began to shake. "And where did you read it? Medical journals? Which ones?"

"If I'm remembering correctly," Lux said, going back to her

purse and digging around. She let her sentence dangle in the empty air before letting out a hum of satisfaction as she pulled out a crumpled journal: *National Soulmate Scientific*. Throwing it at Eliza, she continued, "It should be about halfway through that edition. But this is a worst-case scenario."

Eliza had snatched it from the air easily and was already rifling through to the section Lux had indicated. When the pages settled, her eyes grew wide and I bit my lip nervously. She and Alexander were two rows in front of me, sitting just slightly too far away for me to see the title of the article. All I could make out was a banner that held a crying couple and a graphic of a ripped page.

Eliza pointed at the title, looking a little pale. "You think it's Split Soul Syndrome?"

"I think we need to entertain the possibility."

Theo sighed. "Okay, I don't keep up with this stuff. What's Split Soul Syndrome?"

"It's a soul disease," Lux answered, her brown eyes steady on Theo as she spoke. Theo's brow furrowed as a look of horror painted over his face. "The circumstances have to be very specific for it to happen."

"What are they?" Ronan asked, his voice was even but I could feel the worry churning in his mind.

"The disease is genetic," she explained, and Theo winced. Lux continued like she knew stopping at this point would be worse than continuing. She sighed before ripping the bandaid off. "It's usually the consequence of an unbroken familial curse, usually generations in the making. The split bond, if the article is to be believed, is almost always a personal punishment from a god. The godsplit soul, which the lead researchers call the Central soul, is attached to both its Original soulmate and the Extra addition to the bond."

"So, a god had to be paying attention to the Ceremony?" Tori asked, raising her eyebrows. We all turned to look at her in surprise. Her mind had followed the train of thought much faster than mine, but Cult of Dionysus members understood godly punishment more than most. Dionysus was, above most things, vengeful like his stepmother. "Well then, we can rule this out. There's no way an Olympian would be paying attention—"

"Uh, actually," Alexander interrupted. "My mother is a goddess. She makes a pretty big deal about being involved in the Ceremonies of her children, so there's a pretty good chance she was paying attention."

"And you didn't want to mention this earlier?" Tori snapped at him and Alexander shrugged helplessly. I didn't blame him, how could he have known it would matter?

"Which goddess?" Ronan asked, struggling to keep his voice level.

"Aphrodite."

"Fuck." Theo pressed the heel of his hand into his eyes. "Well, that's one of the requirements."

"What's next?" Eliza asked Lux.

"At least one of the souls must be damaged by some sort of trauma for another bond to attach. It would have to be something major that literally splinters someone's soul into pieces so that it could attach to the others. Dr. Holcomb suggests this usually stems from the loss of a soulmate, either platonic or romantic—"

Theo stood up, looking as if he wanted to run out the door. "Fuck."

"So that's a yes?" Eliza asked, her face now unnaturally blank.

Theo took a step toward the door. "*Fuck.*"

It was Tori that answered, voice tight as she pulled him back down into his seat. "Yes."

"Bad enough to…?" Alexander asked. His voice was hesitant, like he didn't want to ask.

"Bad enough," Theo answered.

"That's two," Ronan said, and I could feel the pressure he put behind the words building under my skin. Everyone leaned forward but I could tell they were keeping their eyes on me and I knew without checking that I was now blushing. "What's number three?"

"One of you must carry the punishment."

Everyone gave up on subtlety as they turned their heads towards me.

"To be blunt, has someone in your family line pissed off Aphrodite?" Eliza asked with a blonde eyebrow raised in my direction. I shook my head and she pressed harder. "Your parents? Your grandparents? How are their bonds? Their careers? Their fertility experiences—"

"Eliza," Alexander admonished, frowning. "That's rude."

"It's okay," I interrupted, and he swallowed his words. "Everything's fine. My grandparents just celebrated their fiftieth anniversary and they renewed their vows for the third time. My parents met before their Ceremony, when they were sixteen, and they've been happily married since before I was born."

Eliza nods. "By all measures, they sound *blessed* by Aphrodite."

Everyone sighed. Lux relaxed her shoulders. "Good, as long as your Ceremony went according to the guidelines—"

My heart stopped and then re-started as Ronan's eyes met mine, a question in them. Should I tell them? I thought back – the long wait for the fire, the whiteness of the Priestess' eyes. The darkness and the cold, ancient words that had poured from her mouth.

"—I think it's safe to eliminate this from our—"

"It didn't," I burst out, cutting Lux off mid-sentence. Everyone looked at me again. This time with shock and horror. My words were breathy as I grabbed on to Ronan's hand for support. "Not at first, anyway. The blood offering didn't catch on fire when it should've. We waited and it was only when I prayed to Aphrodite for help that things went... poorly. The Priestess was touched by some kind of divinity. She spoke Ancient Greek, too fast for me to understand, and I heard a laugh as the cloth finally caught alight."

"You should have told me," Ronan accused, eyebrows furrowing.

"But after, it *did* burn?" Lux said and they all waited for the answer, jaws tight and fingers tapping.

"It burned."

"And you didn't want to mention *this* earlier?" Eliza said icily.

"I didn't think it mattered. It worked," I said, swallowing heavily. "She accepted my blood."

"That's three," Alexander exhaled. "All three requirements for SSS."

Everyone was quiet for a few seconds, thinking about what exactly that could mean for all of us. Even Lux looked a little panicked – like she'd never expected it to actually be this. Worst-case scenario, she had said.

"What are the symptoms?" Ronan's voice cut through the silence like a knife.

Lux blinked, coming back into her own mind. "Until a cure is administered, the Central soul – I think that's you, Vanessa, because of what happened at your Ceremony – will feel the effects of having two soulmates essentially. It's all there in the article, but soulmate abilities can emerge for the Central with both of the other souls."

Goosebumps popped up as I hesitantly asked, "What's the cure?"

A prolonged silence. The overhead lights flickered from the storm outside.

"Divine intervention?" Lux answered tentatively. Eliza

frowned, not bothering to write that down. "No one really knows. This phenomenon is rare, like I said, and only a few people in the world are studying it. But I met a few people at a conference last year that have been doing some research. I'll reach out to them and Dr. Holcomb—"

"What do we do until then?" Tori demanded, smacking her palms on the desk in front of her. "We aren't going to stand around and do nothing."

Lux sighed, rubbing her temples. "I was hoping it would be something simpler. Something I could help you with right away. I'll keep looking into it but at this point, the only thing I'd suggest would be to test the bonds. Vanessa, if you tried to figure out which of them was meant to be your soulmate. The Original…"

I stared at her. Bonds were, for the most part, best understood after a kiss between soulmates and the gods considered a bond completely locked into place after sex. Most abilities appeared by then and if they hadn't, they always showed during or close after the consolidation of the bond. "You want me to *what?*"

"Erm," Lux tried again, grimacing at the way the words came out. "Get to know each other. Maybe if you found that you connected with Alexander or Theo more than the other, we could figure out who is the Original. Maybe then, we could break the artificial bond with the Extra."

"How much of this is guesswork?" Eliza asked.

"More than I want to admit to my students," Lux said but confidence returned to her voice as she looked us over with pity. "Give me a few days to see what I can find. In the meantime" – she looked at Alexander – "perhaps it's best to try to reach your mother. If she's the goddess who set this in motion, she's probably the only one with answers."

"I've been trying," Alexander admitted, frowning. It was a strange sight, like the clouds covering the sun. "But I just keep getting random assistants. I try to tell them I'm her son, and they keep saying, 'Yes, we're all children of Love' and then hang up on me."

Theo snorted. "This is a *fucking* nightmare—"

"Is there anything else we could be doing?" Tori asked, looking at Theo with an expression so worried, it looked alien on her face.

"While Alexander and Vanessa are working on their causes of SSS, it might be helpful for Theo to work on his," Lux said, her voice gentler. "Whatever your trauma is, you could try to lessen that soul-splitting damage. Maybe that'll help us figure this out too."

Theo nodded and Lux continued, "I'll go and call those other professors now. On the record, I'm not recommending this at all, but kissing your soulmate is what sparks other parts of the relationship – keep that in mind. Call me if you need to."

We waited until the clicking of her shoes disappeared completely before we began talking. Eliza and Tori spoke at the same time, arguing over which of their plats should kiss me first.

My fear spiked and my heart pounded in my throat. For a second, I imagined a golden lioness and a black panther fighting over a piece of meat. Didn't I get any say in this?

"Both of you," Ronan shouted in that authoritative voice of his and they paused and looked at him, "knock it off. This conversation doesn't even start until Vanessa decides it does. Then Alexander and Theo have to decide, too."

I stayed silent, struggling to think past my embarrassment. Alexander was staring at me when I finally looked up from the desk, whereas Theo's eyes were on anything but me. I glanced at the whiteboard where the dashes connecting our names looked so fragile, a representation of the impermanence of everything between us. I suppressed the sudden urge to erase the entire thing. My first kiss was supposed to *matter*. It was supposed to be *perfect* – not some experiment.

"Ness?" Ronan asked gently. The old nickname was only ever used in the most severe of circumstances to soften the blow of something life-changing. He'd used it only a handful of times. Once, when my dog died in middle school and once when he'd gotten Sam's information in the mail. His concern tasted like vanilla and cinnamon in my mouth, warm and soothing. The soft skin of his palm pressed against mine, keeping me grounded as I swallowed dryly.

I looked up at him, searching for something, anything, to help me decide what I should do. He gave a small nod of encouragement and my breath stuttered. It probably seemed stupid to anyone else, but this was yet another moment I had defined my life around and it was being taken from me. Ronan's confidence strengthened, our bond buzzing as steadily as ever in the front of my brain. I pulled my thoughts free from my nervousness. *It could be worse,* I reasoned. *It could even be... fun*. Decision made, I stood up and braced myself to kiss two of the most attractive men I'd ever seen.

8

THE JUDGEMENT

"Who first?" Eliza asked, raising her eyebrows at me in a way that seemed half-envious and half-pitying.

I opened my mouth to answer, but I wasn't sure what words would come out. Theo answered instead, "Alexander should go first. Chances are if it is a clerical error, he's the real soulmate."

"Chances are?" Alexander stared intently at Theo, who looked away uncomfortably.

"Don't," Theo demanded, his jaw clenched. "Don't ask."

Theo was right and his return to logic soothed me. If reason was determining this, it should be impossible for Theo to have another romantic soulmate. Whereas Alexander... but it didn't seem like reason was determining much anymore. This was Fate, vindictive as ever.

I shook my head slowly. "Maybe it should be you, Theo."

Alexander's face flashed with hurt before he pulled his features into a stony expression. He turned his head away to stare out of the window, even his profile was ridiculously perfect.

Theo frowned. "Why?"

"You're the outlier here," I explained, and his eyebrows

pulled down as though my words displeased him, despite him previously saying pretty much the same thing. "Alexander and I, we've never been…" I shook my head, trying to get him to understand what I was saying without having to actually say it. "You should go first. If the connection does happen—"

Then we know this is something beyond any clerical error, I thought.

"Okay, yeah." Theo blew out a harsh breath. "Fuck it, yeah, okay."

"Can we—" I licked my suddenly dry lips. "Can we have the room?"

"Of course," Ronan murmured, patting my head. He gestured for the others to leave ahead of him. Eliza shoved Alexander, her small, sharp hands on his shoulder blades. He threw a glance back over his shoulder but I avoided his gaze, unable to bear looking at him. Tori paused, checking in with Theo before she left. He nodded, and with a glare in my direction, she swept from the room. Ronan closed the door behind them.

Silence descended. I felt like my breaths were too loud. I was still standing and Theo sat sprawled in the chair next to me, I blushed as I turned to him. Our eyes met for a long moment before he snorted, slamming his head into his arms folded on the desk and laughing.

My cheeks burned hotter. "Something funny?"

"No," he said, voice muffled. The curve of his back as he leaned forward reminded me of a Roman arch and my muscles ached with the desire to trace the line of it. "And that's why I was laughing."

It didn't sound like an insult, but I bristled anyway. "If you don't want to do this—"

He cut me off with another laugh, bitterness poisoning it. He stood in a sinuous motion that drew my gaze, stretching as he took a step closer to me. The corner of one collarbone was exposed by the low zipper of his sweatshirt and the black edge of that damn hidden tattoo peeked out as the fabric moved. My eyes flicked to the sad smile on his face as he said, "Oh, I'm interested. I just shouldn't be." His smile faded and his face became serious, brow furrowing as he chewed on his bottom lip. The air in the room felt still as he spoke, like we stood on a precipice, not knowing how far we'd fall. "I know you're doing this because you feel like we have to, but we don't. Tell me to stop and I will. At any point. I'll tell them that it was me."

His dark eyes were as warm as the emotions I could feel coming from Ronan on the other side of the door. He meant it, and that made this an easy decision.

"I do have to," I murmured, matching his mood. We stood so close that his breath fanned my face, smelling like strong coffee and the faintest hint of cigarette smoke. Cool, but not unpleasant. "But I'm also doing it for me. Does that make it better?"

"Yeah," he said, leaning in closer until I could see the gold in his eyes forming rings around his pupils. "I think so." He tucked a piece of my hair behind my ear and let his hand linger on my cheek. "Is this okay?"

I made an approving noise as my hands found purchase on the cotton of his shirt. His body shuddered, swaying toward mine as though magnetized. He placed a warm hand on my waist. "Are you sure?"

"Yes."

"Vanessa?" he asked, close enough now that his nose brushed mine. His hand moved down to my neck, sending tingles across my skin until I felt dizzy with excitement. With possibility. It weighed down my eyelids as I blinked slowly up at him. My breathing quickened as the hand on my waist began to rub small circles into the yarn of my sweater. "Can I kiss you?"

His lips brushed mine as he spoke, and a flare of heat bolted through me. Unfamiliar but entirely welcome.

"Yes, please."

The kiss was soft and light, different to what I'd expected. Theo's mouth moved slowly, giving me every opportunity to pull back or push him away. I didn't. Instead, I slid one hand up to wind around his neck, fingertips skimming the soft, dark hair at the nape.

A sound emerged from his lips, a little bit like a moan and a little bit like a sigh. It vibrated against the sensitive skin of my lips as he pulled me firmly against him. I bounced on the heels of my feet. I'd been dreaming about this moment my entire life, like every soft-hearted little girl. There was a lot of pressure in the simple meeting of lips. *What if I'm not doing it right? What if he hates it? What if—*

He pulled away just far enough to whisper, "Stop worrying. You're doing fine. Just relax."

I tried to follow his suggestion, keeping my eyes closed as I clumsily tugged him back to kiss me. A huff of a laugh pressed against my mouth, and then Theo was kissing me again. This time it was different, deeper. A spark lit in my chest and my nerves began to buzz alongside his. The kiss moved through me, exposing me like a nerve but Theo's touch was gentle and I wasn't afraid. I gasped into his mouth as his tongue brushed mine and his hand tightened on my waist for an instant. I leaned into him completely, balancing on my toes to deepen the kiss.

There was an open line from my heart to my mind and Theo was everywhere in between. My whole body hummed, resounding with happiness, and the pleasure of the scruff of his beard against the soft skin of my face. It was a perfect first kiss. Because he was my soulmate, and he was warm and happy in my arms, kissing me like I'd always imagined he would.

You imagined this?

It was his voice in my head. A caress against my temples, the barest brush of a kiss. His mind sat across from mine amidst the chaos of the bond – dark and rich and fragile like coffee grounds – and he was beautiful. Absolutely stunning.

I've been waiting for you my whole life.

It was too honest, too open, and he froze, uncomfortable. One thought flashed through his mind then. One that he couldn't hold back. It was just a name, but it was a reminder.

Margot.

A shield. A barrier. It meant everything. I shivered as pain rushed through me and I gasped as Theo's mind closed off, leaving me feeling lost in the chaos between our souls. He pushed his body away too – gentle, but firm, his hand on my hip settled the distance between us. We were both breathing harder than seemed reasonable.

"Well," I said, wiping my mouth and turning away from him to hide the hurt on my face. I felt him reach out before letting his hand fall to his side. "That answers that question."

He opened his mouth again to speak as there was a knock on the door, and Ronan called out, "Guys?"

"We're done," I replied and the door opened almost as soon as the words left my lips. Alexander, predictably, shouldered his way through the door first, eyes wide and curious. Eliza still had her hands on his back, steadying him. There were a few feet between me and Theo, the kiss we shared felt a million miles away.

Alexander swallowed. "So?"

Theo stayed quiet so I assumed it was up to me to answer. "A bond formed. We're soulmates."

"Abilities?" Ronan asked as the blood drained from Alexander's face. Eliza's muscles tightened as she held him upright. His eyes fluttered shut and, gods, the only thing stopping me from crossing the room and comforting him was the knowledge that it could hurt him more.

"Mind reading," I said and shook my head to focus.

"That was quick," Ronan said, attempting a smile that faltered when neither of us returned it.

"Test it," Tori commanded, watching her plat with worried eyes. Everyone turned to her in confusion and she shrugged. "See if you can do it now. Sometimes the circumstances can determine how it works. Do you need to touch to hear each other?"

Can you hear me? I tried, pushing my thoughts towards him.

Yes, he responded dryly. *I hear you loud and clear.*

"We can hear each other," I answered, keeping my eyes on Alexander who seemed to be concentrating on his breathing. I held my hand out to Ronan, and he closed the distance between us in a few steps.

"Do you need a couple minutes?" Ronan asked, lips pressed to my hair.

I exhaled. I did want a break but I knew I'd chicken out if they gave it to me, so I shook my head and squeezed him tighter for just a moment before releasing him. "No, I'm ready. Alexander?"

His shoulders moved up and down with each deep breath. "I'm ready, too."

Everyone made their way back out the door in an awkward shuffle that would have made me laugh under any other circumstances – this was like the most serious game of *Seven Minutes in Heaven* that had ever occurred. Eliza stopped briefly to ruffle her plat's hair affectionately and Alexander smiled down at her sweetly.

Theo paused just before the door closed, his face carefully blank. "Try not to think too loud, okay?"

My face burned as I nodded. It was going to be a miserable couple of minutes for him, but I would try to do what I could to make it easier.

Alexander stood still on the other side of the room, his hair had lost its perfect wave and his clothes, still expensive and designer, had wrinkles. He drummed his right hand against his thigh nervously, and I couldn't stop the wave of guilt that hit me as I took in the pale tinge to his skin and dark bags under his eyes. He seemed frozen in place, unable to decide whether to run away or move closer.

I took the first step forward and hesitantly opened my arms. "Come here," I said and his eyes grew wide. I made a dissatisfied noise when he stayed rooted to the spot. "You look like you're about to face the executioner. Come *here.*"

Alexander took one step and then two, and then suddenly my arms were full of six-feet-and-too-many-inches of shaking college athlete. He buried his face in my hair, his long arms closing around me. The muscles in his back trembled under my hands. We breathed identical sighs of relief as our shoulders slumped.

"I didn't like that," he murmured, breath ruffling my hair.

"I know. We won't do this again." I pulled back just far enough to see his face as I ran my fingers through his hair. "Are you okay to... continue?"

He swallowed again and his cheeks turned pink. "Yeah, it's just that I, uh, haven't done this before. I mean, I know you have—" He cut himself off as he realized how strange that sentence had the potential to be. He coughed. "I just mean, I might not be very good."

A bubble of hysterical laughter. "Theo said I did okay."

He groaned as if in pain, pressing his cheek to my head. "Please don't joke about that."

"Sorry."

"It's okay," he sighed. I couldn't see him from where I was squished against his much larger frame but I could picture him, blond and tall and everything I always imagined my soulmate would be. The perfect compliment to my dark hair and brown skin. A living daydream.

After a moment he pulled back, tilting my face so that I could see his eyes. My nerves sat sour on my tongue, but Alexander touched me like I was made of glass and crystal and everything precious in the world. "I keep meaning to tell you," he said, his voice barely reaching my ears, "how beautiful you are. Better than any dream I've ever had."

It was so close to what I was thinking that my heart faltered in two painful thumps. "Alexander…"

"Vanessa," he murmured, pressing his forehead to mine. "Can I—"

"Yes, of course."

A pause. His mouth quivered a little, embarrassed. "So, uh, how should I—"

"Just lean down a little? Okay, a little more – *Zeus*, you're tall."

"Like this?"

"Yeah, like that. Ready?"

"I think so?"

"Okay."

Our noses met as our mouths did. *Which did not happen with Theo.*

And then I felt horrible for even comparing the two. To make up for it, I pressed myself closer to Alexander and let myself fall into the sensation of being so close to him. He moved his mouth slowly, like he was waiting for me to take charge. Small movements, unsure. It could feel good, but the angle was wrong. He was just so damn tall and we were both struggling with it.

I pushed him back just enough to say, "Let me get on the desk."

He lifted me by the waist as if I weighed nothing and a small thrill swept through me. *He was so strong.* His muscles barely flexed with the movement. He stepped closer again so that my thighs were bracketing his, and my breaths came faster.

Our lips met again and we both sighed at the tingling sensation that took over our bodies. It wasn't like it was with Theo, which felt like a sudden click into place. This was a slow, consuming sense of balance. He fit me. We matched. Our minds didn't blend into each other with the rushing speed of Theo's bond, but as we kissed my mind expanded and I could feel that there was room for another.

Theo's bond buzzed, squeezing and contracting to make room for Alexander, and my heart felt like it could beat out of my chest. Alexander's bond was all gold and soft-pinks and seafoam green. The colors exploded as we kissed, like a sweet glimpse into his very soul. He was a quick study and soon he was licking gasps and little sighs from me. My hand on his neck scratched in his hair and he pressed in closer, thumb stroking my cheek the way someone would caress their finest treasure.

This, I thought probably too loudly, *is my last first kiss, just like in the fairytales.*

I pulled away again, trying to stop the smile that threatened when I heard him take a few stuttering breaths. Keeping my eyes closed, I reached out into the dark with my soul and felt his response, eager to please and connect. The sound he made was sinful, low and rough. He leaned his forehead on mine and I couldn't stop the smile this time as I rubbed soothing circles on his back.

"Thank you," he murmured, pressing a kiss to my forehead. "Thank you."

There was a knock on the door. Ronan's voice called out, "Guys?"

Alexander didn't move but his entire body tensed. The magic in the room that had thickened until it curled around the desks like fog, smelling of sea salt and orange trees, thinned until it was almost a memory of itself.

"Alexander," I said because I liked the way my tongue

wrapped around the syllables of his name. "It's not fair to make him see us like this. He didn't do that to you."

"None of this is fair," he sighed but stepped away. His hand lingered in mine for a moment but he let go with another surge of strength and shoved it into his pocket. "I just wish... I'd always imagined—"

"I know. Me too," I said, sparing another second to smile at him. It took him a few seconds but his mouth curved into a smile too and my chest felt lighter. "Come in, guys."

Only Ronan and Eliza entered. "Everything okay?" my plat asked.

"What's the verdict?" Eliza asked at the same time, eyes on Alexander.

"We're soulmates," I answered, trying to see around them into the hallway. Alexander's mouth pulled into a larger grin, almost bashful, and Eliza's eyes softened from jade to grass, her mouth lifting at the corners.

Ronan's eyes remained neutral. "Are there two bonds?"

I nodded, swallowing and pressing a hand to my warm chest. "Yeah. Two."

His mouth set into a line as he nodded. "Okay, so I think we can rule out clerical error."

"And confirm that it's some form of SSS," I said, biting the inside of my cheek. I glanced behind, noticing a distinct lack of brunettes. "Where's Theo? And Tori? They should know."

"You were, uh, projecting," Eliza said as delicately as she could and I turned red as I wondered what Theo had heard. "He went for a walk. Or, you know, sprinted away in the hopes that the distance would weaken the strength of your shared thoughts."

"Fuck," I sighed and Alexander's head whipped in my direction, looking shocked at the word coming from my mouth. I ignored him. If I concentrated, I could sense Theo's bond. It was muted and much further away than before.

You can come back now, I said to him through our bond.

Need a few minutes. Sorry.

You don't need to say sorry for protecting yourself.

Just a few minutes, please.

Okay. Did you hear—

Yeah, Vanessa. I heard.

"Have any abilities manifested?" Eliza asked and I got the impression she'd make a fantastic doctor, methodical but with just enough care to take the edge off. "No immediate telepathy?."

Alexander shook his head. "No, not yet."

"That's totally normal," Ronan assured us both. "You know, it took me and Sam almost the entire 24-hours after we kissed to get our emotion-sharing ability. It doesn't mean anything."

"I know," Alexander answered him, frowning.

Theo walked back in a moment later, his face and mind wiped free of whatever he'd been feeling before. Tori trailed behind him, looking unsure as to whether coming back was a good idea.

"What next?" I asked, feeling breathless as I watched both of my soulmates fidget under my gaze. Theo jammed his hands into his pockets and Alexander couldn't contain his energy, teetering from one foot to the other. "Where do we go from here?"

"It's probably best to streamline our conversations," Eliza answered, pulling out her phone and gesturing for us to do the same. "Not that I don't enjoy our panicked phone calls, Vanessa, but let's make a group chat so that we all have a chance to see information at the same time."

We all pulled out our phones. Alexander's was brand new, still shining from the plastic screensaver. Theo's was cracked and at least a few years old – functioning but definitely worn.

When Eliza finished putting all the numbers in we all split into our plat pairs. Ronan threw an arm over my shoulder, protective and supportive. "Okay," he said to everyone. "Then we'll go our separate ways, but when an ability manifests between Alexander and Vanessa, we'll contact each other."

"And if one doesn't?" Theo asked, not unkind but curious.

"Then, we'll deal with that, too," I answered him, watching Alexander's face fall. Theo mentally cursed himself for the unintended bite of his words and I glanced up at him in surprise.

"Lux said to explore the bond," Alexander said in the sudden quiet, fidgeting when we all looked his way. "So, we should probably see each other again, soon, right? I have a practice Saturday. It's stupidly early, but if you wanted to come…"

I smiled as I answered, "I would love to."

He smiled, a delicate hummingbird of a thing. "Great. I'll send you the details—"

"If he gets time to explore his bond," Tori interrupted, her pretty face pulling down into a dark look, "then Theo should get the chance, too. Don't you have that gallery thing downtown next week?"

She posed the question to her plat, who thought another curse before answering. "Tori, she doesn't want to come to that. It'll be boring as hell. You know that nothing even sold last time—"

"You should go," Ronan advised me, cutting Theo off and making Tori grin. "Spending time with them – both of them – should help you flesh out the details of the bond, right? Test the bonds. See if you get along with both or either of them." He smiled down at me. "You know how Sam and I are. You feel it through me. See how it happens with them."

"Smart," Eliza said, narrowing her eyes at Ronan. "If you do feel it with one, it'll be easier to tell who the Extra is and then—"

We all frown, looking away from one another uncomfortably. It would be easier to separate that soul from the others and snip it away from the bond like it was a tumor or a piece of string held by Atropos.

It's me. Theo's thought was clear of static and hesitation.

I cast a glare at him. *You don't know that. Don't say that.*

I don't get another chance at all this. A pause. *Or, at least, I shouldn't.*

Knock it off. We don't know anything, yet.

Silence from him. He seemed better at cutting his thoughts off than I was. I felt a stab of envy, but it also made me wonder what his soulmate ability was the first time around. And if, like our kisses, he prefered what Margot could do.

Same as us. Telepathy, he answered the first but left the second blessedly unanswered.

"I'll go," I answered Tori out loud, before looking at Theo again. His face remained blank, and I doubted myself. "That is if you're okay with it?"

He shrugged. "It'll be boring as Hades. But sure." A thought flitted through his head so quickly that he couldn't hide it from me: *I'm excited.* And then, when he realized I'd heard it, *Fuck.*

His mind cut itself off from me, a block going up between us so that I heard nothing. My mind sat empty, waiting for his to open up again. Theo clenched his jaw and looked away from me.

Ronan must have felt my frustration because his arm tightened around me and he shepherded me towards the door, away from both of my soulmates. A strange thought. "We'll see you soon. And if anything happens, use the group chat."

"Sir, yes, sir," Tori muttered but allowed Theo to lead her out. He pulled her arm, and though it was faster to go out the door Ronan directed us to, he led her in the other direction. Alexander and Eliza walked with us until our paths diverged and they headed to the parking lot.

"I'll see you tomorrow," Alexander murmured to me. "Bright and early."

"Bright and early," I repeated, smiling up at him.

Our bond sang between us as he smiled back, bright as the rising sun. As they walked away, Eliza said something to him and he threw his head back with a laugh. I smiled wider as I watched them together.

On the other side of the building, Theo and Tori disappeared down the path leading to the Cult Houses. In the darkness of the night, shoulders slumped and thoughts shut off between us, Tori's mouth moved and Theo's head bobbed in response, agreeing with whatever she said. The block between our minds held. We were soulmates, but by all means, he felt further from me than ever before.

9

BETWEEN SLEEP AND WAKING

I dreamed in darkness like the shading on the edge of a charcoal drawing. Variations of gray danced in Van Gogh stars. Between heartbeats, they began to evolve into new colors – jewel tones, opaque pastels and earth tones that seemed as real as anything I'd witnessed with waking eyes. Chaos into cosmos.

Black abyss melted into the ground as Gaea did a million years ago. Painted flowers at the edges of the endless horizon swirled into shapes in the sky, clouds and birds and trees lingered on the skyline. A table began to form on the ground, growing up like an organic creature right before my eyes – a picnic table with room for a family and a whole meal to satisfy them. The smell of the food wafted to my nose and even though I knew I was dreaming, I could still taste the salt of the cheese and the sweetness of the apples and the bitterness of the pomegranate seeds.

A shoulder brushed mine as a new shape formed, solid and familiar at my side. I recognized his soul before I saw his face or the golden curls hanging over his forehead and ears. He smelled like mint gum and expensive cologne, and the warmth of clothes fresh out of the dryer.

For a moment he just blinked at me. "Vanessa?"

I laughed, spreading my arms wide as the world breathed. "Did you do this?"

He nodded and then shrugged. "I think so? I just thought that you didn't deserve to dream in darkness."

I smiled at him and offered my hand, he took it without hesitating. I liked the idea of being second nature to him. Like the ancient stories, the words of Homer and Hesiod and Plato were right. The way our bodies were molded by the hands of the Olympians, we'd always been a part of each other. Like my hand was his hand and my heart was his heart and my dreams were his dreams.

I led him to the bench by the table, holding his large hand in both of mine as I urged him to sit. I settled close, my thigh brushing his, and pressed a kiss to the back of his hand. His breath stuttered.

"So dreamsharing, huh? What do you think about this?"

Alexander laughed and it rang a little sad. "I think I got the short end of the stick here. He gets you all day. I only get you when you're sleeping."

"Hey," I admonished, squeezing his hand before brushing a lock of hair away from his eyes. "Don't say that. Whatever the reason this is our ability, it's just for us. It's a gift from the gods." I paused and gave him a grin. "Besides, what guy doesn't want their soulmate all night?"

That startled a real laugh out of him, making his face look like a sunflower, blooming as he blushed. I leaned forward and brushed a kiss across his right cheek, knowing I likely wouldn't have been so brave if I were awake. My heart pounded but it felt good, the beat reverberating even in my toes.

"You're right," he agreed with me, closing his eyes and letting his thick lashes brush against his cheekbones. He sighed and the leaves in the oak trees around us bent with his breath. When his eyes opened, they were a little glassy. His voice was a whisper as he reached out to touch my cheek. "I can't believe you're real. That you're mine. I've spent my entire life waiting for you and listening to my mother's stories about the greatest loves in history – Achilles and Patroclus, Hector and Andromache – but you're better than

anything I ever imagined. Because you're mine. Because you're real."

I swallowed, my emotions rising up too thick to speak. Our bond pulsed, almost tangible between us. "Alexander..."

His mouth lifted and he pressed a kiss to my forehead. "It's okay. I understand. You don't have to say anything." He's so obviously a child of the Goddess of Beauty and I sighed as he lifted up my hand to play with my fingers. Every line of his body was cut from marble with care, a mix of sensuality and sweetness and power. His body could only be described as divinely inspired – but his soul was even more beautiful. The colors of it framed the edges of the dream, painting us in a gorgeous glow that I knew I'd miss when I woke up.

"Do you think time passes the same here?" he asked as if following my thoughts.

I shrugged. Dreamsharing was a rare ability that only manifested for soulmates with long-intertwined souls. Ancient bonds. Movies talked about dreamsharing, occasionally using movie magic to try to recreate all this. Only, now I knew it didn't compare to the real thing.

"I hope you're actually rested tomorrow," I said finally, letting go of his hand to reach into the bag of cherries that were suddenly sitting next to me, enticingly open. Cherries were my favorite and I had no idea how he knew that. "I don't want you drowning on me at practice."

He laughed. "I promise I won't drown. My mother was created from the sea itself. I'm pretty sure it's actually impossible for me to die in the water. My body is ridiculously buoyant."

"Does that count as a performance-enhancing drug?" I joked, popping a cherry into my mouth.

"You laugh," he mocked, bumping his shoulder into mine. "But it was a serious debate when I first started competing at the collegiate level. My mother had to get Zeus himself to sign off on it. But, to be fair, if we banned every demi-god from sports, the Olympics would be incredibly boring."

I laughed at that, thinking how regular humans would look

*participating in the big events at the Olympics, like Nereid catching
and trireme oaring. Ridiculous. But it did remind me of something.
"Wanna hear about the time I accidentally challenged a daughter of
Poseidon to a swim race when I was in preschool?"*

"I want to hear anything you want to tell me."

*The bag of cherries never emptied and the sun didn't set, even
when my mouth and teeth were stained red from cherry juice and
Alexander had to catch a drop from my bottom lip. He said nothing,
just licked the drop from his thumb and managed a wink when I
blushed, though the gesture was a little clumsy. He was as new to all
of this as I was, but it felt right in my soul – our soul – to learn
together. The world was left suspended while we dreamed and I had
no clue what was waiting for us when we woke up, but even sleeping I
couldn't help but begin to love this golden creature.*

Though I had been a student at Golden Valley for a few years
now, I'd never made it far enough into the recreation center to
see the swimming pool. I got lost for about thirty seconds as I
explored the labyrinth of halls underneath the main exercising
area and pulled out my phone. I was mid-text to Alexander
when the faint smell of chlorine wafted by me. I smiled as I
walked, remembering only the vaguest parts of our dream last
night – golden blond hair, a checkered tablecloth, soft smiles. It
was a first date in a world that didn't exist outside of us, but I
couldn't wait to see him again.

I followed the smell to a pair of glass doors. It was early –
stupid early, actually, just as Alexander had warned – but the
entire swim team had turned out, wading in the shallow end of
the pool. A soft smile spread across my face as I watched my
soulmate lecture them.

One of the ten swimmers looked my way and tapped the
shoulder of the guy in front of him, they both grinned as they

turned to Alexander. He was smiling already, enjoying the simplicity of the practice and the jokes lobbed between team-mates. But as he turned to spot me, his smile grew and our bond buzzed happily between us. I blushed as I finally looked away. Everyone on the team was looking over at me and I figured I couldn't hide behind the doors anymore.

"Hi," I said, walking over to him. Ignoring the giggling that surrounded us, I hoped they would mistake my blush for warmth as I moved further inside the pool area. "Good morning."

"Good morning. Hi," he responded, eyes wide and his team laughed. Alexander frowned and pointed to the other side of the pool. "Alright, start your warm-up. The person who finishes last has to organize the weights for the varsity team."

As they groaned, pushing off the wall and racing each other down to the other side, Alexander walked over to me. I closed the distance and wasn't sure whether to feel relieved or disappointed that, unlike the rest of the team, he was wearing sweat-pants and a t-shirt. Then my brain took over, imagining Alexander standing in front of me dripping from the pool and I looked away hastily. Yeah, maybe I wasn't ready for that yet.

"Hi," he said again, anxiously drumming his fingers against his arms.

"You already said that," I teased, opening my arms for him to step into them. The warmth of his skin radiated through the thin t-shirt and I pulled back enough to look at him and asked, "Is there a reason you aren't swimming?"

His cheeks turned pink and I wondered briefly how far down that blush went before wrangling my thoughts under control.

"Yeah, I realized that maybe it was a little creepy to invite you to hang out when I was almost naked. This is the JV practice that I usually help coach."

I was a bit disappointed that I wouldn't get to see him

showing off in the pool for me, but I was mostly just glad to see him. We needed to talk about our new ability and text the group chat too. Shock flared briefly when I realized I had been so excited to see Alexander this morning that I hadn't even taken a moment to text Ronan about it.

"So, dreamsharing, huh?" I said quietly, despite the fact that most of the swim team currently had their heads underwater. Talking about your abilities in public wasn't taboo, but it definitely erred on the side of flirtation.

Alexander blushed harder, leaning toward red this time, and I grinned, loving that I had that effect on him. His hands encircled my waist, his thumbs nearly touching as he pulled me slightly closer. "That must mean our bond is strong, huh? Ancient, maybe."

My brain kicked into overdrive, thinking a thousand sappy thoughts and an entire line-up of movie moments just like this. Before I could respond, Theo's voice sounded in my mind, slow from sleep and sweet-sour with reluctant affection: *Sweetheart, could you keep it down?*

The nickname was new and my brain bounced excitedly. *Sorry! I'll try!*

Kay. His thoughts slowed and I realized he was asleep again.

"Vanessa?" Alexander asked, eyebrows furrowing.

"Sorry," I apologized. "Theo asked me to think quieter. I think I woke him up."

Alexander's eyes lost their softness. The same protective look on his face that I'd seen in class. "It's not really his place to tell you how to think."

"He can't help it. He shouldn't have to wake up this early just because I can't keep the volume of my thoughts down. It's probably good if he tells me. That way I can work on it."

"Work on being less excited to see me?" he asked, and I could tell it was supposed to be a joke, but it fell flat. His eyes had lines around them from his pinched smile, like he had something to say but didn't want to make me angry. I wished he would, just to get it out. I couldn't read *his* mind.

"On not projecting it," I clarified patiently, pulling back a little more. "How would you like it if you had to hear every thought I had about Theo? If you had to hear what I was thinking when we kissed?"

He shrugged, letting me pull away without any hesitation. "It'd probably be better than wondering what you were thinking. Not having any idea what was happening on the other side of the door of that room. Just waiting was one of the worst things I've ever done."

"I'm sorry."

He shook his head and his blond curls bounced. "It's okay. Well, I mean, it's not *okay*, but you didn't want this to happen, either. Neither did Theo, I know, but seeing as he's probably the Extra soul in the bond—"

I stepped away, surprised and a little offended on Theo's behalf. "You don't know that."

"It just makes sense," Alexander said, and I grit my teeth at his tone of effortless condescension. "There was a goddess present for your ceremony. Why else would my mother be there if it wasn't because I was the Original soulmate? As far I know, Theo isn't particularly close to Apollo."

My heart fell to my stomach, weighed down with disappointment, and I moved a few more steps away. Heads began to turn in our direction and I lowered my voice for Alexander's sake. "We don't know anything about this bond yet. As far as I can tell, he's my soulmate too, and I don't want you to talk about him like he's some sort of impermanent fixture to get rid of—"

My volume increased despite my best efforts and Alexander winced. "Hey, shhh, okay? I'm sorry, but it's the obvious answer—"

"Nothing about this is obvious," I sniped, blowing out a

breath of air with annoyance and pushing my hair out of my face. The humidity of the pool had felt pleasant after the cold weather but now it felt suffocating. A few of the swimmers were treading water, waiting for further instruction. They ducked their heads to murmur between glances in our direction. "And don't shush me."

Alexander's face paled slightly and he took a step forward as I moved a step back, opening and closing his mouth like I'd caught him completely off guard.

"I'm going to head out." I moved back a few more paces towards the glass doors with as much grace as I could manage. "It was good to see you, I guess. I'll text the group chat and let them know that our ability manifested last night. I have to go study. I'll see you later."

"Vanessa—" he tried, unsure.

"Goodbye, Alexander," I cut him off and ignored him when he called my name. I swept through the doors, leaving steamy handprints on the glass.

"Wasn't she supposed to stay for the whole practice?" I heard as the doors closed behind me.

Several voices chimed, "Anderson, shut up."

Quieter, Alexander said, "Yeah, she was."

10

BITTER TO SWEET

I felt dazed as I caught the bus downtown, not even really sure where I was headed except *away*. Rain began to drizzle as I found a seat. I let my mind clear a little as I watched the trees through the window, their shapes changing as the water made them bow. The words Alexander and I had said played on a loop in my mind, but worse was the way I felt every emotion afresh. I wasn't sure I recognised the person who had so easily spoken their mind to Alexander. Was it because he was my soulmate? Or because it was easier to defend Theo than it would have been to defend myself? I was still reeling as I dashed through the rain and into the first cafe I saw, my feet carrying me in as if on autopilot while my brain remained rooted in the moment I had shouted at my soulmate.

If Alexander couldn't get hold of his mother... I needed our Detroit trip to be tomorrow, not in a few months.

The cafe was small, decorated with pinks and grays and only a handful of seats. I squeaked into one of the booths as I shrugged off my wet cardigan and promptly began to shiver. The rumbling of conversation and the espresso machine were soothing, and I finally felt my tension begin to ease. It flooded back when I remembered I still needed to message the group chat.

I sent the message and silenced my phone as a pretty waitress with dark hair and skin drifted over. She placed a menu and a glass of water on the table with a smile.

"Any idea what you want?" she asked, and I wanted to simultaneously laugh and cry at the loaded question.

I shook my head. "Not yet. Thanks."

I was in the middle of deciding between wildberry and lemon-mint tea when Theo's end of the bond buzzed to life. It was still relatively early and I could only hope that my brooding on the bus hadn't woken him. I had no idea how to block my thoughts from him yet.

It didn't, he thought, inner voice somehow sleepy. *Morning.*

Good morning, I thought back, relieved. His thoughts faded to background noise and I ordered the lemon-mint tea with a splash of milk and honey at the waitress' recommendation. An acoustic cover of an 80s rock song pulsed over the speakers, soft and somehow familiar. The colorful artwork on the walls captured my attention for a while as I procrastinated, musing over the juxtaposition of pastel colors in some and deep charcoal lines in others. I sighed and finally pulled out my Latin textbooks from my backpack – I hadn't lied to Alexander if I actually *did* study. I tried to translate some of the mass before me, feeling strangely on edge, looking up and at the door several times before glancing back down.

The waitress brought over my tea and a small plate of cookies and I smiled my thanks, looking up from the text gratefully. I tried one while I waited for my drink to cool and groaned at the sweet and buttery taste as it crumbled in my mouth. My tea cooled in just a few minutes, and I was already nibbling at a second one when Theo spoke up again.

Where are you? You feel... close.

A cafe downtown. I think it's called Golden Rings?

No shit, he responded, amusement laced throughout the words. *You gonna be there for a while?*

A few hours at least, I whined in answer. *I don't know why I took Latin this semester.*

Theo's thoughts faded back to a hum, and I got caught in a rushing sensation like maybe he was driving somewhere. The waitress brought over another plate of the butter cookies a few minutes later and I thanked her, already shoving another one into my mouth.

"They're delicious," I complimented her, spraying crumbs.

"Thanks!" she laughed, a bubbly sound. "I wake up early to make them every day."

"It's definitely worth it."

"I'll keep them coming then," she winked before going back over to the counter to rearrange the display of cakes in the glass case. There were a dozen different designs, all mirror-shiny and beautifully colored. Edible works of art that made me wonder if she was Cult of Apollo.

I didn't look up when the bell above the door rang, too focused on trying to figure out all of the ablatives in the sentence I was reading. It wasn't until the new patron sat down on the other side of my booth that I looked up distractedly to see Theo. The bond in my breast throbbed as if in welcome.

"Of all the cafes in all the world," he greeted me, voice even but eyes crinkling in happiness, "you walk into mine." His dark hair was up in a bun and small droplets of rain were caught in the wisps that hung down on either side of his face.

He had on a black t-shirt with the name of the cafe embroidered on the left shoulder and a matching black apron was thrown casually onto the table between us. My eyes dipped unbidden to where his forearms rested, exposed. Strange tattoos twisted over his skin, dark red and serpentine, glimmering with the occasional burst of gold. They were artistic offerings to the gods. A request for magic to improve his art –

judging by the bursts of laurel leaves and symbolic pythons, likely to Apollo. They slithered under the hem of his short-sleeve, and I burned with the desire to know what they looked like in their entirety, curling my fingers in to stop myself from reaching out and touching one.

"Your cafe?" I asked, blinking up at him.

"Well, Tamara's," he clarified, tilting his head towards the smiling, bronze-skinned woman behind the counter rear-ranging the display of cakes. "She owns the place, and I guess I'm cheap labor because I'm biologically obligated to help her out."

Once he'd said it, I could certainly see the resemblance between them and tried to think back to whether I'd done or said anything too embarrassing earlier. It was still early, but things were picking up as we spoke. Coffee orders were grunted and boxes of donuts were bought for offices. I half-worried that Theo's sister might call him to help, but she was the picture of ease as she handled the customers.

"I like it here. Nice ambiance, good cookies," I said honestly, touching the sides of my mug to see if it was cool enough to hold before moving its warmth close to me. Goosebumps still covered my arms and Theo frowned when he noticed them, immediately sliding out of the booth. "If you don't mind the smell of coffee, I have a sweatshirt in the back that you can borrow?"

The thought alone warmed me. "I'd love that."

He was gone for only a few seconds, disappearing through the door behind the counter and ducking away from his sister's gentle slap. I didn't hear what Tamara said to him as he came back through, just his laugh as he told her to stop. His eyes were still crinkled at the corners as he approached me and I smiled as I accepted the sweatshirt, tugging it on over my dress. The name of the cafe was embroidered across it in blocky letters like a Greek epigraph. I caught the quick surge of pride that Theo felt at seeing me in it – like I was his and he could keep me. The thought was a little possessive and arrogant. It was so different from his usual attitude toward me that it made me laugh.

"Sorry," he said lightly, a faint hint of a blush staining his cheeks.

"It's okay." I reached out and squeezed his hand for a second. I intended to pull it back, but he laced our fingers together and warmth fluttered through me. We were both a little surprised at his gesture, but neither of us moved away.

I took another sip of my tea, trying to keep my mouth busy so I wouldn't speak and ruin the moment. But I nearly spat it out when he said, "You're here pretty early. There a reason you aren't at his practice?"

I hesitated and his thoughts were soft when they reached out to me. *We don't have to talk about it if you don't want to.*

My knee-jerk reaction was to brush it off. But Theo was my soulmate too and if I was going to talk to anyone about this, I supposed it should be the person who could literally understand my mind. *It, uh, didn't go well.*

He raised his eyebrows. *I wasn't sure the golden boy could do anything wrong. What happened?*

I wasn't sure what to make of his response, he'd sounded almost... jealous. I thought back to the pool this morning, how it had started and how it ended. *It started out fine. I was excited to see him—*

I remember, Theo thought, amusement coloring his tone and softening his lips as he watched me.

Exactly, I continued, pacing myself with another sip of the sharply refreshing tea. *After our ability manifested last night, I was, you know, happy to see him. But then, after you asked me to, uh, lower the volume, he got weird.*

His thumb began brushing over my knuckle. *How?*

He thinks you're the Extra in the bond, I thought.

Theo was silent, only raising one eyebrow.

Anyway, he was really arrogant about it. I probably overreacted, but I don't like him thinking that you're something extra. I don't want him to think that he's more special to me than you are.

He was quiet for a few moments, a brick wall of silence in his mind stopping me from knowing what he was thinking. Slowly, as if giving himself permission, words trickled from his mind to mine. *He's probably right, you know.* Theo pulled his hand away. *I've already had my chance at all this.* I felt his hesitation before he added the next part, like he couldn't decide whether he should be so open. *I'm just happy we have this time together.*

I already had one dramatic exit today and I don't want to do it again. I thought with a tight jaw. *We have no way of telling who's the Original and who's the Extra, so don't count yourself out, yet, okay? It's in the hands of the gods.*

The gods haven't been too kind with my soul in the past.

Alexander would understand that if you told him.

No, he thought and the word was firm. *When people find out, they ask questions that I don't want to answer. Some people on campus remember me and Margot being together, they look at me funny. If Alexander looked at me like that—* He shook his head.

So, you'd rather keep this between us for now?

His smile was sad, teeth tugging at his lip in something similar to regret. *Yes, thank you. I'm just already sure this is all going to end badly – like the first time. I don't want to see their looks when it turns out that I've lost two soulmates.*

I leaned over the table and pulled his hand to my mouth, brushing my lips to his knuckles until low-boiling affection replaced the grief in his mind. *Have faith that it can be different. For me?*

For you, he thought and smiled, the smallest, sweetest thing in the world. It wasn't brilliant like the sun, but it made my heart and soul burn slow and hot. It had only been there a second, but it made me shiver with something that had nothing to do with the cold weather and all too much to do with this man in front of me.

I'm fond of you, I thought and it was like a caress to my psyche when I felt his brain do the same exclamation mark thing my own had been doing all day. He coughed lightly, looking off into the cafe where his sister was handing someone their change, like that would help control his emotions.

Thank the gods for small miracles, he thought.

I snorted and threw the nearest napkin at him, laughing as he swatted it away. He had to let my hand go to do it, so I grabbed the last butter cookie while I could.

"You want me to get more?" he asked, glancing at it.

I shook my head. Tamara was already coming over with a new plate. She switched them out and ruffled Theo's hair, laughing as he tried and failed to pull away. On the plate next to the small pile of cookies were two chocolate-covered cherries, and I sent her a beaming smile as I popped one in my mouth.

"Cherries are my favorite."

"I know," she said, laughing at her brother when he groaned and placed his head in his hands. His bun flopped forward comically, and I hit the heel of his foot with my heel, delighted that he'd obviously been talking about me. "He told me you mentioned it to him at the tattoo place."

"Tam, please—" he started, and she laughed again.

"Alright, I'll stop embarrassing you," she gave in, heading back to the counter to serve a couple with matching gold bracelets. "But five more minutes, okay, Romeo? I need your help with the cinnamon buns in the back. I promise I'll let you take as many breaks as you need."

"Sounds good, Shakespeare," he snarked.

"Watch it, kiddo." But there was no heat in the threat, and she grinned as she walked away.

Sorry about her, Theo apologized, and I could tell he was blocking me from whatever he was thinking again. Disappointment unfurled for a moment before I could stifle it. *She can be... nosy, I guess. But she means well, I think. It's hard to tell.*

I don't mind, I admitted, *I'm jealous, really. I'm an only child, so I could only dream of having someone embarrass me like that.*

Careful what you wish for, he thought darkly but there was a fond undercurrent. There was an odd humming in his mind like he was thinking of something I couldn't hear. It reminded me of earlier when he'd blocked me from hearing his morning routine.

You're so good at that, I said to him, noticing the way a blush highlighted his cheekbones and the clean line of his facial hair at even the smallest compliment. *Editing your thoughts, I mean. I'm sure mine must be like the worst run-on sentence.*

I had a lot of practice with Margot, remember? he answered, surprising me. *And don't worry. I was like that in the beginning. She made fun of me all the time for how often I thought about color theory.* I laughed and he continued, *Your thoughts are cute, though, and very honest.*

What do I think about?

Ronan but that's not a bad thing. You love him a lot. It's nice.

I do. He's my favorite person in the entire world.

She'd pretend to hate to hear it most likely, but that's how I feel about Tori too.

His phone vibrated against the table.

Speaking of plats, he thought and gave me a small smile. *You might want to text Ronan about all this. You silenced the group chat right? He wants to know how you're doing.* A small pause. *I like him. He seems like good people. Sam, too.*

I'll text him. Promise.

Our gazes met and held each other for a long moment. His lips twitched up into a smile and mine followed. No words were exchanged, but happiness vibrated through our bond.

Still, he sighed and pushed himself out of the booth. He tucked a strand of hair behind his ear and ran his eyes over me once more. "I gotta go help. But stay as long as you like. I can stop over again if you want?"

"Always."

"Uh, good. Great." He paused and tilted his head back. "I'm going now."

"Okay," I suppressed a laugh.

"Okay," he said hesitantly, like maybe he actually wanted to say something completely different. Theo turned around and walked away but before he disappeared behind the door again he thought, *I'm fond of you, too.*

My heart bounced in my chest at the confirmation. I did know that, or at least I'd hoped. My tea was cold when I took another sip, but it was still sharp and sweet and I liked it all the same. Theo's sweatshirt kept me warm, and I buried my nose into the collar of it, inhaling deeply. He was right. It did smell like strong coffee, but I thought that maybe I could like the bitter drink after all.

11

THE GENTLE GOD

In Olympia, a thousand votive offerings sat with the names of oath-breakers carved into their busts. They were a final warning to all Olympic competitors to stay true to their word – their names, fathers' names, and hometowns all announced to the world. It was a practice still used. There was no hiding deceit from god or man with the King of the Gods watching over you.

In my elementary school, we'd had a similar hallway filled with pictures and the names of students who'd cheated on their standardized tests. Words, to me, were not clever things to twist and play with. Honesty was clarity. To me, a promise was an oath to Zeus, and it made being caught between two soulmates even harder.

Tamara wandered near me as I started organizing my Latin papers. I glanced up with an apologetic smile as she moved to clear one of the now empty plates of cookies Theo had brought over earlier. But she waved me off.

"Listen, consider this place your second or third home, okay? My little brother is your soulmate. You're family," she said, her face stern but sincere until she suddenly smiled brilliantly, revealing dimples. "If you need help with your vocab, let me know. I loved Latin in college."

I laughed but it faded quickly the moment I turned my phone back on and a dozen messages popped up. Everyone but Theo had responded to the text about the dreamsharing and Alexander had texted me privately a bunch of times.

Alexander: Hey, I'm sorry about this morning. I was a dick. I don't want you to think that I see Theo as lesser than me or anything like that. I'm just struggling with this whole thing more than I thought and it took you leaving to make me see it. I'll do better though, I promise.

And an hour after that:

Alexander: I saw your text to the group chat, and I just wanted to make sure you got home safely? When you see this, will you let me know? The weather is bad today :(

And then another half-hour later:

Alexander: I'm guessing you've silenced your phone because you're not looking at anyone's messages in the group chat. I feel horrible about this morning. Will you let me apologize in person?

And then another hour later:

Alexander: Or over the phone, if that works better? I'll do whatever you want. Just let me know.

I finished reading the texts as Theo slid into the seat across from me. I must have been frowning at the messages, or maybe he just picked up on my thoughts because he asked, "What's wrong? Your face is sad" as he undid his bun to shake his hair out and massage his head.

I was so distracted by the way his hair looked – *had I seen it down before? Would he let me touch it?* – that I forgot he'd asked me a question. There was a smugness to the hum of his thoughts that he didn't bother hiding. He liked my reaction to him. Liked that he could make my stomach flip and my cheeks blush.

Instead of responding to his thoughts, I slid my phone over to show him the messages from Alexander. He sipped from a mug of coffee as he read and almost offhandedly thought *Apollo, he's wordy.* But to me, he asked, *So what are you gonna do?*

I shrugged. *What do you think I should do?*

It was easier to ask him for advice like this, mind to mind. If I had to have this conversation out loud, I likely would have stumbled over my words or blushed or both. I just had to feel it, think it, and Theo knew exactly what I needed. I laughed a little as I wondered how we must look to the other patrons, silent but laughing, staring across our mugs. Our ability was rare, with most people receiving something simpler, like emotion-sharing rather than telepathy. Including Ronan and Sam.

Let him apologize, he thought after a few moments, sliding the phone back to me. *He was a dick this morning. But, you know, this isn't easy to deal with. He's getting only half of your attention. Think about it. He's probably spent his whole life dreaming of you. Now he thinks he's losing you.*

I guessed Theo of all people understood what it felt like to actually lose a soulmate.

I texted Alexander that I could meet later and he responded almost immediately, offering to come to my apartment. I sent him a time and my address and slid the phone back for Theo to see.

He nodded approvingly. *Good. Talk to Ronan yet?*

I shook my head. *I wanted to deal with this first.*

Call your plat, Vanessa, he thought and I could tell he was serious even though the words were soft. *You have more emotions than anyone I've ever met. He's probably confused and worried. You'll feel better if you call.*

I reflected on my exit from the pool. The broody bus ride. The surprise at seeing Theo.

Fuck, I thought and Theo choked on his coffee.

"I've never heard you swear. You look like someone who doesn't swear."

I shrugged. "Yeah. The skirt and the knee-high socks can be deceiving."

You're telling me, he thought and from the speed of it, I could tell he hadn't meant to let me hear it. I stared at him in shock as another thought slid my way – a picture. It was nothing vivid, just a sketch of me with bare legs. It wasn't particularly sexy or anything, but it was intimate. Or, at least, the desire for something intimate, and that was new.

I raised my eyebrows at him. *Really?*

He winced. *Sorry.*

It's okay, I thought, almost wanting to laugh and thinking about all the things I probably thought during our kiss and when his hair was down for just a few seconds. Though it was doubly flattering that he couldn't control his thoughts even after years of practice. *Go back to work. I'll call my plat.*

Yeah, yeah, he agreed, standing and stretching. My own mind caught on the way his shoulders filled out the t-shirt and the lines of ink swirling on his skin. There was a smugness to his thoughts again as he walked away and out the back. *Tell him I said hi. Sam, too.*

Ronan answered on the second ring. Though we were separated by a few city blocks, a rush of relief came over me and I honestly couldn't have said if it was from him or me. "There she is! I was wondering if you fell off the edge of the world."

I laughed, shoving my textbook and homework into my bag and clearing what little mess I'd made from the table. Talking to him, the minutes easily passed into hours.

When the sun dipped, I said goodbye to Tamara with Ronan still on the other end of the line. I laughed as she pressed a bag bursting with cookies into my arms and told me to come back as soon as I could. Theo emerged from the back and promised to text me the details about the gallery event before pressing a soft, buzzing kiss to my cheek.

The drizzly ride home slipped by easily while Ronan and I chatted. It wasn't until an hour or so passed, video chatting him and Sam as I snacked on hummus and pitta in bed, that the doorbell rang and I remembered inviting Alexander over. I said a rushed goodbye and hurried downstairs, running my hands through my hair anxiously. Alexander stood just outside my door, head bent and dripping, his hand raised like he was unsure whether to ring the doorbell again. Despite this morning, I couldn't help the flood of happiness that filled me when I saw him. His hair hung lower than usual, curls straightened by the weight of the rain, making him look younger and his eyes bigger, more vulnerable.

Still, my face must have betrayed my forgetfulness, because slowly he said, "You did say six, right?"

"Yes!" I answered, wincing at the eagerness in my own answer and his mouth twitched upward. "I did. I, uh, just got home and was talking to Ronan on the phone. I completely lost track of time. Just plat things, you know?"

He was beginning to shiver from the chill in the air and I quickly moved to the side, holding the door open wider as I beckoned him in. His body relaxed as the warmth hit him and I inhaled the scent of his cologne as it drifted past me.

"Can I get you anything to drink—"

"Look, about this morning—"

We both stopped short and the silence stretched until I laughed, flustered. Alexander rubbed the back of his neck, a gesture that I was starting to recognize as his default during awkward situations.

"Water," he answered, swallowing. "Water would be great."

"Okay."

I walked him to the small kitchenette and stifled a laugh at the sight of his large frame in my kitchen. Alexander was tall, he had a few inches on Ronan and a kind of shining presence that created an illusion of occupying more space. With him in there, it was almost claustrophobic.

I gestured to the bar stools in front of our short counter and he sat, fidgeting with his hands. I popped some ice in his glass before moving to the sink. His voice followed me as he scrambled to apologize again. "I know I said this over text this morning," he said, "but I really am sorry for what I said earlier."

"I forgive you," I said, sliding him the glass and smiling when he began to draw squiggles into the condensation on the side. "I understand this is hard, but I also can't listen to you talk about Theo like you did. How would you feel if someone talked about me like I was something frivolous on the side for you?" Thinking about the language Lux used in the classroom, I added, "Like I was a tumor growing where it shouldn't be?"

Alexander frowned but nodded like he'd reached that conclusion on his own already, and I breathed a small sigh of relief.

"I wouldn't like it. At all. Which is why I feel so bad about what I said." He sighed deeply before looking into my eyes. "Look, this situation sucks for all of us and I made it worse on you this morning by making you feel like you had to choose. You don't. None of this is really up to you."

I frowned. "Thanks?"

He blinked as if only just hearing his words and then groaned, putting his head in his hands. Water dripped on the counter, and I wondered if I should offer him a towel. "Gods and my mother is supposed to be charming. I guess I didn't inherit any of that, huh?" He gave a weak laugh and I smiled gently. "What I was trying to say is that it wasn't fair of me to make it feel like it's a competition between me and Theo and I'm sorry for assuming that I was the Original. You're right. There's no way for me to know that."

"Thank you for apologizing," I allowed, the words coming

out too fast. "I'm trying my best to figure all this out and I know you are too. But until it is, I need you to treat Theo like he's a real person and not your rival or something. He's a good guy and if you two could just talk to each other..."

In my head, I heard a reprimand, *Vanessa...*

I ignored Theo and continued, "An apology would be a good place to start."

"I don't know if I can be friends with him," Alexander admitted, unaware of what was happening in my head as he waved his hands in front of him like he was painting a picture. "You saw us even before all of this happened. We were at each other's throats about something as dumb as scheduling a time to meet for our project." He shook his head. "But, you're right and I'll try. I'll apologize to him too."

"Thank you," I said, reaching for his hand. "It would mean a lot."

His thumb rubbed the same spot Theo's had earlier and a shiver ran down my spine. His eyes filled with an emotion I couldn't translate and his words fell heavy in the quiet of my kitchen. "As I said earlier," he whispered and my heart clenched in my chest. "Anything for you, Vanessa."

ΊΣΤΟΡΊΑ - ἈΜΦΌΤΕΡΟΣ

BOTH

The men in Attica were secluded in their giant cities and imprisoned by the neighboring lands, lacking the freedom of island life. They wrote in choppy sentences about how a good woman should act, though most had spent too few minutes with real women to have experience in the subject. But that did not stop them from writing.

They said their women should not be outside the home, should not speak with other men, should never bare their skin to the world. They said their women should be passive and pale and without a clever bone in their body.

Vanessa stripped her own clothes off at the cliffs. Her orange chiton, new sandals, and simple copper necklace hit the ground unceremoniously. She unpinned her curls, letting them unravel until they covered her breasts and below. The waters around her island home were always clear, the color of Alexandros' eyes, or perhaps, like the jewels that his mother wore on her neck, wrists, and ankles. From the highest point of the cliff, Vanessa could see the rocks at the bottom and the silver-scaled fish darting in and out of shadows for food and safety.

She had feared the waves for almost twenty years now. Her

mother, overprotective and who deferred to the King in all matters pertaining to her daughter's rumored beauty, had instilled a love of the dirt and roots and earthly miracles. They spent their midnights with the other women of the island, calling out prayers to the goddess of such things.

Vanessa held more privilege than most girls, unmarried and unmothered at the age of seventeen. She declared herself eleutheria when foreign suitors came to her king, asking for her hand.

But this love of land came with an ignorance of the sea. She knew nothing of saltwater serpents, even those that swam up to the nexus of the waves.

Vanessa did not swim. But today, she would.

She tilted her head to the sky, asking for a blessing, and jumped from the cliff to the sea below.

The chill of the water was a balm to the dry heat of the wind, rushing over her exposed skin like a caress. She didn't touch the sand at the bottom but she could feel herself sinking lower and lower. She had never been submerged before, not like this. The local river ran a few miles from her home and she had snuck off to it with her hand-maidens on occasion. But all they ever did was splash around and wet their tanned toes amongst the minnows. This was nothing like that.

This, she thought, was death.

Because Vanessa did not swim and today, she was drowning.

She opened her eyes under the water, the pain of the salt surprising her. She screamed and lost the air that had been trapped in her lungs. She thrashed her arms and snapped her eyes shut again, calling for anyone, god or man, to help her. To save her. But water filled her mouth, her throat, her chest, and the damage was done. She floated in the dark and her last breath trickled out like the blood of a sacrifice. The current slammed her against the side of the cliff. The rough edges of the rock and the coral slicing her skin to ribbons.

She could not help the images in her brain, stolen from the stories of sailors. The ones she'd eavesdropped upon as they were drunkenly shared at the king's dinner table. The sailors spoke of things like *sirens and sea monsters and the blue, bloated bodies of their dead friends. She thought of their fingers, gnawed down to half by the beasts of the deep. Then her thoughts drifted away and she was no longer human but a nameless body, bobbing in the waves like a fisherman's line.*

"Oh, hello," a voice spoke in her mind, sounding surprised. She imagined warm brown eyes surrounded by dark lashes that blinked at her. "You aren't supposed to be here. Not yet. Not for a while, Vanessa."

She remembered hearing this voice before but did not know when. She had lived on the island all her life and could count her female friends on just her hands. But this voice did not belong to any of them.

"Who are you? Where am I?" Vanessa asked.

"Where do you think you are?"

The darkness began to take on different flecks of color, jewel-toned and metallic. The endlessness began to sharpen at the edges, forming corners and boundaries, creating a definite space. And then the black wasn't black anymore, but dark brown filled with roots and crushed leaves. It was soil, almost loving in its familiarity to her. Then shapes began to form in the soil, long and white and calcified. Bones, she thought, a tibia here, a femur there, drowning in exotic fabrics and jewels. Branches of trees grew around the bones, red fruit plump and crowned.

I am with the dead, she thought without speaking.

"You are," the voice replied kindly. "But you won't be for long."

"Am I dead?"

"No," the voice said. "You have much to do before I can greet you in person, I hear. But we have only a few minutes together. Do you wish to ask anything of me or my husband? I get to meet so few of my followers while they still breathe and I am feeling generous today. Whatever you so desire, it can be willed."

"Who are you?" Vanessa repeated, but she knew. Had called her name into the caverns between tree stumps every night for years.

She'd spent her entire life hearing about this voice. The one that used to speak to women and children nightly, but who was now usually as silent as the rest of the gods.

"I am the Goddess of Opposites," the voice answered. "And I protect your island home. Tell me, Vanessa, daughter of Demetria, what do you want more than anything in the world?"

She thought of golden hair and a brilliant smile, long legs striding next to her as she carried a bucket of ewe's milk. But as this thought appeared, another joined its side, slower but steadier. The image of dark curls and an artist's hands, covered in clay at the potter's wheel.

"Perhaps I misspoke," the voice amended. "Not what do you want, but whom?"

Her thoughts snapped forward and backwards like the head of a striking snake, intent on killing its prey. The decision, in equal measures, felt like poison and hands around her throat.

"I can't decide," she gasped into the darkness. Her mind raced, she couldn't refuse the goddess this answer. "Please, please – I do not wish to insult you. Give this offer to another. I cannot—"

The voice paused. "You are the only human to ever decline my gift."

"I'm sorry—"

"You are not what I expected," the voice became emotionless for the first time. "I will remember this. When you are at your wit's end, when your heart is breaking, and you have no one to turn to, when you reach your Fate with shaking hands and bleeding soul, remember the name of the goddess you rejected and what she offered you, once upon a time. Remember that a goddess' word is never broken."

The threat rushed at her like an angry boar, tusks curled and aimed to puncture. She flinched, raising her arms and legs to block the attack. It never landed.

12

STUMBLING WORDS

My mother answered her phone after the third ring with a gentle hello that instantly made me homesick. With fall firmly in place, the trees at the edge of our property would be blooming, attracting people looking to pick apples, drink craft beer and take pictures in front of an aesthetic background. If I closed my eyes, I could almost smell the richness of butternut squash soup, followed by the turkey with cranberry sauce that my mother and grandmother would be preparing in their restaurant for the season.

"Hey, Mom." I relaxed into the couch and muted the TV. One of my favorite movies was playing. The heroine cried silently as she discovered her soulmate was none other than the arrogant, prideful gentleman of their neighborhood. I'd seen it so many times I didn't need the sound to know what was going on. Two romance novels lay discarded next to my feet on the coffee table, their spines cracked. I had been trying to keep my mind off my own soulmates before finally giving in and picking up the phone for advice. "Do you have time to talk?"

"For you, always," she answered. A door closed and the chatter in the background disappeared. "What's up?"

Thankfully, Ronan had taken the task of filling her in when we had found out my soulmate results. She'd only let him off the phone after he'd promised I would call as soon as I was ready.

I'd put it off for too long and I sighed as I relayed what had happened over the past few days, getting a little choked up again. Her opinion was that Theo shouldn't have run and that Alexander was likely right. This was all just a clerical error. I winced at her words before telling her how annoyed I'd been when Alexander had said the same thing that morning. By the time I finished explaining, she was humming in a vaguely disappointing way. "Well, that was a bit self-centered, wasn't it?"

I nodded before remembering she couldn't see me. "It was, yeah."

"But?" she asked, laughing lightly. "I can tell you want to defend him."

"He felt bad right away. He apologized to me and agreed to apologize to Theo."

"So, he's a little arrogant, maybe," she deduced, "but not purposefully malicious."

"Right," I said, clutching a nearby pillow to my chest. "Honestly, if I didn't like Theo so much, I would probably agree with him. But when I'm with Theo... I don't know, there's just something about him that I can't ignore—"

"You like him then?" Her tone was teasing, and I could easily picture the twinkle in her dark eyes as she asked the question.

I could still smell the coffee on his sweatshirt and I breathed it in as I replied, "I do."

"More than Alexander?"

I was instinctively shaking my head before I could even think anything through. "No. I like them the same."

The quiet on the other end of the line told me that was the wrong answer. "Vanessa, you do realize that one of them isn't your soulmate? At some point – and we should be hoping for sometime soon – you'll have to say goodbye to one of them."

"Mom," I complained loudly, knowing the truth of her words but feeling their sting nonetheless. "I know—"

"I just hope you're taking precautions with your heart," she insisted. Something squeaked in the background and I imagined her leaning back in her office chair, eyes now on the ceiling. "And I don't want to be the bearer of bad news, but if Theo did already have a soulmate—"

"Mom!"

"—then it might be time to start hedging your bets with Alexander," she finished, and I could hear her frown through the phone. "Theo might be a handsome bad boy with a leather jacket – which I get, so was your father – but I looked up their pictures online and Alexander is so tall and he has the kindest eyes and I don't want to sway you but—"

"But what?" I said and it came out sharper than I had intended.

"But Alexander didn't run."

For once, I had nothing to say in response.

"So what are you going to do now?" she asked after a few moments of silence.

I knew she wasn't asking in a hypothetical way, but a part of me still wanted to respond with *I don't know, give up?* Instead, I sighed, flopping totally back into the couch. "Alexander can't get a hold of Aphrodite and things keep getting more confusing. Our packages after the results had the wrong number of bracelets and when I kissed Theo and Alexander I got abilities with both of them—"

"What abilities?" my mother asked, curious.

"Theo and I got telepathy," I said, a blush rising to my cheeks.

An impressed noise. "That's amazing. Congratulations. And Alexander?"

"Dreamsharing," I answered, blowing out a lungful of air.

She was quiet for a long moment. "That's incredible, Vanessa. An ancient bond?"

"Maybe," I answered, deflating. "We don't know. We don't know *anything*, really. At this point, our only plan is to meet with Aphrodite during our trip to Detroit for this stupid group project, so she can help us sort this whole thing out." I paused, sighing louder in my empty apartment. "I just wish a god could come down now and tell me who to pick."

"Well, are you praying?" she asked.

I snorted. "To who?"

There's a pause, and I knew she must be thinking through her answer or trying to soften her words. I bit my lip as I waited to see which would prevail.

"I think you need to initiate into a Cult this semester, Ness. I know you should have until you graduate to decide and I normally wouldn't pressure you if I didn't think it would help, but now is the time to have a deity on your side. Let me call the Cult of Demeter representative in your county, and I'll have them make some introductions."

"Okay, Mama," I said, sighing into the pillow. My movie called my attention back for a moment and I smiled as the hero swept onto the scene, pulling the heroine into a dance across a marble ballroom. Her dress fluttered and her impassive expression cracked when she saw his Cult of Aphrodite dove necklace. There was so much you could tell about someone's soul based on their Cult and I wondered what it said about mine that I had yet to fit in anywhere.

Our next class could've been penned by Euripides, it was that much of a tragedy. I found my seat early, as always, and was laughing with Ronan as he pulled out his phone to show me the photos he'd taken last night. They'd hosted a Star Wars themed event at the tattoo parlor and we were cracking up over photos of Sam dressed as Princess Leia, complete with the white dress and two fake buns affixed to the side of his head. Sam's makeup, much like his tattoos, was a work of art.

My stomach hurt from laughter as Ronan told me how two different Han Solos had attempted to initiate the declaration of love scene, only to be scared away by Ronan's Chewbacca impression. Theo walked in just as I started to wheeze from lack of air and I had to pause to wipe the tears from my eyes before I could see him properly. He sat down in the chair behind me, kicking my ankle and looking unperturbed at the glare being directed his way by the guy who usually sat there.

Hey, Theo greeted me, and I turned to find his eyes warm on mine while I tried to catch my breath.

Hey, I smiled, glad thoughts couldn't be breathless. *You're here early.*

He shrugged but kicked me lightly again. *Wanted to see you.*

Ronan carried on with his Han and Leia story and I nodded in all the right places as I responded to Theo, trying to keep the smug smile from my face. *I know.*

Other people began to trickle in, filling the seats. Tori sat down behind her plat and offered me a wink that took me aback. There was nothing behind it except casual acknowledgement, but I was pleased anyway. She flashed a grin down at Ronan, a jokingly-flirtatious thing and I sighed, *I think their project is going better than ours.*

Alexander walked in later than usual. The room was already full and he was only a few moments earlier than Lux. Instead of sitting down, he walked determinedly over to me and Theo. He was worrying at his bottom lip as he stopped next to us. I opened my mouth to ask if he was okay, but he spoke before I could. My heart lurched as I realized he was here to talk to Theo and not me. *Shit, he isn't going to try and apologize right now, is he?*

"Hey, man," Alexander said and people were turning their heads to watch, eyes curious. Panic overwhelmed me as I realized that was exactly Alexander's intention. "I just wanted to say that I'm sorry for what I said to Vanessa yesterday—"

Oh, Hades, no.

"You don't have to—" Theo tried to interrupt but Alexander talked on. A steady stream of cursing pounded in Theo's head and he sank back into his chair, making himself as small as possible. It seemed like he knew Storm Alexander simply had to be weathered. Tension lined every inch of his body and I wondered how Alexander couldn't see it. I wanted to say something, do something, but I was frozen. I didn't want to pick sides and Alexander was only really doing what I'd asked of him. The problem was that they just didn't know each other at all. Anyone who'd spent even an iota of time talking to Theo knew he loathed public spectacle and here Alexander was, throwing him in the middle of one.

Alexander's eyes were wide and sincere. Theo's were tight with panic. Guilt ate at me, knowing that I had set this in motion.

"I want you to know that I think you're an okay guy," Alexander continued, completely oblivious to my panic and Theo's reaction. Everyone's eyes were on us, even Lux made eye contact with me, raising her brows. "Besides, we're both compatible with her according to the split—"

"Alexander!" I hissed, finally cutting in and yanking on his sleeve until he fell into a nearby seat. "Be quiet, please."

He frowned, his cheeks flushing as he looked at me with a little hurt. But he lowered his voice slightly and I breathed a sigh of relief – until he continued. "Anyway, Theo, I think this could be the start of a decent friendship, or a decent partner-ship for this project. Gods know that we need it. Vanessa, in our dream—"

"Alexander," Eliza snapped, stressing the middle syllable of his name. I prayed for a god to come down to stop this, like Athena in the Odyssey or any other deus ex machina.

But nothing came and he just kept fucking talking, "—made a point that you're not as tough as you seem on the outside, and I like her and she likes you, so I think, mihi soulmatae est tibi soulmat—"

"Okay, class, let's begin!" Lux called out, interrupting him with her cutting voice. But it was about three seconds too late and Theo stood up, grabbed his bag, and walked toward the door with his head down, face inscrutable. "Sorry," he said to the professor without slowing. His mind was closed off from me, the static louder than anything he'd used before.

Tori's glare ricocheted between me and Alexander as she grabbed her stuff and bolted after Theo. Lux began speaking but the words didn't reach me as I stared at Alexander in horror and shock. What had he been thinking? The rest of the class turned, their stares gone but whispers just beginning and I sighed, poking gently at the mental shield between Theo and I and finding no give.

"Huh," Alexander said, looking at the door to the classroom and frowning. He reached down to get his stuff out of his back-pack, apparently clueless about his own role in this. "I don't think he forgives me."

Eliza's jaw clenched and her manicured nails tapped against her desk, unusually irate with her plat, and I yanked on his sleeve until he looked at me. Alexander's eyes widened when he took in my expression – half-angry and half-pained from the tension of the bonds in my chest. Already, the stress of the interaction was giving me a headache.

I kept my voice low and pointed as I said, "After class, we need to talk."

He couldn't read my mind or feel my emotions, but whatever he saw made him swallow and nod, his head bowed in submission. He licked his lips. "Uh, sure, okay, whatever you want."

Lux continued with class as if nothing had happened. Alexander took fastidious notes, following the lecture, but worry prevented me from learning a single thing.

I wrote down the title of the lesson – *what the gods do for you* – but my mind spun and by the time the lecture ended, I just had a page of doodles.

Ronan tilted his head, silently asking if I was okay, and I attempted a smile. I took two extra copies of the assignment being passed around to give to Theo and Tori later and ignored Alexander as he tried to catch my eye.

Images of the gods filled the pages – classical statues like the Olympic Zeus, modern photographs like Zeus giving his State of the World address in a sharp business suit – and small descriptions about each of them and their roles with soulmates. The Aphrodite section stretched for three pages and the urge to pull my hair out was renewed. I couldn't even get Alexander and Theo to sit in the same room for longer than two minutes, let alone work on this project.

Theo? I tried again and the static paused briefly. *I have our assignments from class for you and Tori. I know you probably don't want to see me or Alexander, but we need to go over our plan for this soon.*

Okay, the static shield snapped back into place almost immediately after the word.

I sighed and Ronan reached across the aisle of our desks to offer his hand. I took it and a wave of comfort fell over me, the pounding against my temple growing weaker.

When the clock struck the end of class and our classmates exited the room, Alexander turned in his seat to look at me.

Before I could say anything, Eliza spoke, "Alexander, darling, you have no idea what you did wrong, do you?"

Alexander looked between us all, eyes wide as he shook his head.

And just like that, I couldn't be mad at him. I'd seen his soul and basked in the lightness of his dreams – he was good to his very core. This wasn't an act of revenge to spite his competition, he was just only working with part of the information and it had spiraled out of control.

"Theo," I tried to explain, choosing my words carefully as the static in my mind quieted, "is an extremely private person. You bringing up this whole situation in front of twenty-something strangers is like a nightmare for him."

Alexander glanced around the room, and I knew he was imagining it full, taking in its size for the first time. Still, he asked, "Why would we hide this?"

"He doesn't think of it as hiding," Ronan answered for me, and I wondered if Theo had talked about us during his last tattoo session. "It's just not anyone else's business. If you want to talk about your bond with Vanessa I'm sure he wouldn't mind, but the split bond shouldn't be something you talk about without his permission."

Alexander nodded. "I guess you're right. Gods, I didn't even consider…"

He paused and looked at me, frowning even more. My hands vibrated with the urge to smooth out his brow, but I let him process the situation without anything more from me. "Do you think he'd let me apologize again? In private this time."

"I'll ask," I said. *Theo? Did you hear that?*

Yeah, he responded, the static breaking for a moment. *I need a bit of time though.*

"He needs to cool off a little." Alexander's shoulders slumped, guilt written across every angle of his perfect face. This time, I pressed a palm to his cheek, unable to resist soothing him any longer. "Hey, you didn't mean for this to happen."

"I didn't," he said it like an oath. "And I'm sorry to you for continuing to put you in a place where you have to choose whose side you're on. I said I wouldn't do it again—"

"You didn't mean to," I repeated. "I forgive you. I'm sure Theo will, too."

Ronan frowned but said nothing and I knew I needed to ask him about that look later.

"I have to get to work," Eliza announced, pulling Alexander up by his arm. He let himself be moved, eyes still downcast and fingers drumming against his thigh. "We'll see you—"

"Wait," I interrupted again and they both hesitated. "Eliza, I was wondering if there are any Cult of Athena events going on. I need to initiate somewhere soon and I figured—"

"That I might be a good guide?" she filled in, stopping me from droning on.

"Exactly."

"Crest Industries is hosting a meet-and-greet with some of the movers and shakers of Golden Valley's business sector. I'll text you the details," she glanced at her watch and then started dragging Alexander out again.

I nudged Ronan with my shoulder. "That was a dramatic class."

His laugh surprised me. "Every other class seems boring in comparison to this."

I couldn't stop the grin forming as I looked at the now-empty classroom. "You know, I think I like Eliza."

Ronan snorted and put an arm over my shoulder. Maneuvering us out of the classroom, he said, "Of course you do. I don't think you've ever met someone that you don't see the good in. Now, how do you feel about macaroni and cheese with broccoli?" I must have sent a wave of hunger at him because he threw his head back with laughter again. It soothed my headache even more. "Yeah, I thought so. Sam has a batch baking now and wants your opinion on this floral piece he's working on for a Cult of Aphrodite member."

I couldn't imagine a better distraction. "You're too good to me."

In the worst Han Solo impression I'd ever heard, he said, "I know."

13

MONEY AND BLOOD

My last class on Thursday ended early but my good mood soured once I got home, a note was left on the refrigerator informing me that Ronan was spending the night with Sam again. I crumpled the note in my hand and threw it in the direction of the trash can, sighing when it didn't quite make the journey. I pulled a can of lentil soup from the cabinet, ready to warm it up and spend a night watching the newest rom-com. I had just resigned myself to another night alone when my phone rang.

Alexander's name flashed on the screen, and I answered with surprise, "Hey, what's up?"

"Hey," he responded, his voice soft. In the background of the call, there was a laugh and then the sound of someone shushing someone else. "I just found out that my swim practice got canceled, but I was already on campus, and well, I planned on working on our project tonight anyway, so I was wondering if maybe you wanted to work on it together? If you're not home, I totally understand, but I just thought that it might save us effort if we could just—"

"Alexander," I interrupted, holding back laughter. When we

first met, his rambling would've made me question his sanity, but now I understood that he only did it when he was nervous. He stopped talking and waited for me. "Yes, I'm at home. Yes, you can come over to work on the project."

"Oh," he said. "Good. Uh. Cool. Give me ten minutes?"

"Ten minutes," I agreed. "See you then."

True to his word, he showed up in exactly ten minutes. He knocked three times, and I raised my eyebrows at the paper bag sitting in his arms when I opened the door.

"I brought food from the Chinese place down the road. Eliza said it's rude to visit someone's apartment without bringing something and since it's dinnertime..."

I held the door open and stepped aside. "Thank you. That's really thoughtful."

He winced at the word but said nothing, following me as I led him to the kitchen. He set the bag down and started unpacking the cartons while I pulled a few plates from the cabinet. There was more food than either of us could eat in a few meals and about a thousand fortune cookies fell out of the bag as he tipped it upside-down.

He caught my look and turned red. "I wasn't sure what you'd like."

I opened a drawer and pulled out two forks. Handing him one, I said, "Next time, just call and ask me, you weirdo. You didn't have to spend a fortune on fortune cookies." He looked down, nodding. I touched his arm and his eyes moved back to my face. "I appreciate it, though. You've saved me from another gourmet dinner."

His eyebrows scrunched, and I nodded toward the can of soup still on the counter and one of those brilliant smiles took up half of his face. "No problem, really. I'd spend my entire trust fund on fortune cookies if it made you happy." He paused, his cheeks going pink as he realized that might seem a little full-on. "I mean – it's just that—"

"Alexander," I laughed, and our bond vibrated with happiness. There was an openness to him that made him feel more honest than anyone I'd ever met. A total lack of contrivance that made him clear as diamonds and just as precious. Not once had I ever doubted he was being completely transparent, even if it made him sound jealous or vulnerable or weak.

He sighed. "I meant exactly what I said and there's no point in pretending otherwise, huh?"

"No point at all," I agreed. "Tell me what you got."

"Well, like I said, I wasn't sure what you wanted, so I got a little bit of everything." He pointed out the eggrolls and the fried rice and the beef lo mein and the pork chow mein and the sweet and sour chicken and the Buddha's delight with tofu. He was about halfway through his list when I realized that he had no idea I didn't eat meat. In the end, I ended up with the rice and tofu dish.

I led him to the couch after he filled up his own plate to bursting. Our thighs brushed as we sat, and my chest warmed at the sensation of his jeans against my bare skin.

"What did you want to get done in the project?" I asked him, setting my food down on the coffee table to pull out my binder. It contained all the instructions for the project and everything we've done so far, including in-class notes on Aphrodite and the smaller assignments Lux had given us the last few weeks.

As we reached the beginning of October, the Detroit trip grew closer and closer. Still two months away, I was both eager for it and dreading it at the same time. While it meant that we would get answers sooner, I couldn't deny the fact that those answers would mean losing either Alexander or Theo. No matter how often my mother reminded me, I couldn't decide which I wanted to keep, couldn't even imagine picking between the two of them.

He blinked at me, mouth full of eggroll, and then said, "Right, the project. Um."

I couldn't stop my grin from spreading across my face. "Alexander Crest, did you use this project as an excuse to come over?"

His shoulders reached his ears, but he admitted in a small voice, "Yes."

With slow hands, I took his plate from his hands and set it down on the table next to mine. He let me do it with a mix of trepidation and reverence on his face, the same way the priests look at statues of their gods. When I was certain that I wouldn't spill food all over us and my couch, I threw myself into his arms, tugging him into a tight hug. He sucked in a breath, wrapping his long arms around me, and I marveled at the etched muscles of his body against mine.

"Next time," I said, repeating my words from earlier with more weight. "Just ask. I won't say no."

"Don't make a promise you can't keep," he said against my shoulder. His body shuddered, mimicking our bond. "I won't be able to stop myself from asking constantly. I always want to see you. I like being around you. It makes me happy in a way I've only ever dreamed about."

"I want to see you, too," I said, swallowing the swell of emotion in my throat. "Awake or sleeping."

He made a sound at that, and his hand buried itself in my hair, not pulling but tangling in the curls until they formed rings around his fingers. "You always say the right thing. You make me feel like this whole mess will be worth it in the end."

"It will," I said firmly. I refused to believe otherwise.

"I envy that," he whispered and I took in a big breath, my nose tucked into his chest. He smelled like oranges, bright and fresh and clean. "I say all the wrong things. I keep fucking up, and you keep forgiving me. I'm afraid that, one day, I'll finally do something that can't be forgiven and then I'll lose you."

"Forgiveness isn't a finite resource." I pulled back to touch his cheek with my fingertips. "It won't run out. We're all trying to understand what's happening and it's okay to make mistakes. You apologize and do better every time. I can't stay mad at you for that."

"My father doesn't have a soulmate," he said abruptly and I blinked in surprise, the change of topic like the lash of a whip. But he didn't say it with sadness. He said it like any child talked about their parent's tragedy, with forced ease, the way a narrator says 'the end'. "Gods don't love like us. They can't love selflessly. My mother, the Goddess of Love, destroys soulmate bonds the moment she falls in love with someone."

I looked at him, horrified, but he continued, "So I grew up with the idea that, for love to be real, it had to hurt. That it destroys. Love, as they say, is the worst of all the gods. My mother is famously jealous – she's destroyed cities for not naming her the most beautiful being – and that's half my DNA, you know?" He shook his head and his blond curls bounced, reminding me of that damned Cupid. "I wanted a soulmate so bad, even though I know first-hand what love can do to people. But then I met you. And, gods above, I know we're just getting to know each other, but I think I'd rather burn my own heart out than ever hurt you. I can't imagine—"

He cut himself off. "Anyway. I just wanted to say that, if it ever starts to feel like that for you, if you ever start thinking that the bad in me outweighs the good, that being with me hurts more than it heals, I want you to end it."

"Alexander," I said again, shaking my head. "It won't."

"Promise me," he said. "Please."

I didn't like it, but I nodded. "I promise."

He let out a sigh that I felt in my bones. "Thank you."

We were quiet for a while. His heartbeat matched mine and our bond ached with his vulnerability, but it wasn't a bad hurt. It was the kind that led to healing.

"What was it like?" I asked, words muffled by cotton. "Growing up with a dad without a soulmate?"

"Eliza jokes that we didn't grow up with a father, not really," he answered, smiling sadly. "We grew up with a CEO who we saw at dinner. He took over the company when he was young, when I was just a baby, and my mom was never around very much. She saw me on my birthdays, maybe, and took a few pictures with me at graduation, but she was always more like a patron than a parent."

"I'm sorry," I said, boldness encouraging me to press a kiss to his shoulder. A lifetime with Ronan by my side caused me to push a wave of comfort at Alexander, and unexpectedly, he sighed, relaxing slightly. His eyes fluttered shut, lashes like the wings of a golden butterfly, and his arms readjusted, loosening. "You deserve... well, more than that." I paused, thinking about the event I was supposed to attend with Eliza soon. "I'm sort of worried about the Cult of Athena conference Eliza wants me to attend. From the Society for Ethical Sacrifice I've heard that they, you know, participate in the old traditions."

He frowned. "You mean the sacrifices?"

"Right," I agreed, shivering at even the thought. "I keep having dreams about it. I haven't seen a live one since I was a child, and honestly, I'm hoping to never see one again. The blood alone... Did you know that they were the reason I became a vegetarian?"

His eyes widened, moving toward the buffet of food he'd brought over. "I didn't know. I'm *so* sorry, Vanessa—"

I shook my head, stopping him. "The tofu was delicious. Thank you."

"You're welcome," he answered, green eyes locked onto mine. "I'll do better next time."

"Alexander." I laughed, hiding the sound in his shoulder. "You're perfect. Shut up."

He looked like he wanted to apologize again, but I stopped him with a pleading look. He was quiet, thinking through something that caused a strange, serious face to overcome his perfect features.

"My father never stopped loving my mother," he murmured, and it was the first time his voice didn't shake. "He gave up his soulmate – his only chance at human love – for her, and I don't think he's ever regretted it." He pulled back and brushed my cheek with his thumb, the same way I had earlier. "I guess what I'm trying to say is this – men in my family don't know how to love in halves. Once we're in, we're in forever. And Vanessa?"

"Yeah?" I asked, blinking at him.

He smiled and it was the look from before. Terrifying and worshipful. Half-man and half-God. "I'm in."

Friday came around quicker than I expected it to. Classes trickled by, slow but steady, as the weather began to change. The rain didn't stop, but the last traces of warmth from summer lived in shorter days. It got darker earlier, Artemis fighting with her twin. Ronan traded his short-sleeve button-downs for sweaters and I started wearing wool tights under my dresses.

I didn't hear from Theo all week, though his mind buzzed alongside my own. Ronan and Alexander invited me to check out events with them for the Cults of Hermes and Aphrodite. Tori, though somewhat reluctantly, extended an invitation to me for a giant party she was having after midterms. According to her, it was a better way to experience the Cult of Dionysus than any formal event.

Theo remained silent through it all. I missed his thoughts in my head. I missed *him.*

My dreams with Alexander seemed to go well, though I had little memory of them when I woke up. I didn't think we were dreamsharing every night. Apparently, most soulmates couldn't sustain nightly dreamsharing, it was too invasive. The internet said it's bad for the soul and bad for a budding relationship.

But on the nights that we did dreamshare, I woke up with a warm heart and a fluttery stomach. I could feel the bond solidifying, growing from a piece of yarn to a cord of rope to a bungee cord. I had no idea what the final result would be, but I worried about what would happen if it snapped. Would it be the small sting of a rubber band or the impact after your parachute straps broke?

Though I met Eliza downtown in the middle of the afternoon and Helios still warmed the earth from above, I needed a jacket and a scarf to keep out the cold. The face of the hotel smirked at me, over-carved Corinthian columns bracketed the marble entrance, and two doormen stood resolute in front of the mahogany door itself. Their hands rested on the mostly-decorative spears at their sides.

A single sign, printed on a cream-colored poster board with wine-dark lettering, proclaimed to all visitors that the semi-annual Cult of Athena Festival could be found in the Center Concourse. Registration required. The doormen, who looked more like Praetorian Guards, narrowed their eyes as they looked at me.

"The Grand Cleo is closed to unregistered guests," one said. "We will open to the public in three days, after the Festival—"

"Thank you," Eliza said, pushing the doors open and holding them with one sharp stiletto. Her pale blonde hair was twisted into a tight chignon and her red lipstick matched her confidence and the bottom of her shoes. "But she is registered with Crest Industries. Vanessa, darling, come in. The weather is dreadful out here, and I don't want the wind to mess up my hair."

The doormen stepped back and I walked between them. Eliza's heels clicked as she led me across the marble floor.

We got to another set of fine doors, this time with the Center Concourse written above it and that same sign we had seen outside propped up to the side. When she opened the door to let me in, quiet chatter and the scent of expensive cologne seeped from the room. I couldn't tell if the ceiling was covered in gold paint or whether they used real gold leaf. Images of the Egyptian queen were painted in the corners, eyes dark and clever as she watched over men with a fraction of her power. Her gaze seemed to judge them and their practiced, polite laughter.

"Welcome, Vanessa Reyes," she said, dryness in her words that said she could sense my nervousness, "to the Cult of Athena." There was an order to the chaos of the room. People dressed in clothes that cost more than my parents' house chatted to each other, standing in evenly spaced hexagons. The stage at the front of the room stood empty except for a thick, plastic tarp covering the floor. Horror washed over me as I realized what it was there for. My anxiety about the sacrifice mounted as the chatter grew louder with our arrival.

No one but Eliza wore a color other than black, gray, or navy blue. She stood out in her cream and seafoam blazer, but more than that, her blonde hair and timeless beauty caught the eye of every man in the room. She ignored them and made a beeline to the center of the floor, continuing, "These are the top hundred business owners in the city. All of whom are in the running for more Department of Athena grants for the next six months."

"Ah, Miss Crest," an old man with white and wiry eyebrows said, approaching Eliza. "I'm glad you're here. The new PR Manager is telling that damned golf story again. He's in the corner over there, and the Department representative is falling asleep into his bourbon. I think you should remind him about the Crest Cyprian villa that's available after the grants go out."

She touched his arm, eyes hard. "I'll deal with it. Thank you for letting me know."

He nodded and moved away. I stopped Eliza before she headed in their direction. "How is any of this Cult activity? It just feels like seedy backroom deals, Eliza. And why are you involved with it?"

"I have sort of an unofficial role at Crest Industries," she explained, gesturing to all the men in the room, who snuck glances at her whenever they thought she wasn't looking. There was a glint in her eyes that suggested she knew exactly how much they were. "Alexander is being primed to take over for our father as the proper CEO. But he's a little too... good to handle some of the unsavory parts of the business."

"The woman behind the man?" I asked, frowning.

Her mouth twitched upwards. "That's what the Cult of Athena is – a systematic trading of power. For the Goddess of Wisdom and everyone that follows her, business and religion are synonymous. The rich are the most devoted worshipers." My reaction must have flashed across my face because she continued, "Listen, there will be a religious sacrifice later if that'll help with your judgment of the Cult, but let's just see if this aspect makes you want to join or not. Deal?"

My stomach dropped at the thought of watching the sacrifice so closely. I was sure my smile was watery, but I said, "Deal."

With that, I let myself be led to the hexagon in the corner where a man in a pinstriped suit with an empty glass of alcohol was talking to a silent audience. His arms waved as he weaved his tale. He was probably in his early twenties, but there was a familiar arch to his brow and cleft of his chin that screamed old money. "And then we're at hole sixteen and—"

"Vassilis," Eliza interrupted and honest to gods, one of the other men sighed in relief. "As lovely as that story is, you seem to be out of bourbon. Do you know that the Grand Cleo has an exclusive partnership with the whiskey company in Wisconsin? Have you tried their black label? Crest Industries is, of course, responsible for their safe travel over the Great Lakes. Perhaps, you should go get yourself a glass."

The man, Vassilis, glared but didn't manage to refute her before the man with the Department of Athena badge asked, "I was just reading in the recent catalog that your company was delayed in releasing the new model of the lake freighters. These are the same ones that carry the bourbon, correct?" He punctuated the sentence with a swallow of drink.

Eliza's eyes glinted with the challenge. "Oh, that's true, but it was a purposeful delay on our part. We discovered that the steel we were being sold contained more than the recommended percentage of sulfur, which would have reduced the lifespan of the vessels if left unchecked." Another man joined the group and extended his hand for Eliza to shake. She did so, keeping her eyes on the department representative. "We decided to hire a new supplier. Much better product."

He nodded but asked, "And who discovered this impurity?"

Her smile was absolutely shark-like. "I must confess, it was me and my platonic soulmate."

That made my eyebrows rise even as I was half-hidden behind her tall frame. Billions of drachmae saved, probably. A number so unfathomable to me that it almost made me take a step back. I had grown up comfortably, but their money was beyond anything I could've dreamed as a child. It felt like a different world and I had no idea if there was a place for me in it.

The representative's face changed, too. "That is the young Mr. Crest, is it not? The child of Aphrodite? I believed him to be more detached from the company as he is finishing college." His eyes narrowed. "That's what the news led me to believe."

"Oh, no," she corrected, laughing in that same challenging way and I listened just as eagerly as everyone else as she continued. "Alexander and I are very much involved with the company, even as we pursue our degrees. He knows more about water vessels than anyone other than Phillip, so he recognized the error immediately." She paused and her next words lost some of the measured manipulation. Even I could tell she sincerely meant her next words. "Crest Industries will only continue to grow with him steering the ship."

The Department of Athena representative nodded at her, wrote something down in the small notebook in his hands and turned to the next group. But even as one businessman began to talk to him, he glanced back at Eliza. She caught the look and sent me a smug grin before starting to talk to another person.

I stayed tucked into her side, worried that someone might ask me to comment on the prices of the newest cruisers or the top speed of their sailboats. I had none of the ruthless words Eliza wielded and, to be honest, no desire to learn them.

I was considering ducking out of the room and finding an armchair to curl up in to text Alexander when the lights dimmed and a spotlight was aimed at the stage. It took up all of the north wall, jutting out into the rest of the room, and I understood why when two men dressed in priest's tunics came out. Their owl jewelry sparkled in the bright light.

"Butchering and consuming the meat of cows is an essential part of being in the Cult of Athena," the lead priest said to the audience, who nodded and clapped along with his words. "Like Odysseus, we are the chosen ones of our great goddess. The smart, the cunning, the powerful. The kings of the modern world."

The men all looked pleased with the priest's words. Eliza didn't react, but I couldn't stop the frown from forming on my face. The words sounded like a bad mantra of the chronically insecure. I leaned further into Eliza and said, "They're really eating this up, huh?"

She snorted in that prom queen way of hers, turning her head until her mouth was nearly tucked behind my dark hair. "They don't realize they can't all be the king. None of them are nearly as difficult as Phillip nor as powerful. Certainly, none of these idiots have ever managed to make a goddess fall in love with them."

"And we thank her for these gifts with our continued sacrifices," the priest droned on, before turning to the side of the stage and calling, "bring out the ox."

Another man led the ox to the center of the stage, and my entire chest tightened as horror bloomed. Images swirled in my head of the rituals I had seen as a child – I had always been inconsolable, crying into my mother's neck or running away with Ronan. From wherever he was, Ronan sent a wave of concern, but I couldn't respond as the gentle creature's soft eyes found mine, and I could see its fear. Eliza watched with little reaction, though her brow furrowed when she saw my face.

To distract myself, I asked, "How is Phillip difficult?"

She didn't answer for a moment, grabbing two glasses of bourbon from a server and pressing one into my hand as the priest carried on, talking about cutting sinew properly, and I lost my appetite completely. I took a too-large mouthful and swallowed it as I waited for her response.

On the stage, the younger priest placed one drop of water on the animal's forehead. It slid down its face as he nodded, trying to get it off, but it didn't matter. He nodded. The crowd applauded again. My stomach heaved.

"Alexander's capacity for love is... fitting for a child of the Goddess of Love. He struggled when he was young with Aphrodite being so busy and Phillip doesn't really have the temperament for being a single father," Eliza said, and I was grateful for the distraction. "Phillip adopted me when I was young. He doesn't have a soulmate, but he's close to his plat – he values that bond more than anything. Even parenthood."

She took a breath and let it out slowly.

"So, when it comes to Alexander, all he knows how to do is push him – to be more handsome, more athletic, more pious. Which, in some ways, is good. He's very accomplished, your soulmate," she teased, and I laughed with her, wanting to hear the rest of what she had to say. "But it also makes him eager to do well in absolutely everything. He can't handle disappointing people."

The priest drew a bronze knife across the ox's throat and blood covered the tarp. The ox cried out, and I slammed my eyes shut the moment his eyes became glassy. *Don't think about it. If you think about it, you'll cry and that'll embarrass Eliza. Distract yourself.*

I thought about Alexander. His slumped shoulders and sad eyes when we berated him for his public apology to Theo suddenly made a lot more sense. So did his commitment to his education and the overeager participation that had annoyed me at first. He was the best in the class, but he'd always had to be. His parents never gave him a choice.

"He's also the most hopeless romantic I've ever met, though Ronan says you could be a contender. Alexander's been obsessed with soulmates since his mother told him bedtime stories about Psyche. So, he's always been a good worshiper of all the gods. He loves them for giving us mortals our other halves back."

It also explained why he and Theo couldn't get along for more than a couple of minutes. Alexander loved the gods. He believed in the idea of happy ever after, but Theo had been hurt by them in a way that would kill Alexander to even think about.

The young priest continued to slice and chop. Bones snapped.

"All he ever wanted was to have a soulmate of his own," Eliza said, and the word choice was deliberate. *Of his own.* "And he cares about you, but you have seen as much as I have how this is affecting him. You two are similar. Your emotions control you. You don't have one deceptive instinct between you."

The air smelled like blood and my mouth tasted like sour alcohol. My head spun with sadness for the innocent creature. This was the power of tradition. No matter how horrifying the act was, we all sat in silence and watched it happen. Just because it had always been done this way. The gods never encouraged deviation from the old ways.

"Vanessa, you're looking a little green," Eliza said like she was commenting on the weather. Her eyes were still settled on the ostentatious display of knife skills in front of us. "I don't mean to be rude, darling, but I don't think the Cult of Athena is for you. A little blood is necessary to succeed in this crowd."

"So we must find the balance," the priest announced, spreading his arms wide to draw attention to him and his message. "Between our own greatness and our gratefulness to Athena, beloved daughter of Zeus. With the meat and burning smoke of this animal, may she bless you, your families, and most importantly, your businesses."

"No," I agreed, throwing back the rest of the drink. "I don't think it is."

14

SHE AT THE CROSSROADS

A stream of customers filtered in and out of the Laurel Leaf on Saturday. Sam's machine hummed, and I was getting ahead of closing, organizing the receipts for Ronan, when I heard a thought from Theo: *That art thing is tonight. At 8:00. Wanna go?*

The static in my mind, which had faded to background noise without a pause since he'd left the classroom on Wednesday, ended abruptly. The bond between our minds opened like a road during a storm. I was envious of his ability to open and close it at will, but more than anything, his lack of communication angered me.

My phone had been buzzing all day with texts from Alexander and the conversation glided from one topic to the next. He didn't hesitate to ask what he wanted to know or respond to my questions. It wasn't a competition. I knew that. But if it was? Alexander would be pulling ahead by an inch with every message.

I sighed. I needed to be fair. To give Theo a chance to explain. To talk.

I was due to work until 6:30, but if I left right on time

instead of waiting around for Sam and Ronan to clean up the studio like I normally did, I might have enough time to run home and get ready.

Dress code? I asked.

Semi-formal? he said it like he was unsure. *Tamara said to wear a dress and heels, I guess.*

That probably meant that I needed to do my hair and makeup. *Let me ask Sam.*

Theo didn't respond. Shocker.

I knocked on the door to the studio in the back and walked in when Sam called.

"Hey, Bossman," I greeted him. He had his head down, concentrating on the triangular piece that he was doing, but he grinned at my words. "Theo asked me to go to his art thing tonight. Do you mind if I leave like a half-hour early today?"

"No problem, kiddo," he answered. "I'm sure we can manage without you for a second."

"Sweet, thanks!"

I can make it. Where should I meet you?

I can pick you up from your apartment. 7:30. More static.

"Hey, Vanessa, can I talk to you for a minute?" Ronan said as I sat back down at my desk. His head popped out from behind the door and there was a strange, nervous energy about him as he chewed his bottom lip.

"Sure?"

He came to stand by my desk, and I wanted to laugh as I realized he was doing the same thigh-drumming thing that I'd seen Alexander do a few times now. "So I've been meaning to talk to you about this, and I know this is a pretty chaotic time to ask, but how would you feel about moving downtown with me next semester?"

It was an unexpected question for sure. "Downtown?"

"With Sam," he clarified, sitting down on the extra chair next to me. "We both work down here and all my accounting classes are here, too." He tried to grin but kept shooting me worried glances. "Not to mention that I, uh, would like to live with Sam. I spend half my week at his place, anyway, and if we all go in on rent, we could get a nice place—"

"My classes are still on campus in Golden Valley," I said, frowning a little. Taking the bus from downtown to campus every morning would be a lot of work. Not to mention that the Society for Ethical Sacrifice usually met at night.

"I know! And I get that this is a better deal for me than it is for you," he admitted, still tapping his fingers. I reached out and stopped them and a wave of nervousness rose from him to me. "But I hate being away from him when I spend the night on campus. It'd be a change of scenery and when you do decide on a Cult, you'd be able to go to more events—"

"I'd be further from Alexander," the words tumbled out as I thought them.

"There's a fifty percent chance he's not your soulmate—"

"And a fifty percent chance that he is."

We were at an impasse. On the surface, it was a nice offer, but when I looked a little deeper, it was just more proof that he was moving on to the next stage of his life, with or without me. He was forging ahead, whereas I was caught between Alexander and Theo. I sighed. "Look, can I think about it? When do you need an answer? Maybe once this whole soulmate thing gets figured out, my head will be a little clearer."

"Of course," he said. "We'd probably need to sign a lease by November."

"Okay," I agreed. That was more than an entire month to figure this out and surely it wouldn't take longer than that. "Then, by the end of October, I'll have an answer for you."

"Okay."

There was more silence, and tentatively, I sent out a tendril of comfort. It took him a moment to respond, but then he accepted it, pushing back with a feeling of pure hope.

"I'm gonna go back in there," he said, standing up and brushing invisible dirt from the knees of his salmon-pink pants. "Gotta make sure that Sam doesn't throw any artwork in for free."

"That sounds about right," I said, and he gave me a faint smile before heading back to Sam. When the door between us softly closed, I dropped my head down on to the edge of my desk and groaned.

At 7:30, there was a honk from outside my apartment. I smoothed my hands down the front of my dress, glancing in the mirror one last time before I left and locked the door behind me. Gray clouds consumed the sky as a half-liquid, half-sleet precipitation sank down onto the skeleton trees and brown grass. I shivered, stopping for a few seconds to pull my jacket closer to my body and stopping short at the silver car waiting for me.

Wow, I thought without hesitation, having grown used to having the bond closed. The silver paint of the car glittered even in the low light of the streetlights and the sheet of ice over the hood melted circles into the driveway. *Nicer than I expected.* A hint of amusement came through the bond, and I remembered he could hear every word I thought. *Fuck. Sorry.*

Don't worry about it, Theo's mental voice was somehow scratchy from disuse. He was well-dressed in a charcoal-colored jacket and evenly ironed slacks. His shirt underneath was an interesting pattern, snakes eating their own tails. *It's Tamara's car. Figured my bike was a bad idea. It's chilly.* He held open my door for me and I gave him a small smile as I climbed in.

An image of a red motorcycle entered my thoughts, and I analyzed it with interest. It wasn't brand new, the paint chipped around the wheels, but the obvious affection Theo felt toward it made me like it anyway. I heard a thought in his head, and though I'd promised myself that I'd be a little tougher on him for literally running away from me for half a week, I had to laugh as he settled behind the wheel. "You named the motor-cycle Atlas?"

He snorted, pulling out of the driveway. Light guitar music started playing and I felt myself relaxing back into the seat.

"Margot named it," he told me. "She had hers first. Named it Pleione. The Nymph of Sailing. She hated the water but always wanted the freedom of being out at sea. She thought riding was close to the feeling."

I now understood the affection for the bike. "I like it. It's weird."

"Yeah," he agreed, the corners of his mouth curving up but his bottom lip drew into his mouth, ending the smile before it could completely form. My fingers ached to stop him. "She was weird. It made sense."

Just like with the motorcycle, there's another image in my mind. It was a girl in her twenties, maybe a few years older than us, with short blonde hair in Marilyn Monroe curls and dark lipstick. She had two arms full of tattoos and a goofy grin on her face. It was like looking at a photograph, except lit up with different emotions. Happiness and sadness in equal measures. Grief. Devotion. It was all there in that split-second memory.

The image played out in my head for a few minutes and the sensation was like staring at the sun. How did he stand this? This hurt like it was my own pain. It was like an earache, low and ringing, migrating to my cheeks and jaw and throat until it felt like the nerves in my spinal cord were thrashing against my flesh at the electricity of the pain. Their broken bond. Theo pulled over to the side of the road, calling my name, his hand on my arm. I clutched my temples, unable to respond.

Gasping, I pressed the heels of my palms into my eyes before pulling them away and blinking rapidly. The edges of my sight blurred, but opening my eyes focussed me on the present and physical. *Zeus above. You're walking around with that in your head all the time?*

Thank fuck, Theo thought in one breath, he was holding me by my upper arms and shaking me a little. Nausea filled me and I pushed his hands away. *Are you okay? I don't know how you felt that—*

How long was I out of it?

Only a few minutes, he answered. *What happened?*

That last image hurt. The other ones weren't that bad.

"What images?" he asked. His real words startled me.

My mouth was too dry to reply aloud. *The images that you sent? Like when you talked about your motorcycle, I saw that it was red. It has a scuff mark on the seat, right?*

He blinked at me, wide-eyed to the point that he almost reminded me of Alexander. *Telepathy doesn't work like that.* He paused and then his eyes widened a fraction more. *You're getting emotions from them, too?*

Now I was worried. *Yes. Why? Is that bad?*

Telepathy may have just been the first symptom of something stronger, he thought, starting the car again and pulling back onto the main road, emergency lights flashing. *We should tell the others—*

He made to pull off into the parking lot of the closest store but I stopped him, glancing at the clock. Only a few minutes had passed, but if we turned around now, we were going to be late.

Aside from the most recent image, I thought, recapturing his attention, *they haven't been too bad. I just assumed that your telepathy was better than mine. So can we worry about this after the art gallery?*

148

Are you sure? He looked worried, his hands tight on the wheel and his full lips pressed together.

It's important to you. I don't need to read your mind to know that. And whatever's happening – good or bad – it won't get worse in the couple of hours that we stand and look at art.

He nodded, slowly and hesitantly.

Okay good, then, let's not worry about it. I reached out to squeeze his arm where the muscles were taut and his shoulders lost some of their tension. *Not until you're ready to leave the gallery for real. Okay?*

Okay, he thought and sighed, running his hands over the wheel, the radio and his hair. We said nothing for a few minutes, though I could feel his thoughts building up to saying something, like he was mentally preparing. *I'm sorry about this week. About going radio silent. I needed to think through things. On my own.*

Did you?

Yeah, he thought back, and his gaze was as soft as velvet as it met mine. *I did.*

Night sailed by out of the window. The apology didn't make things better. Not really.

I won't do it again.

Sure.

He fell silent and for the first time, so did I.

15

PAINTED IN OIL AND TRAGEDY

The Galatas Gallery stood taller than the surrounding buildings, looking down on all of us. There was a man in a coat watching the door and checking a list as people entered before us. I suddenly felt a little nervous, not having expected the grandeur.

The Galatas family was responsible for donating a ton of money to hospitals and local festivals, especially to the Cult of Zeus. They're businesspeople, a human dynasty that received quarterly financial blessings from the gods. There were even rumors that they should qualify as minor gods themselves, what with the amount of times the gods had fucked members of the family.

Still, much as I disliked their legacy, I had to admit that they did hire a skilled decorator. The gallery was a dark blue, perfectly complementary to the golden decorations, that somehow managed not to make the large open space seem small.

Paintings took up most of the wall space and sculptures stood proud on the floor. A mixture of realistic and abstract, of black-and-white and delightful color. But one piece, mounted on the first wall of the main gallery floor, made me freeze in place.

The portrait stretched at least eight feet tall, the entire thing done in oil paints. It reminded me of the impressionist pieces that came from the French during the 1800s, or maybe vaguely Renaissance. The artist had mixed the warm reds and yellows with enough gray to make them seem cold, sad. But it's the face of the woman in the picture that made me freeze half in the entrance, pulling Theo to a complete stop.

It was the same woman from the memory that Theo shared with me. In fact, it was the same moment of time. Her hair was the exact shade of blonde and lipstick the same shade of motorbike burgundy. Her tattoos swirled delicately beneath a white shirt, the light fabric making the dark lines look like twisting highways. Laughter glittered in her eyes. Or were they tears?

It was obviously the centerpiece for the collection. *Theo,* I thought through a fog of shock, looking up at the sweet face of the girl that once shared his mind too. *When you said you had an "art thing" to go to, I didn't think you meant that you were the featured artist of an actual gallery.*

He shrugged, either sheepish or just embarrassed by the attention, *It's not a big deal. It still hasn't sold. But the owners, they wanted me to, you know, be here to try to sell it. Though it mostly feels like I'm a showpiece myself. Like, here's the pitiful soul who painted the saddest fucking thing in the universe.*

"No," I disagreed with enough speed that the word came from my lips. I tugged his arm, dragging him closer to look at the art. Up close, the brushstrokes created the effect of mist or clouds. Even without knowing their story, I would have known she was a memory. Or a ghost. *No, Theo, it's beautiful.*

I was just glad I could do her justice.

151

You did. You absolutely did. I paused. *How long did it take to paint?*

A few months, he replied, taking my hand and tucking it into the curve of his elbow. *I had that image in my mind. Couldn't get it out. Sketched her constantly. One of my professors suggested painting it. I did a few smaller copies, first. But they weren't... I don't know, good enough.*

I think she would love it.

"Come on," he said, leading me away from his painting and down the hall. Other pieces of art started to jump out at me. We were surrounded by paintings, but he led me further down the hallway towards the sculptures. *These are my favorite. I wish I could sculpt.*

A few hours passed by as Theo explained the art to me in simple sentences, mostly letting me form my own opinions before telling me what he thought. There was an ugly, yellow sculpture toward the back of the gallery that just looked like meaningless triangles put together to me, but to him, it was profound.

"There's stability in three," he said to me, his mouth pouting as he stared at it for longer than I expected. His thoughts weren't static, but they moved so fast that I couldn't sort through them before they were replaced with something else. Usually, his thoughts were soft and simple, clean-cut colors of grays and blues, but now a thousand colors swirled around his words in my head. It was almost divine, the way he saw art.

He stopped briefly to join in on the small sacrifice to Apollo conducted by some of the other artists in attendance. Thankfully, they only burned barley cakes and blew the smoke toward the altar of the God of Art and the Muses, murmuring low prayers for inspiration in the future.

A few patrons tried to start conversations about Theo's painting, but he didn't seem able to get into the details with them like he had with me. Part of me felt special because of it, but another wished he could talk to more people about Margot's painting. Maybe explaining it in terms of brushstrokes and thickness of paint would help to soothe the sharp pain in his soul.

I knew he could hear my thoughts but before he could respond, a well-dressed couple approached us. Theo stood straighter and extended a hand toward the woman first and then the man, surprising me. I expected the same dismissal he'd given the other artists.

"Mrs. Galatas," he greeted, smiling, but it looked just as forced as the ones in the photos on display around us. The name had me standing to attention. I offered my hand and they both shook it. Her hand was dry whilst his was clammy and I hoped they hadn't noticed my hesitation. "Mr. Galatas. Nice to see you. I wasn't expecting you to be here."

Mrs. Galatas had blond hair, pulled back to show off her sharp jawline and gray eyes. In some ways, she reminded me of Eliza if she lost all her warmth. But she smiled at Theo like they were personal friends, and her voice was pleasant when she spoke, "We didn't plan to, but Theodore, I must say that I was considering buying that spectacular painting of yours."

Surprise. Rapid nodding. "Thank you. It means a lot to me, that painting. I'm glad you like it." He paused and then continued, "I took inspiration from the Leonardos in your family's collection. Especially in terms of posing."

Her eyes lit up. "The Ginevra de Benci, correct? I can tell from the positioning of the arm and the Latin phrases you've woven into the laurel leaves in the background of her tattoos. It's a compliment to your professors, really, Theodore. Apollo must be very proud of you."

"Ah, thank you," he said, shifting uncomfortably at the praise.

"A shame about her death," Mr. Galatas added, and Theo's good mood vanished. A static shield blocked his thoughts from me. "Margot was such a promising artist herself. In fact, if we hadn't been on that vacation in Greece, we'd have gone to her burial—"

"Robert!" Mrs. Galatas interrupted, her voice tight as she glared at her soulmate.

"It's okay," Theo said through clenched teeth. He laughed and it was like sandpaper, scraping painfully through me. "I mean, not everyone knows about her, so I'm just not used to talking about it. But I'm glad you remember her art. She loved drawing."

"We have her charcoals in our summer home," Mrs. Galatas tried to smooth over. Her smile widened and it was a little predatory, like she'd made a decision and expected everyone else to bend to it. "Right in our formal sitting room. And we'd love to add her portrait to our student collection in the new hospital wing—"

"Can I think about it?" Theo interrupted, staring down the hallway towards the painting. "I'm not sure I'm ready to part with it yet. I wasn't expecting an offer at all, let alone at the beginning of the season."

She blinked and I understood – I'd expected him to take the offer right then and there. "Well, I suppose so. But we're looking to decorate the new wing sometime in the next few months, and with the size of your piece, we'd need a confirmation to figure out the rest of the display."

"Of course. I'll think about it."

"You know we'll pay well, don't you, boy?" Mr. Galatas asked, rubbing his gray jaw and his soulmate frowned.

Theo's smile grew tighter. "I know, sir. It's not about the money."

"Everything is about the money."

The words were said in jest but the moment they're spoken, I felt the last of Theo's energy drain away. "Right. I'm going to show my date the rest of the art. I'll be in touch." He nodded at Mrs. Galatas. "Soon."

And with that, he led me away from the richest couple in the entire city and towards another shitty, abstract sculpture on the other side of the room. No one stood near it, but a bright orange sticker had been stuck on the plaque, indicating someone had bought it.

Are you okay? I thought, afraid to ask out loud, in case, somehow, they could hear the tenderness in my voice. They had known Margot and for some reason, I doubted they'd be too understanding about this damn split bond.

He shook his head and I tightened my hand around his bicep. *I don't know. He just thinks that this is all about the money... but there's time and pain put into every single one of these pieces. To him, they're pretty decorations.* He paused, looked closer at the thing in front of us with a tilted head and added, *Or ugly ones.*

He thought of a number then, probably the asking price the gallery set for the portrait. It was higher than I'd expected by two figures and my mind stuttered as he continued. *But if I did sell it, it would make a difference. I wouldn't have to work as much. I just hate that they can just... make me their puppet. With a single check. The cost of divine inspiration.*

I didn't know how to answer. I couldn't imagine having to make that choice. I'd never been talented enough to make art that people would love and I'd certainly never been hurt like Theo.

There's not a wrong answer, I tried anyway. *Whatever you decide, it's okay.*

He said nothing and just stared at the sculpture for a handful of long minutes. I couldn't hear his thoughts and tried to block mine out. If history was any guide, he wouldn't tell me what he was thinking, what he was feeling, so I wouldn't burden him with my own mind. I laid my head on his shoulder and looked at the ugly art, too. We didn't move for a long time. Not until people started to leave and other pieces of art got new stickers that declared them to be sold. Theo's stayed the same.

Margot watched over us as we left, still smiling, but her eyes were sadder than I remembered.

16

ICARUS FLIES LOW

I waited for the elevator, still rubbing my head from the screaming match I had just refereed. Though we were still a few months out from the Society of Ethical Sacrifice event, the arguing between the leaders of the club was only getting louder and more frequent. The elevator opened on the ground floor, and I sighed as I stepped in, trying to prepare myself to study after listening to pointless yelling for nearly an hour.

I had just pressed the button to go up to the top floor of the library when Theo stepped inside. He had earphones in and his head was down, but when he looked up and saw me his smile was wide and automatic. One of his front teeth was slightly crooked, and I couldn't help but feel like it was one of the cutest things in the entire world. His face returned to neutral in less than a second as he caught himself.

"Hey," he stepped closer as the doors shut. "How's your head?"

I laughed. "You can't tell?"

"Oh, I can," he revealed, not bothering to hide his grin. "Those girls can yell, huh?"

"You're telling me."

The elevator stopped again on the second floor, jostling me into Theo's side. With steady hands, he righted me, fingers warm on my waist and a teasing glint in his eyes. "If you wanted to be closer, sweetheart, you could've just asked."

Looking up at him with pink cheeks, I started to respond, but the doors slid open and Alexander stepped in. He looked just as surprised to see us as we were to see him, eyes drawn to where Theo was touching me. He paused for long enough that the doors started to close again and his arm shot out to stop them, but when he stepped inside, surprisingly, he said nothing about it even as I took a step away from Theo.

"Vanessa." Alexander's voice was openly affectionate as he stood on my other side and nodded a greeting at Theo over the top of my head. They were both at least a foot taller than me and could easily see each other with me in the middle. It made me feel small, especially in such an enclosed space. Their broad frames took up so much room. Every time I took a breath, my shoulders would brush against them, sending sparks down my spine.

"Hi," I managed, swallowing the sudden surge of heat inside of me.

Alexander's smile was warm, eyes flickering to my mouth. "Hi."

Unconsciously, I licked my lips. His gaze followed. "Hi."

Next to me, Theo chuckled. A low sound that made me shiver. "I think you already said that."

My blush returned with even more power, but I was mollified that Alexander's cheeks matched my own. My stomach fluttered at the thought when the elevator jerked again, this time pressing me against Alexander's side and Theo into mine, I couldn't stop the gasp from leaving my mouth as both their hands brushed against my skin.

An image flashed across my mind, not for the first time since we'd kissed, of both their mouths on me at the same time.

Theo raised his eyebrows in surprise, pulling his hand away from his temple, and I managed to slam a mental shield into place before my mind could run away with the rest of the fantasy.

Theo's rough palms on my jaw as he pulled me into a scorching kiss at the same time that Alexander's strong arms wrapped around my waist, pressing his lips down my neck and leaving a trail of mulberry red bruises behind. Their bodies bracketing mine, surrounding me on every side until I could do nothing but hold onto them just as tightly.

"Are you okay?" Alexander asked, hand on my shoulder as I steadied myself. His eyes were wide, concerned, and totally oblivious to my train of thought. Thank the gods. "You look a little flushed."

Theo's eyes didn't leave my face but I ignored him as I responded, "I'm fine. Just... a little warm." Shaking my head, I turned back to Theo, doing my best to distract him from whatever he'd managed to see in my head and hoping my heart calmed down. "I forgot to mention, I need volunteers for the event we're hosting if you guys are free that night?"

Theo blinked twice before nodding. "Uh. Sure. I can be free that night."

"What event?" Alexander asked, frowning. "I feel like I missed something."

"Oh," I said, turning back to him with a smile as we finally stepped out of the enclosed space. "I was just telling Theo that my club, The Society for Ethical Sacrifice, is hosting our annual event soon. I just got out of a nightmare of a meeting with them and our heads ache from the arguing."

"You? Arguing?" Alexander asked, eyebrows raised as he turned to me. "Really?"

I shook my head as we found an empty table in the corner of the room. One with a great view of the changing leaves, and the giant river in the background. It was getting cold enough now that the trees were looking a little skeletal, but it was still my favorite view on campus. "Gods, no. The president and VP of the club have very different ideas about how the event should be handled and it's making the whole thing more difficult than it needs to be. I got them to come to some sort of an agreement, but we'll see what they have to fight about next time."

"How'd you get them to stop?" Alexander asked.

"I mean, it doesn't take a genius to suggest getting a bigger room if there are too many people for the one booked. Even if my brain was totally fried from the third straight week of their screaming." I paused, looking at Theo. "Again, I'm so sorry you had to listen to that."

"What's the event about?" Alexander asked, sitting down at the head of the table.

"The usual," I answered, pulling out my notebook for our Soulmates 101 class. "We're putting on this informational meeting. Some of the Cults on campus are supposed to come and talk about the problems with sacrifice on such a large scale. We just need people to greet guests and hand out some information when they walk in."

"Oh," Alexander said. He was quiet for a moment, looking between us. "I can definitely volunteer if you need warm bodies, but I have to be honest, I don't know much about the topic."

"Really? Oh, my gods, that would be amazing. Thank you so much. You don't need to know anything, I promise!" I said with a beaming smile, grateful that the AC was working to cool off my still flushed face.

Alexander's smile was pure sunlight. "Of course. Just let me know when and where."

After the meeting, I was beginning to dread attending the event, even though I had put a lot of effort into making sure the group survived planning it. But now that I knew that they'd both be there, I couldn't stop the burst of excitement coursing through me.

"Oh, fuck, Vanessa," Theo said, both hands going to his head. "Careful, please."

Alexander laughed, surprising me as he threw his head back, showing off the long lines of his neck. He reached into his backpack as he said, "Wow, for the first time, I do not envy your ability to read her every thought. How's your head? I have aspirin if you need it."

"Oh, fuck yeah, man," Theo said, holding his hand out, palm up. "Drug me up."

Alexander poured out the pills and Theo washed them down with a swig of his water bottle. As Theo swallowed, Alexander reached out, squeezed my hand once before he turned back to Theo. "Listen, man, I just want to say sorry for the other day in class. I didn't realize that it'd make you uncomfortable and I won't do it again."

Theo shrugged. "You didn't mean anything by it. It's cool."

"Cool."

They both went back to looking at their notes and neither seemed to notice the baffled look decorating my face. Where was this compromising ability during class? I blinked a few times. Well, I wasn't going to look a gift horse in the mouth. Unless it was from Odysseus.

"I managed to get a hold of one of my mother's assistants," Alexander said after a quiet moment and Theo and I looked up at him hopefully. "They mailed the tickets for Detroit yesterday, so I should get them in a few days. My mom's still not answering her phone, though. I'm sorry."

I placed a hand on his arm and squeezed lightly. "It's not your fault. We'll see her soon anyway." Theo also nodded supportively, and I felt warmth spread through me.

Alexander glanced between us with a small blush forming on his cheeks before giving us a small smile and shuffling some papers in front of him. "We should figure out some of the details of the trip."

Theo shrugged. "Like what?"

"Well, we can use my car," Alexander said, looking at his handwritten to-do list. "I can do the driving by myself. We should try to go the night before, because the major presentation stuff is scheduled for seven in the morning. Does that work for you?"

Theo looked at the dates of the trip and the presentation. I couldn't hear his thoughts word-for-word, but I got a good impression that they boiled down to him wondering if Tamara could manage two days without him. "Sure," he said out loud, typing something into his computer. "I'll let you know if I have any work conflicts. But this should be far enough in advance that it's not a problem."

"Then we have to worry about the hotel," Alexander said and Theo's mouth turned down. He was thinking that Alexander probably didn't want to choose the cheapest option. Alexander seemed to see it on his face, because he said, "Now, my mother will probably pay for our rooms at the hotel that's holding the event but we should talk about, uh, sleeping arrangements."

"What are the options?" Theo asked as I choked on a gulp of water.

"We can do either two fulls or a king," Alexander answered, rubbing the back of his neck and turning pink. Theo blinked at him. The king made no sense, but if we did the fulls, we'd have to decide who was sleeping with whom. "I know, neither are great choices, but—"

Theo shook his head. "Do the fulls. I'll take the one by myself."

Alexander frowned. "Are you sure?"

Theo swallowed. "You guys already spend your nights together. Mentally, at least. What's the difference?" He paused, eyes going wider still as he looked at me. "Or – *fuck* – you can have the bed by yourself. If you're not comfortable with either of us—"

"You really don't think we'll figure out the bond by then?" I interrupted him in a small voice, posing the question to Alexander at first but letting it settle on Theo too. Ronan's offer and my subsequent deadline hovered in my mind. "The trip is right before finals."

They were both quiet for a minute, sharing a quick glance with each other but not looking at me.

"I think," Alexander started, the words coming slowly like he was putting thought into every one of them. "That it's best to plan for a circumstance where we don't know by then." A pause and a sigh. "My mom won't pick up the phone and give us any answers, so I think we need to make her talk to us in Detroit. I looked further into that article in the magazine Professor Lux showed us. They wrote a continuation to it just a few months ago. They still haven't figured out who the Original soulmate is – you know it's hard to get any sort of appointment with a god, let alone the Goddess of Love, to try and sort things out."

Alexander wasn't wrong and I felt something inside me relax a little that at least through him we did have a connection to Aphrodite and could work this out. Hopefully.

Theo frowned. "How long ago did they find out they were soulmates?"

Alexander tried not to wince. "Six years ago."

17

A MOST SOLEMN OATH

Not knowing put us all in a state of limbo. With the three of us twisted into each other's minds and souls and dreams, there could be no happy ending. Theo froze, panic in every limb of his body. He pushed away from the table, eyes even wider. The pen he was holding fell and I didn't need to read his mind to know what he was thinking because his face said it all, *I cannot wait that long.*

You don't have to, I thought, trying to stop him from panicking. *We'll be in Detroit in just a few more weeks, and we'll sort everything out. Theo—*

"Theo," Alexander said, standing up and reaching for him. "Sit down—"

A loud chiming noise echoed around the room, making me jump. It was the sound that announced a god, but it always hurt to hear. Like a piece of Olympus we weren't supposed to experience. A little burning of divinity.

Alexander hadn't winced. In fact, he looked like a little boy on Saturnalia. It took a few moments for the divinity to appear, but there was a hope in his eyes that could only come from the son of a goddess. Even before the Cupid appeared before us, I knew that it couldn't be his mother. That would be too easy. We would just have to wait until Detroit. It was midterms now and December grew closer every moment.

"Late delivery for Vanessa Reyes!" the Cupid announced, his voice as splitting as the chime announcing him. Under one of his golden arms, the winged creature held a cardboard box.

"She's Vanessa," Theo said, stepping forward and accepting the box for me with still-shaking hands. I could tell he just wanted something to do with his body other than worry. Or run. The Cupid handed it over without hesitation, observing our gold bracelets.

"The Delivery System of Olympus, monitored and run by Hermes, Son of Zeus, apologizes for this rare instance of late delivery," the Cupid said, his eyes and voice flat like a recording. "This package was meant to be delivered on the night of Tuesday, the 18th, but it was delayed by strange circumstances—"

"You can open it," I said to Theo, shrugging.

He ripped open the box without hesitation and dropped it as soon as he saw its contents. It hardly made a thump as it hit the table. "What the Hades—"

"—you are legally required to wear it at all times. Thank you, we hope your mind is as pleased as your—"

"Cupid!" Alexander said, interrupting the small creature as he prepared to pop off to another country to make more deliveries for the goddess. Cupid's eyes lost their flat, thoughtless filter and his face relaxed when he recognized Alexander.

"Brother!"

"I'm happy to see you, too," Alexander said, stepping closer to him with outstretched arms. "But I need to ask you something important."

His face fell. "Brother, I must go."

"Where's Mom?" Alexander asked anyway. "Why isn't she answering my calls?"

"I can't tell you—"

"Cupid!" Alexander chastised, his voice stronger than I'd ever heard it. A demanding authority. Whatever relaxation Cupid felt before Alexander began speaking disappeared under his command. His spine straightened and his head bowed, ready to obey any order Alexander gave him. It was obvious that a demi-god ranked higher than a minor god, especially one with such common powers. Aphrodite could create a thousand Cupids in a minute but demi-gods were rare.

"She's busy!" Cupid squeaked, flapping his little wings faster in a nervous tick. "She's working on some restructuring for the department, and she doesn't have time to answer all your questions about your split—" He grew pale and his eyes went wide. "Never mind!"

"She knows?" Alexander asked, wounded. "And she still can't make time?"

Theo shifted, uncomfortable with Alexander's easy vulnerability. His thoughts floated errantly into my brain, an instinctual reaction of *please cover-up, don't let people see*.

My gaze didn't leave Alexander and Cupid, but my hand reached out to grip Theo's arm in reassurance for a moment, and his mental wall shot up so fast that if the situation were at all different, I'd have laughed.

"You know how Mother is," Cupid tried to pacify Alexander. "She's got a million different things going on, and with stepfather acting up in different parts of the world, even life at home is stressful…"

Alexander's face closed off, emptying of all the warmth that bubbled under his perfect skin. He was beautiful but cold with anger, reminding me of the paintings of Aphrodite in wartime. Without conscious thought, my body reacted to the display of power, sending shivers down my spine as I found the danger more attractive than I should have. He'd never looked more like a god than when he dismissed his half-brother with a bored, "Fine. Go back to her."

"Brother—" Cupid started, his face flickering with surprise when Alexander swatted at the air like he could hear an annoying bug, making the creature vanish from above us in a cloud of magic smelling like rosemary, plum and plumeria.

Alexander's face melted back into the warmth that I'd grown accustomed to seeing. His blond eyebrows pulled together as he looked at us in concern. "Are you okay?"

I nodded, still slightly breathless from seeing this other side of Alexander, but Theo replied, "Did you just dismiss a god?"

Alexander, bless his soul, glanced down, bashful. "Not really. The Cupids just listen to me – one of the only benefits of having Aphrodite as a mother, it seems."

"Alexander," I interrupted, trying to keep my voice calm. Emotions clouded his face. Easy for me to read his confusion, anger and impatience with the whole ordeal. I put a hand on his arm, and his eyes fell to it immediately. "Why do you think she's not answering your calls?"

I bit my lip as a new emotion made waves across his face. Embarrassment, shame. I held his hand even tighter in mine. His shoulders fell. "I'm not sure. I'm worried she has bad news for me. Or for all of us. Gods, I have no idea."

"I'm sorry," Theo added, squeezing his shoulder. "We'll talk to her in Detroit."

Alexander swallowed. His jaw clenched. "She can't run from me forever."

"Exactly," Theo said, voice low and soft as if not to spook him. He glanced at me, something apologetic flashed in his eyes before he spoke again. "I know this might not be the best time – I mean, I know it isn't – but there's something else you should know. When we went to the art gallery a couple weeks ago, we realized that our ability had a new element."

167

My heart dropped to my stomach. Alexander's jaw loosened, eyes wide. "What? How?"

"Vanessa can see images in my mind," Theo explained, closing his eyes. "And we don't know how. We were driving to the art gallery and I – I thought about something that meant a lot to me and she could see it too. It turns out that I was sending feelings to her sometimes as well."

I was a little impressed at how much Theo was talking, but I quickly grew concerned as an uncomfortable burning sensation began where mine and Alexander's souls were connected as his dismay grew. I rubbed right under my collarbones where it throbbed, understanding that he probably felt like mine and Theo's connection was only growing stronger – but the same was true for us too. Surely, he knew that?

"You didn't tell me?" Alexander asked. "You didn't want to just, I don't know, text the group chat?"

"I asked her not to," Theo lied. I elbowed him, glaring at him now. But he continued, his nervous words coming from seemingly nowhere. "*Ow.* Fuck. Okay, I didn't, but we never brought it up again, and I didn't know what to do, and now it seems like one of us was hiding it, and I'm pretty sure neither of us was and—"

"Hey," Alexander said, his voice soft and all the anger on his face gone. He reached out and touched Theo's shoulder, shaking him just a little so that the dark-haired man looked at him instead of staring into nothing with panic. "What's going on? Are you okay?"

Theo stood and pushed the box over and it tipped onto its side, revealing another gold bracelet. I blinked at it and took a step back as if it were a wild animal.

Theo spoke again, words bouncing off of me like rubber bullets as I stared at the innocuous bracelet, barely shining under the dull, fluorescent lights of the library. "So, now you have two bracelets and I have two bracelets and Alexander has two bracelets" – he sucked in a gulp of air – "and we're making hotel reservations for weeks in advance and things make even less sense now—"

Alexander pulled him into a hug, his long limbs wrapping around Theo's shoulders as Theo flailed for a second, arms still in the process of gesturing with his sentence. And then he exhaled, a strange sound of half-surprise, half-something like relief and jerked backward like it was instinct, but Alexander held on, his grip around Theo tightening.

Theo didn't relax into it, but he did let himself breathe deeply twice before pulling away and taking a step back. His thoughts were no longer speeding by in barely formed chunks, and the whiplash from the sudden change had me holding onto the table for stability until Theo cut them off from me, putting that impenetrable shield back in place.

"Okay," he said, breathing deep. "Okay."

"You okay, man?" Alexander asked, eyes watching his face.

"Yeah," Theo answered, shaking his head. He tried to clear his throat and got a dry, scratching sound instead. "I'm going to go get a drink of water." A pause. "From downstairs. Two minutes."

He left, nearly jogging to the elevator and Alexander reached for me in the same way he had Theo as he sat down. "He'll be back," Alexander comforted me. "He left all his stuff. He just needs a minute."

"I've never heard him talk that much," I said it like a confession and Alexander nodded. "His mind was like if you threw a deck of cards in the air and watched them fall."

"He's scared," Alexander said gently before shrugging. "I am, too. It's a scary situation."

Sighing, I picked up the new bracelet and clicked it into place on my left wrist, the other warmed against my right.

"What are we going to do?" I asked, my voice small.

"Hey," he answered, pulling me close and pressing a soft kiss to my forehead. "We're going to figure this all out, okay? Aphrodite will have all the answers, and Detroit will be here before we know it and everything will work out. I just know it. And split soul or not, Vanessa, you and I are going to be okay."

I glanced at the elevator. The light indicated it was on its way up.

"And Theo?"

"Him, too. I promise."

ἹΣΤΟΡΊΑ - ΜΈΝΩ

I LIVED

Vanessa's limbs were still flailing when she felt a strong arm wrap around her waist. They tugged her up and up until a gentle breeze touched her face. She would not die this day, but her heart still pumped too slow. When she finally opened her eyes, she was lying on her back and staring up at Alexandros. His face was flushed and his eyes were wide with panic, hands firm on her chest as he tried to push air back into her lungs.

"Vanessa," he called, too loud and too eager. "Can you hear me?"

"I'm alright," she murmured, trying to sit up. "I'm okay."

He pushed her back down as gently as he could, a thank-you to the gods on his lips. "No," he said. The sand scraped against her back and became rougher as sensation returned to her body. "Don't sit up. Theodoros is getting a healer. You almost died."

"It is not my turn to die," she said, blinking the salt out of her eyes. The light of the sun shone through his tunic. His arms trembled where they held her to him. She reached out to grab one of his hands with both of her own. "I'm okay."

He stared at her for a moment, his eyes revealing his panic. "If you had died—" He let out a huff of air that moved the wet strands of his long hair. He was quiet for another moment, tilting his head up to the sky and mouthing something to the clouds. "I swore to my father that I wouldn't do this, or that I would give him more time, but, please, Vanessa, accept my hand in marriage. I could not bear to live in a world that you do not—"

"Yes," she said, the speed of her answer surprising even her. If he asked, if he was the one to choose, to illuminate the path of her decision with torches and oil, then no one could blame her. He was the prince. She would be a fool to deny him. "I will marry you—"

Theodoros arrived then, kicking up storms of sand with every step, a middle-aged woman at his heels. His mouth was tight, which was not unusual, but more emotion swirled in his eyes than she'd seen in years. Maybe more than ever. He dropped to his knees in the sand at her side, pulling a cloak from the bag he carried. It was a deep purple and much too expensive for an artist. There was a golden wave embroidered on the back. He covered her body with it, blocking her from the sun and their gazes and her cheeks heated.

He was always careful with his touches but, as if he could not stop himself, he cupped her cheek in his calloused hand and sighed in relief at the warmth he found. The pad of his thumb brushed something off her face, a droplet of water or debris, maybe.

"You're okay," he murmured, closing his eyes. Theodoros looked to the healer, and she nodded, scooting him out of the way so she could examine Vanessa. His hand dropped from her face, and she missed his warmth. Missed him. She was colder than she should be with the sun blazing so hot above.

"Careful how you touch her, Theodoros," Alexander said, his voice soft but firm, a rock dropped on sand. "She is to be my wife and I will have no one questioning her virtues—"

"Alexandros—" she tried to interrupt but wasn't fast enough. Theodoros' face fell, impossibly open and vulnerable, dark eyes wide and wounded for a moment before they closed off. He snatched his hands back to his body as if she were burning. She tried to protest, but the sound came out as a cough that wracked her chest.

"My Lady," the healer addressed her politely, leaning in to listen to the sound her breathing made. Vanessa closed her eyes. A hand cupped hers and with as much strength as she could manage, she squeezed back. "Can you speak?"

"I can," she croaked. The sound of the sea mimicked a lyre, relaxing her. Sleep threatened. The darkness brooding where it used to comfort. She did not know where the goddess hid with her rejected gifts and scarlet smile.

"Can you breathe?"

"Yes."

"Are you in pain?"

Of course she was. She had been for years now, she thought, caught between them.

"Vanessa?" she heard but had no strength now to answer. She merely nodded.

"She's fine." While Alexandros clutched one hand, the other hand lay with its palm open, empty, and she wished in her weak-minded state that another's hands would touch her too. Was she greedy to want two handfuls when anyone else would be blessed for one? She didn't know. "Her body has suffered but not as much as her mind. She has greeted death, my prince, and I believe that death greeted her in return. Let her rest. You can wait to speak with her."

The last thing she heard was, "I've become good at waiting."

18

WORDS REFLECTED

The next day on campus, a small gathering for the girls in the Cult of Artemis were meeting under the sparsely-leaved trees of the gardens. Only about a dozen girls showed up, wrapped in thick coats, crunching leaves and fallen twigs beneath their rubber-soled boots. The North Wind, Boreas, blew into Michigan as October began and the typical late-night drizzle turned into early-morning frost which covered the yellowing grass blades.

The group dispersed when eight o'clock rolled around, a few of them rushing off to their first class of the day. I walked out of the gardens slower than the others in the group, kicking sticks and fallen pine cones. Still, I didn't feel any more alone than I had during the meeting. It was a long shot, anyway, that I would instantly connect to the Goddess of the Wilderness after a lifetime of disinterest. Frustration made my hands shake in my pockets.

By all accounts, Artemis should've been a perfect fit for me. Her love of nature, her domain over animals, her dedication to keeping the wild in the hearts of all women – that all fit. But there was something about the goddess herself, about her casual dismissal of the importance of soulmates, that had always rubbed me the wrong way. It bled out of the Cult members, wrists bare in the morning light. A girl with two soulmates would find herself lost in a group of girls with none.

The group ended up far enough ahead that I could only hear the occasional burst of laughter and then... nothing. My footsteps dragged, still thinking about what had changed since the first time I explored the large forests surrounding the campus. Almost affectionately, we called them the Ravines, these sharp, pine-covered hills that angled steeply toward the Golden River below. If the students were all quiet, or if I ventured down the trails at the edge of campus, I could hear the break and foam over the rapids.

The thing about being a part of a Cult was that you automatically had a new group of friends. Ronan, a fairly loyal member of the Cult of Hermes, had fallen in with his fellow worshipers during the first semester. We didn't see each other those first few weeks of college, except when he'd stumble home from their late-night excursions.

As a default member of the Cult of Hera, the community was harder to access. We'd spread ourselves too far from each other, scattered in a thousand different majors between this campus and the one downtown. If someone asked, I couldn't tell them the name of the president of our Cult. Or when we were supposed to meet.

I'd spent a lot of time alone during that first year because of it. Too much time, probably. It was hard to be lonely with another person's emotions in your mind and soul, but somehow I'd managed it. Ronan liked to joke about how my emotions could be seen in my every expression, but he had no idea how much I kept back from him. I aced every class that first semester with the amount of time I spent studying, but my soul missed my plat more than anything.

I ambled toward an area of the Arboretum more familiar

than the others. The trees were planted in exact rows and I'd spent hours in the clean lines, among the happily slouching branches of the cherry trees.

During the late summer, the breeze used to lift a gentle sour-sweet smell to my nose, like rotting fruit flesh. Every year, it reminded me of home – of Grandpa's cherry orchard in Traverse City, of Mom's light laughter when I was a kid and how every time she turned her back, I would try to climb up the trunks and my dad would have to pull me down.

It reminded me of family when my plat couldn't. Didn't.

When Sam had decided to finally find out who his soulmate was, and he and Ronan began to spend more time together, he had chastised his soulmate for excluding me. Ronan had apologized and, of course, I forgave him immediately. Without a second thought.

Now, even with Theo in my head and Alexander texting me his random thoughts throughout the day, Ronan's lack of response to my texts still burned. Worse, he could literally feel my loneliness and insecurity, and he didn't send any waves of comfort back or try to reach me.

I sat by the cherry tree in the corner of the space, my back pressed to the trunk. I didn't sleep, but I let my bond expand and reach out into the Chaos without limiting it. There were a few tugs on it in response, Theo or Alexander questioning, and maybe, concerned. I ignored them like Ronan ignored me, twisting my new bracelets around my wrists as confusion filled me at the sight of them and thumped my head back against the tree. I was filled with a strange, violent desire to rip my chest open to see exactly what my split soul looked like. *If I could just see... maybe I wouldn't be so confused. If I could just get my fingers on the pulse of it, I would be able to tell what I really want, who I am—*

Theo's voice interrupted, *That's not a comforting thought. Need to talk?*

I shook my head before realizing he couldn't see me. *No. Maybe.*

Something like a mental snort, and then, *I have some time before my painting studio class. I could come by?*

I sighed and recounted where I was.

Not long after, leaves crunched satisfyingly as Theo's big, black boots carried him to me. I didn't look up until he was right in front of me, holding up a white to-go cup for me to take. A tea bag hung out the top and it smelled like lavender and lemon.

Tamara commanded me to bring this to you, he thought. Pulling out a few crinkled packets of sugar and giving them to me. The smallest tinge of pink touched his cheeks from the wind or from the gesture. *I wasn't sure how sweet you like it.*

In a practiced move, I ripped open and dumped one packet into the top, letting the steam waft into my nose. *A little sweet*, I answered. *If it's too sweet, it'll drown out the actual taste.*

He sat down in front of me, mindless of the melting frost of the grass, crossing his legs and leaning on them with his elbows. His leather jacket grew shiny with moisture and I looked away and into the steam of my tea as he looked at me. *So what's up?*

Ronan wants me to move downtown, I thought and took my first sip of the still steaming tea. It burned but I ignored it until a thought struck me and I raised my brows at him. *How'd you get this here on your bike?*

His earlobes turned delightfully pink. *I borrowed Tam's car again.*

Just to bring me tea?

Just to bring you tea.

I was not exactly in a smiling mood, but there was something about the way he'd said it. Like he knew it was cheesy but as long as I was happy, he didn't care if it made him look soft and vulnerable, or too open, like when Alexander had been talking to Cupid.

Theo cleared his throat as he heard my thoughts and his fingers began to pull the tips off of the dead blades of grass, almost petting them to feel their new texture. *What's the problem?*

I don't know, I repeated. I took another drink to give myself a second before I answered. *You're downtown. Alexander lives here. I told Ronan I'd let him know by November, and I realized yesterday that it's unlikely we'll know by then. It's just scary.*

He nodded and then hesitated. *I think it's scary, too. Not knowing. I'm sorry I panicked yesterday. I know, after I came back, we didn't get as much done as we needed to.* His mouth formed a sad smile. *I'm holding you two back.*

I shook my head. *There's no "you two" in this project. We're a team.* He said nothing, still picking at the grass. *A part of me wants to sit down and consider every possible angle, but I can't get my bearings. Everything is happening all at once and seems to get more complicated by the minute. I'm just trying to survive this semester.*

So let me distract you, Theo offered, glancing around the space we occupied. He asked, *Why the cherry trees?*

My grandparents have an orchard back in TC. I took another sip of my tea. The steam was mostly gone now, the cool, morning air blowing it away. It tasted good and soothed the headache building in my skull. *So, they remind me of home. My parents have lived there together since they met.*

Before their Ceremony, he said like he was reminding himself. My eyebrows shot up. Bashful, he continued, *You mentioned it when we were trying to figure out the SSS stuff with Lux.*

And you remembered?

Vanessa, I remember everything.

I managed to smile into the last cloud of steam, breathing it into my lungs to warm myself. *It's rare to meet your soulmate before the Ceremony, and even rarer to kiss them and confirm who they are before the gods tell you. But my parents have that kind of relationship. A little miraculous. A little strange. A lot of love.* I paused and the next swallow burned my tongue. *A fairytale.*

High expectations was all he added and I nodded, my mind just as silent as his. *Is that why you went so early for your own Ceremony?* he asked after a few moments.

I've always wanted what they had. That easiness and comfort with someone I loved. I was looking forward to having someone that wouldn't—

I cut myself off, thinking about the panic Theo felt when Alexander opened up in the library.

Someone who wouldn't leave, Theo finished anyway, nodding like he was expecting that answer. Maybe I was projecting my thoughts. *But that's what plats are for, too.* There was a split second where he thought about Tori, about meeting her. There was a strong smell of hairspray and paint associated with the memory of their first encounter.

And normally, Ronan is really good about staying in touch.

Normally?

It's hard, I tried to explain without making Ronan out to be the bad guy. Because he wasn't. He just had a life outside the two of us and I didn't. *He's involved with the Cult of Hermes on campus and Sam takes up a lot of his time. We have an apartment together, but he's hardly there.* A pause. *He doesn't need me like I need him. It makes me feel clingy and overly emotional.*

Have you told him this? Theo asked.

I shook my head. *How can I ask him to spend less time with the person he loves because I'm lonely?*

It's not your fault, either.

I ignored that too. *But if I could just pick a Cult, maybe all of this would go away, and I could live with them.* I was upset about Ronan, about Alexander and Theo, but I was mostly upset that my role in trying to figure all of this out should have been easy – find and pick a Cult. But for some reason, I couldn't find where I was supposed to be. The Cult of Artemis should have been right for me. But it wasn't. And I couldn't figure out why.

You can't force it, Theo thought, mental voice soft. *It's like... falling in love. With yourself. It'll just click.* He was quiet for a few seconds, his thoughts closed off from me again. He stilled his hands and asked, *Vanessa, don't take this the wrong way, but do you* want *to live with them?*

I said nothing, thumping my head against the trunk of the tree again and staring at the gaps between the branches above me. We were both silent for a while as we sat and I thought about his question. What did it say about me that I was willing to make an important decision for myself based on what my plat wanted and where my soulmate would be? No wonder I couldn't pick a damn Cult, I had no idea who I was without—

My parents are school teachers, Theo thought, halting my thought. He was playing with something in his pocket and there was a sound like crunching paper. *My mom teaches high school math and my dad is an elementary school art teacher. Both are in the Cult of Athena. We grew up – well, not poor but struggling. We have dinner at least once a week. My mom and dad usually cook. Tam's Cult of Apollo, like me. My parents have a cat—*

What are you doing? I wondered, listening to the words pouring through my mind. They were freer than anything I'd heard from him before, like his panicked blurting at the library, but smoother. Almost liquid, filling up the empty parts of my bond with Ronan.

You wanted to be distracted, Theo said, shrugging again. *So, I'm distracting you. Our cat's name is Achilles and he's in love with the neighbor's cat. I'm from the westside of Golden Rapids and I've never really left. I work in the shop whenever Tam needs me. Which is most days of the week, at least until I graduate. I think she just likes having me close to keep an eye on me after Margot—*

You don't have to do this, I protested, but I was enjoying his rambling. His words, now that they didn't fall with anxiety and panic, had a slow rhythm. I could fall asleep to their sound.

Instead of answering, he handed me what he was playing with in his pocket. It was a small, paper baggie with the logo of the cafe printed on it, slightly greasy, but there were a handful of butter cookies inside still warm. He said nothing, but I accepted them gratefully.

Theo continued, *I'm a senior this year, but my grades were shit all last year before I dropped out so my GPA kind of sucks. I like most forms of art but prefer painting. That's how I met Tori, actually. I was painting the scenery for a play she was in during high school...*

I closed my eyes and leaned completely against the tree, relaxing for the first time in weeks.

The frost was beginning to melt around us and the sun peeked from between the clouds. With every word he spoke, with every new thing I learned about him, Theo was throwing open shades and cleaning cobwebs from an old house, like a man returning from a war that took him away from his family home. There would be clouds of dust when he patted the beds and the books would be stiff from lack of use, but he was making progress.

My phone sounded with a text, but I didn't look at it. Maybe I was cleaning too.

19

BRILLIANT CONTRAST

The hallways of the art building on campus intertwined like the roots of a tree, their endings and openings indistinguishable with only moonlight as a lightsource. Clutching my backpack closer as if it could protect me, I squinted to see the room numbers in the dark.

My feet dragged as I left the main doors further behind. I passed through the main hallway and the next two offshoots before I took the stairs to the basement of the building, each footstep echoing.

It wasn't until I reached the innermost section of the building that a single light buzzed in the distance. I approached, following its path like Theseus until murmuring accompanied it. One classroom hummed with life – the one matching the number Theo gave me when he told me to meet him here. And like a black sail, his voice carried through the space under the closed door. I sagged against the closest wall in exhaustion, closing my eyes.

Shrugging off my backpack, I considered pulling out the papers Lux had emailed us earlier in the week. Personality quizzes, essentially, to get to know myself and my soulmates.

Maybe, she had typed, her tone less forceful than her intentions, *this will help you explore your bonds. To narrow down the Extra.*

"Hey," a voice said as a hand touched my shoulder and I jumped away, heart hammering. Though it took less than a second to recognize Alexander – by his voice, by the way my skin tingled at his touch even through layers of fabric – my mind managed to conjure images of horned hemi-creatures, snorting and enraged. I glared at him but his concerned eyes melted my anger quickly. "Sorry, I didn't mean to startle you. I thought you'd hear me coming."

Before I could answer, the door to the classroom swung open and a stream of students swirled around and between us, eager to leave after their three-hour painting studio class. Once the first wave receded and we stepped into the room, my eyes searched out my other soulmate. Theo, wearing a paint-splattered apron and sporting a smear of gold paint across his cheekbone, was speaking to one of the first-year students.

"I just don't think I got the perspective right," she said, blinking up at him with tears in her eyes. "But it's too late to change – it just feels like there's so much else I could say if I just refocussed—"

"Hey," he stopped her, a firm hand on her shoulder. "You're fine. This is great how it is."

"But—"

"Listen," he said, dark eyes steady as he advised her. "Is a new perspective worth throwing away all the work you've done?" She opened her mouth but closed it when he shook his head. He smeared more paint on his face as he pushed his hair back behind his ear, and I shouldn't have found that so attractive. "You don't have to decide tonight. Think about it. Either way, we can make it work."

She sighed and nodded, packing her stuff. "Thanks, Mr. Patras."

I almost laughed at the disgusted look on his face. He corrected, "Theo."

"Thank you, Theo," she amended, and he gave her an actual smile – the one that crinkled his eyes. She blushed and practically scampered out the door, barely looking at me and Alexander as she left.

He turned to watch her leave, and seeing me at the door, for a second his grin stayed in place, and I thought, *What would the world be like if he smiled like that all the time?* He noticed Alexander and closed off again as the sour, chemical smell of the paint filled my senses.

"Hey," he greeted us. "You can come in. Let me just clean up."

"Oh, no problem," I said, finding a place at one of the tables. Alexander followed, sitting in one of the chairs next to me and grinning when I found his hand and intertwined our fingers. "Mr. Patras."

Theo shot me a glare over his shoulder as he pulled a few of the easels to the side of the room. Straightening the edges of the paintings to make sure they didn't fall, he cleared the center of the floor but left the station in the middle. One chair sat there, looking comfortable with soft blankets and heaters pointing at it.

"What's that for?" Alexander asked, just as curious as me.

"The nude model," Theo answered, heading to the sink to wash his hands.

"Like… naked?" Alexander's eyes were wide. "Like all the way?"

"That's generally what nude means."

Alexander's head swiveled toward me, voice a whisper, "Did you know? Is that okay?"

I squeezed his hand and pulled out the papers. "Question number twenty-three: *Are you the jealous type?* Nope. Not usually. A nude model doesn't bother me."

The water turned off and throwing his apron into a box with the others, Theo joined us at the small table. He sat on the other side of me, making no move to hold my hand. "Besides," he added to my answer, "it's not like a three-hour painting class in front of thirty freshmen is a sexy scenario."

Alexander frowned, looking at me. "I answered: *Yes*."

That made me smile. "I could've guessed that. Theo?"

"Also yes, but more like a maybe, I guess. Only if I have an actual reason to be jealous."

Alexander snorted at that. "An *actual* reason."

Theo raised one eyebrow. "Why is that funny?"

Gesturing between the three of us, Alexander asked, "Is this not a good enough reason?"

Theo blinked, tilting his head at the question. "You don't think I'm jealous?"

I cleared my throat. "Okay, so how do we want to do this? Start from one? Or jump around?"

"Start from one—"

"Jump around—"

They stared at each other. Alexander sighed but gave in, pulling out a red pen. "Fine, we can do it randomly. I'll check we don't forget any. Theo? Where do you want to start?"

"Twenty-five."

I wondered at the significance of the number but read the question out loud, *"What was the best thing about how your parents raised you? What did it teach you?* I guess for me it was the way they let me talk to them about anything. It was really an open conversation about anything and they never yelled at me for asking things that made them uncomfortable, either. I suppose it taught me how important communication is."

Theo shrugged when I turned to him. "I think it was probably the way they treated Tori like family. We were slightly older when we met than was usual for plats, but they never saw a difference between her and Tamara. Taught me about loyalty."

Alexander's face scrunched. "My answer is actually pretty close to that. My dad adopted Eliza when we met and I'll never stop being grateful for that. I guess it taught me about protecting your own."

Before I could comment, Theo said, "Huh. Didn't know that. You look like you could be siblings."

Alexander's face twitched in surprise and then anger. "We are siblings. Just because we aren't blood—"

Theo held his hands up in surrender. "Hey, I get it. I wasn't arguing against that."

"What question next?" I asked before Alexander could make it into an actual argument.

"It's Alexander's turn to pick," Theo said.

"Twenty. *If you dropped everything and went on a vacation, where would you go?* A slightly easier one. Um, I said my mother's house in Cyprus. It's my favorite place. Mostly because of how close it is to the water. The sunsets are beautiful and the water is warm most of the year. I like being able to get in touch with my family's history."

"I'm a fan of road trips. I'd love to ride to California or something," Theo responded, raising his eyebrows. "My Nene lived by the Taurus Mountains when I was growing up. I've wanted to see the mountains out west ever since."

"Really?" Alexander asked, surprised. "You should. They're beautiful."

"No shit," Theo snarked and I smacked his arm. He tried again, "I mean, obviously."

It's not much better, but I took it. "I said Napa Valley. I just really love vineyards and orchards. So sort of similar. It's still California?" They both nodded but it wasn't convincing. Our answers were still pretty different. "Okay, number six: *What's the biggest sign of weakness in another person?* I said being cruel when you can choose to be kind. And you can always choose to be kind."

"That's a good one," Alexander said, nodding. "My answer was: not going after the things you want."

"Waiting too long," Theo answered, fingers pressed against the skin below his left bracelet. "Hesitating."

My throat closed. "Right. Uh. Number sixteen?"

Alexander swallowed, nodding. "*What Greek hero do you most identify with?* I said Achilles. Demi-god, expected to do great things but mostly just interested in being with his soulmate." His smile was small and soft.

Theo snorted again, surprising himself with it. "I said Hektor. I don't know why. He's steady, I guess. Has his priorities straight, which I always thought was special for a hero. He doesn't die doing something stupid, just protecting his family. I don't know if I identify with him most, but I respect him most, for sure."

And they both died because of the other. I looked down at my answer and bit my lip, unwilling to read what I wrote. But they both looked at me expectantly. "I said Helen. One of the reasons for the war that kills your answers. Let's just pretend I didn't, okay? Maybe – Penelope. Waiting for a happy ending to my story."

"That's not much happier," Alexander murmured.

"No," Theo agreed with him, "it's not. Number thirty-two?"

"*Why did you pick your patron god?*" Alexander read.

"Well," I added before he could answer, "this isn't a question for me."

Theo frowned, but Alexander continued, "Well, my choice was easy. I picked it because everyone said that it should be the god that spoke the most to my soul and my mother has literally spoken to me, so I figured that was a good sign. Not to mention, I figured it wouldn't be a bad idea to have some connection to the water for Crest Industries."

"Some connection," Theo repeated back but it's actually amused this time. "I mean, I haven't spoken to Apollo or anything like that, but it always made sense if I was gonna do art. Plus, Margot was already a part of it and it made taxes easier—"

"Who's Margot?" Alexander asked, brow furrowing.

My heart sank as I saw the look of panic flash over Theo's face. "Doesn't matter."

"I think it *does* matter, right now. What with everything else going on we can't also be keeping secrets—"

"Alexander," I interrupted, seeing Theo's face grow red. "Let it go. Next question. Do number ten."

He didn't look convinced, but he read it anyway, *"What's your favorite color? Why?"*

It broke the tension, just a little. I answered, trying to get us as far away from the topic of Margot as possible. "Oh good, an easy one. I think my favorite color is pink. Not neon pink or anything, but like a baby pink. Soft, happy. Reminds me of springtime. Cherry blossoms, maybe."

Alexander answered, "I like gold. I should probably say something about bracelets, but it just reminds me of this one painting that Eliza is obsessed with, *The Kiss* by Klimt, I think? It's a great mix of Bronze Age style and postmodern ideas of romance. It's my favorite too, actually."

"Huh," Theo said, looking at Alexander with a strange expression. It's somewhere between impressed and confused, and the streak of gold on his cheek glinted in the low light. His mind was closed from mine so I couldn't hear what he was thinking, but he shook his head, pulling himself out of whatever it was and said, "Silver."

"Why?" Alexander asked.

"Been on my mind a lot," Theo said. "The moon. Holiday dinners. Second place."

The opposite of gold, I thought. "Next number?"

"Let's do thirty-five, the last one," Theo said, reading, *"What do you think about this questionnaire?"*

"I'm not sure it's working," I admitted and watched their eyes swing toward me, waiting for an explanation. "I mean, I'm learning more about you both, but your answers aren't unexpected? They're not revealing anything that could help me determine who the Extra is."

Alexander swallowed at the word. "You really can't feel a difference?"

I shook my head. "I can't. How would you answer?"

Theo went first, "None of my answers have matched yours. It clarified what I already thought."

"Neither have mine, though," Alexander argued, surprising me. "But isn't that the point?"

"What do you mean?" I asked.

"Are they supposed to match?" he asked, gesturing to my papers, his light eyes uncharacteristically serious. "The questions? Or our souls, even? Or are they supposed to be opposites – the other half to each other, to something? Like, split in the middle by lightning?"

Theo's gaze wandered to the poster hanging on the door to the classroom. It was a cheap one, edges crinkled with time and disuse, but even a non-artist like me could recognize the color wheel. I couldn't say what colors he was staring at when he said, "Like a complement."

But my eyes couldn't concentrate on those opposite colors. Instead, they got stuck on the dashed lines between the primary colors, reminding me of Lux's handwriting on the whiteboard when this whole thing started. The triangle, more than anything, stuck out as the impossible thing. How does red choose between blue and yellow?

Alexander squeezed my hand once before letting go. "Yeah. Exactly like a complement."

20

LAID BARE

Work the next day slithered along with a painful slowness. I was jittery, anxious without reason, and not even the distractions of the internet sped it up. But three in the afternoon eventually rolled around and I tried not to look too excited the moment Theo stepped into the Laurel Leaf, shaking off the rain with his hands shoved into his pockets. I flashed back to the first time we talked. Unlike then, he'd lost the impersonal expression of a classical hero. When he saw me, his mouth formed a smile as our eyes met.

Hey, he greeted, stepping closer to the desk. He saw the to-go cup and the brown bag sat next to my keyboard and his eyebrows went up in surprise. *You see my sister today?*

Something like that, I answered. I clicked a few times around the appointment page, checking him in. *I dropped off a small bouquet of flowers for her as a thank you for the cookies, but she wouldn't let me leave empty handed.*

Sounds like her.

Sam's just prepping the room. Coffee? I asked, already getting up to grab him a cup. He leaned against the desk, sighing and resting his head against his forearms. Two curls had escaped from his bun and purple circles discolored the skin under his deep-set eyes.

Gods, please, yes.

Our hands brushed when I handed it to him, just as they had the first time and our bond responded to it. He ducked his head into his drink, smiling and remembering, just like me.

Sam came out of the studio in the back, crossing his arms over his chest and smiling at Theo. "Hey, man," he greeted. Theo nodded back at him, his skin paler than usual. I frowned. "You ready?"

"Yeah, think so," he said, downing the coffee with a grimace. The mental shield between us still stood but seemed flimsier than usual, his thoughts pounding against it, demanding to be heard. "And before you ask, yes, I've eaten. No drugs, no alcohol, just a few painkillers."

"Cool," Sam said, starting to turn around and then pausing to look at me. "Hey, do you want Vanessa to come back with us? Ronan can watch the desk while we do this. It should only be about an hour."

"Yeah," Theo said again, shrugging. "That'd be cool."

"Uh okay," I said, blinking in surprise. Though I'd worked here for about a year now, I'd never gone back during the process. The blood alone repulsed me. But as they started walking into the studio, I grabbed my phone and followed them, passing Ronan on his way out to the desk. We hadn't said much to each other today but he sent a wave of guilt toward me, and I was pretty sure it was an accident. I ignored him.

"Close the door," Sam told me as he snapped on a pair of black, latex gloves. A silver tray with all his supplies stood next to him, and Theo avoided knocking into it as he lay on the bench. Sam asked Theo, "You comfortable?"

Theo nodded. The buzzing in his mind was growing more intense.

I sat on the stool next to him. Theo flipped his other hand over, palm up and thought, *Please?*

Of course. I twined my fingers with his and he squeezed.

Sam grabbed a piece of paper off the tray, a print out of the tattoo design. It looked simple, but I could see the lines carefully etched into the circular drawing. The magic of Apollo, specifically designed and harnessed by Sam for this piece. He pressed the stencil onto Theo's wrist, careful not to smudge the purple ink. It contrasted with Theo's bronze-gold skin.

In the forges under volcanoes, cyclopes crafted the regular bracelets, both gold and silver. Their magic seeping into the soft metal as they worked. For gold, the magic strengthened the bond between romantic soulmates. For silver, it covered the splintered ends of a broken bond, easing the pain of a literal broken heart for the surviving soulmate. Theo's tattoo should do the same.

Sam prepared his machine. When he tested it, the buzzing nearly shook the room. My thoughts scrambled for a second and so did Theo's. At the sound, he closed his eyes and breathed out unevenly.

You doing okay?

The gods did not often give their approval for these tattoos. The magic of the bracelets seeped into your skin over time, but tattoos forced the magic into your blood with needle and pain. The pain of the broken bond would disappear faster after the application, but the actual process had been described as torturous and unpredictable. No one reacted to magic the same way.

I will be, he answered. *It'll get worse before it gets better.*

"Ready?" Sam asked as the buzzing grew louder.

"Yeah."

The moment the needles pressed against his skin, Theo's body tensed and his back arched in pain. He bit out a curse word – an ancient Greek *malaka* – and his hand squeezed mine. I tried not to wince at the strength of his grip.

"Scale of one to ten," Sam said, eyes still focussed on the line he was drawing. "How bad?"

"An eight," Theo responded through gritted teeth. *I don't know – ow, fuck, ow – if I can stop my thoughts right now. Sorry. Leave if it hurts.*

I'm not leaving, I thought back, though I could already feel pressure building in my head as memories started to travel through the bond. *I'm here until you're done or I pass out. Which-ever comes first.*

He didn't respond and I took it as acceptance. Sam kept his head down, working the ink into Theo's skin with precision and speed. He held Theo's arm against the table with all the strength in his biceps, only moving as the design demanded. He was going as fast as he could, but the pain cracked across Theo's face and body.

Images tangled with his thoughts. Other than a low-level sadness that always came through when he thought about Margot, no emotions transferred through the bond. Nearly every image was of her, smiling or laughing or crying. A few showed her grimacing in pain or snarling in anger.

The thoughts came and went randomly. Little things, giving a location to the images, or maybe a date. They'd only had a year together but they must've done a lot. A lake, an art museum, a canyon, a bedroom with a view of the downtown skyline. Those gave me pause – they weren't meant for me to see.

After fifteen minutes, Theo got used to the pain of the magic. His spine unbent and though his breathing was still deep and focussed, his grip loosened enough for me to relax.

Then the machine turned off. Sam leaned back, stretched his shoulders for a minute, and dipped the needles in a slightly darker ink. "That was the first layer, just setting the area for the stronger stuff."

Theo's bitten lips were red and swollen from holding in screams already, but he answered, "I'm ready."

The machine buzzed to life again, and suddenly, I wasn't in my mind anymore but Theo's.

*　　*　　*

"Hey," we said, attempting a smile at the girl in the bed. She was paler today, her eyes wider and bluer and meaner. Her hair had been braided down the side of her head, like cornsilk and lacking its usual shine. It'd grown much longer than we'd ever seen it before in these last few months. "How are you feeling—"

"Oh shut up, Theodoros," she snapped, pronouncing his name with a thick, Greek accent. She was not Greek, not really, no more than anyone else. She was born and raised here, in Michigan. But she slipped sometimes. The doctors thought she was connecting to a past life. One we couldn't remember. "Do you come from the fields, having seen your noble bitch?"

We sat at the edge of the bed, trying to be gentle even as our bond throbbed at the words. We couldn't take anything she said personally, her mind no longer belonged to her. "I haven't seen anyone today, Margot. I just came from work. Tamara says hi, by the way—"

"I grow so weary of your excuses," she said, sighing and turning away from us. She stared out of the window, watching the winter storm brew in the distance. "You should have never married a woman whom you do not love—"

"Margot," we said, painfully gentle. "I love you. I've only ever loved you—"

"Stop your lies," she said, mouth curling in anger, but refusing to look at us. We were used to this – whatever it was. But that didn't soften the blow when she hurled insults at us. "Just because she died..."

The scene changed and suddenly we were somewhere else.

The hum of the motorcycle beneath us. Clear roads. Melted ice in the ditch. New buds in the trees. Margot, sitting behind us with her arms wrapped around our waist, song lyrics in her mind and ours. Something slow and alternative, a favorite of Margot's.

We slowed as we began to pull over to the side of the road, Margot indicating with her thoughts the right moment to pull off the larger road onto the bumpy dirt path. It's nothing much, but it's one of her favorite places in the world. We'll like it if she does.

A small stream, babbling over riverstones. Her backpack and three small tupperware dishes containing snacks. We sat by the edge of the water. We were quiet most of the time, but she was usually bursting with energy. Not today.

"Do you remember," she started, picking at the grass with a violence we don't understand, "last week when I had to cancel dinner with your family? The night we were supposed to celebrate selling the painting to the Galatas woman?"

"I remember."

"I lied to you about why I canceled. When I told you I had a meeting with a professor." She took a deep breath, the earth beneath her hands now bald, the grass laying dead around it. "I had a doctor's appointment."

"Oh," we said. "Are you okay?"

"No, Theo, I'm not," she said, her words blunt. "You've noticed my headaches, how tired I am all the time. I thought, I don't know, that I needed more vitamins or maybe to eat more iron or something."

"What's wrong?" we asked, our heart plummeting.

"They did some blood work. They called me last night. There's something wrong. They don't know what exactly," she explained. We stayed quiet, unsure how to even begin processing this. "But I only have a few months left."

"Until what?" we wondered, oblivious, stupid.

She blinked at us. "Until I'm dead, Theo."

The images flashed by too fast, dizzyingly quick, making

our – no, *my*, stomach roil until it settled on one more memory.

Her heartbeat stopped. The nurse checked her pulse. We fell to our knees. Our sister supported our upper body as it sagged forward. She clutched us, crying, to her chest. Tori screamed at them. Demanding they do something. Anything. We screamed as the bond cracked. It splintered, the frayed edges stabbing the vulnerable soul around it.

AN AGE OF SILVER

I snapped back into reality, my eyes focusing. Theo was puking into a bucket that Sam was holding. My hands shook like I had just run a marathon, vision blurred at the edges. My cheeks were wet, though I didn't remember starting to cry. Theo let go of my hand to clutch the edges of the trash can but I couldn't bear not touching him, so I rubbed his back in wide circles.

"It's okay," Sam said, his voice cool and level enough to make me believe it. "We knew this was going to happen. We still have a little more to do, but take your time. We're in the process of exposing all the damage done and your soul is seizing in your chest."

Theo nodded like this information was familiar to him. It wasn't to me. I stood up on shaky legs and made my way towards the door. Sam's eyes followed me and I could tell he wanted to know if I was really leaving in the middle of something so painful for my soulmate.

"Water," I said as an explanation, throwing open the door. With clumsy steps, I went to the watercooler and downed two glasses before even thinking about stopping. Washing the taste of blood and pain from my mouth. I drank a third to wet my lips.

"Are you okay?" Ronan asked, standing up so fast that he almost tipped the chair backward. He reached out to touch me, to grab my arm to help steady me, but I shook my head. A wave of worry floated my way and I pushed it back. I already had so many of Theo's feelings inside my head, I didn't want any more.

I filled up my cup again and then filled another before making my way back to the studio. I pushed the door closed behind me with my foot, and Theo pulled away from the trash can, face still pale.

I offered him the cup and he accepted it, sipping a few times, the plastic dimpling under his fingertips. I sat down next to him again and he thought, *I should have warned you. I'm sorry. How much did you see?*

I offered my hand again. He took it. *Most of it, I think. How are you feeling?*

Exhausted.

The machine started again, the buzzing bounced off the walls and my skull. My head pounded but Theo's hand gave me something to hang on to. To ground myself with. "Ready?" Sam asked, already leaning over the tattoo and getting into position to finish.

"Ready," Theo said, bracing himself as the ink and magic stabbed his skin. He tensed and arched again. His hand turned mine white. He had no control over his thoughts or the emotions pouring into me. The images, some the same as last time and new ones intermixed, fell like bombs. The impact hurt, but the effects were worse. His grief, her pain. He'd felt them all before – a thousand times, but they were new to me and each exploded in an array of agony.

It lasted maybe another thirty minutes but time became meaningless at some point, spanning both only seconds and several hours. Yet, it came to an end as everything must. At some point, Sam told us that he was finished cleaning the ends and was moving on to cover them with another layer of magic. With each stroke of the needle, his nerves recovered.

"Like putting rubber over broken wires," Sam explained. "They'll still be broken, but they won't hurt anymore." Every moment, Theo's body relaxed more and his breathing came easier. The machine wound down, the buzzing fading into a soft sound before going silent. Theo was panting, his body slumped.

"We're all done," Sam announced, rolling back in his chair and taking apart his machine. His hands moved with practiced motions and by the time Theo groaned and pushed himself up into a seated position, Sam had started applying lotion to the new tattoo. "Keep it clean. Use the ointment whenever it dries out, but remember: moist not saturated."

Sam turned Theo's wrist back and forth, checking out the work. The silver gleamed in the white light of the studio and the faint lines of magic sparkled. Theo looked down, too, eyes captivated by it. Sam asked him, "What do you think?"

"It's nice," Theo said, turning his wrist over again and again. He pressed his hand to his chest, where the soul bond remained, broken but covered, and his eyes fluttered shut for a moment. "It doesn't hurt like it did before. It just feels sore."

Sam wrapped his wrist in plastic before snapping off his black gloves and throwing them into the trash. "It'll be tender for a while. Give it a few weeks and if you're having any residual pain, we'll take a look and make sure the skin is healing properly." He reached over to the tray next to him and picked up a gold bracelet, handing it to Theo. "You can put this back on. The gold is enchanted, so won't cause any problems touching the tattoo."

Theo slipped it over his wrist, letting my hand go to do it. The silver and gold looked good together, surprising me. They meant opposite things, but they both complemented his skin and the dusting of dark hair there. *Thoughts?*

It's beautiful, I admitted, nodding towards his water. "Drink more."

Sam made a noise in agreement, handing him the cup. "She's right. You need fluids and rest, now. This was a small trauma, basically, to your soul and mind. Are you scheduled to work today?" Theo nodded, wincing. Sam advised, "See if you can take the day off, or at least take it real easy while you're there."

"Would it be okay if I went with him?" I asked Sam, still unhappy with how pale Theo was. "I'll make up my hours after this week. But I don't want him riding there. I'll walk with him."

"Good idea, Ness. Just come in early with me on Saturday. You can come over and spend the night Friday." Sam stood, stretched, and offered Theo a helping hand. Theo took it, wobbly but getting stronger every second.

Sam helped him to the front of the shop and I hurried ahead to figure out the payment side of things. Ronan was on the phone, answering a question about our minimum charge policy, so I pulled out the paperwork. They'd discussed the price during their first meeting and had signed a contract for it too.

Sam leaned Theo against the counter before moving to the other side, where he could put his hands on Ronan's shoulders. Theo got his wallet out and his card and I queued up the bill. But before I could submit the price, Sam added, "Take twenty percent off the top."

Theo blinked in surprise. "But we agreed on—"

"Sure we did," Sam agreed. "But that was before you were family. Ness, twenty percent—"

"Sam, you can't give everyone discounts," Ronan started, crunching numbers in his head.

"Theo's not just anyone," Sam said, shrugging. "He's her soulmate, and I graduated with Margot. We weren't friends exactly, but Golden Valley is smaller than people think it is. We had our senior showcases together." His eyes clouded over, remembering. "She was going to be a tattoo artist. Doing this for Theo is doing it for her, too."

I had no idea that he'd graduated with Margot. Soulmates wove a tangled web of acquaintances. The chain of soulmates and plats went on and on, connecting every human with another. Some cynics think it's the actual reason why the gods gave us our other halves back, so that we'd be too involved with each other's emotions to risk anyone's deaths in a rebellion against Olympus. Perhaps I was naive, but I preferred the more romantic version of the myth.

Theo didn't argue, though I'd expected him to. Instead, his dark eyes were serious as he nodded at Sam. I approved the bill with the extra cost taken off. Theo stuffed the receipt in his wallet with his card. "Thanks, man."

"No problem," Sam said, massaging Ronan's shoulders. The door dinged as his 4:00 appointment walked in. "Now, get out of here. Vanessa, take care of him, yeah?"

"Will do," I murmured, moving around the desk to help Theo. The color was starting to come back to his cheeks but I still insisted on helping him put his jacket on before slipping on mine. Theo lifted his arm and I stood under it, letting him use me as support as we walked to the door. "Bye! I'll see you on Friday!"

"See you, kid!" Sam called out as the door closed behind us, Ronan didn't turn away from the customer, and I felt a momentary flicker of worry before I refocussed back on my soulmate.

The rain had picked up, but not by much. More than anything, the wind was blowing at our backs as we walked toward the Golden Rings Cafe. Theo's steps were naturally longer than mine, but he was slower than me now. It took us double the time it should have to cover the distance.

We walked in silence and the occasional grunt of effort from Theo as he struggled with the dizziness and I struggled to support his weight. But soon enough, the lit sign of the cafe came into view and Theo sighed in relief. The moment we stepped inside the smell of butter and sugar and coffee greeted our noses.

"Theo!" Tamara called from behind the counter. About a half-dozen people were waiting in line and a few other people were waiting for their drinks to be made. "Perfect timing! Can you start the coffees?"

I led him over to the counter and then behind it. There was a small stool tucked under one of the back counters and I pulled it out for Theo. "He's a little unsteady after the tattoo. Can I help?"

"Shoot," she said, moving to start a cappuccino and pushing the stool nearer the register. "Here, sit down and run the register, Theo. Vanessa, do you mind getting the desserts out? We need, uh, one blueberry muffin, one plain scone, one double chocolate cheesecake…"

She continued, and I slid the glass cabinet open to get the desserts out. The register dinged once and then twice. The steamed milk screamed and for the next few hours, I thought of nothing else besides the rhythm of the orders called out. Neither Theo nor I had the energy to think about anything beyond types of milk and blends of tea.

Eventually, I lost the power to distinguish his thoughts from mine. Like where gold met silver on his wrist, we blended together. Perhaps we only existed at the same moment, in the same place, because of a history of suffering, because of a tragedy worthy of the gods. But, like a tattoo, the end result was nothing less than a masterpiece of flesh and magic.

TRADITION AND RENEWAL

M idterm season crashed into our lives like a storm at sea and the library became its first victim. Students and professors alike snarled over their territory, guarding their precious stations with teeth and coffee breath.

Bypassing all of them, I headed to the private room Alexander had reserved weeks ago. Always prepared, my Alexander. The room sat empty as I approached, avoiding the glares of those who hadn't thought so far ahead. Alexander arrived a few minutes later, before my tea had even cooled and sat across the table from me. He murmured a greeting, but it lacked any of his usual energy. There were dark bags under his eyes, wrinkles covered his designer clothes and they hung from his frame without the usual tailored perfection. Even so, he was still beautiful.

"Hey," I said, reaching across the table and grabbing his hand. "Are you okay?"

He smiled but it fell too fast to be convincing. "Yeah, just tired. Bad night. I was nauseated all of yesterday. Nightmares." He rubbed his thumb across my knuckles and frowned at his watch. "Is Theo going to be here?"

I opened my mouth to respond, unsure of his intentions and, of course, that was the moment Theo walked in. He paused in the doorway, face going purposefully blank upon seeing our hands intertwined together, but moved ahead, grabbing the seat next to me.

"I was working," Theo answered, swallowing. He dropped his bag on the ground next to me and, with shaking hands, pulled out his computer and notebooks. "Sorry I'm late."

"It's fine," Alexander murmured, leaning back and closing his eyes. "I didn't mean for that to come off so rudely. Just tired today."

Theo nodded, rubbing his eyes. "Oh gods, me too."

Opening one eye, Alexander looked at the table in front of Theo. "No coffee today?"

Theo blinked in surprise, shrugging. "Didn't have time, I guess."

"I'm almost out," Alexander offered, holding up his own coffee cup. Theo leaned back in his chair, almost mirroring Alexander, but I could tell the exhaustion was even heavier on his eyelids. "I'll buy you some after this, if you want?"

Theo scrubbed his face of emotion again, but I could still see the surprise in his eyes, right alongside a deep twinge of gratitude. Coffee was the quickest way to his good side, it seemed. "I – sure. That sounds great. Thank you."

"No problem."

I stared between them for a moment, shocked by how civil they were being. Clearing my throat, I said, "Okay, so, we turned the last assignment in on time, but it was a close call. You saw that Lux posted grades, right? Good. We got a B, but a low one and I think we could do a little better. This assignment is a short summary of the project. Have you guys started your sections?"

"I did," Alexander answered, pulling it up on his computer

and showing me. "I also outlined a little bit of the actual project based on what I think we'll do for the summary. We can change it, of course, but I thought it might be nice to have a framework to work from."

Theo swallowed. "I, uh, haven't started, yet."

Alexander nodded. "You're good, dude. It's not due for a few more days."

I waited for Theo's snapping comment about the nickname, but he didn't seem to notice, so I continued, "We just need to make sure it's cohesive to pick up our dropped points. It's only supposed to be a short summary of the important steps of libations and sacrifices to the gods, with like 500 words at the end about the specifics for Aphrodite. I think she wants us to focus on how it connects to soulmates."

"From, uh, our own experiences?" Theo asked, eyes shifting to his wrist.

I shook my head. "I don't think so. Just in general. Like how soulmate sacrifices and offerings differ from, like, marriage or childbirth sacrifices to the gods. Lux can't assume everyone in the class has found their soulmate."

"Besides," Alexander added, tone uncharacteristically bitter. "What could we even write about our own experience? *Sorry, Professor, the gods decided that they hate us and have trapped us in a constant cycle of doubt and misery regarding our own souls so... looks like this project can't be completed! Give us an A anyway?* I doubt that'll go over well."

"It hasn't been all bad," Theo tried, making both me and Alexander stare.

"Really?" Alexander asked; the question dripping with disbelief.

Theo's cheeks went red, the words spilling out. "I don't know. I just mean... Look, we're trying our best, right? We're doing our sacrifices. You and I are praying to Apollo and

Aphrodite as much as we can and Vanessa is figuring out which Cult she wants to be in. I know Tori and Eliza have been looking at our family trees just in case there's a latent curse hidden in some distant branch we didn't know about. We're *trying*. So, yeah, it sucks, but…"

He rarely spoke so much, and there was an urgency to his words that I wasn't used to. That I didn't expect. Whether it was because of exhaustion or some realization after yesterday's whole ordeal, there seemed to be some change in him. The bond in my chest felt warm, like tea on a winter's night or the burst of cinnamon in a holiday dessert.

I reached out to squeeze his hand. He squeezed back but his eyes stayed on Alexander.

"But it hasn't been all bad," Alexander finished for him, unable to stop his smile from taking over his face. Though his eyes were still dark from lack of sleep, some of his usual light-ness returned to him with the expression. "You're right. I'm sorry. I shouldn't be so negative."

Theo's laugh seemed to surprise even him. "I think we switched roles today."

"I guess it's my turn to be the broody one," Alexander returned, throwing his head back with a laugh at his own joke. I snickered as well and then we were all laughing.

It was no more than a few seconds, but it was the closest to peace we'd ever come. The color was returning to Alexander's cheeks and Theo's hands weren't shaking as much. It felt like I could breathe for a moment, unworried that they would somehow hurt each other over me.

When the silence after the laughter extended for just too long, Theo gently kicked one of the legs of my chair. "Come on Ness, back to the homework. What do we have to work on?"

"The directions are a little ambiguous, and we have to turn it in by the end of the day. If we can all agree on how to write it best and give it a lot of thought, she'll probably take it. Her comments for dropped points last time were mostly that it read like three different people had written it instead of one group…"

"I wonder why," Theo added, rolling his eyes playfully, glancing meaningfully at Alexander. "We've only ever gotten along as a group. I can't remember there *ever* being any tension or conflict or anything—"

"Shut up," Alexander wheezed another laugh. "Oh my gods."

"Boys," I interrupted with amusement, making them both look at me. "Concentrate."

"Sorry," they muttered together, only to make themselves laugh again.

"I think we should just write it together," Alexander finally said, shrugging at the confused looks he got in response. "I already started it so it should be easy to finish pretty quick. We grab a couple sources, I can talk about some of the more basic rituals and then we can talk about our trip to Detroit at the end of the semester. Boom. Done. Party time!"

"Boom," Theo repeated with raised eyebrows. I could tell he was holding in another laugh. His repetition was dry, not nearly as enthusiastic as the original, but his smile softened his mocking tone.

Alexander opened his mouth, but I cut him off, afraid to lose their focus again. To Alexander, I asked, "You're sure you're alright with doing more work? Theo and I can do the rest, if you want?"

He shook his head, shrugging again. "I don't mind. I'm not sure if you understand how much I like talking about this stuff. During a normal semester, I would've shown up to this meeting with the entire project finished already, probably, and personal quotes from my mother."

"You are such a weirdo," Theo snorted. "Gods, get a life."

Instinctively, I opened my mouth to correct him, to tell him to be nicer to Alexander, but Alexander's grin only grew at the simple taunt. It took me a second to realize that this *was* nice for them. As long as no one's feelings were getting hurt, it was probably better if I just let them exchange harmless barbs.

"We have the room until eight, right?" I asked Alexander. He nodded then shook his head at the dumb face Theo was making in his direction. Theo threw his arm over the back of my chair and Alexander pressed his foot against mine under the table. Neither of their expressions changed and the invisible cord wrapped around my lungs lessened.

Though the weather outside was growing darker and more charged with frost and lashing winds, though tests and exams made Chaos out of my brain, at least we were all at peace.

"Then let's get to work."

When the assignment was completed and submitted, we began to pack up our stuff. It had gone smoothly, their ideas for the project so different but strangely compatible. They moved around each other seamlessly, unplugging cords from outlets and gathering their school supplies from the table, narrowly avoiding touching hands as they sorted through any papers we had used for the project. In the end, they both stood around, waiting for me to finish packing up and donning gloves and hats for the cold of the fall.

"See?" Alexander said to Theo, bumping his shoulder into him as I hurried to pack my backpack. "I told you. Don't you feel so much better about the weekend now that the homework is done? Like I said: Boom. Done. Party time."

Theo rolled his eyes at the teasing tone of his voice. "Yeah, yeah, yeah."

"You're such a jerk," Alexander responded with no heat in the words. Even though I wasn't facing them, I could hear the smile in his words. He sighed, loud and overdramatic. "But I still owe you coffee."

"You don't owe me—"

"Okay, let's go—"

Theo and I both stopped to let the other finish, making Alexander laugh again. I shoved his shoulder, barely moving him, and he pulled me into a hug. Where my face was pressed against his chest, I could smell his expensive cologne and feel his chest move with each breath. I sighed into the feeling, and wrapped my arms around him.

I could feel his chin move as he said to Theo, "Coffee?"

I realized that this was maybe the first time that Alexander had been so touchy right in front of Theo and started to pull away, but Theo just snorted and held the door open for both of us.

"Coffee sounds great," Theo answered, allowing us to move toward the elevator. Once the doors had opened and we had all stepped inside, he pressed the button down to the bottom floor. The elevator jerked but with Alexander's arm still wrapped around my shoulder, I hardly moved. I looked up at him, smiling, and he grinned right back.

"Speaking of party time," Theo said, rubbing the back of his neck and Alexander and I looked away from each other to blink in confusion at him. "The Cult of Dionysus on campus is throwing one of their parties tonight and, uh, Tori asked if you still wanted to come?"

"She did?" I asked, raising my eyebrows. It had been so long since I'd asked about a Cult of Dionysus event that I had practically forgotten. "Really?"

Theo's mouth twitched up into a grin. "Really... and I guess I'd like you to come, too."

I thought through my plans for the night and distantly remembered that Ronan was supposed to be at the apartment tonight for once. I didn't want to chance not being able to see him. "Can Ronan come?"

Theo shrugged, but his smile was sweet. "I'm pretty sure

Tori already invited all our plats, what with them being on the same project."

I had never been to a party before, let alone a proper Cult of Dionysus party. A thousand questions swirled through my mind: my wardrobe, what I should expect, what kind of alcohol did he prefer? And then I noticed Theo's thoughts, the nervousness radiating from him with my lack of answer.

"I'll be there," I answered, grinning up at him. "Happily."

"Good," he answered, smiling down just the same. "I'm glad."

After a few seconds, he turned his gaze to Alexander. "How about you?"

Alexander's entire body froze. "What about me?"

"Are you free tonight?" Theo asked, coughing and staring straight ahead at the elevator buttons in front of him. The number ticked down steadily. Alexander seemed at a loss for words and Theo swallowed. My neck hurt from glancing back and forth between them. "Like I said, I think Tori already invited Eliza, but if not you could come together? If you wanted. No pressure—"

"Yes," Alexander managed, interrupting him quickly. "I'm free. And I'll be there."

I swallowed, a new round of nerves wracking me at his answer. It was hard to imagine the inside of the Cult of Dionysus house, but it was even harder to imagine walking its halls with both of them at my side. Even now, just dressed in casual clothes to study, Theo with his worn leather and Alexander with his pristine collar, they tempted me with their closeness. My hands ached to touch, desperate to feel the buzzing of our bonds in my chest. Throw in the alcohol and revelry of Bacchants…

I hoped Aphrodite would be gentle with us all.

"Cool," Theo answered, unable to hide the way his smile grew.

"Cool," Alexander echoed, the doors of the elevator opening. He cleared his throat. "Coffee first?"

Theo laughed again. It was a different sort of laugh, relieved and happy. "Coffee first."

THE BLOOM OF RUINATION

The bus stop was just a few minutes away from our apartment, though the walk felt much longer as the temperature continued to drop. I pulled my thin jacket tighter. Ronan had mentioned how warm the parties would get, warning me against wearing a real coat, but the cold wind was starting to convince me it would be worth running back and grabbing my winter parka. Luckily, the bus arrived with brakes squealing in the slush on the road before I could give in to the cold.

The ride was as silent as our wait. An odd tension filled the air between us that refused to let up. The bus screeched to a stop outside the Cult of Dionysus house and the driver hesitated as we stepped back into the cold. "Y'all be careful, alright? I see the kids that come stumbling out of there. Make sure you get a ride home."

I shivered again and this time it had nothing to do with the weather. The legend of the Cult of Dionysus parties carried a lot of weight in the small college town and from what I'd heard, Tori's place as president was a big part of that. Dionysus was often just thought of as the God of Wine and Theater, but he was also the God of Madness and these parties were celebrations of that identity too. The lines between good and bad decisions were blurred and with blessed wine and liquor in your system, it was easy to lose your head.

Ronan smiled politely. "My soulmate is on speed dial for the night. Thank you!" He helped me off the bus, making sure I didn't slip on the slick ground. Voice low, he asked, "You seem nervous. Are you alright?"

I was grateful for the break in silence as I stared up at the looming house. There was already excess noise coming through the windows and double doors of the three-storey white building. A mix of plants and wildflowers grew around the outside, some of them artfully reaching into the walking path to the door, though the cold should've killed them months ago.

"Yeah," I lied, swallowing my nerves and attempting a smile and Ronan eyed me doubtfully. "I'm alright."

There were two doors on either side of us as we walked inside, but there was music coming from both. The pounding music made me raise my voice, "Any idea where we should go?"

Ronan tilted his head to the right and led us that way. Portraits of the presidents of the Cult cluttered the small hallway, stretching back to the beginning of Golden Valley in the sixties. At the very end was Tori, smiling in a frame like she had a secret.

The hallway ended just after her picture and we found ourselves in a giant kitchen with about thirty other people. I thought to Theo, *We're here.* A girl threw up in the trash can. Two of her friends holding her hair back. *Didn't this thing just start?*

Welcome to the Cult of Dionysus, he responded, catching my disgust. *I'll be right there.*

And he wasn't lying. He came around the same corner we had, holding a bottle of beer with a label that read "Green

213

Sphinx." It looked too expensive and pretentious for my taste, and I had to stop the swell of affection I felt for him. From the look Ronan sent me, I didn't block it completely.

"Hey," Theo said. Except for the braided gold circlet around his forehead, he hadn't dressed up for the party and I'd bet my left arm that Tori made him wear the accessory. It complemented his skin tone the same way his bracelets and new tattoo did. *And besides*, I thought to myself, *he looked so good in his usual dark-wash jeans and black t-shirt, why would he want to change?*

"Hi," I said, my cheeks flushing pink at the sight of him.

Neither of us said anything for a second and in an almost-Alexandrian gesture, Theo rubbed the back of his neck with nerves. He thought, *You look nice.* But his eyes didn't wander down to my neckline, where the lace hinted at the rare cleavage I was showing off. I didn't let my disappointment color my thoughts.

You too.

A guy came up to Ronan and they greeted each other. They said something about being in class together, and Ronan told me he was going to dance. The guy had a gold bracelet on his wrist too, so I didn't worry about him. Mostly, I thought he was giving me and Theo a minute to talk.

Theo thought, *Want anything to drink?*

I didn't bring anything.

They supply it all here. I can open the fridge and anything you want will be there. So what'll it be? He moved to the fridge, slapping a hand on the shoulder of the guy in front of it to move around him. The guy turned as red as his drink as he checked Theo out. My sympathies went out to him.

Theo was opening the door as I answered, *Something with cherries.*

He came away from the fridge holding a wine glass full of a thick, dark liquid. He handed it to me and the first sip filled my mouth and covered my tongue with the sweet, sharp tang of cherries and wine. The alcohol hit my mostly empty stomach and I grinned at him.

It's good, I thought. Another sip. *Really good. Thank you.*

Theo took a step closer. Already emboldened by the wine and atmosphere, I took a step back, putting my back to the edge of the counter. Someone bumped into him and pushed us closer and I curled a hand around his bicep to stop his retreat. It was the closest we had been since our kiss and there was a tension in his shoulders that let me know he was thinking the same thing. Still, he leaned in, one hand resting on the counter behind me, boxing me in. His cologne smelled like smoke and whiskey and pure heat settled in my stomach as he stared down at me.

"I mean it," he murmured, stepping even closer until our chests brushed with each breath. I wanted him closer. "You look good." Where my hair hung past my shoulders, he wrapped a curl around the tip of a finger, and I followed his mouth as he brought the beer to his lips again. "Really good."

The music was deafening, but he was thinking his words as well as speaking them aloud so I could understand what he was saying. I did the same, echoing my own words with my thoughts as my hand slid up his arm to land on his shoulder. Blinking up at him, I asked, "Thank you. Do you like my dress?"

His eyes darkened as they roved over the neckline of my dress. *Finally*, I thought, though I knew he would hear it. Gaze trailing over the lace, he answered, "Love it. Very pretty." A noise escaped me and his eyes grew even darker as he pressed even closer. Without meaning to, he tugged on the strand of hair wrapped around his finger and a gasp escaped me. He hummed. "So fucking pretty, sweetheart."

I opened my mouth to respond, still unsure what I wanted to say, when someone loudly cleared their throat behind him.

Eliza, dressed impeccably in a designer bodysuit, raised an icy blonde eyebrow. Theo swallowed, taking a step back from me. We both took a long drink and looked away from each other. "You look like you're having fun."

Theo huffed an awkward laugh. "Hi, Eliza. Glad you could make it."

Eliza rolled her eyes. "Yeah, I'm sure I'm the one you're looking forward to seeing."

"You are," I said, smiling warmly at her. Her eyebrows raised again, this time from surprise. "Thank you for looking into the family trees. Theo mentioned it earlier and I just wanted to let you know how much I appreciate it. I know it was a dead end, but genuinely, it means a lot that you tried."

"Of course," she responded, softer than I expected, her voice nearly carried away with the cacophony of electronic music. "We're all in this together, right?" She paused, a slight smirk on her glossed lips as she tilted her head to the door. "And besides, we're the only ones not operating on lust and jealousy right now."

Alexander entered the kitchen before we could say anything, wearing a nice button-down shirt that had been ripped open, a glittering handprint showing on his stomach. Theo swallowed at the same moment I did. Eliza snorted delicately, grabbing a glass of something white and cloudy from the enchanted fridge and leaving the kitchen.

Alexander called out to her, "I told you not to leave me alone! I have glitter in my underwear now!" He coughed as his gaze widened on mine and Theo's. "I mean, uh, hey. You look nice, Vanessa."

Their similar greeting was funny to me, so I said, "Thanks. You look nice, too. Love to see people so... open with their bodies." I looked pointedly at his exposed stomach and abdominal muscles. My tongue went dry at the sight and I swallowed more of my drink.

His face got redder and he pulled the shirt closed. "I ran into a group of Cult of Aphrodite followers and they can get, uh, touchy." He shuddered as he flicked glitter off his skin. I tried not to track the movement with my eyes, knowing Theo would hear those thoughts in my head. "Man, glitter is the worst to get off."

Theo, with his usual timing and glassy eyes, said, "Uh, hi?"

Alexander looked up from his stomach, his hands covered in purple glitter, and stared at Theo for a second with wide eyes. They didn't say anything for a second, just stared at each other across the loud space. Alexander, blinking out of the weird pause, stepped closer to us. Then he stopped, turned to the fridge, and pulled out a glass of amber liquid. He downed it like a shot and then reached for another before coming over to where Theo and I were still pressed against the side of the island.

"Hi," he said, holding the glass to his chest. His bare chest. *Gods above, how is that fair?*

You're telling me, Theo thought back. *Was he modeled after a Bernini sculpture?*

For my own sake, I asked, "Do you, uh, want help buttoning?"

Alexander looked mournful. "They popped the buttons off."

Theo was already taking off his top layer, a red and gray flannel, and handing it to Alexander. He was wearing a black t-shirt underneath, so at least I didn't have to worry about both of them being shirtless and tempting. Alexander started to protest, but Theo insisted. "I'm literally begging you to take it."

"Alright," Alexander finally agreed, taking off the buttonless shirt and shoving it in the nearby trashcan before shrugging on the plaid. It didn't fit perfectly, of course, but I felt like I could breathe again when the buttons were done up. "Thanks, man."

"No problem," Theo responded, his voice tighter than I expected. I looked at him, confused, and he cleared his throat.

"You look, uh, nice too. In my shirt." A pause, a cough, another drink of his beer. "I mean, dressed. In clothes. I like the glitter."

Alexander blinked, mouth twisting into a half-smile. "Thanks. You, too."

Alexander looked over him, no doubt taking in the same stretch of the fabric at Theo's shoulders, the tight fit of his jeans at his thighs, the spirals of ink curving around his collarbones. He took a sip of his drink but choked a little when he saw the silver of Theo's new tattoo.

His eyes widened, recognizing the significance of the color. He looked back up at Theo, their eyes meeting for an extended moment. I waited, unsure of how he would react. When he spoke, his voice was quiet, each syllable measured.

"I wish you would've told me," he shook his head. "I guess I understand why you didn't, but... I wish you had."

Theo pulled his hand closer to his body almost protectively.

I stayed silent, watching them with a hummingbird in my chest.

"I just figured—" he started, cutting himself off with a sigh. "I just figured that, once it was done, it'd be the first thing people would notice about me. I wanted more time without people knowing." His eyebrows drew together. "I'm sorry. You're right. I should've said something."

Alexander's face crinkled and for just a second, I worried that tears might fill his eyes. But he swallowed, straightening his spine and closing the space between all three of us. Theo froze next to me. Alexander, moving slowly, reached a hand out, gaze flicking down to look Theo in the eyes. "Can I see?"

The unspoken question seemed almost too loud: Can I touch?

I turned to Theo. *You don't have to—*

Theo nodded, offering his wrist to Alexander palm facing up and the moment his fingers touched his skin, index finger following the swirls of magic ink and hidden veins, they both let out a sharp breath. Alexander pulled back, but Theo shook his head. "It's alright. It doesn't hurt."

"Good," Alexandered murmured, tilting his arm to watch the metallic material catch the light. I understood the urge, it was a tragic piece of work, but so beautiful. "When did you get it?"

"Yesterday," Theo answered, the word a quiet confession.

I felt the need to say something. To moderate this strangely intense, peaceful moment between them, only to be interrupted by a loud banging from upstairs. People around us looked up, laughing, and it popped the bubble.

"What was that?" Alexander asked, braver than I.

"I think Tori is running a game of truth or dare in the other room," Theo said with a current of nervousness. "We could go watch, if you want? It can get kind of crazy. Some of the shit they do gets the cops called."

They both looked at me and I stilled at their combined attention. My nerves flared again in my stomach, warning bells ringing in my head. "Uh. Sure?"

"We don't have to," Theo clarified quickly. "I know it can be a lot—"

"Are you scared, Theo?" Alexander asked, a glint of challenge in his expression. He nodded toward the stairs, just on the other side of the wall. Arrogance dripped off of him in a way that I knew was just to piss Theo off. "I'm not."

Theo's hand wrapped around mine, eyes darkening with the taunt. "Not at all. Let's go." He navigated us through the crowds, leading me with small tugs. Alexander, behind me, placed his hand on the small of my back when we passed a cluster of screaming Dio-Bros.

Upstairs the music was quieter, barely a hum, but the stench of weed and other incense fogged the air. I coughed and Theo continued to explain, "The games used to get huge when the last president was in charge but Tori tries to keep them more lowkey. There's only so much they can get away with in the name of Cult activity."

Only a dozen people sat in a circle inside the small lounge, some smoking but most drinking out of a cup of wine they passed around. As we walked in, a dude in a beanie dared a girl in a spaghetti-strap shirt to text a naughty picture to her ex. She did it, laughing loudly and drunkenly, and sent a sarcastic prayer to Dionysus. Everyone laughed and it filled the room.

Growing up, we'd all heard about the Cults of the Olympians in our history classes. Members of the Cult of Dionysus were, statistically, most likely to wait until their twenty-fourth birthday to do their Soulmate Ceremonies. Bards sang about their legendary parties and most porn-writers looked to them as their Muses. Their activities, though entertaining to hear about, had never really appealed to me.

Theo stopped in the doorway and I stood on the very tips of my toes to try and see over his shoulders. The room wasn't very big, a bunch of mismatched furniture was spread across the floor. Couches, loveseats, armchairs, even beanbags. The other people sprawled across each other on all of them, touching constantly.

Tori wiggled in the lap of another girl with tattoos up and down her strong arms. She grinned, loud and obvious, when she saw her plat. "Theo!" she called, patting the spot next to her. "Come sit down! And you brought the wonder duo! Great!"

It seemed a little sarcastic but Theo just rolled his eyes and led us to sit by her. Behind me, Alexander muttered the words "wonder duo" to himself in amusement. His chest pressed against me as we entered the room and his hand sat low and possessive on my back. I felt greedy, wanting more.

"Hey, Tori," I greeted, sitting down in a way that I hope didn't flash anyone. Tori was wearing less than I was – a black bandeau shirt and a jean skirt with sewn patches of theater masks. "I like your skirt."

Her grin wasn't sharklike like Eliza's but instead a little wolfy. She didn't bother hiding her big scary teeth. "You look hot, too. Or, at least, Theo thinks so. You walk into a room and his emotions go—"

"Victoria," Theo interrupted. "Knock it off."

"Alright, *Theodore*," she laughed. She turned her gaze to Alexander, who leaned his back against the wall with his legs spread open, relaxed even in a place very much not his own. I envied him, making myself smaller in the space. "Alexander Crest. Interesting to see you here. I don't remember inviting you."

Alexander didn't even blink. "Theo invited me."

Tori snaked an arm around the waist of the girl she was cuddling with, "Oh, did he? Well, house rules say that it's mandatory for first-time partygoers to join the game."

Someone started, "That's not a house rule—"

"I'm the president," she snapped at them, eyes sharpening. "And I say it's a rule. Which means you have to join too, Vanessa, sweetheart."

I winced. Coming from Theo, the term was a comfort but from Tori it stung. I agreed anyway.

She continued, looking at her plat, now. "So, you might as well join, too, Theodore."

Theo was frowning, but he only said, "Fine."

"Ooh," a girl giggled from the couch, where she was tucked into the armpit of a guy wearing a bro-tank and a Cult of Dionysus hat. A Dio-Bro, if I'd ever seen one. "I love when Theo plays. He's the best kisser—"

Someone talked over her, truth or daring someone in the circle. I swallowed my emotions, trying to ignore the jealousy shooting down my spine, and Theo put his hand on my thigh, low enough that it wasn't inappropriate, but his fingertips buzzed against my bare skin. Alexander stretched, pushing his thigh until it touched the other leg and I flushed, glancing between them.

"Sorry," Theo murmured.

I didn't respond. A few turns passed. Two truths revealing nothing interesting. Someone dared Tori to give the girl a lap dance, which felt pointless as she was already on her lap. She fulfilled her dare, grinding her hips to the music. Theo grimaced and drank more beer.

"My turn to ask, now," Tori announced, her dark eyes landing on me. She sipped her drink, some bright purple mix, and licked her lips like a lion going in for the kill. "Vanessa. Truth or dare?"

MORE THAN TRUTH

"Truth."

"Boring," Tori sing-songed. "But fine. Who's a better kisser, Alexander or Theo?"

I blinked. Theo protested. Alexander tensed next to me. "I don't know," I said, still frazzled by the question. Everyone was looking at me. "I didn't really consider comparing—"

"But you have kissed them both?" someone asked, laughing.

I blushed. "Yes."

"Victoria," Theo started again and I wished the shield between us would let up for a moment.

"Answer the question," she taunted me. "Or drink. That's the punishment for not answering."

"I did answer," I said. "I don't know."

"Rules say that's not an answer!" someone calls.

"She's telling the truth—" Theo tried.

"I'll drink then," I offered, lifting my glass to my lips.

Several people whooped. Someone got up and pulled a red Solo cup from a minifridge and the guy handed it to me with a wink. It was brave, considering I was bracketed by two soulmates.

"Not your cute little wine," Tori explained. "This is our special T&D mix."

I sniffed the liquid. It was almost black and had the texture of tar. "What's in it?"

She snorted. "What isn't in it? And no baby sips, either. A full mouthful."

I made eye contact with Theo and he shrugged, helpless. I winced as I swallowed a mouthful of the stuff. It burned like hydra fire and tasted like the bottom of a wine barrel, grainy pieces of grapes that hadn't been completely juiced.

The moment the taste started to fade, something happened. I got a flash of something. A memory, maybe. Or a remembered sensation. Running through the woods barefoot, ripping the head off a beautiful prince in the woods. I almost spat the drink back out.

"Hades below," I cursed. "That's vile."

"Enchanted liqueur," someone explained. "A gift from the big guy, himself."

"Answer next time," someone else responded.

"Anyway," Tori interrupted. "It's your turn to ask someone."

"Okay. Alexander, truth or dare?" I asked, hoping I could think of something to appease the eager crowd.

"Truth," Alexander said, sitting up a little bit.

Help. Please.

Ask him who his best kiss was.

But he's only—

I know. But they'll like the drama of the answer. It's not really about being honest. It's about putting on a good show. They thrive off blatant sex and seduction stuff.

"Who was your best kiss?" I asked him.

"You know the answer to that," he said, raising his eyebrows, but his eyes flashed with something that made me warm. He leaned forward just a little, pressing his thigh into mine more. I was entranced even as Theo's hand squeezed my other thigh. Not possessive but encouraging, and I felt dangerously alive being held by the two of them. "You. Of course, it's you."

Our audience catcalled. Tori's eyes narrowed, but she didn't say anything. I took it as a win.

"My turn, right?" Alexander looked to Tori. She nodded. "Cool. Theo, truth or dare?"

"Dare."

"Oh," Alexander said. "I thought you'd say truth."

"Thirty seconds to come up with something," Tori informed him. "Or you forfeit your dare to the person to your right." That person happened to be the girl who'd complimented Theo's kissing earlier. Alexander's and Theo's faces pulled into the same expression at the realization.

I'll drink before I kiss her, don't worry.

"Uh," Alexander said at the same time. I could tell his mind was spinning even if I couldn't read his mind, too. The girl Tori was sitting on dragged her hand up her thigh, revealing more skin. Alexander noticed too and said, "Most of the party downstairs has already seen me shirtless at this point. Level the playing field. Take your clothes off."

People laughed but there was a rough edge to it and a few people, men and women, leaned forward. The shield in my mind flew up with record speed, but Theo still shot me a look.

"All of them?" Theo asked, a little incredulous. But he was standing up next to me and pulling his shirt off. The expanse of his bronze skin was on display, revealing the dark hair that dusted across his lower abdomen and a black tattoo across his right shoulder, unfamiliar to me. It was something in Ancient Greek, the lines almost archaic.

My face felt hot and my mouth went dry, so I took another sip of my cherry wine.

Quickly, Alexander amended, "Keep your underwear on."

Before I could stop it, I thought, *Oh, thank gods.*

A few disappointed sighs. I tried not to glare at anyone.

After taking off his shoes and socks, Theo let out a huff of a laugh as he unbuttoned his pants and lowered them past his thighs. More dark hair, another tattoo on his left thigh. Medusa holding Perseus' head in her hand. I thought another completely inappropriate thought. Another chuckle. Everyone must have assumed it was from amusement or embarrassment but he thought to me, *Thanks, sweetheart.*

Another sip of wine. *Uh, you're welcome.*

Apparently committing to the dare completely, Theo took off the snake necklace fastened around his neck. Somehow that was what made him look truly naked. When only a pair of black underwear and his gold bracelets remained, he sat back down next to me. To Alexander, he said with one raised brow, "Satisfied?"

Alexander's entire face was the color of roses. He coughed out, "Yes."

"Good," Theo said, placing his hand on my thigh again like nothing had changed. Another sip of wine. With his other hand, he grabbed his beer and took a long drink. I stopped myself from following the movement of his throat. "My turn. Tori, truth or dare?"

"Truth," she answered, though she'd teased me for it earlier.

"You turn twenty-four next year," he said like he'd planned for her to answer with that. When he spoke there was an obvious mocking to his tone, but my vision blurred and I didn't process it. "Are you just, like, super excited to find your soulmate?"

She scowled. "No."

"Awe," the girl whined, tightening her arms around her. "What are we going to do when our local sex-goddess is on lock-down? Who will pleasure the masses with her lovely fingers and tongue?"

Theo scrunched his nose, grossed out. A predictable reaction. The bond between platonic soulmates was, by definition, opposed to romance. I would feel the same if someone spoke about Ronan like that.

"Weep," Tori responded, deadpan. "Melony, truth or dare?"

The game went on for some time. A girl named Morgan confessed that someone named Sean gave her an STI. A guy named Steven confessed to his nipple piercings being the most painful of his metal accessories. I sipped my wine a little but the glass never seemed to drain. The black substance in the red Solo cup bubbled, and I questioned the life choices of people who willingly played this game.

Eventually, the girl under Tori got asked a question that she didn't want to answer, so she was also handed a cup of the vile substance. Her friends mocked her. When she was done, she asked Theo, "Truth or dare?"

"Truth."

"How many people have you had sex with?"

I turned to look at him, just as curious. Alexander stared at the wall, refusing to pay attention. Not for the first time, I appreciated his sensitivity to the situation. Theo didn't flush, at least, not right away. First, he asked, "What are you defining as sex?"

"Anything below the belt."

He thought for a moment, thoughts still blocked. "Ten."

The group heckled him and one of the girls, the one with dyed red hair, looked smug. A sip of wine caught my throat and I coughed. People looked at me. Theo reached for me, but, without thinking about it, I scooted closer to Alexander. Theo's face cracked, and where his hand still rested on my thigh, I intertwined our fingers. An apology.

After Margot, he started, rubbing the skin of my thigh until goosebumps broke out across my skin.

You don't owe me an explanation.

But I want to tell you anyway, he thought and continued, *things were bad. Sex without feelings was fun for about three months and then it sucked. It didn't help. It just made me feel – guilty, I guess.*

So, the redhead?

Yeah. His mental tone was bland, but his thoughts were still shielded.

Cool, cool. I took a much larger gulp of wine. *Thanks for warning me.*

Vanessa—

"Dude," one of the nameless guys said. "You gotta ask someone."

"Fine," he said. "Vanessa, truth or dare."

"Truth," I said again.

"Do you want to get married?"

I choked on my wine again. "Are you *proposing* to me?"

The crowd cackled. Alexander shifted, coughing. Theo laughed, too, his head thrown back and hair falling around him. Maybe it was the wine, but he looked like Dionysus, young and beautiful and free. "No," he answered, grinning at me. His teeth were a little crooked, sharp at the canines and totally human. "Well, not yet. I was just wondering. Not everyone gets married. But some like to."

Mind loose, I thought of the pictures of my parents' wedding sitting on our fireplace back home. Our family gazebo stood in the middle of a well-trimmed field. Cherry trees, on the precipice of fruiting, perfumed the air. My grandfather married them five days after my father's twenty-first birthday, when the gods confirmed what they both had known since they'd first brushed hands in high school. Blessed soulmates, each drawn to their other half so strongly that they found them early.

"Yes," I said, trying not to imagine who would stand across the aisle. I didn't count myself as a traditionalist, thinking that sex should wait until after the ceremony, but the night *after* did cross my mind. I skimmed past the thought. "I think I would. Just not yet."

Alexander cleared his throat. "Ask someone, Vanessa."

"Tori?"

"Truth."

"I want you," I said, thinking on the fly. I must have used more gravitas than I intended to because people leaned forward, hyenas waiting for a juicy morsel, "to tell us all why you're so afraid of finding your soulmate."

Uh-oh, Theo thought before mentally shutting up. By the shock on her friends' faces, no one had ever touched on the topic before. I didn't back down, though my first instinct was to cower behind her plat. Surely, she wouldn't murder Theo to get to me.

Her eyes were wide for a moment before they narrowed. If she was a wolf, she'd have been lunging for my throat already. "No. Actually, fuck no. I'll drink instead. Give me your damn cup." Wordlessly, I handed her the red Solo cup. She sniffed it and shuddered, then took two swallows. Her eyes went glassy for about three seconds. Her friends fell silent, anticipating. She snapped back into reality and shuddered. "Lord Bacchus, why do we even keep this shit around?"

Tori hasn't had to drink since freshman year. She brags about it all the time. Or, bragged, I guess.

"Moving on," Tori continued, wiping her mouth with the back of her hand and downing the rest of her drink. Rum and coke, it smelled like. "Theo, remember that conversation we had last night? Tell us all what you really think about Alexander, here."

I tensed and so did Alexander. *Uh-oh.*

Theo, unblinking, said instead, "Dare."

A few people laughed but the air was suddenly tense. Because Theo and Tori were looking at each other like they could speak with their minds too and whatever she saw in his, it made her smile, baring her teeth.

"Fine," she conceded, her voice sickly sweet. "I dare you to kiss Alexander."

IN VINO VERITAS

He was surprised for about two seconds. And then he got angry. "Victoria—"

"Theodore," she mocked. "Come on, are you really going to chicken out?"

"Give me the damn drink—"

Alexander interrupted, shrugging. "I'm okay with it, if you are. It's just a game."

Theo stopped and so did I. I would have paid an unfathomable amount of money to know what Alexander was thinking right then. His third glass of bourbon sat by his side, empty. Where the top two buttons of the flannel shirt were undone, a soft pink blush rose up over his collarbones. But still, he gave the offer without any reluctance, sitting forward and leaning toward both of us.

Theo asked, "Are you sure?"

"Why not, right?" he answered, clearing his throat.

Theo looked at me. I said nothing. I was pretty sure I'd crossed the line from tipsy to drunk about three minutes ago because the ceiling was spinning. Theo's thoughts probed mine and wanting him out of my head I thought, *It's fine. Do it. Give them a good show.*

Theo stared at me for a long moment, taking in my finger's nervous drumming, but when Tori opened her mouth he gestured to Alexander. "Fine, come here. I'm not crawling across the floor in my underwear." A disappointed sigh sounded from the redhead, and I shot her a glare.

Alexander followed Theo's command and I switched spots with him, almost slipping on the floor as I sat back. The guy from earlier winked at me again and I didn't even bother hiding my disdain.

The moment Alexander was in front of him, Theo leaned forward with purpose, connecting their lips. He pulled back a second later, glaring at his plat. Alexander blinked, his brain looked like it was trying to figure out what happened.

"There," Theo said. "Done—"

"Nope!" someone called. "Kissing dares require tongue."

"House rules," Tori said, teeth still showing. "Try again, Theodore."

"He didn't agree to that," he tried to protest. "I'll just drink—"

"S'alright," Alexander slurred slightly, reaching out to cup Theo's jaw in his hand. Theo tensed, hands clenching at his sides. Alexander moved closer, their faces just a breath apart. "Theo, it's *okay*."

"I don't know if this a good idea," Theo murmured, unable to look away from Alexander's mouth. Still shaking, his hands found their place on his slim hips, keeping them both from swaying with the alcohol. "I'll just drink—"

"Stop being a coward," Alexander huffed, blinking long lashes as the slightest smirk curved his mouth, "and just kiss me."

Theo's eyes flashed with the challenge. With a hand on Alexander's jaw, he tugged him forward. Their lips met again and Alexander's eyes widened. I thought he was going to push Theo back, but he didn't. Instead, his hands gripped Theo's broad shoulders. Theo sighed and opened his mouth, coaxing him into the slow rhythm of the kiss, and settled his wide hands on Alexander's waist. His eyes fluttered shut and his fingers pressed white prints into Theo's skin, but he stayed where he was, opening his mouth in return.

They both made a small noise of surprise and desire and my head throbbed in time with the bonds in my chest. I blinked and it must have lasted longer than a second, because when I opened my eyes Theo had two hands under Alexander's shirt, touching as much naked skin as he could manage, and Alexander's fingers were buried in Theo's hair, the inky strands covering his gilded skin. His shoulders trembled, the same way they did for me, but his breathing remained slow and steady. He looked, for lack of a better word, intoxicated by the kiss.

Theo pulled back for a second and, immediately, Alexander pulled him back. A flash of pink tongue. A groan, low and hot. There was glitter in Theo's hair, on their hands. My head throbbed again and somehow it felt like a reminder. Like an alarm going off, trying to wake me up. I ignored it and closed my eyes again.

"Yeah," one of them said, laughing a little. It was weird, directionless. They pulled each other in again.

I felt my stomach flip. People chuckled around me, wrapping me in their silk-and-sandpaper sounds and I had to put my head in my hands to stop myself from passing out right there. From the other side of the door, Ronan's concern enveloped my thoughts and its sickly sweetness tasted worse than the hallucinogenic black liquid of Dionysus.

"Theo!" Tori said from beside me, her voice loud and cutting. She was skittering off the girl's lap to pull them apart. Their faces were as open and confused as a season's end. "What the fuck? What are you doing? Vanessa—"

They both turned their heads to look at me and realization sparked in their expressions. They threw themselves apart, but their red lips and the blooming beard-burn on Alexander's jaw made me want to crawl out of my skin. The world was tinted jade. My stomach flipped again and I pushed myself up to my feet.

"I'll be back in a minute."

Stumbling over outstretched limbs, I ducked out of the room and dodged their concerned voices. Vaguely, I remembered passing a bathroom on the way to the lounge and my feet took me in that direction. By the mercy of the gods, it was open and I slammed the door shut behind me.

Immediately, I pressed my forehead against the cool marble of the sink, trying to steady my mind and my stomach. Everything replayed in my mind, repeating the kiss with devastating accuracy. The looks on their faces, the noises they'd made, all echoing around the small room as my head spun and spun.

I dove for the toilet. I emptied my stomach for a few minutes, feeling shame and sickness take over me. I closed my eyes, pressing my too hot forehead to the cool of the ivory toilet. The alcohol churned in my stomach, throat, mouth, but my chest burned and then I was gasping but no air filled my lungs.

I slowly realized that someone was pounding on the bathroom door. Yelling. Two voices. No. Three. Two men's voices outside and one very persistent one in my head. I pushed myself into a sitting position, wiping the back of my hand across my mouth. My wrist wobbled, barely supporting me.

Please stop yelling, I begged, clutching my head. *It hurts.*

"She's awake," I heard from outside the door. *Sweetheart, can you unlock the door?*

A stone wall. A kiss. Way too much alcohol.

Go away.

A new voice said, "Ness, please, open the door. I just want to make sure you're okay."

Ronan. I tried speaking, but it came out as a gross cough. I pressed my forehead to the seat again, trying to muster the strength to say an actual word. A few murmurs, the softest wave of comfort and concern from Ronan. I managed to say, "No one else."

"Just Tori," Ronan said after a few tense moments, "in case I need help. Okay?"

We're going. Can you call me tomorrow?

I slammed my shield in place without replying. For the first time since our kiss, I was totally alone in my head. It didn't feel nearly as good as I'd hoped.

Shuffling footsteps. My thoughts tasted like resignation and I crawled from the toilet to the door. The moment I unlocked it, it swung out and revealed a blast of comforting, cool emotion from Ronan and a red-faced Tori. Theo and Alexander weren't in the hallway. Vaguely, I sensed his concern from the closest bedroom and my stomach roiled at the thought of them together in bed, me on the sidelines once more.

"Oh, shit," Tori said, kneeling down and pulling the skirt of my dress to cover more of me. "Hey, how are you feeling? Do you need to puke some more? No shame in it. There's nothing I haven't seen before."

I shook my head and held my arms out to Ronan. "Just want to go home."

He brushed my hair off my sweaty forehead and pressed a kiss there. He was sweaty, too, and I remembered he was dancing before my dumb soulmate drama interrupted his life. Fucking again. Tears welled in my eyes without my permission and then he was reaching to lift me from the ground to his chest.

"Aw, kiddo," he said and I muffled my sob into his shoulder.

He was rubbing my back. "Let's get you out of here, then we can get you cleaned up and cry together as much as you want. Do you think you can walk?" I shook my head because my legs were already trembling. "That's okay. Just let me know if you need to puke again. Tori—"

"Gotcha," she said, already helping him to get my arms over their shoulders. We left the bathroom, and I tried to apologize to her for getting sick, but she just shushed me. "It's okay. I was the one who fucked up."

I shook my head and then stopped as it made me feel sicker. "No."

"No?" she asked.

"No," I said firmly, not inclined to say anything more. I closed my eyes, and the next thing I knew, I was in the back of a cab. Ronan was holding me against him. I missed him.

"I miss you, too," he answered. Fuck, I'd said that out loud. "Even if you're so wasted you won't remember anything from tonight, I miss you, too. Don't worry. We'll talk about it in the morning."

"Okay," I said again, drowsing on his shoulder. When I woke up, Ronan was prodding me, asking me to open my eyes. When I did, I saw we were in front of our apartment. Sam was standing outside, leaning against the door with gathered eyebrows. As Ronan helped me out of the car, I said, "Don't worry. I just drank too much."

"That's why I'm worried, Ness," Sam answered, coming to lift me out of the car. He sent a disappointed look to both Tori and Ronan. "How much did she drink?"

"Bottomless cups," I answered, leaning my cheek against his shoulder. "Wine."

"And a mouthful of the Dionysian Juice," Tori admitted, getting out of the car, too. When she got close enough, I reached out and patted her cheek. She was very pretty. She should be a moviestar. She looked at me strangely. "I didn't know she was a lightweight."

"Lightweight?" Sam asked, lifting me completely in his arms. "I think the only thing she's ever had to drink is wine at Cult services during the holidays." I nodded and Tori winced. "Do you mind coming up? She should shower and she'd probably be more comfortable with you doing it."

"I'm not sure about that," Tori said, following us into the apartment anyway. "She and I went back and forth a lot tonight and it's my fault that—"

"No," I denied again.

She sighed. "Yes, I shouldn't have let that kiss go on for that long."

"Not your fault," I repeated, finally giving into sleep. Sam or maybe Ronan smoothed my hair back. In the darkness of my eyelids, a gleaming smile bit at my memories, all sharp teeth and sweet fruit. The sounds of bacchic frenzy danced in my head – pounding drums, rattling instruments, echoing uvulations. Somewhere in the chaos of the music, Dionysus whispered to me. Things that I wished weren't true, things that I was still too terrified to acknowledge in the daylight. But it remained.

"In vino veritas."

ἹΣΤΟΡΊΑ - ΠΛΕΟΝΕΞΊΑ

GREED

S he had done nothing wrong. By the order of the King, she had only been exploring the halls of the palace that would be hers in just a few short hours. But now, with her back pressed to the cold stone and ears straining to hear the urgent whispers, she couldn't help but feel as though she was living in a mistake.

"You cannot say things like that, Prince Alexand—"

"I told you, Theodoros, call me my name without my title," Alexandros interrupted. She couldn't see them, but she heard someone shift. Maybe a step closer. Maybe a step further away. "And I can say anything I please. I am the son of Aphrodite."

"You are to be married tomorrow," Theodoros snapped, "to Vanessa." He said her name like it meant something else, like it stood for something besides just her. Later, she would wonder if it was meant to be a remark about her gender or her station. "How can you be so arrogant to demand us both?"

"I demanded nothing," Alexandros answered, his voice so soft that she almost couldn't hear him. But, as if carried by the wings of Fate or Pain, they landed in her mind anyway. "I only asked. I only begged. But, if you can tell me that you are not filled with longing whenever you see us together—"

"Of course, I am," Theodoros snapped at him. "I have loved her since we were children. I loved her before I knew what love was. Before I left for Athens and you decided to give her the attention she has always been worthy of—"

"If you can tell me that you are not filled with longing whenever you see me," Alexandros amended, his footsteps quiet against the stone floor. A soft thudding, a back against the wall. Another shuffle of feet. His words grew rougher as he continued his thought, "Then I will leave you alone, now and forever. I will be nothing but your prince—"

There was a rustle of material and then silence. The same thump against the wall and a low groan. They were kissing, she knew it. Because they loved each other. She held in a sob, biting her fist, not sure whose hidden love she was mourning, and moved to leave before they heard her.

"Are you greedy enough to want us both?"

"If I am greedy," Alexandros whispered, "so are you."

"Then so am I," he spoke with tears caught in his throat. "But I am not the son of Aphrodite. I cannot afford to be greedy. I proposed to Margarita today. She accepted. We plan on marrying and then moving to Athens. Soon, Alexandros, you will not even be my prince."

Something ripped inside her. Something tore in two. Death, she thought, would be less painful.

She begged her goddess to drag her down to her groves underground.

Her goddess did not respond.

WHAT IS DIFFICULT

Thirst woke me first but was shortly followed by the aching in my neck and back. Someone had piled several heavy quilts on top of me, tucked tightly. They held me in place on my side, so tight that I felt the bruise my own elbow had pressed into my ribs before I could even open my eyes. My mouth tasted like cotton balls and bad decisions.

As I was trying to lift myself out from underneath the pile, someone said, "Woah, hey. Water."

I blinked my eyes open. Ronan was holding out a glass of water from where he was sitting on the floor of my bedroom. Blankets surrounded him and about every other pillow in the apartment laid under him. Material lines creased his cheeks.

I took the water with two hands and gulped it down. It got rid of the scratchiness but did little to ease the regret. "Did you sleep in here last night?"

"Yeah, I wanted to make sure you didn't choke on your own vomit."

I grimaced. "Ew. Thanks."

A knock sounded at my door and Sam popped his head in. "How are you feeling?"

"Head hurts, mostly, but I'm okay."

He shook a bottle of aspirin and pulled a bottle of water from his back pocket. It was sweating with condensation and my mouth watered at the sight of it. "So, I can't interest you in one of these?"

"Oh my Gods," I said, already sitting up for them. "Yes, please."

He came to sit by me on the bed, pouring two pills out and handing me the water. "Slowly, Ness," he warned, pulling another bottle from his other pocket and tossing it to Ronan on the ground. Ronan caught it with one hand and downed it like I had the glass. Sam put his arm around my shoulder and pulled me into his side.

"Thank you," I said. "Sorry about being a mess last night. I don't know what got into me."

Ronan frowned, which just looked cute with how sleepy he was. "How much do you remember?"

As if the words were an injection of a different kind of medicine, the events of last night caught-up to my hungover brain. The kitchen, the game, the way Theo and Alexander had kissed each other…

"I remember enough," I said, sighing into Sam's shoulder. He was dressed to go to work, but didn't seem to be in any rush.

"How are you feeling?" Sam asked again, and I knew he was enquiring about more than just my hangover.

"I'm not sure," I admitted. I put one hand to my chest, where my stupid split soul rested and it reacted to the attention, pounding against my palm. "Everything is blurry, so maybe it wasn't as bad as I remember—"

My phone started ringing, a sure sign of the gods laughing at me as the sound clanged through my head. We all looked at each other and the phone rang three more times before I reached for it. Eliza's name was on the screen and I hesitated. If she was going to yell at me, I didn't want to answer.

"Give it to me," Ronan said, a kind command, and I handed it over. He cleared his throat as he greeted, "Hi, Eliza. This is Ronan. What can we do for you and *not Alexander* this morning?"

It was the least subtle thing that I could imagine, but it made me laugh. Sam laughed too, and pulled me back to him. Eliza said something and Ronan's face remained impassive. He shook his head, though she couldn't see him.

"I don't think she wants to. It *is* her phone. She gave it to me for a reason—" He stopped, listening again. He sighed and held the phone out to me. "She says she wants to talk to you. Says it's very important."

"Fine."

He slapped the phone into my hand. Pressing the speaker button so they could both hear, I took a deep breath before I answered, "What is it, Eliza? You probably know that I'm really not in the mood for this today."

"I wouldn't call if it wasn't necessary," she promised me. Her voice was tight and a little scratchy. "In fact, I spent all morning questioning my plat while he vomited into the toilet. And then I got a call from Tori, who said that Theo was sick this morning, as well."

I frowned at his name. "So?"

"That's what I said, too." I could hear the sound of her heels clicking as she paced. "But she's informed me that Theo has been to many parties in his life and when he got home last night, he wasn't even tipsy anymore. He didn't drink much." Well, there went my *they were drunk* excuse. "So, why would he be getting sick, Vanessa?"

"How am I supposed to know?" I snapped. Sam rubbed my back, and I took another breath and tried to think it through. I felt sick this morning, but there's a good reason for that.

Alexander didn't have much experience drinking either, from what I could tell, so that's why he was sick. But Theo? "Maybe because he felt guilty—"

"You're smart," Eliza continued. "I thought that, too, until I smacked Alexander on the shoulder when I was on the phone with Tori and Theo asked if she'd hit him."

"Why would Theo—" Ronan started to wonder out loud before his face paled, and he dropped the water bottle he was holding. I stared at him, confused and a little scared. He jumped up, moving his long limbs with a tired, jerky energy as he ran to his room. Sam called after him, but he was back in ten seconds, clutching a stack of papers. "These are from the meeting we had with Lux. The scientific articles she gave us."

"Ronan?" Eliza asked. "Good. So you know what I think I know."

"Stop being vague," I snapped at her. To Ronan, I said, "Continue."

He explained, "There are only a few known, published cases of SSS, right? But one of them, the one that was published about two years ago, talks about the abilities the triad had between them. Between two of the members, there was something called physical collaboration, meaning they could feel what the other felt physically, but only if they were in trouble, like an evolutionary protection against predators—"

He kept talking for a few more seconds, flipping through the papers, but my ears stopped working. Because he was implying something about Alexander and Theo. He was implying something that made me nauseated all over again. My hands were shaking and Sam took the phone.

"Eliza, this is Sam, Ronan's soulmate," Sam said, his voice level and serious just like when he was permanently marking someone's skin. And maybe he was, because his next words burned as much as Theo's tattoo. "Are you telling us that, after they kissed during a stupid fucking game of truth or dare, Alexander and Theo got a soulmate ability?"

"That" – the click of her heels finally stopped and my heart jumped in my chest as she shushed a voice in the background – "is exactly what I'm saying. How soon can you meet us at the Ceremonial Building?"

When we walked into the lobby, the Priestess saw us, stood up from her desk, and asked, "Vanessa Reyes?"

"That's me," I said. The only thing I was sure of at this point.

"Okay, you can follow me," she said, moving towards the door behind the desk. We headed in her direction. "The rest of your group is waiting in the private room with our Head Priestess."

"Where is everyone?" I asked, gesturing to all the empty seats.

"Your friend, Eliza," the young Priestess explained, "came in and offered two thousand drachmae to anyone who left. Everyone accepted."

"Holy shit," Sam said, agreeing with my inner thoughts. We stopped outside a familiar door. The Priestess left with a reminder to let her know if we needed anything. Ronan's hand was on the door knob when the reality of the situation hit me. Alexander and Theo were on the other side.

"Wait," I gasped, pressing a hand to my still-throbbing head. "Give me a minute."

He pulled his arm back. "Ness, what's wrong?"

"I don't want to talk to them," I admitted, trying to stop my eyes from watering. "I don't know what's going on, but I – it's just… everything is *so unfair* and I—" I took another deep breath. "I don't want to talk to either of them. Please. Not yet."

"You don't have to," Sam assured me, placing a kiss on my

forehead and holding my hand. "We won't let anything happen that you don't want to. We can leave anytime. But I think we all have to figure out what is going on, Ness. This is so far out of anyone's experience. And, to do that, all three of you have to be there. Okay?"

"Okay," I said after a minute. And though it hurt to do so, though it was one of the hardest things I'd ever done, I straightened my shoulders and nodded. My words still came out shaky but Ronan's eyes glittered with pride. "Lead the way."

Ronan pushed the door open. I looked straight ahead, keeping my chin up but couldn't help a small glance at each of my soulmates. Alexander was sitting on the recliner in the corner, his eyes closed and throat exposed as he faced the ceiling. His lips moved in a whispered prayer. Eliza balanced on the arm of his seat like it was a throne and petted his sweaty hair. Still, her shoulders were tense.

Theo was on the ground in front of the couch, head between his knees and hands in his hair. He muttered something too low for anyone to hear except Tori who sat by him, rubbing his back.

All of them looked at us when we walked in the room. Alexander's eyes were red and Theo had dark circles around his. Alexander reached out, but Eliza pushed his hand down. Theo closed his eyes and muttered a curse.

They'd left the couch open for us and Sam and Ronan corralled me into the middle seat, bracketing me and blocking my view of everyone but the strong-shouldered Priestess sitting opposite us all. I started bouncing my leg and then tucked it under me when Sam noticed.

"Thank you for coming so quickly," the Priestess greeted us. "Eliza mentioned you were bringing the case studies your professor recommended you read. Do you mind if I look them over for a few minutes?"

"Of course," Ronan answered, pulling the papers out of his

messenger bag. He handed them to the Priestess and she settled back into the couch. "I've highlighted the sections I think are relevant."

"Thank you," she answered before focusing on reading. It was quiet and Ronan placed his arm over my shoulders just as Sam had this morning.

The silence stretched for a tense moment until Alexander broke it.

"Vanessa, I'm so sorry—"

I hadn't realized how much I'd needed to hear his voice, even as it sliced through the mental protections I had put into place, but it felt wrong to want to touch him when he didn't belong to me.

Eliza interrupted him, her voice a hiss, "Alexander, shut up. We talked about this."

"I know," he said, his words coming out fast like he was afraid she might try to gag him. I wouldn't put it past her and wasn't sure if I'd be grateful for it. "But, Vanessa, I need you to know I'm so sorry for everything—"

"Alexander!" Eliza said again, her voice snapping like a whip.

But he kept going, "If I had any idea this would happen, I would never—"

"Stop talking," Theo growled, head falling back into his lap, "and stop yelling. It hurts."

Alexander shut up for a second. "I'm not yelling."

"You are," Theo growled again, his voice shaking with some kind of restraint. My fingers curled into my palms, cutting into my skin as I tried my best to block out the sound of his voice and I wished Tori would shut him up. "In your head."

I pinched Ronan's thigh, wanting to know more but not yet ready to engage with him in a way that I knew would show my own hurt. He startled and asked, "You can hear his thoughts?"

"Yes," Theo muttered. "Obviously."

"I can't hear yours," Alexander said, his voice now a whisper.

The Priestess finished reading and to Ronan and Eliza, she said, "I think you're right to assume this is a soulmate ability. I would say it was something residual from the original bond. Physical collaboration is one of the oldest abilities, usually only appearing in bonds with the most ancient history."

I made a wounded noise involuntarily. Theo flinched.

"What does that mean, though?" Sam wondered, frowning.

"While only the Great Goddess can truly answer," she said, sighing and looking at me with pity. My gut tightened. "I would say it probably means that the bond between Alexander and Theo is the Original."

"I'm the Extra," I said out loud and suddenly I was a ghost in Cupid's home. Disembodied. Something in my chest felt hot and wet like a stab wound. Theo and Alexander made low noises of pain. My hollow laugh followed. "It's me."

CRACKS IN THE WALLS

E veryone started talking all at once.

"This shouldn't be possible," Theo groaned, head falling back into his hands. He sounded tired. I wanted to say something but couldn't find the words, lost in my own panic. "I already had a soulmate—"

"That's what you said when this whole thing started," Eliza pointed out, glancing at his two bracelets. "And now—"

"And now," Tori cut her off, rolling her eyes. "He gets three? Something has to be off—"

"Come on, guys," Ronan tried to calm everyone down. "Let's just talk—"

I stood, brushing Ronan's hand off my arm and stepping around Theo to make it to the door. I walked to the bathroom, half out of my mind with confusion. My hands felt sticky and unclean, like I had blood on them, and I pumped the soap dispenser three times until the coconut smelling liquid lathered around my hands and overpowered the room and my thoughts with its scent.

The door opened. "Ronan—" I started to protest.

"Not Ronan," Tori said, pushing the door with enough strength that it marked the wall.

Eliza walked in behind her and shut the door with a sense of finality.

"Go away," I muttered, scrubbing my hands even though there was nothing on them. "I'm fine. I just need a minute. I'm fine."

"People who are fine don't usually need to insist they are," Eliza replied, hopping up on the sink counter. Her voice was still glass sharp, but her hands were surprisingly warm when she touched my arm. "How are you really feeling?"

"Sick of people asking me that," I snapped. She raised one blonde brow and, deflating, I sighed. The lathered bubbles went down the drain, spinning. "I think I'm cursed."

Tori hopped up on the other side, her grin suggestive. "What have you done to be cursed?"

"I don't know," I answered, shrugging. Tori patted the open space on the counter next to her and I lifted myself up, my legs dangling in the open air. "Maybe it's hereditary. Maybe a god is angry that my parents didn't need their help to find love."

"Probably not," Eliza concluded after a moment of serious thought. "The gods tend to like when humans do things for themselves. Less paperwork for them. Besides, I don't think you're cursed. That's much too simple of an answer."

I sighed. "You're right. Nothing is ever easy for me."

"Oh, sure," Tori said with her usual sarcasm. She knocked her shoulder into mine. "You're so unfortunate to have two hot guys in love with you. It must really suck to be the center of everyone's lives. Poor, miserable, Vanessa."

I frowned. "You think I want that? I don't want attention. I never wanted it. I just wanted to find a soulmate who loved me."

"Luckily," Eliza answered, "you found two."

I let out a grunt of annoyance. "Didn't you hear? Neither of them are mine."

"When this thing first started," Tori said, her voice uncharacteristically serious as she played with the frayed edges of a hole in her jeans, "Alexander assumed he was the Original. Theo understood. Hades, he thought so too. But you wouldn't stand for either of them treating him like he was the Extra. Because he was a part of the bond, either way. Why don't you treat yourself with the same consideration?"

Eliza and I stared at her for a minute. That was the most she'd ever spoken to me and none of it had been rude or sarcastic.

"Because," I said after a moment, "we didn't know then."

"We don't know now," Eliza insisted. "None of this is adding up. Why would all three of you gain abilities? All three of you receive bracelets?"

"Even if you are the Extra," Tori cut-in, and I had to stop myself from flinching, "do you think that's going to change the way they feel about you? Both of them are actually fucking stupid for you."

"They are," Eliza agreed. "To the point where they can't stand to look at each other. Vanessa, they found their soulmate and would rather never touch or look at him again so they don't hurt you."

"I feel like I lost them both," I murmured, looking down at the cracked tile.

"Maybe you did," Eliza said with the precision of a surgeon, "but that doesn't change the fact that there are two very handsome, very upset boys out there who would take on an entire hoplite army if you even hinted you wanted them to. That doesn't sound very lost to me."

"So what?" I asked, exhausted. "I go back in there and pretend like looking at them doesn't make me sick to my stomach with jealousy? I pretend like—" I took a deep breath to push back my sob. "Like I still have a chance with either of them when I'm making them choose me over the literal other half of their soul?"

"Take the time you need to feel better about it. But, if you want them... just don't shut them out," Tori said, shrugging, but her face was gravely serious.

"Can't argue with that," Eliza said. She put one hand on my shoulder and squeezed. "Vanessa, stay the course. This shouldn't change anything. Nothing is any clearer. We still don't have answers."

"Keep getting to know 'em," Tori added. "Just like before."

"Just like before," I repeated. "Except Theo can hear Alexander's thoughts."

Eliza winced. "Poor Theo. I love Alexander, but his mind must be insane. Like a puppy's."

"A Golden Retriever puppy?" I asked.

She snapped her fingers. "Exactly like a Golden Retriever."

That managed to get a laugh out of me. Then we were all laughing and it wasn't even that funny, but it helped to pull the tension out of my chest. My laugh turned into a sigh as I pushed myself off the counter regretfully, "We should get back."

They followed my lead from the bathroom to the private therapy room. I opened the door and everyone looked up again. I folded myself back into my spot on the couch. Ronan held my hand.

"You good?" he asked.

"Yeah," I said, smiling at Eliza and Tori, who were just coming through the door. "I am."

"Have you decided what you want to do?" Sam asked.

I looked at Eliza. She nodded and I answered, "Stay the course."

Ronan ran his eyes over my face, as if checking I'd meant what I'd said, before turning to the Priestess. "So, what's next?"

The Priestess said, "Alexander, have you done your Soulmate Ceremony yet?" He shook his head and she continued, "Your birthday is next week, correct? There's a process to find out the results faster, to expedite the answers, but only in emergencies. I think we can call this an emergency."

"I'll say," Tori snorted, sarcastic. It was so familiar that it almost made me relax.

"How about you follow me to the Ceremony Room?" the Priestess continued, standing up and Alexander scrambled to his feet. "Theodore, Vanessa, I'll be back in a minute to take a small sample of your blood to compare his results with."

We both nodded and they left the room. The rest of us were quiet for a moment. As I secured the block between our minds, I imagined myself building a wall. Brick by brick, impervious to even wooden horses and clever, beautiful boys. My thoughts were soft, delicate like a finely woven tapestry, and I wouldn't expose them to the elements, letting the sun and the rain damage the colors. I wouldn't.

A few, tense minutes passed in silence. Finally, Theo's brows pulled down. "Fuck, Vanessa, what can I do to make this better? Because this isn't going to work for me."

Ronan sucked in a breath and I stayed silent, not sure what to say.

"Alexander and I," Theo said, pausing for a split second at the sound of their names together and even the thought of them without me cut deep, like my soul was slicing into my chest. He continued, "We wouldn't be the same without you. You balance us so well. Making sure neither one of us feels better or worse than the other. Nothing has changed and none of this makes sense. We need you."

I thought about my conversation with my mother – about her warning. About how I liked them the same, regardless of the fact that I'd have to say goodbye to one of them. So much had changed since then. And not little transformations, either. Giant ones. Men into mountains, women into spiders... and what complicated webs they wove. Could I pretend things were still the same?

"Fucking hell, not hearing your thoughts is driving me insane." Theo blew out an agitated breath and my breath hitched. Sam wrapped an arm around my shoulders. "Whatever it is, you can tell me. I can take it. Even if it means—"

Finally, I voiced my thoughts out loud, interrupting whatever fatalistic thing was about to come out of his mouth, "I don't know, okay? I…" I clenched my jaw, angry with myself for how difficult the truth seemed. "To understand this bond, I need to keep spending time with you. But it feels wrong, now. Like I'm stealing his soulmate." *Like I'm stealing yours.*

"Vanessa," he said again, frowning and sparing a glance my way. I couldn't look at him and not want him so *I couldn't look at him.* "You're still in my head. You're still in his dreams. Just because this connection opened up between Alexander and I doesn't mean ours is gone. We don't know what any of this means yet, okay? Detroit is still the goal."

I didn't respond. I couldn't.

"She said she feels like she's losing two soulmates," Tori told him, making me glare at her.

"You know that's not true, right?"

I side-eyed him and finally, words came out of my mouth. "How could it not be true? You're so connected that you literally feel each other in your bones. You hear his thoughts and feel his pain. And who knows what else will pop up on his side—"

"We share memories," he countered, "that's an ancient ability too, you know."

Sighing, I said, "I'm so stupid. From the beginning, I knew this bond was going to end with one of you and I let myself get too attached. When we figure out how to cure the SSS and I'm split from you two, it'll hurt more than—"

"What do you mean?" he interrupted. "Why would *you* be separated?"

"He's your actual soulmate," I snapped at him, guilt boiling under my skin. My hands clenched tighter. "When it comes to it, you'll have to pick him—"

"I'm going to say this one time," Theo said, also speaking through gritted teeth. "Vanessa Reyes, I'd pick *you*."

My throat tightened with the effort it took to hold back a sob, but I tried to explain, "I think for all of this, I've only been here to connect the two of you." His face fell, eyes ready to argue. "I was a placeholder, a stepping stone for him. That explains the bracelet, too."

"What do you mean?" Eliza asked, interrupting for the first time.

"They both got two bracelets in the beginning," I said, holding up my wrists. Ronan's gaze was dark and sad. He was following my logic and his heart yearned to hold me. "I only got one. Obviously, I'm not as much a part of this as they are. I'm the Extra."

No one responded right away. Eventually, Eliza murmured, "That makes sense."

"You're wrong," Theo said just as softly. "I can't tell you how I know it, but you are. I swear, when this is all figured out, I—" He took a breath and his hands were shaking and so were mine. "He and I might have an ability, but…" His voice broke and my head snapped up, meeting his eyes as they looked at me desperately. "I don't want to call him my soulmate. Gods, I don't even know if I like him!"

I frowned. "Theo—"

"Wait, just – just listen, okay?" he interrupted, pushing the words uphill. "My soulmate was supposed to be Margot and even that seems uncertain right now. *I don't know* what's happening between the three of us, but I don't think it's as simple as you're making it out. You're a part of this as much as any of us. You can't look at me and tell me you don't want me... or him."

"Of course I do!" I finally snapped at him. "But what we want doesn't *matter—*"

"I don't believe that you believe that," he interrupted, finally looking at me.

I stayed silent. I didn't want to argue.

"I liked you before this whole thing started," he told me like he was admitting to something illegal. Tears of frustration swelled in his eyes. "Before I knew our souls were connected. You're my soulmate, but I liked *you*. As a person. As Vanessa. And this whole thing with Alexander doesn't change it." His breath came out rough. "It can't."

I opened my mind and he sucked in a wet breath as he tasted the hurt of my thoughts.

"Vanessa," he said, almost gasping it. "I am so, so sorry."

"Stop saying that." I shook my head. His eyes were pleading, and I had to look away to find the strength to speak. "You didn't do anything wrong. I just need time, okay? Just... give me time." I attempted a smile, trying not to choke on false hope. "I'll be okay. We're all gonna be okay."

His dark eyes were heavy and swollen with exhaustion and unshed tears. No one else in the room spoke, but none of them pretended to not be paying attention. "You are too good for me."

I wanted to deny it, to make him see just how much he was worth, but an explosion in the next room cut him off and I covered my ears. The bond in my chest felt like an electrical current and my heart dropped, heavy with fear. *Alexander.* Whatever Theo heard in his mind painted his face gray as he stumbled to his feet and ran to the ritual room with me right behind him.

TRANSLATING ASH

I threw open the door to the room and gasped. A thin layer of black ash covered everything. The altar was crackling, still flickering with a small flame. Everything smelled of burning and blood.

One figure lay crumpled on the floor and one stood in front of the altar. I rushed to the standing figure and grabbed Alexander's face in my hands, Theo following me with just as much urgency. Alexander stared at nothing, eyes glassy, a perfect circle around him untouched by the surrounding debris. There wasn't even a speck of dirt on his clothes.

"Hey, can you hear me?" I asked, touching him softly at his pulse point. It thumped erratically. After a second of hesitation, the others rushed past us to the Priestess laying on the floor. Ronan called out to confirm she was breathing, so I focussed back on my soulmate. "Alexander, please—"

Theo reached out to put a hand on Alexander's shoulder. "Hey—"

Alexander snapped out of whatever stupor had taken him and then I had a sobbing, shaking, armful of him. I somehow tucked him into my body and held on tightly – he was much taller than me of course, but he didn't seem to mind as he cried into the spot between my neck and shoulder.

Looking at Theo, I offered, *do you want to hold him?*

I'm not taking your place, he thought, moving closer and pulling Alexander's gaze to him as the hand on his shoulder tightened. "Alexander, tell us what happened."

The words burst out without any pause or punctuation. "Nothing happened. I mean, like, seriously, nothing. I did the regular process – official introduction, libation, blood sacrifice, but it didn't burn. Didn't even start to smoke. So we asked again, and did it all again. Nothing. Finally, I asked my mother to please help, I told her I'd do anything, and then she" – I thought he meant the Priestess – "just freaked out, her eyes were all white and she was speaking Greek—"

"What did she say?" Theo asked as my own Ceremony replayed in my head.

"Something about a gift and leader," Alexander said, the words mumbled into my skin as he pressed himself to me. I rubbed his back in the same slow circles Ronan and Sam had used with me. Eliza was standing back from the Priestess, her eyes closed and her hands pressing her head, no doubt sending waves of comfort her plat's way. Alexander relaxed slightly. "She said, 'I have given you all you require, a leader and a gift.'"

"And then what, Alexander?" I asked him.

"I said, Mom, if that is you, I need your help. And that's when everything exploded. The blood sacrifice started burning so hot and so fast – it scorched the bowl. It must've gotten too hot because it shattered and then—"

He let out another sob and I held him tighter to me. With a blind hand, Alexander grabbed Theo by the edge of his jacket and yanked him closer to him too. Theo seemed startled, but he let himself be moved. I pulled back slowly, removing myself from his embrace and hurried to sit by the Priestess. Without glancing over my shoulder, I knew Alexander had his arms wrapped around Theo. All for the better.

Ronan checked the Priestess' pulse and urged her to come back to consciousness. Tori looked over her arms and legs to make sure she wasn't bleeding anywhere. The younger Priestess from the desk skidded to a halt at the doorway. She dropped to her knees by the other Priestess and rushed a few healing spells, mumbled prayers to her goddess blurring together. The older Priestess blinked her eyes open and groaned.

Sam's voice didn't waiver as he spoke, "Can you talk? Are you in pain?"

The Priestess groaned again, but managed, "Yes. Burns, I think."

The younger Priestess changed the spells she was using. Eliza pulled a pack of wipes from her purse and handed them to Ronan from where she stood above everyone else. She looked concerned but unwilling to get her pants dirty in the ash.

Sam began asking another question, but something happened and the words dropped into nothing. Both Priestesses tensed and their eyes turned completely white, as if they had no irises or pupils. They were speaking, then, that same rhythmic Ancient Greek, low and much too fast for me to understand. The words pressed on us, a weight on my shoulders until I was practically suffocating. Goosebumps broke out on my skin and the cadence of the speech vaguely reminded me of something.

Eliza's face paled as if she understood. Alexander pushed himself back from Theo, too, like he was surprised by the words.

They repeated the same lines over and over again until their bodies collapsed under the presence of whatever god or goddess was in them. The younger Priestess fell and Tori just about caught her before her head hit the marble ground.

She blinked up at Tori, and with a shaking hand, touched her face. "Goddess?"

Tori's smile was sharp. "Not quite."

The older Priestess gasped and sat up, her burns were gone and her eyes were wild. Before she could say anything, Eliza was crouching in front of her with a savage twist to her mouth. "What did you mean by those words?"

The Priestess stuttered, "I don't – I don't remember what I said."

Eliza repeated the Greek with her usual precision and the Priestess' looked only confused. Eliza sighed, and when she looked up to see the rest of our confused faces, translated, "*Remember the promises of a goddess, the consequences of indecision. I offered salvation and you chose hesitation*. Or something. Maybe hesitation is wrong. Indecision?"

"What does it mean?" Alexander asked, moving closer to the Priestess and almost mindlessly dragging Theo behind him. His feet left lines in the ash as his boots scraped on the ground. "Was it my mother?"

They both shook their heads. "I don't know."

Eliza frowned at her plat. "Who else would it be?"

"I'm not sure, but it didn't feel like my mother. She usually feels... familiar to me. Like, in my soul, I know she means me no harm. This didn't have that. This felt..." He paused to think about it. "The first time, it felt like I was being buried alive."

A silence followed his words and goosebumps spread across my skin once again. If he was right, this was something beyond the Olympian Gods. Beyond the world of humans. Anything that happened underground, in the dirt and soil and the darkness below, polluted the atmosphere with mysterious and ancient magic. Instinctively, humans didn't trust it. The only time someone should go underground was when they died, or, at least, that was what we had been taught to believe. We had a word for the kind of deities who blended this earth and darkness together and even thinking it made me shiver.

Tori, however, was fearless. "You think it's a Chthonic God?"

Alexander's jaw clenched. "Maybe. But I'm sure it wasn't Aphrodite."

"What do we do?" I asked and the question echoed around the room.

The older Priestess answered, repeating Eliza's words back at me, "Stay the course. This proves nothing and solves nothing." She paused, looking at Alexander with a frown. "But be careful. If this deity means to harm you, you should avoid anything that has too much to do with what happens below the grass."

He nodded but then paused, gesturing to his clothes. "They didn't hurt me. They went out of their way not to, actually." He paused. "Maybe I met one accidentally when I was a kid with my mother. Maybe I offended—"

"There's no point in guessing," Theo cut his thought off, shaking his head. As if he couldn't stop himself, he touched Alexander's arm. His eyes were soft, matching his touch. "All that matters is that you're okay. I got you."

It was a shocking reminder that it was no longer my job to protect either of them, that I would now be something *other* in our relationship. I shoved my hands into my pockets and left the room, biting my lip to keep the tears inside, even as they both called my name. A piece of paper crumpled under the pressure of my hands and I thought nothing of it, waiting outside by Sam's car until Ronan swept me up in a hug. It wasn't until I'd gotten home that I realized it was anything of note.

It was a small slip of paper that looked old enough to be in a museum, and there was only one phrase written in Ancient Greek. It wasn't familiar to me but my brain translated the written words without difficulty.

It said: Τί δύσκολον; Τὸ ἑαυτὸν γνῶναι.

What is difficult? To know yourself.

29

REDHANDED

M y dreams, as always, eluded me when I woke up. The smell of oranges vanished as the sound of distant knocking pulled me out of the warmth of my own unconsciousness. After another failed Cult exploration yesterday, I had fallen asleep quickly. I had never expected to like the Cult of Hera – had thought at least exploring a new Cult would distract me from Alexander and Theo, but I'd felt as out of place at their meeting as I did within our own bond. I'd never quite understood the sharp-toothed ambition of Hera's Cult, but it was the default. The simplest choice of making none.

Dark eyes. Golden skin. I shook my sleepy head clear.

Another future I wouldn't be a part of.

My phone buzzed on my bedside table and I groaned at the message. It was time to go.

A few minutes later, after donning the sturdiest boots I owned and pulling on a jacket that would keep me warm in the empty fields of the winter, I walked alongside another one of Lux's students to another event. The Cult of Demeter met on the first Sunday of every month, their members gathered among the tools and hay of the furthest reaches of campus. The campus proper sprung up in the middle of cornfields and organic farms and as my feet crunched the frost-frozen leaves on the path toward the barns. I tried to think of some way to fill the awkward silence.

Emilia, who had introduced herself via text and arrived sharply at seven in the morning to pick me up, seemed a quiet sort. Her light brown braids fell past her shoulders, bouncing with each step, and I could tell she was searching for the right thing to say, too.

"So," I said after a while of quiet, as she directed the both of us to the largest building. Our footsteps echoed in the empty morning air. Beneath my gloves, my bracelets pressed close to my skin. For the moment, I was glad they were hidden. "How much did Lux tell you about me?"

That earned a weird look, but Emilia answered anyway, "Not much. Just that you were getting some outside pressure from parents or something to pick a Cult this year. You're supposed to pick by the time you graduate, but it sucks that someone is rushing you."

That was a good excuse for the whole situation. "Yeah, my parents picked their Cults at eighteen, so they already think I'm procrastinating." Not a lie, technically.

"Are you leaning toward any of the major Cults?" she asked as the path ended and the doors waited for us. She paused, glancing over her shoulder to finish the question. "Or leaning away from any? Which have you looked into?"

I listed the events I'd been to and how none of them seemed to fit. She nodded sympathetically. "I've been looking forward to exploring the Cult of Demeter," I said, another not-lie, thinking of my mother's traditions. Gardening in the spring, harvesting in the fall. Baking cherry pies in the winter. "But I don't know much about it."

"Well," she said, opening the door for me. Immediately, the warmth of the barn flooded toward me. I hadn't realized how cold I was. "Then I'm glad you're here. Welcome to our sustainable farm. It's too cold to grow anything now, but they'll have juice and cookies inside the barn for the talk."

"Thank the gods," I responded, pulling off my gloves and hat.

She reminded me of Tori a bit – if Tori was less about drinking and making my soulmates kiss and more about the importance of organic food. I liked her more because of it. Still, I knew the exact moment she noticed my bracelets. Her eyebrows furrowed.

Clearing her throat, she asked, "So, tell me about yourself. Major? Soulmate? I see you've got two bracelets there. That's a little weird." She paused and her cool demeanor shifted. "I didn't mean weird. Different. Uh, unusual."

I decided to spare her from the awkwardness. "It is a little weird. There was a clerical issue, we think, and my results got messed up. We're trying to fix it now." I smiled at her like my heart wasn't beating harder in my chest and brushed an errant piece of hair away from my face, fighting back a wince as my bracelets clinked together. "I'm surprised more people don't ask about them."

"When did you get your results back?"

"A couple months ago."

She whistled. "Some clerical issue."

I nodded and made a mental note to work on what I'd say when people inevitably asked why I had two bracelets since I couldn't stop wearing them. Most people with soulmates didn't mind wearing their bracelets. They were supposed to be a reminder of your soul being reunited. For the few people in the world that didn't wear them, they could be fired from a government job and made to answer to Aphrodite or Zeus. The worst stories were from those that faced down Hera.

"But I'm a Communications major," I answered her first question.

She nodded, relieved to have an out. "What do you want to do with that?"

I laughed, shrugging. "I'm not sure. I like the idea of working for the city, maybe, or taking a government job through a Cult. A business degree probably would've made more sense, but I'm pretty familiar with that side of things." After all, I had helped sell cherries and wine and all sorts of goodies for the orchard every summer practically since I could talk. "What's your major?"

"I'm an Environmental Science and Soulmate Information double major, but that's pretty standard for the Cult of Demeter. Not that you'd be expected to change. We come in all majors and genders. Though, like most Cults to goddesses, our numbers lean more towards the feminine persuasion," she answered. This part sounded more rehearsed and I nodded in familiarity with the speech. I'd heard the same yesterday at the Cult of Hera.

The chatter inside grew louder as Emilia marched us further into the barn. A decent-sized group of people were clustered together. Some of them looked like they belonged there in their dirt-speckled flannels and thick, leather boots, others looked just as out of place as I was sure I did.

Emilia led me over to a group of girls in flannel. They spoke to each other in low voices, eating only the oatmeal and raisin cookies and drinking from metal water bottles covered in stickers. Each had a different braid woven into their ponytails.

"This is Vanessa, the girl Lux asked me to invite. Vanessa, my plat."

I shook their hands and answered the same questions about my major, my soulmates, and so on. The answers squeaked out a little easier this time. They introduced themselves and explained the line-up of professors, who murmured to each other at the front of the room. Emilia added, "Anyway, they'll start talking soon, so you'll want to get snacks now. I recommend the blueberry juice. It's locally made."

I nodded with a murmur of thanks and walked over to the little table of refreshments. On a tiny, recycled-paper plate, I put a cookie, a few baby carrots, crackers, and vegan cheese. Compostable cups had been laid across the table with juice of various flavors inside – blueberry, cranberry, orange and pomegranate.

The sounds of the professors wrapping up reached me, and I quickly made a selection, reaching for the deep red of the pomegranate before I could think it through too much. The voices around me went quiet for a half second and then resumed.

Emilia nodded to the juice in my hand when I walked back over. "The pomegranate? Not many people choose it over the blueberry."

I shrugged and took a sip. It was a strange flavor, some-where between sweet and bitter, fruity and acidic. It sat heavy on my tongue, slid thickly down my throat. "I guess it looked good."

Emilia seemed to accept this but had a strange smile on her face. "The professor talking now is the chair of the Environ-mental Science major and our faculty advisor for the Cult. She'd be the one to swear you in."

She talked for a while about the benefits of the Cult. After that, she went onto the sustainable farm itself, about the beekeeping unit they had and how much honey they made. She listed the flavors they came in, the flowers that grew around the hives. She had just invited us all back to see the bees wake up in the spring when my stomach cramped.

My breath hitched at the stab of pain, somewhere between a period cramp and what I imagined a bursting appendix felt like. I almost dropped my snacks when I clutched at my gut, trying to hold myself together. Trying to keep my voice even, I asked Emilia, "Is there a bathroom out here?"

She looked a little surprised but answered, "Yeah, third building down the path. Red roof. Can't miss it."

I threw my empty plate away as I left the building but kept my drink instinctively clutched in my hand – the first rule of drink safety. I felt the teeth of the winter air on my skin as I followed the path, arriving at the smallest building on the road with a red roof. She couldn't have been talking about another building but it was dark as I walked inside, only distant lights at the end of the long hallway illuminating the way.

Shadows jumped around me, grinning reimaginings of my own body, and sounds trickled out from the doorway at the end of the hallway – chatterings of birds, buzzings of cicadas. Then human sounds. Voices speaking. Not in English, but Ancient Greek. The same tempo the Priestesses had spoken in and I shivered.

The familiar sound pulled me closer. I needed to hear more. I gathered my strength, my feet carrying me closer to the chanting spilling out of a door that stood ajar, beckoning. Moving as silently as I could, I hovered just outside the door and tried to translate the Greek words. But it made no sense to me, it never did when spoken aloud.

When I got close enough, I leaned into the doorframe to look inside. There was only one light source in the room, the flickering flame of a candle. People and shadows danced together, and my eyes caught the occasional glimpse of dark hair, flowing robes and lips rounded to accommodate the syllables of their chant. There couldn't be more than a dozen people inside, but the whole building vibrated and echoed with their words.

My heart slammed against my ribs and my soul reached out for something, I didn't realize until it was too late that my hands had followed the motion too. Totally forgotten in my hands, my cup was crushed in my fingers and the red juice spilled out. The cold sensation surprised me and I dropped it to the floor with a curse.

The chanting stopped and heads turned.

"Can we help you?" the person in front of me demanded. They threw their hood back to reveal a pale face with big, dark eyes. "Can't you see we're busy?"

"I'm sorry," I said, taking a step back and holding my red hands up. "I didn't mean to disturb you. I was looking for the bathroom and then I spilled this all over me—" I shook my head. "I think I misheard the directions my friend gave me. If you could just point me the right way..."

"Rebecca," another voice came from the group of people. Whoever said it didn't remove their hood, their face remained in shadow, hidden behind the thick fabric. "Look at her hands."

Rebecca followed the command. Her breath caught in her throat when she saw my hands and wrists. The juice had stained my skin ruby red and covered my bracelets too, turning them a strange shade of rose gold. Moving my hands to wipe them on my shirt, I started to apologize again. She snapped her own hands forward and held me in place, locking her grip around my wrists. Even when I tried to pull away, her grip wouldn't budge. Her hands burned my skin where our skin touched.

"What's your name?" she demanded.

"Vanessa," I answered. "Look, I'll just go and pretend I didn't see anything—"

"Let us help you clean up."

She pulled me forward and I lost my footing for a second. She kept pulling until I was in the room completely and the door slammed behind me. The candle flickered with nothing but gray smoke. There was a marble bowl sat beside it, the edges dotted with dried wax.

The rest of the group threw their hoods back. Girls,

women, with young faces and dark, knowing eyes. Ancient eyes. Their bodies were shapeless under the same black fabric but one figure with added decoration stood in the middle of the group. Her hands clutched a long, silver necklace with seven red stones.

She handed Rebecca a metal water bottle. Ice water flowed from the opening, washing the juice from my hands into the marble bowl. Wax floated to the top as she spoke to me, eyes flickering to my bracelets.

"I'm Rose," the woman with the necklace introduced herself. Everyone was silent as she spoke, and the water turned pink in the bowl. "You said your name is Vanessa? Tell me, what do you know of the origin of your name?"

It was a really weird thing to ask, but I answered to distract myself from the way the water was now almost the color of blood. "I think it's Greek. My mother just liked the way it sounded."

"Are you close to your mother?" Rose asked, tilting her head to the right.

Another weird question. "We call a few times a week."

"Do you read Homer much?"

"Enough," I said, shrugging and a little confused at the twenty-questions. "Before holiday meals with the family. At weddings, funerals. Why?"

"Homer refers to kings by a specific term," she explained, rubbing her thumb against the first red stone on her necklace. "It fell out of fashion soon after him. He uses the word "Anax" to talk about Agamemnon and Zeus. But, before the alphabet changed and the digamma dropped out, this word was Wanax."

The random linguistics lesson surprised me into answering, "Oh. Uh, cool."

Rose smiled and it was like a flower blooming. "The feminine version is Wanaxa or, after the Romans corrupted our original language, Wanessa." A pause and the flower turned into a viper. "And then the Germans, Vanessa."

"So it means queen?" I clarified, turning to look at everyone else in the room, to see if they thought this was as weird as I did, but their faces were closed off. There was a sharp pain in my right thumb and I cursed, turning back to Rebecca who just shrugged. A drop of blood mixed with the red water.

"Must've been my nails," she said and I watched her more closely. Her nails were flat, blunt. Manicured.

"No, Vanessa, it doesn't mean queen," Rose answered. "It means king, all the same."

The candle next to the bowl ignited, the flame shooting high. I gasped and tried to step back but was held in place. No one else reacted to it. Rebecca continued scrubbing my hands, even though all the juice had gone. My bracelets shone gold and burned against my skin, just like her hands.

She released me and took a step back. The candle's flame receded to a normal height, and I quickly moved toward the door, jumping when it opened without anyone touching it. "I'm going to go," I told them, stepping out of their circle and gesturing behind me. "Probably missed the speech."

"Probably," Rose said, shrugging like she didn't care. With an easy flick of her wrists, she threw the hood of her cloak back up and only the smallest gleam of a smile showed through. The stones around her neck glowed brighter. Everyone else put their hoods up at the same time in a fluid motion that had me staring as the lights dimmed. "We'll see you soon, Wanaxa."

I didn't bother answering, just tripped over my feet as I scuttled away.

When I got back, Emilia asked, "Did you find the bathroom?"

The pain in my stomach had faded not long after I'd spilled my juice, so I lied and told her yes. I'd missed most of the important information and the session was winding down. I heaved a sigh, not sure I even really cared that I'd missed it all, my mind still on the strange girls in the dark building. The Cult of Demeter locked itself behind a door. Another place I did not belong.

"That's alright," Emilia said as we walked back to her car. "I'm sure you'll figure it out soon."

I thanked her but wasn't sure I believed her.

The smell of pomegranate permeated my clothes, my skin, and the air around me in a way that should have been cloying but somehow wasn't. Lingering late into the night, until sleep arrived and dragged me, unwilling, through ivory gates.

30

ADAMANTINE CHAINS

A tornado siren was screaming on campus as I ducked into the library. The sky was the color of olives as some-where Hera raged. October had turned into November swiftly and project deadlines hovered over my shoulder. A welcome distraction from the nightmare of my love life.

The first time I'd met Alexander in the library to work on our project, it had taken me a few minutes to locate his blond head in the crowd. Now, my eyes found him instinctively. He was sitting at a small table, books and computer taking up exactly half of the space, and he tapped his fingers on his keyboard, writing frantically. He looked... worried, maybe. Nervous.

I wished Theo didn't have to work, if only for there to be a buffer between us.

My feet followed the path my eyes had tracked and he looked up as I dropped my backpack to the ground. "Hey."

"Hi," he responded, sitting up straighter and closing his laptop with suspicious speed. I raised my eyebrows but said nothing. His cheeks went pink as he stood up. "How are you?

Do you want anything from the coffee shop? I was just going to get coffee, so I don't mind—"

I shook my head. "No. I'm okay. I just want to get this over with."

He swallowed and sat back down. "Right. Okay."

I pulled out the syllabus, clicking my pen as I read aloud, "So the next assignment is collecting stories about our deity being involved with the soulmate process. For today, we should just decide on a story and gather some sources. Lux gave a few examples for some of the other groups but I think this will be pretty easy for us. We could explore her friendship with Sappho or how her relationship with Adonis and Pygmalion led to unhealthy—"

"I think we should do the story of Eros and Psyche," he interrupted, the words touching each other as they came out of his mouth. I blinked, staring at him for an explanation. Taking a quick breath, he said, "It's about the marriage between love and the soul and with my mom being the main antagonist in the story, I think it could be an interesting—"

I shrugged, grabbing our textbook for the class. "Sure, but it's not in here."

"I know, but Lux said we could use outside sources if we wanted and there has to be something in her section of the library—"

"Fine. Let's go."

He scrambled to follow me to the third floor and was still at my heels like a puppy seeking forgiveness as I headed toward the row of pink and blue books under the goddess' name.

"You look at the top shelves," I told him and he snapped to attention, searching the spines of the books for anything useful. I was more than a foot shorter than him, so I kept my eyes on the lower shelves – *Aeneas, Adonis, Anchises, Charities, Eirene...*

"Here," I said, pulling the thick book from the shelf. The spine was uncracked and the pages stuck together as I opened it to the title page. *The Tale of Eros and the Soul*, annotated by the god himself. The margins had been decorated with elaborate designs, detailed drawings at the ends of the sections of the labors Venus assigned Psyche: the seeds and the ants, the golden wool caught on biers, the waters of the Underworld... The last caused me to shiver, even as my fingers caressed the image of the rivers connecting and the girl attempting to retrieve what she'd lost.

"Perfect," Alexander said as I stared at the image. He leaned closer, taking a better look at the pinks and golds of the page, reading the Latin with no difficulty. "Hey, can you flip to the back to see if any of his annotations mention the soulmate process—"

He leaned closer, pressing his chest to my shoulder, his warmth seeping into me. I pulled my hands back from the page at the shock of his skin on mine. He sucked in a breath, and then his hand was on my arm, gripping right below my elbow. My breath hitched, almost like a sob, and gods above, I wanted his hands on me, on every part of me, but I couldn't. I shouldn't. *If he is greedy, then so am I.*

I dropped the book and it landed open. The image stared back at me, a momentary distraction as I gazed at the goddess in gauzy fabric – not Aphrodite but softer, darker – it was strange, familiar—

The lights flickered twice and then shut off completely, bathing us in total darkness. My skin seemed to become electric in the silence, the contact with Alexander never having faded but now all I could focus on. The quiet was marred only by our heavy breaths.

I took a deep one to steady myself. "It must be the wind—"

"Are you breaking up with me?"

His words were deafening in the dead quiet, raw and pained. I wondered if Theo could feel them in his chest.

I choked on the air. *"What?"*

"Are you breaking up with me?" he asked again, slowly, like that would help the question make sense. I couldn't see his face properly in the darkness. An emergency exit light gave the faintest guide for my eyes. I could make out the general shapes of his face – the straight line of his nose, the angle of his jaw, his impressive height.

"Why would you ask that?" I demanded, wrapping my arms around myself. "Do you want—"

"No! Gods, no, Vanessa." He took a step closer until the fabric of his varsity jacket brushed against the bulky yarn of my sweater. His hands bracketed my face, forcing my chin up. "But I got here and you won't look me in the eyes and… I just don't know what you want—"

His voice broke. His hands fell away.

My fingers shot out to his sides, and he sucked in a breath at the touch, looking into my eyes. Slowly, so slowly, he reached out again, thumb arching over my cheekbone. My exhale ran away from me, leaving my chest tight.

"I never know what you want," he admitted, jaw trembling.

Even in the low light, barely illuminated by the glow of the flickering exit sign, he was one of the most beautiful creatures on earth. Every inch of him was artwork, living and breathing and so sweet. I licked my lips, thinking about how he had tasted during our first kiss. How gentle and pliable he had been, letting me take the lead. And then how strong he had been as he'd lifted me onto the desk, hands spanning my waist as he spread my thighs, pressing closer.

Mirroring him, I lifted my hand to his face. His skin was as smooth as marble, heating under my touch. Slowly, just as slowly as he moved for me, I pressed the pad of my thumb to his lips. He went still, as if he was afraid to scare me away.

"You," I murmured, close enough now that I could taste the mint of his breath. He stepped forward, our bodies completely flush as the bookshelf dug into my back. "I want you."

Balancing on the very tips of my toes, I pressed a kiss to his lips. Warm, soft, hesitant. His eyelids fluttered shut and I pulled back, lowering myself to my feet. Barely audible even to myself, I whispered, "Do you want me too?"

I couldn't tell who started the next kiss, but it was no longer soft or hesitant. My arms looped around his neck as his found my waist, fingers under the hem of my top burning hot against the skin. The spines of the books behind me formed indents along my shoulder blades that I didn't even feel as the sweep of his tongue along my bottom lip pulled a whine from me.

Then there was no space between us at all. Chest to chest, hips to hips, he barely grunted with the effort it took to lift me and set me on the shaking shelf behind me, stepping even closer. *Greedy*, I thought, sucking his tongue into my mouth and relishing in the sweetest moans I had ever heard, the ones I'd caused. *Greedy, greedy, greedy*, I thought, pushing his jacket from his shoulders.

One hand slid down to the small of my back to knead my ass and my head fell back as I gasped his name, the noise bouncing around the stacks around us. He echoed the sound against my skin, the flat of his teeth rough against the tendon of my throat, soothed by his tongue just a moment later. I clutched at him, golden strands of his hair threaded between my knuckles as I tugged. Another sweet, filthy noise from him and unpracticed hips met mine, the fabric of our shirts rising until the bare skin of our stomachs brushed.

Our shared groan was too loud for how public we were, but in that moment I would've set myself aflame before I separated from him. His mouth covered mine again, muffling the next sound from both of us. The bond in my chest sizzled, like lightning down to the very core of me. Outside the sky grew darker, the storm ravaging the atmosphere as Alexander trembled and

I grinned against his mouth, victory tasting sweeter than oranges and dark chocolate.

A book fell from the shelf next to us. Hippolytus stared up at us from the page, tragic and doomed from his dismissal of Aphrodite. Alexander pulled back to rest his forehead against mine, our breathing labored like ancient heroes.

His next breath shuddered and I felt his muscles tense, tendons straining for control, but his hands on my face stayed gentle. So gentle, always. "Vanessa," he panted against my cheek, a prayer in the darkness. "I don't know how to *stop* wanting you."

I shook my head in the dark, swallowing the shock of hope in my throat as my heartbeat returned to normal. "I was worried that you only liked me because you thought I was your soulmate, and now that you have him—"

Another kiss, bruisingly hard, that left me heaving for air.

"I don't care about the before," he snapped, voice low, "because I like you now. And I don't like you because you're my soulmate. You're my soulmate because I like you—"

"What does that even mean?"

"Vanessa," he said my name the same way he prayed, "I've never felt this much about a person before." A shake of his head, his curls the color of smoldering ember fighting against the dark. "I like you – exponentially. More everyday. Regardless of my relationship with my mother and the other gods, I refuse to believe I could feel that way about someone who isn't my soulmate."

I clutched him closer to me until it felt like I could hear the bonds in his chest – both of them. The fabric of his t-shirt was thin enough that I felt the muscle beneath, warm and strong. I could admit that I was stupid for thinking they'd give up so easily – especially the man before me, who had love woven into his very being.

"Do you remember," Alexander started, knocking his nose

277

against mine, "when I came over to your place – the night we ate Chinese food – and I made you promise something?"

I swallowed. "Yes."

"Do the bad parts outweigh the good, yet?" he asked, the words the coldest thing in the room. "Have you had enough?"

The answer should've been yes. All of this, probably, could be traced back to Aphrodite and this stupidly beautiful boy of hers. They said Eros was the cruelest of all the gods. That only he and Necessity could control the Olympians. Even Zeus crumpled like paper under his influence.

But Alexander was not Eros. He was Psyche, more beautiful than he should be and punished for it. He was everything kind and good in the world, even if he made mistakes and fell in love with people he shouldn't. And maybe Theo liked me first but Alexander liked me now, just as much, with a vulnerable soul and no trace of cowardice in the face of everything.

So was the bad too much? Was that good not enough?

Was he worth more of this pain?

My words shook as I spoke, but I did speak. "I don't think I'll ever have enough of you."

Like he was a bow, pulled taut with the question, he snapped with the relief of my answer. His lips hovered so close to mine, still close enough to kiss, and I opened my eyes for the first time. I wished I could see the color of his eyes as he leaned in infinitesimally. I could feel his gravity pulling me in again—

The lights flickered on and he stepped back. He was stronger than I was.

I grabbed his hand before he could go too far and his smile was delicate, the edge of a knife.

"Come on," he said, grabbing the book and his jacket from the floor. With ever-gentle hands, he led me toward the staircase. There was a softness to him, our skin buzzing where we were connected. "Let's go."

Anywhere, I thought, not glancing behind me. *Anywhere.*

LEFT GASPING

Golden sun emerged its rounded head from the silk-lined clouds. Then purple-crested waves, curls of water reaching toward the edges of the earth. The deep lake contained unknown monsters beneath her sparkling surfaces. Below my feet, sand rubbed against my bare skin, the earth breathed cool air on the thin skin of the arches of my feet. The only comfort in this place of his, nostalgic to him and shiver-inducing to me.

Waves rocked against the metal dock that extended into the sand, over the dunes and the grassy hills sitting proudly above them, until it turned into a stone path. At the end sat a house. As if it grew upward with the heavens in mind. Three stories, maybe, of carved pink granite and driftwood. A living memory of summer, the color of sunset in the glowing sun. Rose bushes and fragrant cherry blossom trees stood guard, warding away anything unbeautiful.

"Where are we?" I asked Alexander, who stood next to me.

"My house," he answered, his soft, deep voice matched the sounds of the lake, "in Grand Haven."

"Is this really what it looks like?" I asked, looking around again. "It's beautiful here."

"Thank you," he answered. "My mother gifted the property to my father when she gave birth to me."

Using whatever authority he had over the magic of the dreamsharing, he formed another shape at the end of the dock. A boat. Its name was on the side: The Defender. It was small, sleek. Built for speed, rather than the luxury of too many passengers.

"She's mine," he announced, looking fondly at it. "My mother buys me a new one for my birthday every year. Or, she used to. Once she gave me this one, I never wanted another. I fell in love on our first trip together."

Grabbing my hand in his, he led me down the metal dock. My knees locked when we took our first step onto it and the water stared up at me, just as unsure. I pulled on his arm and he turned to look at me.

"What's wrong?" he asked.

"I can't swim," I admitted. "Maybe I should stay on solid ground."

"I won't let anything happen to you," he promised, hand cupping my cheek. "But if you don't want to go, we don't have to. There's a pool behind the house and we can just sit and relax. Or we could watch a movie—"

"I want to try," I interrupted, looking out at the horizon. It must be early evening. The sun was warm, the world swelling with the anticipation of the sunset. "But I'm scared. I don't want to drown."

"You won't," Alexander said. "I won't leave your side."

He got on first, keeping hold of my hand, and lifted me up beside him. My legs were shaking as he led me to the captain's seat.

"Just relax," he told me. "I'll take care of everything."

He moved around the boat with an ease that made me jealous. Just as comfortable here as on land, effortlessly graceful.

The motor purred to life and silver-scaled fish darted away. He took both my hands in his and stood me up, whispering praise and encouragement. With calm eyes, he sat himself down and urged me into his lap. One arm held me to his chest. The other led my hands to the wheel before covering it.

"You're in charge," he said, his chin sharp on my shoulder. His words, or maybe the wind, moved my hair. I opened my mouth to protest, but his words were firm. "You decide where we go and how fast. We can stop at any time."

We jolted forward too fast and I slammed my eyes closed, afraid of an impact that didn't come. He placed a kiss on my shoulder as he smoothly took control once more.

I'd made my peace with fire. It burned and it consumed, but even dead you existed as ash and smoke and calcified bone. Water did not consume. It erased. When you're erased, you remember nothing.

"Hey," Alexander called to me over the sound of the waves. "Remember what I said? I created this place for us. And, as the son of Aphrodite, I can't drown, so I can't imagine a place where that can happen."

Somehow, that did comfort me. If it was an unimaginable fate. Surely it couldn't happen in such a perfect place. Eventually, my breathing evened out and I was able to appreciate the purple tint to the edges of the sky, like Tyrian purple dye at the edges of a tapestry. The shades blurred together in the center, but at the edges they were distinct.

The clouds pulled apart and I said, "Here."

Alexander, with swift hands, turned off the motor and dropped the anchor.

"Can I assume you also can't get seasick?" I wondered, smiling at him as we swayed.

"I never have before," he answered, smiling as he leaned back. I followed the movement, tucking myself into his side. He wrapped his other arm around me again and I placed my hands on top of his. "So probably not. Though, depending on how much of my day bleeds into these dreams, it's possible."

"You were sick?" I asked, frowning. "Are you okay? Are you coming down with something?"

He swallowed with a shrug "I think so. I have no idea what it was. It lasted only about an hour and then I was fine. Eliza thinks it was food poisoning, but I didn't eat anything unusual. Unless you count the cookies Anderson baked for the team. You know what? I bet it was that."

"Are you going to be okay for your meet?" I demanded. He was smiling still as I touched his forehead with the back of my hand, taking his temperature. The gesture was so ingrained that I did it despite it being a dream. "You shouldn't swim or overexert yourself if you're not feeling well."

He laughed again, face golden in the sun. His breath fanned over my face, smelling sweet. "The donors wouldn't—"

"Alexander," I said, serious enough that he looked at me with all his attention. "Let me say this once and then never again. You don't live for them. You're a person. A person I happen to care a lot about. So, your health comes first. Got it?"

He blinked at me and his lashes, red with the sunset at the tips, fluttered. "I really want to kiss you again right now."

I bit my lip, turning red. "We shouldn't."

He looked crestfallen. "Why not?"

"I want to remember it when we kiss," I admitted. He reached for my hands and I let him take them in his. "And I want you to remember it, too."

He frowned, deep enough to wrinkle his forehead, genuine confusion coloring his eyes. "What do you mean? Of course I'll remember it."

"While we're here, sure," I agreed, brushing my fingers against his cheek. "But, when we wake up, we won't remember anything."

"Vanessa," he said slowly after a few moments, eyes wide. "I remember everything we do in these dreams."

"You do?" I asked. "How?"

"I don't know!" he said, horror creeping into his face and words. He leaned back sharply and the boat swayed. I gripped him tighter to me, tethering him to me with our hands. He continued, eyes flicking to my lips once, "I thought you did too?"

"I remember the picnic," I explained, trying to soothe the panic in his face. It didn't work. It grew wilder. My words fell faster. "But I just get the barest hints of what happened. I remember the cherries and the sunset on the trees—"

"You're saying that like it was the only one."

"Wasn't it?" His face fell, wind gone from sails. "What else has there been?"

"Paris," he said, matching my hysterical tone from earlier. "Where my favorite painting is. And then Cyprus, where my mother's temple is and where she remembers emerging from the sea. And then there was my New York cabin—"

I shook my head, feeling overwhelmed by the sheer amount of dreams that held no place in my memory. "Alexander, I'm so sorry—"

"I don't understand," he said with anger. Not at me. He was looking at the sky, the unreal purple-pink-sunset, and glaring at the clouds. When he called to the nothingness above us, his voice echoed louder than I'd heard it before. It reverberated the air around us, like the universe was waiting to hear the words he spoke.

"What are you doing, mother?" he called into the void. The sky responded with thunder and the sun retreated completely into the edge of the world, leaving us in the dark. A candle snuffed out. The only light seemed to come from the blond halo of hair around him. "What are you trying to prove?"

Another wave. A bigger push. Something clattered to the floor of the boat. I tried not to shriek, tried not to cry as another and another hit. He yelled again, standing up and leaving me to grasp the wheel for balance. Another wave. The boat turned, rotated and twisted. My stomach flipped.

Another yell into the sky. My feet lost the ground.

And then I was in the water, splashing, but mostly sinking.

Drowning. I was drowning.

I heard him call my name, panicked, scared, but I was a rock.

I sank deeper until I hit something.

The bottom, maybe? But it didn't matter.

Because I couldn't breathe and sirens sung as my lungs filled with water.

I was a ship, embraced by Scylla. Lost to the pages of another person's story.

That was the thing about water.

It erased.

And I was gone.

I woke up with the taste of water in my mouth and thunder reverberating in my ears though the night was quiet. My head pounded absently and I coughed once, twice, and half expected salt water to come up. Lake water. Something.

"I'm okay," I said out loud to myself, willing myself to believe it.

Sweetheart? Theo thought with sleep-slow cadence. *What's going on?*

I don't know. I don't—

I clutched my head as a sharp pain stabbed me. My phone started ringing and I threw myself across the bed to unplug it from the charger. It was Alexander. I answered without hesitation. "What's happening?"

"What do you remember about your dream last night?" he asked in a shaky voice. Exhausted.

"Water," I said. "Not much else. Why? What happened?"

Agonizing silence. He sighed. Infinite patience mixed with debilitating sadness. I could imagine the way his curls bounced with the shaking of his head. "Nothing, Vanessa. Are you still coming to my meet today?"

Vanessa, hey, are you okay—

I clutched my head again. "What time?"

What time what?

"It starts at 3:00, but I don't swim until 3:30."

Vanessa, please—

"Okay, I'll be there."

Be where?

"I'll see you then."

I shoved my face into my pillow and put up a mental shield. Sleep found me again. This time, with a gentler touch.

32

A FEVERISH CHILL

An urgent knock on my bedroom door woke me up hours later and I sleepily called, "Yeah, I'm up!"

"Vanessa?" It was Ronan's voice. "Theo's here to see you."

I stumbled out of bed and pulled the door open. My skin burned but I shivered as Theo's eyes widened, eyes flicking down to my bare thighs where my oversized t-shirt stopped. His cheeks went red and Ronan stepped back up the stairs, eyes curious.

"Are you okay?" Theo asked, frowning with his eyes averted. "You look like you didn't sleep."

"Nightmares."

"What's happening at 3:00?" he asked, shuffling with his hands in his pockets. "Your thoughts this morning were all over the place and you put up a shield. So did Alexander, which he's never done before. I didn't even think he knew how."

"Alexander has a swim meet," I said, opening my door wider. "I need to get ready, but you can come in." I moved from the doorframe and he followed me, leaving the door open like we needed to be chaperoned. I nodded to the bed, the only place for him to sit.

He followed my suggestion, looking around the room. The pale yellow walls usually gave the space a relaxing atmosphere, but they felt claustrophobic now. The matching decor – yellow sunflowers in a crystal vase, fat bumblebees on my comforter – left a sweet taste on my tongue.

I continued, "I didn't know he could put up a shield, either. He probably just needs to focus before the meet. I'm sure you're happy to have his thoughts quiet for a few hours though, right?"

"Right," was all Theo said as I grabbed a new dress in our school colors and socks that matched. "I'm going to change real quick. Make yourself comfortable." I was gone for only a few minutes, brushing my hair and teeth with relentless speed.

He was leaning on my stack of pillows, staring intensely at the ceiling. The two main characters from a soulmate romcom stared back at him, smiling with too-white teeth as they held hands.

"What did Brad Pitt's character in *Touched by the Fates* do to you?"

His gaze shifted to me as he huffed a laugh. "It's just cheesy, I guess."

"All soulmate media is cheesy," I admitted. "You said that the first time we met, remember?"

"I remember," he said. *But I think I get it now.*

I hummed a noise of agreement and put on a small, gold necklace with a peacock pendant – Cult of Hera merchandise that my mom had given me on my last birthday.

"Can I come with you today?" Theo asked, his voice quiet.

I shot him a look. "Why?"

He hesitated, "I think some of your nightmare got into my brain. I don't like the thought of you by the water. But it's not fair to ask you not to go."

I applied a coat of mascara and fluffed some powder on my

face. My lipstick was light pink and tasted like cherries. "Sure. I'm sure Alexander won't mind."

"We haven't seen each other since the Ceremonial Building and he probably doesn't *want* to see me, but" – a deep breath – "if I don't go, I'm not going to be of any use to anyone at work. I'll just worry all day about you." Another pause. "Both of you."

Don't think about the party, I reminded myself.

"We're going to be late, so we should start walking—"

"I borrowed Tamara's car again," he admitted. "I came right after my opening shift. I've been feeling off all day. I'm not sure what kind of nightmare—" He paused and his brow furrowed. "Do you know how Alexander is feeling? My stomach hurts, but I don't know if it's me or him."

"He called me this morning," I told him, rubbing my temple. "He seemed kind of upset, actually. I think it's probably just nerves, though, right? I don't remember any dreamsharing happening last night."

He nodded, but his eyes watched me cautiously.

"Hey," I said as I locked up the apartment. "How are you feeling, by the way? Did you send the Galatas lady your work?"

The car was just outside. As we headed towards it, he said, "Nah. But I'm just glad I don't have to worry about it anymore. They seem to be interested in some of my new stuff, but not nearly as much as the Margot piece."

"I'm sure it's great, whatever it is," I said, sitting down and pulling the seatbelt across my chest. The drive across campus took less than five minutes and luckily there was a parking spot right by the gym doors.

Theo seemed lost as we walked through the poorly lit halls of the gym. He hesitated when we got to the stairwell, one foot swinging as he halted his gait, but he recovered quickly. The sound of a crowd and the now-familiar smell of chlorine grew as we made our way in the right direction.

He held the door open for me and I smiled. I'd been here

more times in the last few weeks than in all the years I'd been a student here. I was used to seeing the pool area mostly empty, but now people were like vines on the walls of the space. Someone announced the start of the 150 meter race and then people were cheering, calling out names. We pushed our way to the front to see the race.

I couldn't tell the swimmers apart, but I did see Alexander on the bench, wringing a towel in his hands and looking nervous. But, when he saw me – us – that nervous look turned into relief. I smiled back, waving, and something in me that had been twitching since he'd called, settled.

"Do you think he minds me being here?" Theo asked, frowning. "I can go to the back—"

"Theo," I said, entranced by the muscle on display, slipping my hand into his. People were cheering, drowning out any thoughts from either of us. The swimmers splashed and their teams called their names in chants. "Please be quiet."

The race continued for another few minutes and he said nothing else, only moving to shrug off his jacket. I didn't blame him, the humidity of the pool was at odds with the coolness of the rainy afternoon. I wasn't sure when I'd become used to it.

The race ended. A swimmer from the other team took first place and ours second. It was a close call though and my mortal eyes had a hard time even telling their times apart. They announced the 50 meter race and Alexander stood up.

He was easily a few inches taller than the next tallest swimmer, his arms long and his body all lean muscle. They took their places and the kids from the other school glared as Alexander stared straight ahead. His gaze focussed on the other side of the pool. Still, he spared half a second to look for me again.

Though I knew he couldn't hear me over the sound of his teammates chanting his name, I called out, "Come on, Alexander! You got this!" He grinned in my direction as I jumped and clapped for him. Theo laughed but let me use his hand to clap.

The whistle blew and they pushed off. He was so fast, curved like a dolphin or a shark or one of those mythical beasts, as he plunged into the water.

I couldn't look at the pool without something seizing in my chest, so I focussed on the way his muscles moved instead. It was almost like a dance. Something ancient and beautiful. It was easy to imagine him as the Goddess of Love, pushing himself from the water onto the island of Cyprus, equal parts sea and god.

Alexander finished so far ahead that he had time to pull himself out of the water and towel his hair dry before the next swimmer finished. He didn't come up for air once, didn't stop for an instant when he flipped around to do the second half of the race. His chest expanded and contracted with each deep breath, effort obviously put in, but I could tell that he was comfortable with his win.

They called the race and announced him the winner. His coach patted him on the back, dark eyes focussed and intent on telling him something important. The easy grin on Alexander's face turned to something more serious. I couldn't hear his coach, but from the way his mouth moved and the look on Alexander's face, he wasn't happy.

The next race began and Alexander sat back down on the bench, eyes to the tile floor.

"What was that?" I wondered to Theo. "What do you think he said?"

"I caught a piece of it before he put his shield back up," Theo said, clenching his jaw. "I guess Alexander was slower than he should've been. The coach told him he shouldn't invite people who are going to be distractions. He's trying to qualify for the Olympics."

"Slower?" I demanded. "He won! He totally beat the others!"

"Yeah," Theo agreed. "He did."

We cheered for the rest of the meet, but without the same enthusiasm. Alexander's smile lacked its usual brightness as he cheered for his team, and I wanted to snap at his coach. The meet ended soon enough and our team was declared victorious.

We waited on the other side of the pool to congratulate him, neither of us wanting to make the coach angrier. It took a while for Alexander to make his way over to us, stopping to congratulate his teammates and thank the other swimmers. They accepted it, grinning up at him.

Then he was standing in front of us, the navy towel over his shoulders bringing out the blue of his eyes. "Hey, guys, thanks for coming – oof!" I crashed into his stomach and chest, wrapping him in a tight hug. He huffed out a laugh and then his arms were around me.

"You did so good!" I said, pulling back just enough to press a kiss on his cheek.

"Thanks," he murmured against my hair.

"You did," Theo added after a small pause. "Great job."

I was far enough from Alexander now that I could see his face slacken with surprise and close enough that I could feel his body tense with the unexpected compliment. He waited a few seconds as if expecting Theo to turn it into a barb or an insult, but he didn't. I turned to look at Theo and he was staring at the ground, hands stuffed into his pockets so as not to fidget under Alexander's gaze.

"Really?" Alexander asked, openly vulnerable in a way that would've made Theo flinch just last week.

Theo, as if he couldn't stop himself, reached out and put a heavy hand on Alexander's shoulder. The moment their bare skin touched, Alexander's eyes fluttered closed and Theo's breath hitched. "Really."

Both of the bonds in my chest buzzed, warm and bubbling

with – something. Where his arm lay across my waist, Alexander's fingers pressed into the softness of my hip. I pressed my hand against his.

"Thank you," Alexander said, voice low, "that means a lot. But it could've been better."

"You're right," a new voice said. We all turned to look as a man approached us. I expected it to be the coach, but this man was dressed in an expensive suit and his watch was made by the same brand as that of the Galatas man. I'd never seen him before, but I knew who he was anyway. "It should have been much better. Alexander, introduce me."

"Father," Alexander started, standing up straighter. Though my instincts urged me to step between them or tuck myself into Theo's side, I didn't. I took one step backward. "I didn't know you'd be here."

33

OF PRIDE

"With how much money I give this school, I think I'm entitled to see my son swim whenever I want," Phillip Crest returned, sniffing like Alexander had insulted him. Alexander's fears about disappointing the donors made a lot more sense. "Your friends, Alexander."

"This is Vanessa Reyes," Alexander said without another hesitation, "my soulmate."

I held my hand out to shake. His grip was firm but not rough. "Hello."

"Ah, the soulmate that Betsy Galatas met the other day at her gallery," he announced to Alexander. His grip tightened around my hand a miniscule amount before he released it. His wrist was bare. "Now, she tells me that you spent the whole night holding hands with some tattooed artist."

"That," Theo interrupted, offering his hand to shake too, "would be me. Theo Patras."

"My other soulmate," Alexander revealed, closing his eyes almost immediately, waiting for a sharp reaction. Theo and I looked at him, surprised. The words came out with more power than I'd expected. More defensive. His shoulders tensed when he heard it, too.

"Wonderful," Phillip said, like he thought the exact opposite. His lip curled in disgust at the sight of all our bracelets, and I remembered what Alexander had told me about his father. "Another distraction. A pretty good one if your terrible performance today was any indication. You're lucky Eliza keeps me informed of your practice schedule, otherwise. I would think you've been so busy with this soulmate nonsense that you've forgotten we have our sights on the Olympics."

"Sorry—" Alexander started.

"His performance wasn't terrible," Theo interrupted with a frown. "He won."

Phillip laughed and it wasn't a happy sound. "You don't seem the type to know much about swimming. I know you haven't known my son very long, but he can do much better." His eyes scanned Theo as he spoke. "He could keep up with one of my yachts by the time he was five years old."

"You made a five-year-old swim in a lake by himself?" Theo asked.

"You couldn't drown him if you tried."

"And did you try?" Theo asked, lip curling.

That actually seemed to surprise Phillip. "Are you asking if I tried to kill my son?"

"Theo—" Alexander started, shaking his head and reaching toward him. "It wasn't like that."

"Then what was it like?" Theo snapped at Alexander. To Phillip, "He kicked ass, today."

"By a much smaller margin than he should have," Phillip snapped back, his blue eyes flashing. "He's the only demi-god on this team and he needs to make sure *everyone* knows it. Do you know how many of his half-siblings are vying for a place on the team for the next Olympics in colleges all around the country? And I promise you, they all gave a better performance today than my son."

Alexander flinched like he was backhanded. Half a second later, Theo did too, and I remembered they could feel each other's pain. Theo knew exactly what Alexander was thinking and whatever it was made the warmth fade from every part of him.

I took another step backward instinctively.

"You actually seem like the type to not understand how unconditional support works," Theo ripped into him with a slow viciousness. "So I'll let that pass, but if I ever see that look on his face again because of you, I'll—"

"You'll what?" Phillip said, stepping up to Theo with his shoulders set. "I could have you expelled in a second. And then what would you have? No education, no job, and no soulmate, certainly. According to Eliza, it seems quite obvious you're the unwanted tumor on this soul bond—"

"Dad," Alexander said, stepping in-between them as I moved out of their way. "Come on, you can't say that. You know mother isn't responding to my calls either. I could be the Extra, too—"

"You're the son of the Goddess of Soulmates," Phillip scoffed at his son, not taking his eyes off of Theo. "You've never been the Extra in your life, even if you continue to be a spoiled disappointment. Apologize now, for taking up my time."

Alexander flinched again, and lowered his hands. "Okay. Theo, please—"

"Take it back," Theo snapped at Phillip. "Take all of that back."

"Just because your first soulmate gave up on you doesn't mean I'll let you take advantage of my son's naivety and money—"

Theo lunged at Alexander's dad and Alexander thrust

forward to get between them but Theo's fist hit Phillip across the face. The blow landed, cracking as it connected. Phillip lunged back, his fist connecting not with Theo, but Alexander. Another crack. Theo staggered back, feeling the hit too and it gave Phillip enough time to hit him again.

They fell back, eyes in front of them as they fought together, pushing me further back. I took another step and my heart caught in my chest when my foot found only air. I sucked in a breath to scream, but the air became a mouthful of water.

My arms tried their hardest to grasp at something but swiped only through the water that stung my eyes. The unnatural blue filled my vision before I slammed them shut. My chest was burning and another bubble of air floated above me, escaping.

An afterimage appeared behind my eyelids: *a beautiful woman, reaching out.*

Someone jumped in. I felt the ripples, rather than saw or heard it. And then there were arms around me, pulling me up and back into the air. I gasped as soon as I could. My ears pounded and my body ached with the burn of oxygen in my lungs. I was crying.

"Get her up," the person holding me in the water said. Alexander. He lifted me, using his legs to keep us above the water. Theo leaned down and got his sleeves wet as he wrapped his arms under my shoulders and pulled me onto the concrete. It scraped against my skin as I shook there.

My hair was plastered to my cheeks. Theo pushed it away from my face as Alexander pulled himself out of the water. He was panting even though the effort to rescue me must've only been a fraction of what had been required in the race. There was something in his expression, though, like a memory of grief.

"Vanessa," Theo said, holding my face in his hands. Water-color bruises bloomed around his eyes and his bottom lip was split, but he paid no attention to the blood. Next to us, Alexander had a cut on his eyebrow, red blood mixing with the water dripping from his hair. "Are you okay? Can you hear me?"

I nodded but when I spoke the words were half-uttered and scratchy against my throat. "I'm okay."

Theo shook his head and called to all the people watching us. Gods, the swimmers from both teams, the coaches, the fans…

"Can I get a medic or something over here?"

Someone came forward, first aid kit in hand. There was the sound of the glass doors into the pool slamming and then shattering. More silence. Alexander let out a noise that was half-laugh and half-sob. "Well, I guess our first meet-the-parents situation could've gone better, huh?"

Theo closed his eyes and a combination of shame-pain-embarrassment passed over his face, but he said nothing.

Alexander's coach politely asked everyone to leave the pool and people left, shooting us looks before stepping through the broken glass on the ground and towards the locker rooms.

Alexander's coach stayed while the medic checked us over, listening to my breathing and bandaging their cuts. Theo had a fist-shaped bruise on his stomach and a small cut in the middle of it where Phillip's class ring had sliced into him. Alexander's blood was more orange than red. When the medic gave us the all-clear and left, the coach said to Alexander, "It's not really my job to tell you how to do anything but swim, but before you invite your friends back, maybe teach them *how to swim.*"

"Yeah, that's probably a good idea, Coach Nate," Alexander agreed, wincing as he sat up, hand on the same place where Theo's worst cut sat, lodged between his ribs.

"I can swim," Theo protested lightly. His hand was wrapped. "I just can't punch."

"I can't do either," I said. After everything, the words were hilarious to me. I laughed and it hurt.

"We know," Alexander and Theo said at the same time.

"I think you should get out of here," Nate said to Alexander. "Get some food. Your muscles need it. You burned a lot of calories today, swimming... and punching your father in the face."

"That was me," Theo admitted. "I punched him in the face."

"We know," Alexander and I said. I snickered and it burned the back of my nose.

Then Theo was laughing too, stopping only when it aggravated his stomach wounds and Alexander grunted in pain. "Sorry. I'll try not to make this worse."

"Kid, I'm really not sure if that's possible," Nate added, not helpfully. "You punched a billionaire. In the face. And broke his nose. And your hand."

"Yeah, I'm really not gonna sell that fucking painting now."

"Nate, please." Alexander sighed, pushing himself up into a sitting position. Nate handed him a t-shirt. He slipped it over his head and then shrugged on a pair of sweatpants. "We'll get out of your hair. I'll pay for the glass door. Just bill me."

Nate waved that off, whistling to himself as he went. Like his star swimmer didn't just massively embarrass the school. Like we weren't the cause of it. Over his shoulder, he called, "That's why we have insurance! And your family paid for it in the first place."

Suddenly it was just us, breathing heavily by the side of the pool. Broken and bruised and water-logged from my near-death experience.

Theo punched a fucking billionaire. Alexander's dad.

I laughed again and it echoed around the empty pool.

ΙΣΤΟΡΊΑ - ΜῆΝΙΣ

WRATH

F ire arched into the sky, a lover's backbone. Feet stomped, the earth pounding even between the moments soles packed the dirt, the only answer they'd receive. The island women, bearing the light of the moon on bare skin, called to the sky, the earth, the waters of the sea and nearby rivers. But only Echoes respond, curling into the angles of branches and the curves of lightless paths.

The fire reached to touch the moon, but no voice responded to their questions, their desires, their genuine pleas for guidance.

"What do we do?" the women whispered among each other, their voices hidden in the wind-rustled leaves. "If the gods don't listen, what do we do?"

"Ask again."

"Beg."

"Forsake them."

Vanessa had anger boiling beneath her skin. Her wedding loomed like a funeral on the daybreak and yet, her goddess cowered in silence. She pulled power from her bones, from her muscles, from her severed soul. It stung her chest like an angry wasp and she pulled away from the women. They watched, their faces pale in the night.

She had been a slave to tradition for too long. She had been diligent about sacrifices, earnest about prayers, loyal and steady about only asking for their help when it was something she could not do herself. And what did she receive in return? Nothing. Emptiness. A life submerged in loneliness.

So here, on the eve of her marriage, she became Euridice and Orpheus all at once, and hiked her skirt to walk further into the forest. Her women called her back, warning her of the mysteries that lay beyond the edge of their kingdom, but she did not stop walking. She didn't stop when the waves in the distance drowned themselves out, or when the screeching of the bats took on a mocking edge, or when the glowing eyes of predators blinked, afraid of what lay in the deepest parts of their woods.

She was not brave. There was no room left in her for bravery.

Only rage.

INEVITABLE

O n Thursday morning, I got a call from Professor Lux.
"I heard back from the professors in England," she said without preamble when I answered, she sounded out of breath and there was an urgency to her words that made me sit up despite the ungodly hour. "There's a cure. Or, at least, there could be. Tell everyone to meet me in the classroom in an hour."

She hung up before I could get my sleep-addled brain to function. I shot off a quick text to the group chat before falling back down against my pillow for another few minutes. Nausea rolled over me as their responses lit up my phone and I prayed to Asklepius for mercy.

Ronan knocked on my bedroom door a half-hour later and we headed to campus together, walking side-by-side in the morning chill. We were both quiet and I wasn't sure how I should have been feeling – relieved that we could potentially have this sorted out sooner rather than later? Afraid at losing two people I'd come to... care about?

"It feels like we're going to a funeral," Ronan muttered, shoving his hands into his pockets. Something crunched. "Oh, right, I forgot." He pulled out a small bag of butter cookies and I smiled. "I worked late last night, so I grabbed some coffee from the cafe down the street. The owner told me to give you these cookies, but you were already passed out when I got home."

"Thank you," I said, shoving them in my own pocket. "She's Theo's sister."

"I know," he said and the silence between us stretched awkwardly on as we made our way to Lux's room.

Theo and Tori were already waiting outside. She wore her red lipstick like armor, and he wore his white headphones like a shield, blaring music as he gave me a quick and shaky smile. Clearly, he didn't know how to feel about all this either.

"Tori, Theo," Ronan greeted, walking over to the door. "Morning. Door locked?"

"No, we're standing outside for the fun of it," Tori sighed, but she lacked her usual bite. She leaned against the wall, looking at her phone for the time. "Where is everyone? We're usually the late ones."

"I'm here," Lux announced, bustling into the building and pulling her keys out. She was still unlocking the door when Eliza and Alexander came in, the former surprisingly put together for the early morning hours. Her hair without a single strand of frizz, even after she took off her winter hat. Alexander, on the other hand, looked nervous, picking at the fabric of his gloves.

Theo caught my eye with a frown as he took in Alexander's unusually nervous countenance, concern deepened his features.

We all stepped inside the familiar classroom and Lux closed the door behind Alexander. He sat on the front row, but scooted his desk closer to Eliza. Farther from me. Theo had his hood pulled up around his head and sat in the back row, equally as far from me. I took my usual seat, Ronan behind me.

His hands found my shoulders, thumbs pressing into muscle but despite the contact, I felt adrift. What had happened to the easy laughter of the last few days? The kiss Alexander and I had shared... were they ready to give all of that up so fast? Was I?

"So, what's the update?" Eliza said, wasting no time. She had a notebook pulled out and clicked her pen into action. "I assume it's coming from the SSS experts in Oxford. Correct?"

"Correct," Lux confirmed as she situated herself behind the podium. "One of the groups with confirmed SSS – the one with two members who also manifested physical collaboration – was able to find a cure but it's complicated. It involves connecting to your past selves and discovering what you did to offend a god."

"And it worked? They're cured?" Eliza raised both eyebrows, and I held my breath as I waited for Lux's response.

"Not exactly," Lux said. "For the cure to work, it has to be blessed by the god or goddess who split your souls in the first place. In their case, according to my colleagues, it was related to a curse on one of their families from Hera. She refused to bless it."

"So, they don't even really know if or how it works?" Ronan asked. We all frowned at him. He clarified, "I mean, does it reveal who the Original and Extra souls are? Does it cut the Extra from the bond? Or is everyone cut from the bond?"

"From the description they sent me," Lux said after a beat, "it sounds like ingesting the potion dissolves all soul bonds. Though this is all guesswork, I'm afraid. They didn't take it, after all."

"What happened to the group?" Tori wondered, a dark look on her face.

"They all married widowed souls," Lux said with a bluntness that made me wince. "They're still connected through their souls and the two with the physical collaboration ability have to see each other every few months to stop themselves from becoming seriously ill." A pause. "But, by their own reports, they live relatively normal, happy lives."

"That's crazy," Ronan said on an exhale. "How can they—"

"You don't think people can be happy without a soulmate?" Tori demanded.

"Of course, they can," Ronan said, surprised at her tone, like he wasn't used to anyone questioning him. "But choosing not to be with your soulmate after you've met them? That must be—"

"One of the hardest decisions in the universe," Alexander finished with a tone that had me on edge. Theo and I snapped our heads to look at him, but he refused to look back. Theo's jaw clenched.

"You just put up a shield. What is it, Alexander?"

"How did you learn to put one up so fast?" I asked, slightly envious. "It took me weeks."

Alexander still stared stubbornly ahead, as if looking at either of us was painful. "Lux gave me a few tips. I figured it would come in handy. It's not easy to deal with my brain all the time." He finally turned to me but his smile was weak. "Like a puppy, right?"

Horrified, I shot a glare at Eliza. "That wasn't an insult, Alexander. No one minds a puppy!"

"I never asked you to shield your thoughts," Theo said, eyes wide.

Alexander shrugged one shoulder. "I figured I'd do it before you asked." To me, he said, "Don't be mad at Eliza. It didn't bother me."

"That's a lie. You're lying," Theo said, frowning and Tori squeezed his hand nervously, like she could feel the tension in the room escalating as much as I could. I spared half a thought on wishing Lux wasn't here witnessing this. "Your shield doesn't stop me from feeling your pain. Do you feel everything like a physical blow?"

"Eliza says I'm too sensitive," Alexander admitted, folding in on himself as he rambled, "but, in my defense, my mom once started a war because she wanted to be called the prettiest goddess. Drama might just be in my genes at this point—"

"Alexander—" Eliza began but he just shook his head.

"I think I'm the Extra."

Theo made a sound of protest at the same time as me. "That doesn't make any sense. Out of all of us, I've already had my soulmate, so I'm—"

I cut him off. "You're both being ridiculous. You guys got all the strong abilities—"

Theo raised an eyebrow and Ronan's eyes were bouncing back and forth between the three of us as if watching a train wreck. "You guys dreamshare."

Alexander let out a sad little laugh and we both swerved our heads to stare at him. Theo demanded, "What's funny?"

"Oh, we don't dream*share*," Alexander clarified and we both just stared harder. He took a sip of water and continued, "I mean, we do. But I'm the only one who remembers it when we wake up. It's not exactly split custody of our dreams."

"I remember our picnic," I protested.

"But not New York or Cyprus or Paris," Alexander said with a nod. None of those places were even vaguely familiar to me. "Yeah, you told me the other night in the dream that you don't remember. I was... disappointed, but it makes sense now."

"Fucking *what* makes sense?" Theo said through clenched teeth.

"That it's me! Our abilities don't work right and you guys are in each other's minds with your powers getting stronger all the time." Alexander sighed again, a heavy sound. "Either way, I'm bowing out."

"Bowing out?" I asked, frowning at him and Ronan squeezed my hand. I ignored his sympathy. I didn't need it, Alexander wasn't leaving us. He couldn't.

"Bowing out of *what?*" Theo demanded.

Alexander gestured to the three of us. "This. Whatever this is. This love-triangle, I guess."

"You can't *bow out* of Fate," Theo said, lines appearing between his eyebrows. "Plus, what about me? I'm in your mind too."

Alexander shook his head. "But you don't want to be. You and I are opposites and not the good kind. If you can tell me right now that you would want me as your soulmate if the universe didn't force you, I'll take it back."

Theo didn't say anything, struggling for words.

Say something. Tell him he's wrong.

He stayed quiet, jaw clenched.

Theo, please!

Alexander nodded but his body shuddered and he pressed a thumb to his tear duct. The perfect cupid's bow of his upper lip quivered. "So I'm out," Alexander concluded, nodding without looking at me. He gestured between the three of us again. "I hope we can stay friends. Just – don't invite me to the wedding, okay? I'm too polite to decline and I don't want to be there."

"Stop it," I said, shaking with some strong emotion. Half of it anger, but the other half was a mixture of confusion, sadness, and desperation. "We don't know anything for sure – we'll go to Detroit and get our answers and—"

"That's the other thing," Alexander interrupted. "There's a reason my mother isn't calling me back, and I think it's because she doesn't want to break the bad news to me." He barked a laugh. "The son of Aphrodite without a soulmate. How disappointing." Eliza flushed red beside him and it was clear she'd had no idea of his intentions coming into this meeting.

"That's not true. Theo!" I snapped. "Say something."

"He's right," Theo said it reluctantly, but I could still see him trying to convince himself. I wanted to scream. "Not about him being the Extra. I still think it's me. But we don't get along. We can barely get through a single interaction without arguing or without me punching his family. This is his choice, Vanessa, you have to let him choose—"

"I don't want to *choose*!" I shouted. Alexander looked between us in something close to horror. I narrowed my eyes and switched to thought, *All he needed was for you to tell him that you didn't hate him. I've never asked for anything but him. And you couldn't even—*

My face must have been a giveaway to our continued conversation because Ronan stood abruptly to cut-off my view of Theo, whose face had grown paler.

Lux cleared her throat lightly and I felt dizzy, like the world was spinning out from under my feet too quickly for me to make sense of it. I wanted to say something to change Alexander's mind, to stop this from all unraveling. *We had a plan*. Go to Detroit. Get answers. Live happily ever after. Any words crawled back down my throat when my eyes met Alexander's and he looked away first, bottom lip trembling. Ronan's hand squeezed mine and it was the only thing that kept me from running.

"I gathered most of the ingredients we'd need this morning," Lux said quietly, as if sensing one wrong word could send us all running. "But we also need to do a spell to find out which god split your souls in the first place. You'll beseech your gods and pray for their help, offering them something valuable for it. The shop in town won't have the rest of the ingredients until Saturday so we can do both then. Does that work for everyone?"

"I... do we really need to do the spell?" Alexander asked with a frown. "It had to be my mother."

"Are you forgetting how your Ceremony went?" Tori asked him, rolling her eyes, and I was surprised she'd managed to stay quiet for so long. I guess, unlike Ronan, she preferred to let her plat fight some battles alone. "Do you really think a Chthonic god just happened to be hanging around at the same time?" To Lux, she said, "Saturday works for us."

"We're free," Eliza said for her plat.

"I can't Saturday night. Sam needs me at the shop," Ronan said to everyone. Tori raised her eyebrows, glancing at me. No one else dared to make eye contact. To me, he asked, "Can you do it without me?"

I swallowed, the prospect of my plat not being there left me feeling untethered. I would be going into this with two soul-mates and by the time the cure was taken, I'd have none. *Gods, I'd have none.* Were we crazy for attempting this? This was... a mess, but I couldn't imagine not having the warmth in my chest where my two bonds now lay.

I could do this by myself but gods, I didn't want to. I wanted him there. I wanted my best friend by my side. But I'd already stolen so much of his time with Sam, needing him for every step of my own nonsense, so I stomached my anxiety and turned back to the group.

"Yeah. I'm good for Saturday. But only after six that night," I answered instead.

"What, hot date?" Tori snarked.

"*Tori,*" Theo barked at her, finally drawing my eyes back to him.

"No," I answered her, even though I knew she was just speaking to be contrary and likely angry because she had a direct line into Theo's head. "I have the Society for Ethical Sacrifice event that night. I've been helping to plan it for months and I'd prefer to avoid questions about why I'm missing."

Alexander looked at me, eyes wine-dark. "That's this week-end?" I nodded, swallowing. Everyone but Theo was watching the interaction, he just stared down at his hands, at his bracelets, with what I imagined to be the same expression

David had worn as he faced down Goliath. "Do you still need me?"

That's a loaded question, I thought and Theo flinched.

"Yeah, we could use you, for sure. The club."

"Then I'll be there," Alexander said, turning back to Lux.

"Okay," I croaked, swallowing again. Ronan handed me a water bottle and I took a swig of water to help my dry mouth. "Does that time work for everyone?"

"Yeah, we can do it later," Eliza said. "Where do we meet?"

"We need a source of fresh running water. There's an offshoot of the Golden River a few minutes walk from the ravines. We'll meet at the classroom at six and then head down that way. The weather shows rain in the morning, so it might be slippery. Wear good shoes," Lux said and attempted a smile that withered in the thick tension still clouding the room.

"Do they need to bring anything else?" Ronan asked and I was glad, my head still somewhere else and unable to focus.

"Vanessa, Alexander, Theo," Lux said. My spine tingled and my heart raced. Something in my breast began to wake and I beat it back down. "Bring a sacrifice of some kind. Something meaningful, so the god that cursed you knows you're serious about this."

We all nodded but said nothing. Lux sighed, "You *are* serious about this, aren't you?" There was silence as we shifted awkwardly in our seats and she looked like she really didn't want to get into it with us, not after having witnessed our fight, but she continued anyway. "This cure isn't something you can reverse after you take it."

"And the abilities just disappear?" Ronan asked, frowning. "Right away?"

Lux looked unsure. "That's what they hypothesized when they created the recipe. But we won't know until it's done." She clasped her hands in front of her as she assessed us. "They've asked that you answer some questions afterwards, so that the academic community might better understand the cure and its effects."

"You want them to be guinea pigs?" Tori demanded.

Theo laughed. "We're already freaks. Why not?"

"So Saturday at six," Lux interrupted before we could begin fighting again, but I didn't have the energy to fight this any more. Neither of my soulmates wanted me and this was happening. There was a knock on the door and we all startled. Even Eliza. Lux opened it and students began to file in as we grabbed our stuff. "See you then."

We pushed through the throng and I hesitated outside the classroom door for a minute. Finally, Alexander said, "What time do you need me for the event?"

I gripped my backpack straps so I couldn't throw myself into his arms like I had after his race. "It starts at four, so maybe a half-hour early?"

"Sounds good," he said and Eliza cleared her throat. "Right. Bye."

"See you," I echoed, watching him walk away. Theo looked at me silently, jaw clenched as if he was holding in his words and then he and Tori walked away. When they were out of sight, I sighed and slumped forward, exhausted.

Ronan pulled me to him. I held in a noise and gripped his shirt in my fists.

"I'm so sorry, kiddo. Want ice cream? I'm buying." A small pause. "Well, Sam is buying. It's his credit card."

"Yes to the ice cream. But I have a question for you," I said from where I was buried in his shirt fabric. "Is the second room of your new apartment still open?"

He laughed, a small sound that I felt more than heard. "For you? Always."

THE SWORD OF DAMOCLES

I arrived at the auditorium at three, so that I could move the seats around before the event. One section would seat the Cult of Demeter, another for Dionysus members and another for those unaffiliated. As I moved the fifty chairs we'd requested, I couldn't help but think we'd overestimated ourselves.

Most were in place by the time the president and the rest of the club arrived, bringing a few volunteers with them. Melissa, took in the room and the perfectly spaced rows of chairs, "Did you do all of this?"

"If you don't like it, we can change it—"

"No, it looks great," she told me, clapping me on the shoulder. She barked out a few orders to the rest of the club and the volunteers, and I went back to the few rows of chairs I had left to organize. It wasn't long before Ronan came by and helped me straighten out the rows. I didn't even notice Alexander arrive until he was right in front of me.

"Uh, hey," he said, rubbing the back of his neck. I looked up from what I was doing and my brain froze for a moment. He looked good. Better than he did on Thursday, for sure. There were still dark circles under his eyes, but the sweats had been replaced by a button down shirt and pressed dress pants. He'd shaved, too, revealing the sharp cut of his jaw.

"Hi," I answered once my voice returned. "You're early."

He shrugged. "Practice wrapped up quicker than usual."

"Hey, Achilles!" Olympia, the vice president, called in our direction. She made a two-finger point from him to a couple of large, black squares and added, "If you're here to volunteer, I need your help. These amps are too heavy for me. You, too, Ronan!"

"I think she means me," Alexander murmured. "Time to do some heavy lifting."

"Okay," I said but they were already walking away. I guessed I should be used to it by this point. I moved on to helping some of the other girls hang posters, stepping back to see if they were even.

"I think they're okay?" I offered as the girls experimented with moving their corners.

"They're not," a voice said from beside me, and I jumped, yelping loud enough that I saw a few groups stop their preparations to look over at me. Theo continued like I hadn't, "They're all leaning to the right a little." To the girl holding the right corner of the poster, he said, "Maybe pull it up, like, three centimeters. There. Perfect."

"You're here," I said, blinking at him.

"I am."

"But why?" It came out a little more forcefully than I'd wanted.

"I said I'd help. So I'm helping."

"Yo, Patroklus!" Olympia called in our direction. She and Melissa were trying to move a table closer to the stage and couldn't even lift it off the ground. Alexander was busy hefting amps. "Get your stupid shoulders over here."

"Am I Patroklus?" Theo wondered.

"I think so."

"Who does that make you?" he asked, raising his eyebrows.

"Briseis, probably."

He frowned, opening his mouth to argue.

"Chop, chop, manbun!" Melissa added, setting the table down on the ground after another attempt to lift it. "Don't have all day."

He looked down at me and attempted a smile. Unlike Alexander, he hadn't dressed up for the event, but then again, I hadn't asked him to. He was dressed in his usual dark shirt and ripped jeans but he'd shaved, too. Not completely smooth, like Alexander, but the scruff was definitely at a more moderate level now. "Can we talk, after?"

"Sure," I said hesitantly. "I'll have to help with the clean-up, but we could walk to the classroom together?"

He nodded and his smile faded before he walked over to Olympia. I turned back to the girls with the posters, and we managed to hang them all before anyone showed up. Alexander had moved on to sorting out the microphones and Theo was setting up the food with the catering team when I felt a tap on my shoulder.

I turned expecting it to be Ronan, but the girl from the Demeter Cult, Rose, was there grinning at me. She was wearing a long, black dress not dissimilar to the cloak I'd first seen her in and the necklace with seven red stones. Her grin was sharp as she greeted me, "Looking good in here, Wanaxa."

Two other girls in dark dresses stood behind her. One of them was Rebecca, looking bored, and the other was one of the other girls from the barn meeting.

"What are you doing here?"

"Oh, we're giving the opening speech," Rebecca answered, examining her blunt nails.

"What?" I asked, looking back at Rose with a mix of surprise and suspicion. "Why?"

"There are a lot of reasons. They'll be clear soon," she said, shrugging like that wasn't weird at all. She looked around the room, her gaze only stilling when it landed on Alexander and Theo, who were now approaching me. "Oh, are these them? Handsome, Wanaxa—"

"Stop calling me that," I begged through a tight smile and Rebecca laughed.

"Hey," Melissa called from the stage to Rose and the other girls. "We've got the mic working. You have a few minutes if you want to come up and get a feel for the stage before everyone gets here."

"Great!" Rose replied, bumping into me as she made her way to the stage. I stumbled at the movement, and she steadied me with a single hand on my waist. "Careful, you never know what a little fall can do." She winked and they made their way up to the stage. I was still staring at them as Alexander and Theo settled beside me. They were both sweating a little and Theo was panting but trying to hide it. I was careful not to look at the way his tattooed arms glinted with perspiration.

"Friends of yours?" he asked, tilting his head towards Rose.

"I have no idea." I shook my head. Focusing back on them, I said, "Looking for another job? People are starting to arrive, so could you pass out some programs as they walk in?"

"I think we can manage that," Alexander said, grabbing a stack and Theo nodded.

"Thanks, guys." I turned to help Olympia seat the Cult of Dionysus speakers and jumped a few minutes later when Melissa tapped the microphone twice and told everyone to take their seats. I sat in the second row with Ronan and the other club members and Alexander and Theo sat right behind me.

Melissa made a quick introduction and surrendered the stage to the group from Demeter.

"Hi, everyone," Rose announced like she had no fear of the

stage and I winced, wondering what sort of weirdness she was about to spout now. Surprisingly, there were more people here than we had chairs, and I really hoped Rose wasn't going to embarrass us all. "My name is Rose and, like Melissa said, I'm the leader of the campus' Cult of Demeter. Usually, the president of our Cult talks at this event, but I'm here instead this year. Lucky you."

A light wave of laughter. She continued, "Now, tradition demands we talk to you about the history of sacrifice and other boring stuff, but that's not what we're going to talk about. We're going to talk about a certain festival to Zeus in Ancient Athens."

Melissa sat next to me as she came down from the stage. The moment she sat down, she flipped open the program and hissed, "This is not in here. People look confused."

"I'm sure it'll be fine," I said, though I didn't mean it. "She seems okay."

"She's not," Melissa whispered. "She's Cult of Demeter, sure, but on the fringes. She and her little clique of freaks pay their dues and never show up to the real meetings. I don't know how she convinced the faculty advisor to let her speak tonight."

That did not bode well.

Melissa's phone rang. She frowned deeper and grabbed it before leaving the auditorium. Just a few seconds later, Olympia, who was sitting in front of me, picked up her phone and left too.

"I am, of course, talking about the Buphonia," Rose continued, looking back at her friends. They laughed lightly like they were a part of some grand joke. "Most of you are probably familiar with it, but let me tell you the details..."

She spoke about the ritual sacrifice that happened at the Acropolis every year in honor of Zeus, explaining how a group of oxen were led to the altar filled with food. The first to eat sealed their fate as the sacrifice and the leading families would slaughter the animal while it ate.

It's an interesting speech, but the problem was that it pushed their time slot from fifteen minutes to twenty and was pushing twenty-five when I realized that neither Melissa nor Olympia were back. The secretary and treasurer, who were both too timid to say anything, glanced back at me with worried expressions and the next speaker was shifting in his seat and glancing at the clock.

"The problem with such sacrifices," Rose said in a way that meant she had no intention of wrapping up, "is that it is impossible for the animal to consent to the act of dying. Even if they did the drip test we all know that's bullshit. Get it, bull-shit? Anyway, even if they did the drip test—"

"Ness," Ronan said from beside me. "I think you gotta do something."

"—they took away the animal's ability to decide the moment they put them on the Acropolis," she continued as if speaking over Ronan. "Because that's what consent is, isn't it? The ability to decide without anyone forcing you to. And that's where power comes from, doesn't it?" She paused extra long here and it felt pointed.

"Alright, I'll figure it out," I said and took a deep breath. There was no part of me that wanted to stand up and make myself the center of attention, but this needed to be done before the rest of the speakers left.

Rose went on, "And by taking that power from someone or something, in this case the creatures that we sacrifice to the gods, we make them out to be less than us, though we all know them to be kind, beautiful creatures—"

I stood up, moving past Ronan to walk down the aisle. Rose saw me, grinned and talked faster. "—and, as the chosen representative of the Cult of Demeter today, I wanted to say that we stand with the Society of Ethical Sacrifice on the matter of making this campus as safe as possible for the sweet, little beasts."

She started wrapping up as I climbed the steps to the stage. "Finally, I wanted to thank you all for listening to our speech today. It means a lot to us, and, wow, would you look at that? It seems we've gone a little bit past our allotted time. Vanessa, I'm so sorry."

There was nothing sorry about her smile, though, and I saw right through her perfect, dark red lip gloss to the cunning underneath. I had no idea what it meant, but I pulled the microphone away from her with the same fabricated politeness.

"Okay, can we get a big thank you for our Cult of Demeter representatives?" I asked the audience. There was scattered applause but it faded quickly. Clearing my throat, I adjusted the microphone so that it was at my own height. Light feedback screeched and everyone winced. I continued, "Thank you—"

Rebecca winked at me. "No problem, Wanaxa."

"Without further delay," I said, gesturing for the Dio-Bro to stand. He made his way to the stage with his crinkled note-cards. "Here's a message from the Cult of Dionysus!"

As I got back to my seat, I noticed the Demeter girls had sat in the back row. But I didn't pay them any more atten-tion. Somehow, the Dio-Bro wrapped up his speech early, making some pretty simple comments about sacrifice, and we were only running a few minutes behind our original schedule when Melissa and Olympia snuck back through the door. As we all clapped, I leaned over to Melissa. "What happened?"

She shrugged. "It was the Financial Aid department telling me there was a problem with my account. They said there was a hold on my Cult scholarships but we got cut off and when I called back the new person couldn't find an issue. Anything weird happen?"

I shrugged. "There was a timing problem, but I took care of it."

She knocked her shoulder into mine like we were friends and said, "I knew you would."

She got up and walked onto the stage. She was still clapping when she announced, "Thank you, everyone! Now, feel free to look at the posters and other presentations we've set up around the room. We encourage you to ask questions and enjoy the catering. There are plenty of great veggie and vegan options, all officially supplied by the Cult of Demeter on campus and our own Society for Ethical Sacrifice." She paused, and sent me a smile before finishing, "And a special thanks to Vanessa for all her help today."

Ronan leaned his head on my shoulder for a second, grinning at me and I laughed, embarrassed at how much I liked the attention.

"You did good, kiddo," he said, stealing the nickname from Sam.

I smiled and nodded. "Thank you. Did you have fun?"

He laughed, throwing an arm around my shoulder. "More than last year, definitely."

Turning around, I saw Alexander and Theo standing. They weren't looking at each other, but there was no uncomfortable air or tension surrounding them. I smiled at them and swallowed my emotions when they both smiled back.

"Hey," I said. "Any questions?"

"I have one," Rose interrupted, moving to push herself into our little group. I tensed but said nothing. My soulmates looked between us curiously. "Did you like leading your group for a moment just then, Vanessa?"

"No *Wanaxa*, this time?" I fired back, frowning. "I just did what I had to."

Her grin widened. "As all great leaders claim. I'm sure Zeus said the same before he smote the Titans and threw his father into Tartarus for all of eternity." That earned a few odd looks from people nearby. It was strange to say the names of such creatures in everyday conversation, but not for Rose apparently.

The other girl that had been with Rose and Rebecca spoke up, then. She had a voice that wasn't as abrasive and there was a calmness to her that made her somehow more threatening than either of the fierce girls. She said, "You did well. A leader not a tyrant."

"Why would she need to be a tyrant for this event?" Alexander answered, face open and curious, like he thought the conversation was an exercise in wordplay. Theo, on the other hand, stared at the necklace around Rose's neck like he was starting to understand something. I wished I could say the same.

"Why, indeed," was all Rose said. She slapped a hand to my shoulder and tilted her head to a poster I'd made the year before, all pastel pink and covered with cherries, about more environmentally conscious agricultural practices for local produce. "It's good to see you again, Wanaxa. I'm sure we'll see you soon."

They walked away and the spot where Rose's hand touched me burned.

"That was kind of weird, right?" Ronan asked, but he was smiling.

The rest of the event passed without much commotion. We'd easily beaten our record for attendance and a few people stepped forward and asked about our meeting times. All in all, it'd been a success.

Ronan had to leave to get to work, but Alexander and Theo helped clean up and it took half the time with them. Occasionally, some of the other girls stopped to watch them lift the heavy things and I narrowed my eyes until they looked away, but it was nothing more than innocent fun. Besides, I liked looking, too.

We were about to leave when I realized that I must've cut myself on one of the posters without noticing. Alexander reached out to help, only to catch himself. Grabbing a napkin, I said to them, "Give me two minutes."

They both nodded. Theo had his thinking face on, but his mind was firmly shut away from mine. Alexander, on the other hand, looked openly worried and conflicted about not helping.

I ducked into the closest bathroom, heading to the sink. The water ran pink when it touched the cut but when the blood was gone, there wasn't even a papercut. Swallowing, I looked over my entire hand, thinking maybe I'd wiped the blood from elsewhere, but there was nothing.

The bathroom door shut and the lock clicked into place, the snap of it was a breaking branch in a dark forest, a growl from the shadows. The third girl from Rose's group, the one whose name I didn't know but whose energy was slow and building like a dangerous current, had walked in.

"I'm sorry about this," she said, her tall stature matching the magnitude of her presence, the words echoing around the small room with chipped paint and ugly, floral wallpaper. I shivered at the sensation of the strange apology, glancing around. Maybe someone else was in the room? But there was no one. Just me.

"About what?" I asked as she took a few steps towards me. Instinct had me backing up, but there was nowhere to go. The corner of the sink stabbed into my back, drops of water wetting my hands as I gripped the edge. The girl didn't answer, her footsteps breaking the silence after the question. That same instinct pounded in my chest, telling me to run. To grab a weapon. I ignored it, glancing at the exit. "Why did you lock the door?"

She pulled something out of the leather purse she'd been

carrying around all night and my stomach lurched at the gleam of silver. A knife. It shone in the light, wickedly sharp and curved like it was made to slice through skin and bone. It was a sick thought considering the event I'd just helped put together and images of bloody sacrifices flashed through my mind. On my head, a bead of water, suspended.

"You'll understand soon enough that it has to be like this."

Move, my brain supplied. *Get out of here.*

And I wanted to listen, but panic locked my knees, rooting me to the spot. I imagined how it would play out. I would weave, screeching past the girl, and throw the lock to escape. I could scream, I thought, when the dense air of the small room no longer clogged my windpipe, and someone would save me. Someone always saved me.

The sink next to me turned on, the water running with such force that it splashed onto the marble floor, running over my hands, sliding between my knuckles. I shook it off, shivering. My eyes darted to the floor and the girl instantly slid closer until the knife was against my throat. The tip was cold as it pressed against my skin, the metal singing like life and death as the girl held it closer.

"You will obey me," she said and my body relaxed even as my mind raced. I couldn't shout and Theo's mind seemed a thousand miles away. That, more than anything, terrified me. "Just for now. Not forever. But you need to know."

"Need to know what?" I begged, wishing my body would thrash, would fight.

"Not what," she responded, moving with a speed I couldn't fathom. The knife's edge pressed into the hollow of my throat and I choked as I suppressed a gasp, the skin of my throat thin and delicate in proximity to the wicked curve. She was taller than me and her arms were like iron bars. "But who."

With a too-strong hand on my back, she pushed me over the counter until my head hovered over the water. My hands flailed behind me, false hope clenching my fingers on empty air. With nowhere else to look but down, the water caressed my face, eyelashes skimming the surface, nose hovering.

Untouched, the water stopped flowing when it reached the top of the basin.

"Who, then?" I demanded, my chest tightening. I managed to tilt my head to the side and I watched water run down the old tile, the scent of moss and decay filled my nose, stagnating below our very feet. The sound of its trickling filled my ears until the dripping became a soundtrack to my panic. "Who do I need to know?"

"It is difficult," she said as if talking to herself, and speaking to many others at the same time. The words paused around us, hovering and repeating like ripples on the water. A dozen voices, low and high and new and ancient. A womb at the birth of the universe, that split open my mind. The knife like a strike of lightning, memories like a blood sacrifice, I was divided. Open. Split apart. "To know yourself."

The water muffled my scream, bubbles foaming to cover my mouth, my nose, my ears. Long fingernails scraped the back of my head, holding me down, down, down, my limbs numb and helpless to do anything but pray to any god willing to listen.

Please, I tried. *Please help...*

Darkness stifled my last chance at salvation.

Silence. And then a single laugh, strangely familiar and warm like rot.

ἹΣΤΟΡΊΑ - ΠΟΤΑΜΟΊ

THE RIVER

The river emerged from the darkness like a beast with snarling teeth. Black as shadows, the water darker, bubbling with silver froth. It was like glass, reflecting the moonlight. Obsidian sharpened its bank.

Nothing lived by the water, not even grass or flowers. If a current were to sweep them up and carry them into the mouth, they would never again see the sun.

Aware of this too, Vanessa stepped into the icy water. The sun warmed the island during the summer, but these streams were immune. The grandmothers on the island whispered about how even the rays of Apollo shrank back from the black water. But like Icarus, Vanessa braved the unknown.

The bubbling quieted when her skin touched the water and grew silent when she submerged her foot to the ankle. But nothing else happened. She rucked up her dress farther, pulling it to her knees. She waded to her shins. Nothing. Then to her knees. Nothing. To her thighs, to her hips, to her breasts. Nothing, nothing, nothing.

Her own face in the light of the moon grinned up at her from below, though she knew she was snarling above the surface. Wide-eyed, she greeted herself and she knew then that she was playing with darker forces than she could've imagined.

Lightning struck, the last sound she heard before she closed her eyes and ducked below the freezing water, somehow distant and impossibly close. Her hands shook from where they clutched at her clothes, holding them to her skin in the hopes they would keep her warm enough to survive this.

She took one breath and opened her eyes underwater. A face hovered centimeters from her own, blinking and grinning. Dark gray and scaled, part fish, part maiden, all-decaying. She wrapped her hands around Vanessa's waist and pulled her deeper into the water with webbed hands. Vanessa's screams went no further than the bubble of air in front of her.

The creature pulled her deeper and deeper into the water until she could no longer see the moonlight. Until the pressure on her temples threatened to explode. Her hands were blue, she thought, though there was no way of knowing.

She was nearly unconscious when they reached some sort of cave, an opening on the side of the mountain, free of water. The creature, face still grinning with needle-sharp teeth, threw her from her arms onto the sharp rocks of the cave floor.

Vanessa coughed out the water. She began to shiver, there was no warmth here and her soaked chiton was no good. There was no light. She could see nothing and was convinced that the creature had brought her here to be dinner for a larger, more terrifying thing.

She wasn't entirely wrong.

A light flickered at the other end of the cave. She gasped and scooted backwards, wanting to throw herself back into the river to escape. But the creature hissed at her, pausing her grin just long enough to do so. The light swayed closer, bobbing up and down.

There were stories, of course, of dragons and hydras and a million other things with powers and teeth that could easily kill a defenseless girl. But the light moved closer and revealed something worse. She must have been a goddess because the woman was at least as beautiful *as Alexandros' mother. Umber-skinned and emerald-eyed. But the Goddess of Love never stayed long and this woman was slow to approach, letting fear and attraction take their time on Vanessa's mind.*

It took only a few seconds for the woman to place herself in front of the shivering, hunched-over girl. She greeted her with a smile nothing like the pointed, terrifying one of the creature, but it was somehow more unsettling. Maybe because she smiled like she had expected Vanessa to come. Like she was pleased by her midnight visit.

"Welcome again, my dear," the woman said, reaching a hand out and brushing a wet strand of hair from her face. When her fingers touched Vanessa, her skin no longer felt stiff and freezing. She burned with Greek fire. "I thought I'd see you soon."

"Who are you?" Vanessa demanded. But the question was pointless, because around her neck was a chain of red stones, each thrumming as if lit from within, the source of the bouncing light. Up close, they were strangely shaped, almost like seeds, and Vanessa's eyes widened with realization.

"I was given the name Kore by my mother," the woman answered. From nowhere, she pulled out a thick, fur coat and draped it around Vanessa's shoulders. "But I am known by many titles now. The Dread Queen. The Bringer of Chaos. Wife of the Wealthy."

Vanessa's body stiffened. She had come to confront her goddess and now—

The goddess continued, "But you worship me as Persephone."

LOOK FAVORABLY UPON ME

A knock on the bathroom door shocked me into my own body. I sat up, gasping on dry tile. My face, my hands, my clothes – all dry. Like a fawn, I made it to my feet and looked in the mirror, flinching back, half-expecting a smile with too-sharp teeth to appear but only my own dark eyes stared back. I was alone in the room, visions of dark caves and glowing eyes dancing behind heavy eyelids. Something was wrong, but I remembered nothing except the taste of river water.

"Vanessa?" Alexander called from outside. "Are you okay?"

I moved to the door and pressed my hand to the knob, catching a glimpse of something in the metal reflection. *Teeth like daggers, a woman in the dark.* I paused to close my eyes and took a deep breath before opening the door with more strength than I intended.

Alexander stood there, hand raised as if to knock again and blinking at my sudden appearance.

"Hi, yeah, sorry," I answered. There was tension in his shoulders, worry in the shaking of his hands, and I couldn't bear to make it worse. I shook my head and forced a smile. "I was fixing my makeup."

"Oh." He examined my face. "Well, you look, uh, fine. Great."

"What time is it?" I asked, stepping outside of the bathroom. I'd left my phone and backpack behind so wasn't sure if I'd been gone for minutes or hours.

"Almost six," Alexander said and I fell quiet once more, unsure what else to say to him.

We walked back towards the auditorium, not touching but close enough that our shoulders nearly brushed. Our footsteps echoed but my ears only rang with the sound of trickling water.

Alexander walked on one side of me and Theo on the other and despite everything, I felt safe between them. This wasn't the end, we wouldn't take the cure today – but it was the first step. The beginning of the end. The sun was half-way through setting, coloring the sky as blue blended into indigo, with darkness soon falling. Moonlight filtered through criss-crossed branches, a weaving pattern of shadows covering us. It was a quiet night, even for the creatures around us, only the occasional rustling of crisp leaves filling the silence of the forest.

My simple combat boots squelched in the thick mud and I shifted my backpack nervously as we followed the path to the river. Thankfully, Theo had remembered to bring it for me, or maybe Ronan had reminded him. Either way, its weight at my back felt comforting. I slipped a little in the mud, and Alexander's hand at my waist steadied me. I sighed and saw my breath fog the air – I should have worn something sturdier. The boots were made for fashion more than warmth, and I could only hope they'd protect my socks from becoming bogged down with river water.

"Thank you," I murmured, disliking how my voice broke through the darkness.

"If anyone is going to fall in, it should be me. Can't drown, remember?" Alexander said with a dryness that surprised me. I did remember, though I wasn't sure where from. "I'll just have to make sure to throw someone Lux's supplies for the spell before I fall."

He laughed lightly, but I thought about how far it was from the top of the cliffs to the surface of the river and didn't laugh. Neither did Theo, calling back from in front of me, "Don't even joke about that. Chance loves to play games with ironic statements."

"But if you do fall," Tori added from her spot in front of him, "throw me the stuff. No one else looks like they can catch. Except for Theo. And that's false advertisement. His arms are good for nothing but the aesthetic."

Theo snorted but didn't deny it. I relaxed until a crack of a tree branch off to our right had my muscles tensing again. The leaves of the forest curled in on themselves now, their fallen brethren covered the dirt path and shadows decorated the back of Theo's coat like the darkness was reaching out for him.

The foliage crunched under our feet and the ground became increasingly steep as we approached the river. The sound of our labored breaths seemed to echo strangely, like they were bouncing off of a wall of darkness, and I shivered as the frost seemed to seep into me.

Soon enough, we stood at the point between the cleared and untraversed paths. A Frost poem in my head, Lux gave us all a look over her shoulder as she led us past the pine branch that blocked the walkway, stepping off of the worn trail. I ducked under low hanging branches, stepped over half-rotted logs and tried to stop the night air from stealing my breaths when I was caught in a spiderweb.

It was likely worse for Lux and Eliza in the front, but they powered through it without comment. Tori swore up a storm, making Alexander snicker to himself as he maintained that perfect, demi-god grace.

I hesitated, half-expecting some other, darker, laughter to sound from between the trees. It never came and I shook my head free from what had to be the aftereffects of whatever that girl had done to me in the bathroom.

The sounds of the river grew louder and somewhere to our right a bullfrog beckoned us closer. We met the edge of the ravine that overlooked the river and all stumbled into each other as Lux stopped at the front of the line. I grabbed Theo's side to stabilize myself and Alexander did the same with my shoulder.

"This is the steepest part," Lux called back to us, and I broke out in a cold sweat, some primal instincts firing off about what attention we might be drawing stood here in the open. "The fall is something like 35 meters from the path to the river. The offshoot we're looking for is on the other side of this cliff, so we'll get to ground-level soon, but we need to be careful. Watch out for each other."

The fall hung over us, making my knees lock and my palms dampen. The dense thicket of trees, roots and dead foliage bracketed us from the right, too thick to walk through but our only safety as we skirted along the edge of the cliff. We began walking slower as we left behind the last of the trees, the rapids below now in plain sight as the water rushed fast and foamed white where it hit the craggy rocks. The wind around us stung as it whipped at my skin. We stepped in each other's footsteps, all of us silent as we attempted to navigate the sloping path that only deepened the further we walked.

By the time those of us at the back of the line put our feet down, the mud had been smoothed into a deadly slickness. I felt worse for Alexander, who held the heavy bag of spell ingredients as he tried to maneuver his body and was panting with the effort. Theo occasionally cursed and implored Apollo, accidentally grabbing a scarlet-tipped hawthorn branch instead of smooth wood. Alexander, surprisingly, asked for no help from his mother, gritting his teeth through the process. I had no one to call on.

The cliff began to even out and then we were on flat ground. The tension in my shoulders lifted and I leaned against one of the few trees near the rocky, sandy shore of the river offshoot. Alexander set the bag down and took a few deep breaths with his hands behind his head. Tori checked her plat for any injuries, frowning at Theo's scraped hands. Eliza stretched like she'd just enjoyed a mildly taxing day of yoga. I continued to shiver against the night air, something inside of me stretching and tensing like an animal readying for a fight.

The little stream bubbled against the dark stones and packed sand of the small shore, illuminated silver in the light of the moon as if Artemis herself was watching over us. The large river still resounded with its force but a wall of boulders cut it off to create the offshoot. Lux crouched down next to the bag and pulled it over to the very edge of the water. She pulled out two plastic bags and slipped them over her boots, protecting them from sand and the small waves that gurgled on the land.

A marble bowl and spoon of some kind, little bags of herbs, a bottle of Greek red wine, a flask of something and several tupperware containers of things I didn't recognize hit the ground at her feet.

"Okay," she said to us all. "I need you three on the shore with me. Grab plastic bags for your shoes, they'll stop most of the water. You might need two, actually, Vanessa." To Eliza and Tori, she added, "You must stay on the grass. Under no circumstances should you touch the water. It'll mess everything up and we'll have to do this again tomorrow."

We tied plastic bags over our shoes before stepping into the very edge of the water. The damp sand moistened the edges of the grocery bags, but our feet stayed dry.

You okay? I heard in my head from Theo, though he didn't even lift his head from where he was double knotting the bag on his right foot. *You're sighing a lot.*

Just thinking about everything, I answered in my head. *It just sucks.*

Theo snorted aloud. *You're telling me, sweetheart.*

Alexander looked over at us. "Are you two doing the silent communication thing again?"

"Yeah," I answered, shrugging.

He sighed, too. "I'm not going to miss that."

It made us all frown.

Lux cleared her throat. "Okay, you all brought your sacrifices, right?"

We nodded and, with the deafening sound of the crinkling plastic, walked over to our bags to retrieve them. Alexander had a Ziplock of golden sand. Theo had a clump of charcoal.

I had put my sacrifice – a small bottle of cherry wine from my family's orchard – in the front pocket of my backpack. But when I stuck my hand in the pocket, I didn't touch the bottle. In fact, the strange texture waiting for my hand made me pull it back into my side. I opened the pocket fully and a bright red pomegranate fell to the forest floor.

"Interesting," Theo said to me with raised eyebrows as he looked at the fruit.

"I didn't bring this," I answered. Lux frowned at the words. "I mean, I brought a bottle of wine. I don't know where this came from." The fruit seemed to grin up at me, mocking me and reminding me of my sticky, red hands.

"Do you have anything else to sacrifice?" Lux asked. I remembered her warning in the classroom to bring something meaningful. I shook my head, sighing and picking the dumb fruit up. "Then we'll have to use that. Do you need a knife to cut it?"

"Yes, please," I answered and she handed me a pocket knife. I cut into it – a circle around the crown and then down the sides in sections. The juice dripped down around my fingers, staining my nails pink and red. It looked like blood. I kept cutting through the dense outer flesh and when it was finally sliced into its natural sixths, I looked up. Theo and Alexander were staring at me.

"What?"

"You a big fan of pomegranates?" Theo asked, nodding to the perfectly sliced fruit in my hands.

I blinked down at the murder scene of my hands. "Not really."

"Huh," Alexander said. "Well, you did that pretty fast. It would've taken me like fifteen minutes and I would've only ended up with a few seeds. You have a lot to sacrifice now."

"Yeah," Theo echoed, still staring. His frown is deep. "Good."

"Come on, let's get this over with," Lux urged. "Bring your sacrifices over here." In the time it'd taken me to cut the fruit, she'd set up the bowl and the spoon over a makeshift altar. We offered a piece of our sacrifices in the small bowl – a pinch of sand, a corner of the clump of charcoal, seven seeds – and then she instructed us to throw the rest into the water. We did so and my hands felt strangely empty.

She set the contents of the bowl on fire and the smoke that billowed out was dark, nearly black, and smelled sweet and strange. It faded into the air within seconds. She said something in Ancient Greek and the water hesitated in its next wave, as if listening to her.

"Okay," she said to us, tilting her head towards the water. "Step into the water now as it accepts your gifts. I'm going to start the ritual, brewing a potion to connect your minds with your ancient memories. It won't hurt, but it might be intense. Prepare yourselves."

We stepped into the water. Even though I stayed dry, it made me shiver. Alexander pulled off his coat and then his sweatshirt underneath. He shrugged the outer coat back on but handed me the sweatshirt.

"You'll freeze," I said, shaking my head in denial.

He pressed a warm hand to my cheek. "I'll be fine. You're like ice."

"I have a flannel in my bag," Theo added. "I'll give it to you when we're done."

I sighed in reluctant acceptance but stopped myself from grabbing the hoodie. It was dark blue and white, our school colors, and I still had bright red juice all over my hands. "I don't want to stain it," I told Alexander.

They both shook their heads, working in sync to pull the sweatshirt over my head and arms without me touching it. They worked so well together when they weren't screaming at each other. Soon, I was drowning in the fabric and with Alexander's residual body heat still lingering, I could have fallen asleep in its warmth.

Lux had nearly finished mixing the potion in another bowl. The last ingredient was the liquid in the flask. It was a red-brown color and my stomach rolled. Catching my expression, Theo asked, "Is that blood?"

Lux nodded. "From an ox."

"Can we do it without it?" he asked. "Vanessa is a vegetarian."

She shook her head and my stomach dropped. She poured the blood into the mixture and the thickness made me want to gag. "No, I don't have an alternative. But there's enough wine in this potion that you shouldn't be able to taste it."

"It's not about the taste," I replied, but I took a deep breath. "It's fine. I can do it."

"Are you sure?" Alexander asked. "You look a little green."

"We don't have a choice," Lux said. She had three plastic cups and poured a third of the potion into each before handing it to us.

Whatever god we'd pissed off must have been powerful. Half-gods could be worshiped with wine, perhaps, but real gods demanded blood.

Standing up straight, I held the cup with both hands. Lux was right, anyway. The only thing I could smell was wine. "What do we do?"

She pulled out a notebook. "I'll read this Greek to invoke their presence. When I finish speaking, you need to swallow all of the potion. Its purpose is to connect you to your past self, and if drunk right after the invocation, it should make you remember the moment you interacted with the god."

We all nodded and the cup dimpled with the pressure of my fingers.

She started speaking and the water grew quiet, the small waves by our feet swelled with hesitation. I only understood a few of the words. She said things like "please" and "help" and "repent". When she was about to finish, she raised her hands and nodded her head at us.

We raised the cups to our lips and blood filled my mouth.

ῙΣΤΟΡΊΑ - ΔῶΡΟΝ

GIFT

Vanessa pressed her forehead to the ground in respect, muttering her praises to the Goddess. Persephone allowed it to happen for a second before pulling the girl upright again by her shoulders. Her hands were soft and warm, a comfort even while they held enough power to destroy her.

"You need not speak your prayers to the ground," Persephone said to her, brushing the girl's dark hair back from her face. "There is no one below us to listen, but I appreciate them all the same."

"You bless me by meeting me here," Vanessa responded. "Thank you."

"I do not come to merely visit," the goddess responded with a sad smile. "There will be time for that soon, I am sure. For now, however, we must discuss the reason for your presence. Though you showed your respect to me now, anger boiled your blood when you stepped into the river. It is the only thing that kept you alive."

The girl swallowed. "I am angry."

"With me?" the goddess asked, her eyes sparking. "Why so?"

"I have given you my life," Vanessa explained, shaking from fear but continuing to speak anyway. A bold claim to the Queen of the Dead. "I spend my nights with your followers. I've burned meat and

335

poured wine for you at every meal. By the first time I bled, I was the most dedicated of your worshipers. Your women hail me as their leader."

"I know this," the goddess said with a raised eyebrow. "I appreciate it."

"Yet, still, you do not answer," Vanessa continued, the words emerging in one long breath as if she pushed them out before they could sink back and away. "I've done all this for you and I have received nothing in return. When I was happy, I did not mind, but now? I suffer."

The goddess, almost wistfully, stroked on the glowing stones. "Don't we all?"

"It feels as though my heart is breaking," she said, barely holding back a sob. "And you offer me no aid, though I have loved you for my entire life. None of the gods respond. Some people – those on the mainland, the Athenians and the Lakedaimonians – speak of rebellion, of terrible acts against the gods. We love you. Why do you not return this love?"

She shook her head. "My father fears your power."

"Why?" Vanessa begged.

"When the traitor, Prometheus, created you," the goddess said, sitting back and sighing with the pressure of the tale, "you were strange, ugly creatures. Four arms, four legs, two heads, with all and no genders. You spoke of rebellion then too, and for it, Zeus struck you with his powerful bolts, tearing you in two."

"That's what my soul feels like now," Vanessa murmured. "Torn in two."

Persephone sighed. "You are still so powerful, you little humans, even in half. But now, you are never satisfied, never happy, because you are missing half of your soul." She frowned, her beautiful face growing wrinkled with concentration. "Do you remember the day you became engaged?"

"The day I drowned."

"Indeed," the goddess said, nodding. The cave shook and the water

from the river splashed onto the stone. "You died that day, though I made sure you did not remember it. We met upon your death and I, so pleased with our meeting, offered you a gift."

"What gift?" Surprise tinged the question.

"Anything in this world or the next," Persephone described. "You did not take it."

Horror filled the girl's face and heart. "I am so sorry—"

"And I tell you now what I told you then," the goddess said, her dark eyes now burning as bright as the stones around her neck. The cave shuddered and her skin began to glow gold. Her power made the air sizzle. "You are at your wit's end. Your heart is breaking and you have no one to turn to. You reach to your Fate with shaking hands and a bleeding soul. Now you remember the name of the goddess you rejected and what I offered you, once upon a time. Now you remember that a goddess' word is never broken."

37

HOLY MYSTERY

M y first thought coming back into my own body was of Pausanias, who traveled Greece and relayed his visions to the world. He saw great art and architecture and heard a million tales of the gods, believing few of them himself. As I opened my eyes, I became to myself such a tale. Mostly forgotten, scarcely believable, lost to the years between two times.

"What do you remember?" Lux asked us, dumping water on the burning offerings.

"Ancient Greece," Theo answered, rubbing his temple. A curl was escaping from where his hair was pulled back. His eyes were red from tears. "I married someone I shouldn't have. Someone I didn't love."

"I was in Greece too," Alexander replied. There was a red flush to his cheeks, high and bright against his skin. In the approaching darkness of evening, it only highlighted his bone structure. He no longer looked completely mortal. "I cheated on someone. My wife, maybe? I'm not sure."

Everyone looked at me and I concentrated, only half-formed images flashing in my mind. Nothing certain, nothing concrete. I wanted to scream, to scare birds from trees and bats from caverns. Instead, I muttered, "I don't remember. Does that mean I didn't offend anyone?"

Lux nodded and put the remnants of the ingredients back into her bag. She kept a couple out, laid on the wet sand, and pulled out a bag of hypodermic needles. "I think so, yes. Theo, Alexander, which goddess did you talk to? Which god split your souls?"

"Aphrodite," Theo said, refusing to look at Alexander.

"Aphrodite," Alexander answered at the same time, his face heartbroken.

They both looked at each other. Lux's face tightened as she looked up at the sky, her lip curled with annoyance. Maybe anger. It was a rare sight, this emotion, and her apology stung like disinfectant. "I'm sorry, Alexander."

Alexander closed his eyes and his body shook with the effort it took to hold back his tears. He didn't quite manage and one slipped down his cheek. He didn't move to brush it away. "I hoped – gods above, I prayed *so hard* that it wasn't my mother. I can't believe—" A sad, bitter laugh that sounded wrong coming from him. "No, that's not right. I can believe she'd do something like this. I just don't know *why*—"

I couldn't stop myself from wrapping my arms around his waist, pulling him as close as possible until I could hear his heart thundering even under layers of thick, warm fabric. He pressed his face into my hair and hugged me back. Another angry laugh. "Gods, I'm sorry you got dragged into this, too. You didn't offend anyone, you didn't do anything wrong, Vanessa, and you're still her victim."

"Please don't apologize," I begged. "It's not your fault."

He swallowed and nodded. With my face buried in his chest, I didn't see him look at Theo, but I felt it when Alexander lifted his chin from my head, and then I felt Theo along my back, his head buried in my shoulder and his arms around us both. He let out a wet huff of a breath too but held back a sob, and I ached for them, unsure if it had been a blessing that I could remember nothing.

"I'm sorry," Lux interrupted and she sounded it. "I don't want to do this to you. I know you need to comfort each other, but we need to make the cure."

We pulled away from each other again, but not completely. Alexander kept one arm over my shoulder. Theo kept his fingertips pressed against my hip.

Keeping my voice as even as I could manage, I asked, "What do you need us to do?"

Passing out a needle to each of us, she instructed, "I need a drop of blood from each of you. I'll mix it with the ambrosia and a few other things to make the cure according to the directions of the other SSS groups. Like I said before, this is nothing without the blessing from the goddess that split you in the first place." She huffed and her breath turned into a white cloud. "Not that we know why that is."

"You guys are going to see Aphrodite soon, though," Eliza piped up from her spot on the blanket. For the first time since this started, I paid attention to their plats. Eliza was laying on her stomach, legs up in the air and crossed at the ankle. Tori leaned back on her hands from her seated position. "Just ask her then."

I noticed that she didn't call her Alexander's mother. Like she knew it would only hurt him right then.

As we waded out of the water Lux mixed things together in the new bowl and, when our feet were secured on land, held it out to us. We pricked our fingers and let the blood well into fat drops that hissed when they touched the other ingredients. She added a splash of the dark wine and, finally, a square of something golden with the texture of the richest cake. When she dropped it into the bowl, it bubbled and disappeared. The mixture turned from a gross shade of brown-red to the same shade of gold as the ambrosia.

Lux poured the frothing liquid to the top of a clear, glass bottle. She sighed in relief as she screwed the lid into place and muttered a spell to lock it. "Alright, it's done. Who will be able to care for it most responsibly?"

"Eliza," Alexander said right away, looking at his plat. "Please."

She blinked at him and stood to retrieve it from Lux's outstretched hand, wrapping it carefully in the bubblewrap Lux supplied and placing it gently in her backpack. She was silent throughout, the weight of the responsibility suppressing her words.

When it was secure, Eliza looked up and asked, "Is that all?"

Lux nodded, picking up her now mostly empty backpack and slinging it over her shoulders. We marched back along the path behind Lux, retreating in the same order as we had approached. I somehow felt more on edge now than I had as we had made our way here. Why couldn't I remember my past life like the boys had?

I glanced about, my eyes unable to penetrate the thick darkness. Rumors spiraled in my mind about the ravines surrounding our campus. Crazy, ridiculous things, only spoken of by the Cult of Dionysus members after too many drinks and puffs of smoke. Monsters, some would say. Myth, fools would clarify, disbelieving that our origins were in monsters and their thirst for blood. How could you discount the idea of Medusa when Athena spoke to us about the state of education in our country on the nightly news? How could we discredit the existence of the Hydra when Hera's comments about her distaste for the minor god Herakles were famous in the 90s?

Perhaps during the day I had no fear of these creatures, but once Apollo had fallen asleep in Olympus beside his lovers, the briefest glimpses of shining eyes amongst the branches of the skeletal trees suggested their presence.

I wanted to pull my hands inside the holes of my coat, wished I had thought to bring gloves like Eliza, but I kept them out so I could feel my way through the path I could barely see. It was only Theo's low voice, pitched below the sounds of our footsteps, that warned me of branches and logs. The hoarse river still rumbled, hungry.

Soon, just as before, we reached the summit of the cliff. Lux murmured a low warning, nearly the same as the first but with an emphasis on watching out for each other. We walked for a few minutes, moving only an inch at a time. There were no trees now to block us from the edge.

The moment we were about to reach the apex, I slipped on something below my feet. A bony-fingered, grasping hand if I was letting my imagination terrify me. But I steadied myself and Alexander caught my elbow.

A laugh coughed out of me. I couldn't see him in the darkness, but the line of him behind me was my resting place. "Sorry," I murmured to him, breaking the tension with a rueful laugh.

He laughed, too, something low and rough. "I've got you."

A memory hit me.

I was lying on a white-sand beach. I was wearing nothing, but the sun was warm on my skin. I struggled to breathe, but I knew Alexander was beside me. He looked different, his hair a few shades lighter, his skin much tanner. He had a scar on his shoulder. Theo was on the other side of me, draping me in a luxurious cloak as purple as violets. He looked different, too. His face more open and hands rougher as they brushed against my wet skin.

I was caught between past and present, swaying as my mind struggled to align itself with the here and now. I had jumped from a rock. Or had I? I was the daughter of a local family, rich but not royalty. *No.* That was the past wasn't it?

I was young, unmarried, but just now engaged and bursting with the love of gods and kingdom and these men. I knew they said my name on this island with respect and affection. Theo painted on pottery, and Alexander was going to be the next king of my island home.

I was myself but not me. What had the potion unlocked? What had been waiting inside me?

A thousand memories, a thousand moments, snapshots of time in my first life, rushed into my brain like a wall in my head came crumbling down and they stampeded through my reality. It felt like a physical blow, the most painful thing I'd ever experienced, wringing a scream out of me that would make even the gods wince. Worse than when the Cupid read my results. Worse than the secondhand pain from Theo during his tattoo. Worse, even, than seeing them kiss at the party and forget me.

I jerked back in surprise and Theo grunted in pain, feeling my mind split open like a pomegranate under a knife. Alexander whined, feeling my agony through Theo, and his hand fell from where it held me at my elbow. I took a step backward, clutching my head. Theo cursed, calling my name as they both crumpled to their knees. Lux demanded an explanation. My foot found a hold on nothing, though I scrambled for any sort of purchase. A craggy rock, a grounded root, a strong hand, but there was nothing. Nothing but two sets of eyes, all dark in the night, staring at me with horror and a dangerous hope that I could save myself. Their faces blurred, the space between us growing and growing until there was nothing but the echoes of their cries reverberating through my present, my past.

Because I was falling.

The wind ghosted over me, ripping the air from my lungs, screams lost to the rush of gravity. A lifetime passed in no seconds at all, the world a swirl of stars above me. Andromeda wept, cursing the water once again.

And then I was drowning.

I had drowned many times before, but that didn't stop my limbs from freezing the second I was submerged in the water. My skin split open from the impact and my scream was lost in the water. It was so cold. Cold beyond words, beyond description. My blood felt like it had solidified in my veins as I sank in both the present and the past, colliding with such vigor I could have been dead or dying already but instead hung suspended between.

The cold felt like needles, like a tattoo inked into every inch of skin on my body. Unlike the sea, unlike the pool, this river was rocky, and my limbs hit the stones with such force that I imagined I was being ripped apart and scattered like paper in the wind. In my mind, images flashed like turning pages, chapters of my own story that I could only now read. Water in my lungs, both here and now and then and always. So many years lost, so many memories faded. I was a ghost of myself as the dark water erased me.

I tasted blood in my mouth, along with dirt and water and panic and sweet-bitter fruit. The cold shocked, the pain numbed, and I grieved for them and for myself all at once as I found the weakening tether between me and my soulmates. My senses maxed out in less than a second. I felt everything and nothing.

And then I was dead.

ἹΣΤΟΡΊΑ - ΠΡΟΑΊΡΕΣΙΣ

A CHOICE

"Are you going to kill me?" I asked the goddess, shrinking back from her words until my back pressed against the wall of the cave. "Or am I already dead? Did you draw me here with your magic?"

She laughed and the cave shuddered again. "No, you came of your own will."

The words were ironic and unbearably sad. "What is my punishment?"

She blinked. "Punishment?"

"For rejecting your gift," I clarified. "If you're not going to kill me."

"I never made that promise," she said with a grin. She slid closer to me until I couldn't stop the tear from falling. "Unlike my husband, I will not take you into my home without your consent."

"Please," I said. "What do you want?"

"No, sweet Vanessa, what do you want?" she returned. She wiped my tear away with her finger and then stuck it into her mouth. She grinned at the taste of my fear. "I offered you anything in the world and you never answered me. This is why I cannot answer your prayers. It is your turn to speak."

"To speak what?" I asked.

"I offered you a gift," she said slowly as if speaking to a child. But, to the gods, mortals are little more than shortly-lived infants. "And a goddess' word is never broken. I cannot retract my offer any more than you can retract your decision to seek me out in this land unmeant for mortals."

"What do I want?" I echoed back.

Her grin widened. "Or perhaps who?"

Her meaning was clear then, and I shook my head. "I cannot choose between them." She looked eternally disappointed for a small second. "But I don't want to. I know what I want. I want to stop feeling like I'm being ripped apart."

Her eyes, dark and glowing at the same time, grew wide. "What?"

"You said your father ripped us mortals apart," I continued, the words pouring out of me like water from the mouth of a rough river. "Because he was afraid of us and thought it would make us weaker. But it did not. This grand scheme has hurt us all." I took a deep breath, breathing in the musty air of the cave. "All our pains – the gods not responding, the threat of human rebellion, your gift, my indecision – require only one solution. You give us our soulmates back."

"How?" she asked, face open and curious.

"Humanity would be grateful to Olympus – indebted. We would sacrifice every day to the gods – not just small Cults like mine but everyone! Your power would grow and we'd never worship another—"

"Vanessa," she said with pity. "I cannot do this. It is not in my power—"

"You offered me anything," I reminded her. "This is my choice."

She stared out into the dark water of the river. Thinking to herself, her hands moved at her sides like a scale, testing the balance of the world and my request. Finally, she swallowed, just as anxious and afraid as I was.

"Give me a moment," Persephone said. "I will return."

She blinked out of sight, making no move to hide her divinity from me. She was gone for only a second but deep inside my chest, I felt something begin to buzz, to shake. Air meant nothing to me as eagerness filled my lungs, my ribcage, my throat. This was right.

The goddess returned with a blank face. "I have discussed your wish with my father."

"And?" I begged. Hope filled my chest and weighed me down.

"He has heard your proposal," she answered, "and accepts."

I smiled at her, young and happy and stupid. "Persephone—"

"But, as always with my father, there is a price for such a wish."

"What is it? I will pay anything."

"Your death," she said, swallowing. The hope turned to dread and, gasping, my bones softened with the meaning of her words. "What you asked for would change the world, Vanessa. I offered you anything and you asked for everything." She took a deep breath. "I would make it painless for you. But it would have to be now. Zeus does not wait at the discretion of humans for very long."

I thought about the people I would leave behind. My mother would scour the earth for me, I was certain. I was her only child, the only one to carry on our family into future generations. My father would grieve for me beyond sanity. But many parents survived this particular tragedy. In the end, they would be happy and healthy, their souls connected by the gods.

And then, of course, there was Alexandros and Theodoros, whose reactions I could not begin to imagine. Theodoros would move to Athens soon and, perhaps, be too busy with his handful of children and destined bride to remember me. Alexandros would find another wife, as bright and kind as he was. He would be King. He would not have time to remember the girl he once claimed to love.

"I will not get to enjoy my own wish?" I asked, my words brushing against my lips.

"Not in this lifetime."

"Do you know who my other half is?" I asked, swallowing my tears.

She nodded, "It is already written—" She cut herself short with a shrug and a pause. She continued after a few seconds of thinking, "I can give you another life in the future. Your story in Greece will not have a happy ending. It is to be a tragedy."

"For me? Or for everyone I know?"

"Both."

"So I will be dead," I said, clarifying, "but waiting for another life."

She nodded. The cave shuddered again. "You will remain at my side when I am in my husband's home and I will provide something to pass your time while I am with my mother." She offered a hand to me. "And, as soon as the world is ready, I will give you another chance to find those you love. To understand your soul."

The choice was not an easy one to make, but the choice was mine.

I took the goddess' hand and we walked into the darkness together.

I remembered Paris. New York. Cyprus. Grand Haven. The sunset at our picnic.
I remembered moments stolen from me by sleep.
I remembered everything.

ἹΣΤΟΡΊΑ - ΠΊΠΤΩ

I FALL

"What happens now?" I asked the goddess. The world had been reshaped by countless millennia, but the cave had not changed. It was still dark and the water lapped at the stone, making small noises. The only light came from her necklace, which I had never seen removed in our entire companionship.

"Now," she answered as we edged closer to the water, "you return to your home."

"But I do not know my soulmate," I protested, reaching forward to grab her hand. I was not a human any longer, but an idea of one kept alive through her will. A soul floating in nothingness, caught between distant lifetimes. Still, she allowed me to touch her. I was the only one she permitted to do so, except for her husband. "How will I recognize them?"

The goddess grinned and then we stood at the opening of the river. At her nearness, the water grew wild with excitement. The waves crested with foam and, all this time later, it made me ache for the golden-haired boy I had left behind to make the world whole. She placed her hands on my shoulders, pulled me into a quick, final hug, and whispered, "You never know what a little fall can do."

She pushed me back with the force of an immortal.
I hit the water and gasped in a mouthful of it.
And then I was living.

38

(I MUST SAY NOTHING)

I was swimming.

My head surfaced first and I sucked in a few lungfuls of air. It took a while for me to process what was happening, but by then I was already moving. The currents pulled and pushed me in every direction, but there was power in my limbs now along with a skill I had not learned and should not possess. A dark laugh filled my mind, warm enough to keep my heart beating.

The river carried me until I was able to find a weak point in the current where the water had less pressure and didn't dominate my body. Soon, I was able to pull myself onto the sandy beach.

The water licked at my feet, and I knew I was not safe from death. It was too cold to survive, drenched and vulnerable. My breathing jabbed into my skin, hard and painful, but it was nothing compared to what I now knew I had survived.

My brain spun with everything. Memories from a thousand missed moments swirled and each burned energy and sanity as it made room for itself inside my head. Whatever power possessed me to swim disappeared and I no longer had the energy to move my limbs. There was no benefit to death by hypothermia except, perhaps, I would not know fear. It would happen when I closed my eyes to sleep.

And I did want to sleep. My eyelids weighed down toward it already, and I couldn't control them. My breathing evened out after a few long minutes. Death, once again, came for me. *Thanatos, my old friend.*

Something rustled in a bush or tree. I didn't open my eyes, but I begged the gods to kill me before I had to endure the feasting of wild animals.

I braced for pain, wondering how my brain could possibly take more but it never came.

Instead, a familiar voice said, "Finally. I thought maybe we really killed her this time."

My curiosity motivated me just enough to open my eyes.

Seven glowing seeds.

Pulsating light in the darkness.

She reached for me.

I was not dead.

But I was unconscious.

When I woke up, I was bleeding sweat. The warmth had me in its claws and I pushed against the heavy fabric holding me down, thrashing to escape the prison. The forest stared at me from above, leaves like curious eyes, waiting for me to stare back.

A heavier weight landed on my hips and I grunted with it. My eyes felt sandy and rough, and I winced as I attempted to see whoever was straddling my waist and holding my arms down. She was familiar, but it took some time before I could place her face. And when I did – when I remembered the curved knife in her hands and the way she'd held my head under the water of the bathroom sink, I began to thrash with renewed vigor.

"Stop resisting," the girl said. At her side, she carried the same leather bag that had held the knife and I whimpered, trying to pull away. "You need to conserve energy. The healing spell needs it to work. And if you want to live, you *need* it to work."

"Maia, you're scaring her," Rose said from somewhere out of view, and I called out to Theo with my thoughts but got no response. His mind felt open and searching, but I couldn't think with enough strength or coherency to send anything to him.

Maia rolled her eyes. "Of course, I am. You insisted on being weird and sneaky about all of this instead of just being honest." She tucked the blanket under my thighs until I had no room to even struggle. "Maybe if you'd just explained it to her—"

"I was going to explain it to her, oh my gods," Rose snapped, but she sounded affectionate. Suddenly, there was movement and the weight of several people shook the ground like a goddess' nod.

My head was too heavy to lift and Rose's face filled up my vision as she leaned over me, still grinning. The earth was a barrier stronger than my exhausted body, stopping me from running away from all that was new and scary. And there was a lot that was new and scary, my mind opening up and revealing all the hidden crevices that death had hid. But right now, the scariest monster was a group of girls, cloaked in black and burning with magic, running around a forest at night and casually mentioning my murder.

"Hey," Rose greeted, as if we were bumping into each other at a supermarket. "Glad you pulled through, Wanaxa. It was touch and go for a while." She tapped her temple with her index finger. "But I knew you'd be fine. The voices in my head said so."

Maia snickered from just outside my vision. "You mean you could feel that I wasn't worried."

Rose shrugged, turning to her and winking. "And I thank you for not panicking, babe. Your magic saved my ass. Well," she reconsidered, "it saved Vanessa's, but I'm pretty sure I would be dead right now if I accidentally killed her."

"What the fuck is going on?"

"I guess that sounded rude," Rose agreed, "but she did choose you."

"Who chose me?" I demanded. "And for what?"

Rose blinked at me like *I* was the one who'd said something strange. She looked around, presumably for the rest of her followers, and asked, "Wait, she was supposed to get everything back, wasn't she? Shouldn't she know?"

"Know what?" I demanded, loud enough to shake the leaves on the ground.

Her dark eyes were back on me. "Yourself."

I paused and considered again that she might just be actually insane. Like, medically. Because none of this made sense and the more she talked, the less it made. I steadied myself with a breath and tried a different approach. "Look, I appreciate the blanket and the warmth, even though I feel like I'm getting heat stroke—"

"A symptom of hypothermia," Maia interrupted. "Should pass soon."

"—but I fell off a ravine in front of my soulmates and I'm sure they're worried. Can you let me go so I can let them know I didn't die?" I finished, trying to smile at Rose. "Please?"

She blinked again and then let out a loud burst of laughter. So did the other people around me. Between waves of laughter, she said, "Yeah, they're worried. You died in front of them. At least, they think so. But don't worry about that. We have other things to talk about."

She sobered herself and continued, "I'm talking about Persephone. You do remember all of that, right? She said you would." I thought for a moment about the cave, the river and the men I'd left behind.

Rose continued, "You were supposed to remember after the bathroom thing but nothing happened. We figured you'd need a bigger push, and luckily, I always have a back-up."

"You made me fall in the ravine?"

Rose's grin turned into a smirk. "One of the girls works at a local magic shop. She told your professor that the spell she was doing for you had to happen by a moving source of fresh water. The river was the obvious choice. The fall was... harder to guarantee, but everything worked out in the end, right?"

"How many of you are there?" I asked. The group hadn't been that big when I first met them in the barn at the Demeter event, but what were the chances they'd just have someone in the exact magic shop we needed for our soulmate stuff? "Did you guys do something to cause the SSS?"

"That double soulmate catastrophe?" I heard someone ask. One of the other girls. It sounded like Rebecca, and I craned my head, but couldn't see anything against the dark. With a huff, Rose pulled me into a sitting position and propped me against the nearest tree.

What looked like thirty girls in total, all dressed in those thick, black cloaks, stood in a circle around me. A campfire blazed just a few feet from us, adding to my warmth and a collection of magical items covered the earth, not dissimilar to what Lux had used earlier.

Rebecca eventually shook her head. "No, your bonds remain a mystery to us, as well."

"So why am I here?" I demanded. "If this isn't about the spell—"

"You're here," Rose interrupted, rolling her eyes, "because we wanted to welcome you to the Cult of Persephone—"

"And the Cult of Hekate!" Maia added.

"And the Cult of Hekate," Rose amended. I looked around at the full group of girls. I could not differentiate between the two. I wondered if they could. "And offer you a place among us. As one of our sisters."

I blinked at them. "You want to initiate me? I thought you hated me!"

It was Rose's turn to look surprised. "Hate you? Why would you think that?"

"Because you've tried to drown me!" I blurted out. "Multiple times."

"Sure," she conceded. "But not maliciously. That was for your benefit."

"I am…" I blew out a breath. "Very confused."

"Our Cult," Maia said when Rose didn't, "both of our Cults, are selective. They require more from members. An offering to the goddess, something more painful than anything else. It requires a remembering."

"Remembering what?" I asked.

"Your past, your present," Rose added.

"Life and death," Rebecca explained.

"Who you were in your first life," Maia continued as if uninterrupted, "and who you are now. It is only through death that the goddess collects the offering of the most difficult thing in the world. Τί δύσκολον;"

"Τὸ ἑαυτὸν γνῶναι," the Cult echoed back. The red necklace pulsed.

"What is difficult," I said and the words set my soul afire. "To know yourself."

"You passed the first test during that Cult of Demeter interest meeting," Rose said with a wry smile. "We offered everyone the drinks. Most were normal, but the pomegranate juice was enchanted. Though the regular members push the blueberry juice, the people who have compatible first lives will reach for the pomegranate juice."

"You belong with us, here, in the Cult of Persephone," Rebecca said and it felt right. A mystery Cult, hidden in plain sight within the Cult of Demeter. It seemed nothing about my place in life would ever be simple.

The first version of me, the one on the Greek island, had been a member of the Cult so much a part of me, my soul, maybe, had always belonged to this goddess. If my memories were to be trusted, and I thought they were, I'd spent thousands of years as the goddess' companion in the world beneath the mortal earth. For the first time, my soul sang, like two pieces of a puzzle fitting back together in my chest.

"And Hekate," Rose added, winking at the other girl. "So, what do you say? Ready to join us?"

"Right now?" I asked, looking around.

"A goddess doesn't wait very long for the decisions of mortals," Rebecca snarked and heard the words echo in my memory.

I shuddered. "What do I need to do?"

"Oh, it's easy," Rose said with a grin. From a hidden pocket of her cloak, she pulled out a metal flask. I couldn't see the contents, and after Lux's blood-flask, I was more than a little hesitant. "Don't look so scared, Wanaxa. It's pomegranate wine. All you have to do is drink it and swear your loyalty."

"That's it?" I asked, accepting the flask when she handed it to me. "How much?"

"Just a sip," she explained. "You can't drink too much or it doesn't count as consent."

I put the metal to my mouth. "I want to do this."

"Then drink," Rose said and the necklace glowed brighter in the dark forest.

I drank. It was a bitter, strangely sweet taste and it coated my mouth like sin. My skin buzzed, and I was pretty sure there was something magical about this mixture, too. When I swallowed, the residual pain in my body – things I hadn't even realized I was feeling, like my stiff neck and a scrape on my elbow – vanished.

I felt new, born again. Considering my drowning and the way I'd clawed my way back to this life, maybe I had been.

Rose nodded at me and I said aloud, "I swear my loyalty to Persephone and her Cult."

Why? I heard in my head. It wasn't Theo, but something ancient and unknown and yet so familiar.

"Because my soul knows her," I answered and they all hummed an agreement. "Because she is a girl and a queen, a lover of spring and the most dreaded creature in the darkness. She is the Goddess of Contradictions and she doesn't have to choose."

39

TO THE SUN, TO THE MOON

Something sparked inside of me and I gasped. The world trembled around us as power claimed my soul, burning like lightning and purring with pleasure.

"So it is true," Rose said with a grin that no longer seemed scary or threatening to me. Rather, it looked a little proud and a little sly. Like we were part of the same inside joke. "Now, we can move on to the next order of business."

She took the center seed from her necklace in hand and it pulsed three times. She cupped it, rubbing a finger on its glassy surface and said, "These are seeds from the same tree our goddess ate from when she was still Kore. Wearing them marks someone as the leader of a Cult of Persephone. If someone tried to wear them without the goddess' permission they would supposedly bring a curse down upon their family that would last for generations."

Rose's voice was a little quieter as she went on, "I was chosen by our goddess last year, but my time comes to an end soon with graduation in the spring. Without a leader, our Cult cannot run, understood?" I nodded. "So we did a ceremony, as is our tradition. I was put into a trance by our Hekate members and I spoke to the goddess."

"You spoke with the goddess?" I asked, wide-eyed.

She nodded. "And she told me I would catch our next leader *red-handed*."

"What does that mean?" I asked.

"At first, we assumed she'd be a thief of some kind. I work at a coffee shop, maybe she would try to steal someone's coffee? Or an item from the magic shop? But then, well, you appeared quite literally red-handed."

My arms were still bundled in the blanket, but Maia allowed me to pull them out as I looked at my hands. They were small and lightly tanned even as winter approached and dirty from the river, but when I looked closer I laughed slightly.

Some of the red from the pomegranate sacrifice had stained the thin skin of my cuticles, and I let my smile grow as I remembered the crumpled cup of pomegranate juice clutched in my fingers the first time we'd met.

Before I could say anything, Rose continued, "You remember our first meeting?"

I did. *Look at her hands, Rebecca.*

"Me?" I dropped my hands. "Why?"

Rose shrugged. "That was for the goddess to decide. She chose you. Now it is your turn."

"To decide if I want to lead?" I asked and everyone nodded.

"Power is in your blood, *Wanaxa*," Rose told me. "You just have to decide to take it."

She took off the necklace and offered it to me. It pulsed even faster, the seeds desperate for someone to wear them.

"I'm not ready," I told her and she frowned, but I continued before she could argue. "I can't choose. Not yet. Something tells me – I'm not ready. I don't know myself well enough, not yet."

She pulled the seeds back an inch. "What do you need from us in order to decide?"

"Time," I said. "Please."

"We cannot make you take the power," Rose said, slipping the necklace back over her head. "You have to take it for yourself. Power is nothing but useless energy if you have no desire to wield it."

"But we need to know soon," Maia added with a raised eyebrow. "Four weeks."

I swallowed. "I can do that."

"Then we have a plan," Rebecca said with a grin. "Do you have any questions for us?"

Though I knew it was futile, I asked, "Do you really not know anything about my soulmates?"

Rose managed to look apologetic when she shook her head. "After we met in that godsforsaken barn they threw us in, we asked around about you. You're a quiet girl, Wanaxa. The people we asked – an old roommate, an old professor, your Freshman RA – they all said the same thing. Good, kind, soft but unsure of her abilities."

She paused and Maia took over. "When we asked for more, people mentioned the rumors of your two soulmates. If it was meant to be a secret, you did a poor job. The whole university is talking about your demi-god and widower."

"Don't call them that," I said, automatically. "I just wish... I wish we had more answers."

"I'm sorry," Rose said. She looked at Maia. "We can't help you with that. All we can do is get you home safe. Maia? Has she healed enough to return?"

Maia took my temperature, pressing the back of her hand against my forehead. She nodded, seemingly satisfied with the result. "I think so. She might need help on the walk back. It'll take a while for her mind to heal enough for her soulmate abilities to return and her cell phone was destroyed in the fall."

"That's fine. I'll walk her back," Rose said, helping Maia unravel the blanket around me. The cold air brushed against my skin and I should have shivered from the temperature but didn't. Whatever magic was in the pomegranate wine still flowed in my blood and kept me warm. One of the nameless members handed me an armful of black fabric and I shrugged the cloak on over my head. It fit perfectly.

As we walked away from the circle of Cult members, everyone bid me softly goodbye. Somehow I'd been chosen by their goddess to lead them, but I didn't know if I could. I had my memories now, maybe. I had died, giving my sacrifice to our goddess, but I was still a mystery even to myself.

Rose and I walked for less than an hour. It was dark, but her necklace lit the way and I trusted her not to get us lost. Her footsteps were sure and she never hesitated on a turn or hill. She led me and I allowed her to. I understood why she was chosen. Other than her necklace, only the moon lit our way. We didn't say anything on our walk, focusing on the destination ahead, but worry began to creep into my thoughts at the prospect of returning to Theo and Alexander.

Soon enough, we reached the line between the forest and the campus, the only thing separating the wilderness from civilization. Street lamps had been lit on campus, creating shadows and revealing to me the small circle of people huddled together outside our classroom building, desperate voices arguing about what they should do. Lux's voice cut through them all, wavering as she spoke to someone on the phone.

"That's them," I said to Rose, nodding my head in their direction. "I should go."

"You should," she agreed. "But remember, we need an answer in four weeks."

"A decision," I repeated. "I'll let you know."

She retreated into the woods, her dark cloak blurring into the shadows of the overarching trees. Over her shoulder, she called to me, "Oh, and Wanaxa? In case it wasn't obvious, you're part of a mystery Cult now. Don't tell them who you were really with. Not yet. Say it was hikers who found you."

She gave me no time to ask any questions about that before vanishing into the dark, the only thing left to do now was face my soulmates. I did not allow myself a moment to pause, because I knew that if I hesitated, I would stand frozen here all night. Instead, I marched towards the group, making sure that my footsteps were loud and my voice carried when I greeted them.

They turned to look at me, a mixture of emotions on every-one's faces. Our professor looked confused, surprised. Eliza's eyebrows raised nearly to her hairline and Tori's mouth gaped.

Relief poured across Alexander's face, tears welling in his eyes even as he moved towards me with his arms wide open. He pulled me to him and the wetness of his eyes froze against the crook of my neck. I wrapped my arms around him, holding him just as tight, reveling in the warmth of his dry clothes.

Though it was difficult to move in his embrace, I lifted my head just enough to see over his shoulder. Theo, like his plat, stared at me as if I was a ghost. He reached out a trembling hand to his plat and Tori, in an uncharacteristically soft gesture, kissed the back of it, calming him.

"You're alive," he said, the first to break the silence. He took a stumbling step forward and then jerked himself back, blinking away the tears in his eyes that sparkled like gemstones. I heard nothing in my mind. "How are you—" He swallowed, shaking his head. "You fell. Your mind was... gone. Empty. Like Margot. How are you alive?"

"When I fell into the river, a group of hikers helped me out. They had some extra clothes including this…" I thought about it for a moment, this didn't look like anything except a cloak belonging to a mystery Cult member. I tried anyway, "Coat."

"You floated down the river. You," he started, pausing to

take a breath, a wet sound, just on the verge of tears, and Alexander sighed contentedly into my skin. Theo continued, shaking his curls. "You hit the water and your mind just... emptied. We didn't see you come up. I thought you—" He paused again. "Did you *swim?*"

"I did. Down the river. There was a bank that some girls were camping at. I think they were Cult of Artemis, enjoying the forest before the first snow arrives."

"How are you dry?" Eliza asked, frowning at my hair.

"Sat by the fire," I answered. Theo still looked upset, horrified, like he was grieving, but I could tell Alexander had no intention of letting me go. So instead of moving to him on my own, I murmured into Alexander's ear, "Can he hold us both?"

"Oh gods," Alexander said, lifting his head enough to look me in the eye. He moved so that he had an arm around only half of my body, cheek pressing into the top of my head, and left the other half open for Theo to fit in. "Of course, he can. Come here, Theodore."

Theo, apparently overwhelmed with his own relief, said nothing about the use of his full name. In two long steps, he had pulled us both into his chest, stumbling with the force of it. I didn't look to see Tori's face, but I was certain she wasn't enjoying the flood of emotion coming from him.

"Well," our Professor said to us all as she made to leave. "I'll call the police back and let them know you're okay. I trust you'll take care of Vanessa – make sure she eats and stays warm. I have to get home to my sister's kids. I'll see you all in class." She paused, face cracking as she took me in. Quickly, she squeezed my shoulder, her exhale revealing her relief. "I am so glad you're okay."

Once she was out of sight, Eliza moved hesitantly to her plat's side. "Alexander, what do you need?"

"If I could... Vanessa, could we go back to your place? I'm not... I'm not ready to say goodnight yet." His hands tightened around me and I understood the feeling, I'd almost lost them both. Again.

"Yeah, that's fine. Ronan won't be home tonight anyway." Theo tensed and started to pull away but I held on tighter. "You too, Theo."

He shook his head. "I can't. I took the bus today and they stop running soon."

"I can drive you home," Alexander said, voice low enough that only we could hear him, to put Theo at ease. "Do you want to—"

"Yes," Theo answered. "I – yes."

"Great," Tori said, readjusting her backpack on her shoulders. "Well, I'm heading back to the Cult house. The near-death experience ruined my buzz, and I like my buzzes pure. Blondie, want to walk back that way with me?"

Eliza rolled her eyes in the most dignified way. "Sure."

They left the three of us under the flickering light of a streetlamp and we stayed still for a few minutes more as Theo's panic began to edge into something less intense, more of a fizzing worry under his skin. Then I pulled away to hold their hands and start down the path toward my apartment. "Come on. I'm still cold."

Theo flinched like I'd struck him and Alexander did too, feeling his pain as Theo let go of my hand to pull a red flannel from his backpack and drape it around my shoulders.

The walk home was surprisingly quiet, the leaves barely rustled and the birds didn't caw. Only Theo's occasional curses filled the air, low and rough as he attempted to fight off his adrenaline crash. I murmured back small bits of comfort, trying to keep him upright and Alexander still buzzed with energy, saying nothing.

By the grace of Hermes, the bump in my pocket turned out to be the still-wet fabric of my lanyard and the bronze key for my apartment. I sighed in relief as I let them in, warmth rushing over me as we moved across the threshold.

Alexander turned on the television, a meaningless romantic comedy, and the heating on high. "I can't cook, but if you wanted, my nutritionist could bring us—"

"I'll cook," Theo said, moving to the kitchen. There was some clanking of cabinets as he figured out where things were, but I couldn't see what he was pulling out. "Just make sure she's warm enough."

Alexander placed his warm hands on my shoulders and looked into my eyes with a deep earnestness that tugged at my heart. "Do you want to stay in your, uh, coat?"

I shook my head, not really knowing what the procedure was for post-drowning comfort. For me or for them. "Not really. I just want to get the sand and dirt out of my hair. Can I take a shower?"

"Why are you asking me?" Alexander asked, frowning. "You're in charge."

Thinking about the offer from Rose, I smiled tightly at him. "Right."

The shower felt like it was burning my skin after the cold night air, but I was whole and unscathed, my bruises faded and my scrapes cleared. I covered up as much skin as I could when I tugged on some comfy clothes. There was no way I could explain how I'd healed so quickly, and I wasn't yet sure what or how much to tell them.

Theo's flannel caught my eye from where it sat crumpled up in the hamper and, for a moment, I stood and stared, realizing why it looked so familiar.

It was the same one Theo had given Alexander the night of the party and I wasn't sure if I loved or hated it, but I crossed the room to retrieve it anyway. I took off my sweatshirt and put the flannel on, letting the remnants of Theo's comforting scent wrap itself around me and then felt my body jolt as my mind sank effortlessly into his.

I gripped the bathroom counter and closed my eyes, breathing deeply to control the wave of nausea from the intense psychic connection. I saw through eyes that weren't my own.

His hands shook as he poured coffee into two mugs and the liquid spilled on the countertop. Grief crept up his throat, wild and untamable and leaving him confused because *she was fine.* A white mug of tea sat alone on the edge of the granite and Alexander's voice carried over, the words resounding in my head at the same time they hit his ears.

"Theo?" Alexander asked, reaching out to place a hand on Theo's shoulder. "Hey, what's wrong?"

"Nothing," Theo gasped out, waving a hand as if brushing Alexander off, but he was in the same position as me, head pressed to the coolness of the counter and trying to control his panic. "I'm fine. I'm *fine—*"

Alexander grabbed him by the shoulders and pulled him up. Theo's hands steadied themselves on Alexander's arms and his head sank down, pressing against his collarbone. "Theodore, what's wrong?"

"She died," Theo shook between wide mouthfuls of air, hyperventilating as his eyes closed and skin turned pale. My lungs matched his and stars twinkled at the edges of my vision. "She was dead and you were going to throw yourself off the fucking cliff too—"

My heart stuttered in my chest.

"She can't swim," Alexander said in a low voice. "I was jumping in to save her—"

"I almost lost you too!" Theo snapped, immediately flinching back from the strength of the words. "And it was so selfish of me, I watched her die – *we* watched her die and you were readying to jump into that damn river, and I could practically imagine you hitting your head and dying and your thoughts going silent too, and all I could think was *how many soulmates do I have to lose?*"

"You're not going to lose either of us—"

"Of course I am!" Theo bit back, voice even louder. He jerked himself back, but Alexander kept his grip on his shoulders. Keeping him steady. "I have a week until Detroit. Until I lose you both—"

"Theo, please," Alexander tried again. "You have to calm down—"

"Calm down?" Theo laughed hollowly and I was caught in the tidal wave of his emotions, gasping and shaking as I tried to pull back. "I'm a fucking cosmic joke, Alexander. The gods are sitting on Olympus, laughing at me, because I can't manage to keep my soulmates alive, let alone happy—"

"We're happy," Alexander said, but neither of us believed him. "Well, this whole situation sucks, but neither of us are unhappy with you. We're unhappy with my mother, with the whole split part. None of this is your fault!"

Theo's next laugh was almost a sob. "That's what Margot used to say. *This isn't your fault.* Like I don't know how much easier this would be for everyone if I wasn't involved. You and Vanessa? You make sense. You're both brilliant and happy and so sincere about everything. Gods, if you knew how often I prayed that I could wake up and you two could just be happy together, without me—"

Alexander grabbed him by the jaw and slotted their mouths together in a clumsy, earnest attempt at a kiss. I felt their teeth click together in the roughness of the movement and something inside of me twisted in envy. They pulled back and looked at each other for a minute, eyes and minds speaking volumes in a way that was completely separate from me and what we meant to each other, like I didn't speak their language anymore.

You belong with us, Alexander thought. *You belong here. Stay.* I wanted to respond, but I could only think in his thoughts. Again and again. *Stay. Stay. Stay.*

Then Theo yanked Alexander back toward him, leading the kiss into something more graceful. More powerful. Like that moment in a movie, where it all makes sense and the main characters will live happily ever after from this moment on.

Everything that I'd always wanted.

The first kiss after the one to confirm a soulmate bond was important. It meant 'I don't just like you because I have to' and 'I'm glad we met and you're in my life', and typically, it meant 'I love you'. In the darkness of the library, storms and sirens screaming outside, Alexander had kissed me. I thought that was what he had meant. That he'd chosen me. But now, as he fell into Theo with white-knuckled hands and desperation in his veins, utterly helpless and totally at peace, I knew I was wrong.

This was all theirs, as it was always meant to be. It hurt like drowning, like freezing, but it's not anything I didn't already know. For them, I was a crutch they no longer needed. A catalyst for their perfect The End moment.

Suddenly, a week seemed like much too much time to wait to cure them of me.

All that came out was a single thought, *Oh.*

Theo pulled away from Alexander just an inch. *Vanessa?*

I wiped my eyes with my hands, not sure when I'd begun crying and when I'd found my own thoughts enough to not be lost in him. In them. My heart was breaking and the shards of it ripped into my soul. I tried to block it all out. They deserved this happiness, this moment, and each other, but Theo's eyes flashed open wide as he threw himself away from a very confused Alexander.

Vanessa, oh my gods, I'm so sorry—

I'm not angry, I thought at the same moment Alexander spoke.

"Theo?" Alexander swallowed, worry bright in his eyes and lips still swollen and well-kissed.

Theo's thoughts span too fast for me to follow. "It's Vanessa—"

I'm not angry, I repeated. I couldn't continue as their crutch, not now, not when the water of the river and the edge of the cliff and all my lives before lived so fresh in my mind. *But I need you to leave. Both of you.*

"Is something wrong?" Alexander asked, turning to look toward the stairs that would take him to me.

"She's in my head," Theo said, *Let me explain, please—*

I don't need you to explain, I responded. *I just need you to leave. Please.*

"She, what? Saw us?" Alexander touched his mouth with his fingers, and we watched them tremble.

"I think she saw everything."

"That's not how telepathy works," Alexander murmured to himself. "Is she angry?"

"No," Theo responded. "She wants us to leave."

I'm going to bed, I said, leaving the bathroom and going into my bedroom, locking the door behind me as exhaustion finally sank into my bones.

"Vanessa!" Theo said out loud and I sent him a wordless plea. I just needed to be alone.

My bed cradled me and the darkness was welcome as I pulled the blanket over my head. I wanted to cry, but not yet. I buried my face in my arms, *Please.*

Theo didn't respond, instead cutting me off from his thoughts. I heard a muted conversation below me and the sound of the front door closing as I shrugged off Theo's shirt and laid it down next to me before finally allowing the tears to come.

A part of me wanted to laugh at the way history repeated itself. Their kiss, a river, a Chthonic goddess. In thousands of years nothing had changed and in the end, the result was always the same.

I was alone and the reason for our bond was something of a holy mystery.

PIERCED

I showed up late to work the next day. I'd forgotten to set my alarm after crying until I'd fallen asleep and then the downtown buses were slow in the fresh snow. With the baleful winds, the world pulled me back every time I tried to step forward.

I was never late. It made my skin itchy and my palms sweaty. My mother liked to joke that I was even early for my birth by almost a month. Ronan knew this. Or, at least, he should. He'd sat through my mother's well-intentioned birthing stories more than once, nodding along politely and grimacing at all the right parts.

Still, when I arrived he shot me a dirty look and pointed to the sign beside the door as he got up from my seat at the reception desk. It advertised today's piercing special, which explained the group of college freshmen in the lobby, their giggles filling the space like bubbles.

"Why are you late?" he demanded as I sat down to check one of the girls in. She passed me the exact amount of drachmae and her ID and I tried to shove down my irritation as she continued snickering with her friends.

"Bad night of sleep," I said with a shrug, not wanting to worry him. He hadn't messaged me yesterday to ask how the spell had gone, hadn't even checked-in when the bond between us had likely fallen silent. I could tell he'd grown tired of dealing with all of this, and honestly, I couldn't blame him. I was tired too. Our relationship going back to normal was the light at the end of this horrible soulmate tunnel. "I'm sorry."

He looked away. "It's fine. I need to help Sam prep the equipment." He left the lobby through the door to the studio and though it wasn't dramatic, the slam of the door seemed to reverberate in my head.

The group of girls took forever to check in and my shaking hands weren't helping. Their perfume was warm and sweet and smelled too much like *pancakes for dinner*. But eventually, with Sam's needle skills, they were all happily stabbed in various places. I was pretty sure they were all Cult of Aphrodite and the thought reminded me of Alexander, making me frown as they left.

I got up to refill the coffee now that the girls had cleared out. *Great goddess, how much sugar did they need?* The bell rang at the door behind me as I was in the middle of counting scoops, it smelled heavenly, with a Golden Rings design stamped on the side of the brown bag. I called over my shoulder, "I'll be with you in a minute! Can you pull your ID out so I can check it?"

"I'm not here to get anything," Theo's voice came from behind me.

I didn't drop the bag of coffee, but *Hades* if I hadn't come close. I tensed up and knew he could probably see it. I set the bag down and rolled the end up tightly as I mentally rehearsed what I was going to say. My shield slotted into place without a thought.

I turned around, settling on, "What can I help you with?" Reluctantly, I brought my gaze to his face.

Unfortunately, he was just as beautiful as always. The light snow of the November storms still dusted the shoulders of his jacket and the snowflakes melted as the question hovered between us. His eyes were dark and there was no doubt that I was the reason.

"Sam called me," he answered, lifting one shoulder in a nonchalant movement. He paused, grinding his jaw, and continued, "Asked me to come in. I don't know what you can help me with."

I nodded stiffly. "He'll be out in a few minutes. Coffee?"

Our minds shuddered as one and we were both remembering the first time we met. It seemed like years ago and also just like yesterday. The girl that stood in this spot was now a stranger to me, young and naive and hopeful. Would I recognize her now if I ran into her on the street? Or vice versa?

"Yeah," he answered. "Coffee."

The pot gurgled behind me and coffee poured into the glass container. "Have a seat. Sam is just finishing clean-up from the piercing event."

Theo nodded and sat down as I made up his coffee. Black, not completely filling the cup, and I prayed my hand wouldn't shake as I handed it to him. "Here you go."

He took it but reached his other hand out to take my arm in his hand. It wasn't rough in any way, his calloused hands soft against my skin, but I flinched away from the buzz of our bond as he murmured my name. Sam and Ronan walked out of the studio, cutting through the odd tension, and Theo's mouth closed, saying nothing else.

"Sam," he said. "What's up?"

Sam looked between the two of us before speaking, taking note of our dark eyes, my rumpled appearance and the tight clench of Theo's jaw. "Are you two alright?"

"Fine," I answered with a shrug and Ronan's mouth pulled down. "We're fine."

"Yeah," Theo echoed. "Just fine."

Sam's brows were still furrowed, but he nodded, walking from the doorway to sit on the couch opposite Theo. More delicately, Ronan sat next to him and I remained stiffly standing as Sam asked, "Do you remember our last conversation?"

It sounded vaguely threatening, but Theo nodded in response. "Sure. You asked me to see if I knew anyone from the Cult of Apollo who would be interested in working for you or being your apprentice."

"And?" Ronan asked, leaning forward.

"I asked around," Theo answered, frowning at them both and leaning back into the dark leather of the couch, body tight, giving off the image of a tense panther. "But no one was interested. Sorry. I promise I did ask."

Sam sighed but didn't look surprised.

"You don't have to be sorry," I said to Theo, and he blinked up at me. "You tried your best."

"My best," he echoed back in that same distant way as before. "Right."

"Actually," Sam said eagerly as he leaned forward like a mirror of Ronan. "I have an offer for you. I know you said that no one wanted to do this job, but have you considered doing it yourself?"

"Samuel," Ronan said, smacking his arm lightly, "that sounds bad."

"Right, I'm not very good with words," Sam admitted and shrugged. "What I meant was, I want you to work for me."

"Uh," Theo answered eloquently. "I'm confused."

"Why?" Ronan asked, tilting his head to the side.

"I haven't graduated," Theo tried.

"But next semester, right?" Sam asked. "That's fine. You can start training now."

"Right," Theo said slowly, "but I don't know anything about tattooing. I'm a painter."

"Exactly," Sam agreed. "I do line work. I'm looking for someone with a more artistic, painterly aesthetic. I can teach you about tattooing. But I already know you're a great artist." He paused. "We went to the Galatas gallery a few weeks ago. Your painting of Margot? It's beautiful. Looks just like her."

I had forgotten that Sam knew her. Small world.

Theo answered, "Thank you. But this was her thing and—" He shot me a look. "I'm not sure what Vanessa's told you about all of this, but we plan on curing this split bond in a week. I wouldn't want to make it awkward for her."

"We're not offering a job to Vanessa," Ronan answered. "We're offering it to you."

That, for some reason, rubbed me the wrong way and Theo grimaced too. "You're her family. I couldn't – I *won't* do that to her. It would be like if she took a job with my sister or something. I'm going to politely decline your offer. But thank you. I mean it."

"Now, hold on," Sam said, frowning deeply. "I'm gonna say something you both might not agree with, but I think it needs to be said. You can't make your life choices based on your soulmate."

"It's not about the soulmate thing," Theo said, shaking his head. "It's about space to heal."

"You're throwing away a great job opportunity," Sam argued, sitting up straighter but looking no less serious as his deep-set eyes stared us all down. "I love Ronan of course, but if I thought he was choosing to stay at the Laurel Leaf for me instead of making a career choice that makes sense for him, I wouldn't let him."

"You think Ronan dreamed about running the finances of a small business?" I asked him and immediately regretted the sarcastic bite of the words, but it didn't change the fact that I was upset. They were basically saying *fuck Vanessa*.

Ronan's blue eyes looked unimpressed. "I didn't know what I wanted to do."

"Exactly," Theo said. "I just think she means that being around your soulmate was a good incentive to use your skills to help him... and being around an ex-soulmate would be the opposite for us."

"Margot was the one who did your Ceremony, right?" Sam asked Theo, who nodded. "You were probably just about twenty-one at the time, but she was my age, so a few years older. I'm the only one of us here who waited until I graduated and knew who I was by myself before looking for my soulmate. I had the time to put myself first. So just because you've got a soulmate for now, doesn't mean you shouldn't do the same. Theo, you should take this job."

"Why?"

"Because you won't have a soulmate in a week," Sam responded and I flinched. "You'll need something to throw yourself into. It was painting before, but you've already accomplished what most artists want to: you've sold your work to a great collection and did something meaningful with your grief. But it's time to move on."

"From painting or from me?" I demanded.

Sam's gaze was level but Ronan rolled his eyes. "Both, Vanessa."

It's almost as if he'd slapped me. "You don't think it'll affect business if I can't look at your new artist?" I asked, lip curling with anger and Theo paled a little but I continued, "If I can't even say his name to a customer without it being physically painful?"

Ronan snorted. "You're being dramatic."

"Theo," I said, turning to my soulmate. "Did it hurt yesterday when our bond stopped?"

"Yeah," he answered, face slack with the memory. "It hurt."

"Do you think it'll hurt when all of us are snipped away from each other?" I snapped.

"Yeah," he answered, looking anywhere but at me, mouth tight.

"Oh, don't pretend you care about this business—"

"Ronan," Sam said in warning.

"What's that supposed to mean?" I asked, hands curled on my hips to stop them from shaking. Power flickered in my chest, throbbing in time to my anger like red seeds on a necklace.

Ronan leaned back even more, looking casual and not at all like we're in the middle of a disagreement. It pissed me off even more. "You've been so out of it for the last few months, with all this nonsense—"

"Nonsense?" I demanded, voice raising and Sam's eyebrows lifted. I never raised my voice.

"—and, even today, you were late because of it—"

"For the first and only time!" I snapped. "Yesterday sucked! I forgot to set my alarm—"

"Oh, what?" Ronan said sarcastically and Sam attempted to rein him in. "Did you fall even more in love with two handsome men, and man, your soul is just so sad that everyone loves and takes care of poor, sweet Vanessa—"

"I died!" I yelled at him. He stopped talking. Everyone stopped talking. "I fell off a fucking cliff in the middle of winter and I can't swim! I drowned and you weren't there! You know what? Fuck you, Ronan. I quit." I moved to grab my purse from the desk and snagged my coat from the back of the chair, too.

Theo's eyes were wide and his chest was still like he'd taken his last breath when I screamed those words, but he reached out to grab my forearm again and looked me up and down, terrified. "I knew it. It was just like with Margot…" He trailed off, but shook his head. "How?"

I yanked my arm away. "What does it matter? In a week—"

"*Vanessa*," he snapped for the first time ever, sending a dark look in my direction. "You died. How—"

"Vanessa," Sam stood up and made his way over to me. He placed his hands on my cheeks and tilted my face, checking me for scrapes and bruises while Ronan stayed frozen in his spot on the couch. "Are you okay? Are you in pain?"

"No," Ronan said at last, "she's not."

"Just because I let you feel some of what I go through," I snapped at him. "Doesn't mean you know what it's like for me. You have no idea what this—" I cut myself off, shaking my head. The thought of anyone's hands on me made me shake with sickness. A current of something like electricity flowed across my skin and both Theo and Sam jerked back as the scent of pomegranates filled the air.

"What in Hades—" Theo stared down at his arm and the hair that was standing up.

The power in my chest pulsed at the name.

"I'm leaving," I told the room. "Don't follow me."

Chimes rang as I left and none of them followed, watching silently as I walked away. I had no idea where I was going, no plan except *escape.* Eventually, whatever bravery it took to say those things, to react that way, receded and left me feeling even more alone, hollow, than before.

I had no job. No plat. And, in a week, no soulmates.

So I did the only thing I could think of.

I called my mother.

41

FRUITS OF GAIA

The drive from Traverse City to Golden Valley's campus was three hours. Demetria Reyes did it in two and a half. She arrived at my apartment with her usual air of concern and worry, told me to put my coat and gloves on and led me outside.

When I first moved onto campus during my freshman year, she and my dad explored campus more than I did. My mom, being the daughter of an orchard owner and a proud Cult of Demeter member, picked the Arboretum as her favorite place and I couldn't help but relax in the space that was so reminiscent of home.

It was bitterly cold, the ground frozen and branches bare. As we walked the dirt path leading to the cherry orchard, my mother began to speak without turning to me, leaving me with only her profile to study. Her nose was small, like mine, but her face slimmer. Her eyes were the same, wide and brown, surrounded by dark lashes.

"Tell me about them," she said to me. So I did.

I told her about Alexander, his perfect face and his excitement for everything. How fast he could swim. How he relaxed when his plat walked into the room. I told her that he was half-god, half-human, but the best of them both.

Then I told her about Theo, about his gentleness and his talent with a paintbrush. He was steady and broken in some ways that I was only just beginning to understand. We were a mess of a trio, honestly, with all our history creating a labyrinth of obstacles. *Death*, I thought to myself, thankful to have my thoughts alone for the moment, *was a constant for all of us*. I opened my mouth to tell my mom all about it, the fall and the goddess and the dying, but I couldn't. Not when it was still so alive in my mind. Not when they didn't know.

"When did you fall in love with each of them?" My mother asked as we stepped into the section dedicated to cherry trees. Her eyes sparkled at the sight of them, though they are gray and empty of sweet fruit.

"Mom—" I objected, and she pulled me over to a bench. Sparrows, the last of the season, jumped around on the tree closest to us, tweeting in urgency. The sky was gray and swelling with the promise of more snow.

"You aren't fooling anyone," she interrupted me, rolling her eyes and nudging me with her shoulder. I bounced in the opposite direction but leaned back into her, she was warm and smelled like home. "You talk about them like they hung the stars."

"Can you even be in love with two people?" I wondered.

She shrugged, "They're your soulmates. Why not?"

"Mistakenly," I said.

"Oh, honey," she said, wrapping her arm around me. "Love is never a mistake."

"This is," I said, swallowing. "I was so stupid. I knew this couldn't end well. I knew someone would have to choose and someone would be left out." I blew out a puff of air. "I just didn't think it would be me."

"I'm sorry," she answered, the point of her chin digging into my head as she pulled me close. "But you do love them?"

"Of course," I admitted, the words low enough so only we could hear, though the sparrows looked over at us, eager for gossip. The admission stung across my bonds like a curse. "But it doesn't matter. Mom, they had *the* kiss. They care about each other more than they care about me."

"I think you're wrong," she said, "but they're fools if they don't love you."

"They make sense," I told her, and I almost wished I was lying. "Together, I mean. They would work without me. I can see how they're soulmates. They're opposites that just…" I sighed, thinking back. "Complement each other."

"You don't have to be opposites to make sense," she corrected with a soft smile. "Love isn't about being perfect on paper. It's about working with each other when real life happens. Take me and your father, we aren't opposites. Do you think you make sense with them? If your soul was intertwined with only one, would it work?"

I thought about how my life with Alexander would be, if it were just me and him. We'd have met in class. I would have got the results, we would have dated for a while, going to fancy restaurants. He'd take me to meet his father in a non-swimming-related context and he'd have held my hand the entire time. We'd make plans to move in with each other right away and in just a few months, a marriage proposal would have come.

I'd be at every practice, he'd sit with me for hours and help me figure out which cult I wanted to be in. Eventually I would join his mother's and then we'd move into a giant house with marble countertops. We'd be happy and in love. We'd make sense.

I considered my life with Theo. We'd meet at the tattoo shop and he would have accepted Sam's job offer. He'd bring me tea every morning and we'd go to art shows to get to know each other. We'd move into a shitty little apartment somewhere on the East Side of the Golden Valley. I'd deal with dinner with Tori and enjoy hanging out with Tamara. Eventually, I'd find my way to Cult of Demeter, following in my mother's footsteps, and money would be tight, but we'd be happy and in love. We'd make sense, too.

"Yeah," I said with a sigh, "it would."

"So, if you had to choose, you couldn't?" she asked.

The question was completely innocuous but it brought back the memories of where this had all begun. Jumping from a Greek cliff and my first meeting with the Goddess of the Underworld. If I knew myself at all, I knew I'd rather piss off the Dread Queen than pick between the golden demi-god and the dark-eyed artist.

"I've tried," I answered her and my voice shook. "I've begged and begged that my heart could just pick. But I can't."

"Oh, honey," she said, "you seem so sad. What is it?"

"Everything," I hiccuped as my chest seized with a sob.

"You know being vague doesn't help," she said as she rubbed soothing circles into my back and shook her head. "Tell me, exactly, what are you afraid of? The cure? Them staying together after the cure? Being alone?" She paused. "You aren't alone, you know that, right? You and Ronan will be fine. He's your soulmate, too."

I swallowed, turning my face into her shoulder and hoping I wouldn't cry. "I don't know, Mom. We've never yelled at each other before."

"He won't stay mad forever, but don't deflect – you didn't answer my question."

"I don't know what I'm afraid of," I sighed. "I guess... being inconsequential. Being forgotten." I shook my head. "I want, more than anything, for them to be happy. It just sucks to know that they don't need me for that."

"Have you said this to them?" she asked. "From what you've told me about them, Alexander sounds like he may be too focussed on himself – not in a bad way, but he's had to rethink his entire life because of this, especially with his mother. And Theo probably blames himself." She smiled cleverly. "He seems the self-sacrificing type."

"He is," I agreed, thinking about his marriage to Margarita before and about his immediate belief that he was the Extra. "I haven't really talked to them." The wind blew through the branches, whistling around and it sounded like the voice of another, ancient mother. "But I will. I promise."

"Good," my mother said with a nod.

We were quiet for a while and then she asked, "I wasn't going to mention it, but maybe I should with all of this going on. New paperwork was delivered at home for you – Cult of Demeter ID. Why didn't you tell me you were joining, sweetheart?"

I winced. "It's complicated, Mom."

"How can it be complicated?" she asked, laughing. "It's just joining a cult, unless you joined one of those insider mystery cults. Lots of Cults have them—" She cut herself off when I looked pointedly away and the wind grew quiet. "Oh, *Demeter*, really? You've never been able to pick the easy road."

I laughed then, because she was right about that, and she joined in.

"You know, only girls with a strong sense of self and a good relationship with their mother can join the Cult of Persephone. That must mean I did an okay job."

I rolled my eyes. "Mom—"

"Oh, shush," she said with a grin. "Let a mother be proud."

42

THE SISTER OF THE EARTH

At three o'clock on Saturday, I stood waiting with my suitcase for Alexander to pick me up. Last night, he'd emailed us our tickets and hotel reservations for the Aphrodite event. The text conversation between the three of us had been stilted and awkward, but we decided he'd pick up Theo first and then scoop me from campus.

Tapping my foot, I checked the charge on my phone again and re-read the text from Rose that had been waiting on the new phone I'd found sitting in a box in my apartment. *You're welcome. Four weeks, Wanaxa. Don't forget no one can tell you what to do. The choice will always be yours.*

I sighed. I was not looking forward to a three hour drive with them without any escape. I clutched my headphones in my hands like they were a lifeline. The only way I was getting through this was with my music deafening enough to drown out the sound of the empty space.

With the first-snow seal broken, the sky seemed to be addicted to dropping it all over the state. The slushy, gray stuff had already bled through my boots to wet my now-wet socks and a few more drops splashed onto my kneesocks as Alexander pulled up.

He stopped the car and got out to help me load the suitcase into the trunk. Theo opened the passenger door and started to step out and I raised a brow. "What are you doing?"

"Getting out," he answered. "You can take the front seat."

"I'm sitting in the back." I waved him off, already moving to the back door. "You can stay."

"Fine," he said shortly, closing the door again.

Alexander, wordless, slid back into the driver's side. I took one deep breath as I pulled open the door. Three hours. I could do this. The quiet cords of *Narcissus and the Pool Boys* slipped out of the speakers as I slid inside. "Oh, Theo's controlling the radio?"

Alexander shrugged, but his hands tightened on the wheel. "I don't care what we listen to. I like all kinds of music." He paused and glanced at me in the rearview. "If you don't like it, you can—"

I held up my white headphones. "No, I'm all set."

"Then why ask?" Theo said through gritted teeth.

I popped them in my ears. "Just curious. It's cute you're sharing playlists."

Theo turned to me slightly as I searched through my music. "I thought you weren't the jealous type?"

I ignored him, irritation burning in my stomach as I turned my music up to full volume and closed my eyes, more feeling than hearing him snort at my non-response. I leaned against the window, hoping to nap before we arrived. Two hours and fifty-nine minutes. I knew I would feel each one.

One hour and three minutes into the drive, my phone screen turned black and my music stopped. *Great,* I sighed, about to say something when the boys' conversation filtered back to me and I hesitated. For a few seconds, I let their voices wash over me without any consequences.

"—your art," Alexander was saying. "Went with Eliza to the Galatas gallery."

"Oh, thank you," Theo responded, sounding surprised and a little proud.

"Vanessa mentioned you were selling it?" Alexander said.

"I got an offer. But I'm not ready to let go of it yet."

"Still," Alexander said, taking an exit and grinning at Theo whose own smile was softer, less enthusiastic, but just as beautiful. "An offer is great. Was it a private collection or a business? Or something else? I'm not sure how the art market works."

"A private collection," Theo answered. "The Galatas family wants it for their summer home."

"Oh, really? That's so cool. The Galatas clan are regular customers of my family's business." He patted the dashboard of his car. "Their monthly subscription to our catalog paid for this baby."

"I think I'll probably be in the market soon."

Alexander glanced at him. "Oh yeah? Why's that?"

"Selling my motorcycle," Theo answered. "Riding was kind of Margot's thing and it's only fun if you have someone to do it with. And I don't really imagine–" He coughed, cutting himself off. "My future partner riding, you know?"

"Yeah," Alexander answered, his voice lower. "I know."

I didn't want to hear anymore. They both jumped when I cleared my throat and sat up straight. I dangled my phone and headphones in my hand. "They died. I guess I didn't charge it right. Weird."

Theo swallowed. "Yeah, weird."

"Technology tends to crash around me," Alexander admitted. "Hephaestus doesn't like me much. Or any bastard of his wife's, really."

No one said anything more and Theo eventually reached out and turned the music up. It was something plucky and hopeful and I wanted to throw the CD out of the window. Ten more minutes passed and Alexander turned the music back off. I would have laughed if it didn't spell trouble.

Alexander's words came out so fast that they became impenetrable. "Okay, so what we're not going to do is be weird about this. We kissed again! It was stupid to do at that moment, but it did happen! Who cares? So, Vanessa, you're going to stop giving us the silent treatment. And, Theo, you're going to stop pouting every time she talks to you. And break!"

I crossed my arms over my chest and glared out the window. In the seat in front of me, Theo huffed an angry noise. The car was quiet as we both pouted. Alexander's hands wrapped around the wheel in a vicious grip and his fingers drummed a beat not nearly as complicated and perfect as Theo's when he did it.

Neither of us gave in and Alexander's shoulders slumped, his eyes losing their natural sparkle. I sighed and uncrossed my arms, jumping when there was something like a knock on my mental shield. Curious, I dropped it enough to hear Theo think, *Why does it feel like we just kicked a puppy?*

Because we kind of did, I thought back. *I just want to pat his head.*

And tell him he's a good boy?

I snorted out loud, because he wasn't entirely wrong. Alexander looked at me in the mirror, surprised, but Theo just looked smug, proud of the fact that he made me break first. The moment I thought it, one corner of his mouth lifted even higher and I kicked the back of his chair until he laughed, filling the car with the sound. Without permission, I smiled too.

Alexander's eyes narrowed. "Are you doing the mind thing?"

"Yeah," Theo said. "We are."

I expected Alexander to make a comment about how unfair

it was that he couldn't hear us, but his grin was brighter than either of ours. "Good," he said. "As long as you're talking, I don't care how you do it."

"I'm sorry I asked you guys to leave that night." My words were soft. Theo turned around to look at me, and I stared back out the window, hoping my cheeks weren't as red as I thought they were. "It was unfair to you both."

"It's okay," Theo responded, quiet enough that if I closed my eyes, he could have been speaking in my mind.

"I just needed some time alone," I continued, watching the empty fields blur across my window, "to process."

"Hey," Theo answered, tentative as he reached behind the seat to touch my knee, just the same as Alexander was doing for him. It made me want more than I should. "Vanessa, that's okay. You can have space. I just wish... that you had told us what happened."

Just as tentatively, I placed my hand over his. "I wish I had, too." With my other hand, I tapped my temple, looking back to him with an attempt at a smile. "Words can just, you know, get stuck up here."

"Yeah," he said, smiling back. My chest was warm. "I know."

A moment of quiet, small but comfortable. Purposefully, I looked from Theo to Alexander, who was watching and pretending he wasn't. Theo followed my eyes, smile widening into a grin. "I guess that's why we need Alexander, huh? You and I would just brood at each other until the end of the world."

Alexander's smile brightened and I enjoyed the slight flush to his cheeks, "I'm glad I could help."

"You always help," Theo said to him, reaching out to touch his shoulder for a split second.

It was strange to watch them interact in a peaceful, caring way, but it settled something in my stomach. The warmth in my chest – whatever power the Cult of Persephone left in me –

grew hot at the interaction, but it didn't hurt. If anything, it felt a little like happiness.

The song changed on the radio and I relaxed against my seat. "Can you turn it up? This one is my favorite."

Theo turned the dial. "Did you bring the travel questions we need for the presentation?"

I patted my backpack. "Yeah, we're all set. There are a few jobs we need to have covered, according to Lux's instructions. Did you want to do the recording or the presenting?"

Theo shook his head. "The recording, for sure. I'm not great in front of crowds."

Alexander caught my eye in the mirror and mouthed his thanks at me and later, when I put my head down to flip through the assignment, he reached out and rested a hand on Theo's thigh.

My stomach clenched not unpleasantly. Like falling from a cliff, only to be caught safely below.

When we got out of the car, Alexander handed his keys to the valet. I got my suitcase out of the back of the car and slapped Theo's hands away when he tried to take it from me. Alexander tried too, but was restrained with only a glare. We rushed inside once we had everything, ready to be away from the cold air.

Theo jolted to a stop when the decadence of the lobby became visible and I wasn't too far behind him. The entire place was decorated like the Acropolis in Athens, only smaller. Giant marble friezes lined the walls and columns bracketed all of the building structures. On the right was the Erectheon and the Parthenon on the left. The lights mimicked the Mediterranean sun, bright and nearly white. Palm trees stood potted in the corners.

The receptionist wore a chiton and blushed as Alexander approached the desk. He checked us in, hesitating before he said his last name and the lady dropped her pen to the ground in surprise.

"The son of the goddess?"

Alexander, clearly used to this, just nodded. "Yes, ma'am."

"My manager approved an upgrade for your room," she told him, fluttering her eyelashes as she looked him up and down. Her gaze settled on his expensive watch for a few seconds before coming to rest on his cheekbones. His smile didn't waver and I wasn't sure if he'd even noticed the way her smile grew sharper. She slid him three room keys. "The person who made the reservation would be able to have a private room, if that's of any interest to you?"

Theo smiled at her, lifting his arms to tie his hair back and showing off the gold of his bracelets, and I snickered at his lack of subtlety. "I think we're okay with our original room. Vanessa?"

I leaned against the desk, propping my head on my hands. My sleeves fell back and both my bracelets were revealed. Her gaze moved down, taking them both in, and I said, "Yeah, I don't think we have a problem sharing."

Her smile dropped faster than I expected and her face grew impassive. "Have a nice stay, Mr. Crest. Please let us know if you require anything else to make your stay at The Acropolis even better."

"Thank you," he said, distributing the room keys.

"It's my pleasure, Mr. Crest." Her eyes grew wider as she stared at our hands, cheeks red. "I mean, it's no problem."

Our room was on the ninth floor so we took our bags to the closest elevator and I smirked at Theo as soon as we were safely inside.

The doors closed and I thought to him, *Nice hair trick.*

Oh, like yours was more clever, Theo answered, leaning

against the metal paneling.

"You both look insane, smiling at nothing," Alexander said, "just so you know."

"We're just talking about your new girlfriend," Theo teased.

The elevator doors opened, and Alexander gave us the most confused look. It was so genuine, I couldn't help but lean forward and pinch his cheek. He sputtered and Theo laughed as I led them out of the elevator and down the hallway.

"What girlfriend?" Alexander asked and neither of us responded. Our room sat at the end of the hall and Theo gently nudged me out of the way as the roomkey light refused to turn green. He got it on the first try and pushed the door open, the smell of oranges floated to my nose. It was just as nice as I'd expected, except for one problem staring us right in the face.

"Seriously, what girl—" Alexander stopped talking and I knew he'd seen it too. "I forgot about the bed situation."

Two full-size beds sat in the room. We had decided on the sleeping arrangements months ago. Before Theo and Alexander's kiss at the party, before their kiss in my kitchen.

"We can still go ask for the upgrade," Alexander suggested, his voice soft in the room.

"It's fine," I said, placing my bag on the far bed. "I don't mind."

"Vanessa," they both started, but stopped when they talked over each other.

I took off my coat and laid it down on the bed, giving me a few seconds to brace myself for the rest of the night. I turned around to face them and they're both still standing with their bags, eyebrows drawn down and looking unsure. I took Alexander's bags from his hands and held his face in my hands.

"You're very sweet," I said, looking to Theo as he set his own stuff on the ground, "but I'm okay by myself."

And weirdly enough, those words didn't feel like a lie anymore.

43

GODSPLIT

Alexander had made us a reservation at the restaurant downstairs. As soon as we walked in, I was glad I had taken the time to throw on a dress and some makeup. Theo, on the other hand, looked out of place with his ripped jeans and black t-shirt. Alexander always looked like he'd stepped out of a designer ad in those magazines only given to first class flyers.

The lights were a strange blue-green color, barely allowing us to see, and I nearly tripped over the leg of a chair as we approached the hostess. She shot Theo a glare but stopped when she noticed Alexander. He was like a ticket for getting rid of snootiness or at least redirecting it into schmoozing as she led us to our booth.

It was in the back, private, and set for only two people with candles and wine glasses. Her face turned red as she gestured wildly to a waiter to fix it. The waiter asked us if we wanted wine and Alexander handed him a credit card with instructions to bring whatever he thought we'd like. Theo rolled his eyes and Alexander must have seen it because he said, "It's my mom's card."

"We don't need expensive food," Theo argued, tucking

himself further into the corner of the booth. He'd got in first, hiding himself behind Alexander. "Seriously, we could've stopped for something on the way."

Alexander rolled his eyes and I grinned at how much he resembled Theo with the gesture. "Yeah, I don't think so. At least with this" – he held up the menu which didn't even have prices on it – "I don't have to worry about my trainer and nutritionist murdering me when we get back."

"Vanessa," Theo implored, looking at me and I held up my hands in surrender, still looking down at the menu.

"Nope. I'm not getting in between you two." We all paused at my wording and Alexander laughed while Theo grinned. "Maybe that wasn't the best way to say that," I said, feeling the heat of a blush on my cheeks.

"Probably not," Alexander agreed. The waiter reappeared, cutting through the weird tension and took our orders before leaving to put the ticket in. Someone else brought over a bottle of red wine with a label entirely in Italian and poured us the dark liquid in crystal glasses. I took a sip and the buzzing of the alcohol on my tongue was a strange mix of pleasant and painful. The bitter taste coated my mouth as I stared, maybe for the last time, at my soulmates sitting together in front of me.

Theo was fiddling with his left bracelet, spinning the gold and brushing the silver tattoo beneath almost absentmindedly, his face open and carefree. Compared to the art recluse I'd met back in September, he seemed like a new version of himself. This was Theo, but happy.

Alexander had a flush high on his cheeks. His leg was bouncing, bringing the table up and down with it, but I didn't mind. He could pull Theo from his silence with a well-placed comment, could make me feel like my emotions – jealousy, awkwardness, insecurity – weren't too much. He turned his hand over, intertwining our fingers as his shoulder brushed against Theo's.

He knew us, cared for us. And not just because we were his soulmates.

Too bad it doesn't matter after tomorrow.

"Can you not think about that?" Theo said out loud, frowning at me.

Alexander didn't look up from reading the back of the wine bottle – of course he could read Italian. "Context, please?"

"Was I projecting all of that?" I asked Theo.

He nodded. "She thinks none of this matters after tomorrow."

"Why wouldn't it matter?" Alexander demanded, and Theo's jaw clenched but the food arrived before he could say anything more. The plates clinked and the silverware clattered and we were silent. "Of course, it'll matter tomorrow. Why wouldn't it?"

"Why wouldn't it?" I laughed without humor and stabbed at my noodles. "Because we'll be, you know, disconnected in less than a day. Cured. And after this project is over, we won't have a reason to see each other—"

"We're friends!" Alexander snapped at me, still glaring at his sandwich before his shoulders slumped. "I guess, maybe! We don't just have to cut each other off and say none of this happened." He took a swallow of the wine. "Can you really just wake up everyday and pretend that we didn't dream together, that you didn't have his thoughts in your head for the last five months—"

"Alexander, just eat," I said, because if I had to hear the words I couldn't bear to think in my head out loud, I was going to start crying in this stupid, fancy restaurant. "We can talk about this later."

"Fine," he said, "but we *are* talking about this. Tonight."

We finished eating in relative silence and Alexander signed

the check without even looking at the price once our plates were cleared. Theo, still upset from the almost-argument, huffed a complaint about rich people. We made it to the room and I struggled again with the key, hands shaking and huffing with irritation until Alexander placed his warm hands over mine and unlocked the door instantly.

The moment the door closed behind us, Theo scrubbed a hand over the stubble on his jaw and said, "Why are we even arguing about this? We don't know if your mom will bless the cure. We don't even know why she did this in the first place."

"She will," Alexander said, "because I'll ask her to."

I braced myself. "Regardless of what happens with your Mom, it doesn't matter. After this, I'm done."

Theo flinched back and so did Alexander. "What?"

"Why?" Alexander asked, tears welling in his eyes that made my lungs feel tight. "I know what I said in the classroom, but that was before we thought you'd—" He sat heavily on the bed closest to the door and put his head between his legs as his breath came out in unsteady bursts. "If it's me, I'm trying to be better. I promise. If you need me to do more—"

"Alexander," I restrained myself from going to him. Instead, I sat on the bed opposite, facing them. "That's not it at all. You're perfect."

"So it's me?" Theo asked, his voice as cool as the air outside. He looked like his old self at that moment. The one who'd sat across from Alexander in the classroom and instigated fights for the pettiest reasons. Who couldn't speak about his emotions outside of our minds. He was pressed against the door like a trapped animal. "I guess I expected that, but you don't have to be the one—"

"It's not you, either, Theo."

"Then what the fuck is it?" Theo demanded but it sounded more like a plea.

"You kissed each other. You *want* each other. You belong together – and don't try to convince me you don't."

Alexander argued anyway. "We kissed. It was just a kiss."

"I know you. A kiss isn't just a kiss with you." I sat on my hands so I wouldn't reach out, trying to pull my thoughts away from the kiss we'd shared in the library – that had seemed like more than a kiss too, but in the end he was meant for Theo. Not me. His shoulders shook, just like they had when I'd come back from the dead. This felt like another death, but I had to ask, had to be *sure* before I gave them up. "Alexander, can you look at me and tell me that kiss didn't mean anything?"

"Vanessa, please—"

"Can you?" Theo asked, that open, vulnerable look returning.

Alexander shook his head.

I nodded as my stomach dropped again. "Can you tell me Theo doesn't mean anything to you?"

Pain cut across his face, but he wouldn't lie. "I can't."

"Tell me you don't love him."

"I can't! Okay?" he snapped, standing up. Theo's eyes were like saucers and his hand moved to the doorknob as Alexander continued, "I can't. I can't say I love him, but I can't say that I don't. But what does it matter? Just because I" – he shook his head – "with him, doesn't mean I don't want you, too. And, I swear on my mother's divinity, Theodore, if you try to run from this conversation after you started it—"

"I'm not running from anything," he said, but his hand stayed on the doorknob.

"It doesn't matter," I repeated. "I'm done."

"*Why?*" Alexander said again, his voice loud enough that it echoed.

"Because I respect myself too much to be anyone's second choice!" I yelled back. The words were true, I realized, and the power in my chest strengthened my spirit. The next words came easy. "Because I would rather you be happy together than content to be stuck with me. Because I've served my purpose. You're together. You don't need me anymore! That's what being the Extra means!"

"Don't need you?" Theo asked and it was so quiet that it fell like rocks into a river.

"You really think that?" Alexander wondered just as softly, blue eyes wide and soft.

"I was a stepping stone," I said, swallowing my own sadness. "Like the Cult of Hera, I was just preparing you to be ready for your real soulmates. For each other. I served my purpose. You're ready now. It's okay—"

"It's not okay," Alexander said, taking three steps forward until he was close enough to cup my face in his hands. His blue eyes swirled with grief and anger and tears. My hands moved subconsciously to rest on his arms and his skin was river-cold. "If you think any of what you just said is okay, we must suck as soulmates."

"You don't," I objected, shaking my head. My cheeks were wet, but I couldn't remember starting to cry. "I promise."

"We must," he said again and murmured a prayer to the gods before continuing. His next words were everything I had ever wanted to hear and at the same time the stuff of Greek tragedy. The tropes played out in my head: star-crossed lovers, plans foiled by the gods, hubris and, *dear gods*, the fall. "Vanessa, you're everything to me. To *us*. You're not a stepping stone. You're not preparing us for each other. You're not anyone's second choice. If anything, you're the first of everything for me." His shoulders were shaking. "I love you."

"Don't," I protested, shaking my head. "Please don't say that. This doesn't end in happily ever after."

"Then what do you want?" he asked, tilting my face until I had to look at him. He, too, was begging for an answer. For any decision from me. I had dived from cliffs and fallen into rivers and survived it all. Yet, it was those words that felt like a mortal wound.

A goddess echoed in my head: *Tell me, now, Vanessa, daughter of Demetria, what do you want more than anything in the world?* And the river whispered: *Decide, decide, decide*—

But I did not want to decide. What I wanted was impossible. Or it would be on any other night. My chest ached with the desire to have them close, both of them. But I couldn't. At least, not permanently. I knew whatever I did tonight, it wouldn't matter in the morning.

Back at the first meeting, Lux had called my soul *godsplit*. But it wasn't. Tomorrow, when the cure cut me from them and the bonds in my chest were severed by magic and misfortune and the mercurial hands of Fate, then I would be split.

But now? We were together and I wanted to remember that for the rest of my life, this fleeting glimpse of happiness.

"Just one night," I said to them, shaking. "To pretend that we can have everything. Tomorrow we'll surrender ourselves to the Fates and cut whatever strings there are between us. But tonight... I want to let myself believe that I get to have you." I wiped a tear from my cheek. "Just one night."

44

PANDORA

"One night?" he repeated with pain. "Vanessa—

"Please," I begged. "Please."

"Okay," Alexander agreed. Submitted. Surrendered. "Whatever you want, but I'm not sure it'll ever be enough."

I pulled him into a kiss and it was nothing like our first and so much like our second that it felt like coming home. The first was slow, the bond unraveling between us like a delicate thread. This was frantic, clumsy on my part but smoother on his. My fingertips dug into his back as I pulled him close to me, and he moved one arm to wrap around my waist, yanking me closer and then off the ground by almost half a foot to match his height.

He tasted like saltwater and this was a different kind of drowning, lost in him. But, for the first time, I embraced it, pushing myself closer and filling my mouth and my lungs with Alexander.

Kissing him and knowing that, at least for this moment, he was really, truly mine, was a dip into the Lethe, erasing the inevitability of future pain for as long as his lips were on mine. The thing about water was that it erased, but I was not gone with him. I chose to be here, to stay, to share every part of my soul that he couldn't see.

The power in my chest matched the beat of my erratic pulse, part fear, part desire. Alexander had seawater in his veins, but he was born from love itself and love didn't erase. It flowed around us, beautiful and confusing and everything I hadn't known to wish for.

We stopped only when Theo said, "I'll leave you alone."

Alexander set me down, keeping me close to him, his heart beating just as fast as mine. We both turned towards the door that was being pulled open. I wasn't fast enough to stop Theo, to make it across the room before he could step outside, so I did the only thing I could.

I held out my hand. Theo froze, looking at me like snakes had just grown from my scalp.

"One night," I said to him, "to be together."

He stared at my hand like it was both salvation and damnation. "But you two—"

"One night," Alexander repeated, extending a hand too. "All three of us. Together."

Stasis, waves beating both sides of a ship so that it cannot move. Then the boat rocked.

Theo crossed the room to us and lifted me in a kiss. He tasted familiar – like coffee and cinnamon and buttery pastries. Theo's kisses only reminded me of security, of sureness, of the undeniable, indisputable truth of us. Of being safe and warm with tea in my stomach and a hand in mine.

I couldn't let go of Alexander completely, my hand lingering on the hot skin of his waist. Theo didn't complain. He kissed me with one hand and pulled Alexander closer with the other, fingers twisted in the material of his shirt. I scraped my fingers down the back of his neck, teasing a groan from him and slid it to rest on his shoulders. He was as broad as Atlas and just as steady.

Theo pulled away, tucking a piece of hair behind my ear. His gaze didn't waver as he searched for any sign of hesitation, of anything other than desire. Finding none, he leaned down again for another kiss, quicker but no less intense. "Are you sure?"

"Yes, a million times, yes," I said, sliding my hand down to press against his heart. It thundered like Zeus above and his mind opened for me. Our bond pulsed between us as I heard his thoughts. How much he wanted this. How Alexander's excitement poured into his every cell.

I stepped back from both of them and shrugged off my cardigan, their eyes following my movements. There was a bravery in me, radiating from my chest, from the pomegranate-scented power filling the air. My hands barely shook as I grabbed the hem of my dress and pulled it up and over my head, the material coaxing a shiver from my sensitized skin. I wasn't wearing anything fancy underneath – I could hardly say I'd planned for this to happen, though, it felt like it was meant to. My bra and underwear didn't match and goosebumps broke out when my skin was exposed to the air and their gaze.

But I was not afraid, not of my inexperience and certainly not of them.

"Vanessa," Alexander murmured, taking half a step forward.

Theo stopped him with a hand on his chest. His eyes stayed connected to mine, but his mind reeled with the focus required not to close the distance between us. "How far do you want to go?"

"I want—" I shook my head, struggling with the words. "I don't want to choose. I want—"

"Everything," Theo agreed, nodding.

"Together," Alexander reminded us, eyes glistening and then stepped forward, cupping my cheek. I stopped him before his mouth could cover my lips once more.

I was as fragile as the stars.

"Take off your shirts."

Alexander slowly unbuttoned his with trembling hands, but Theo removed his t-shirt in one smooth movement that had me gulping. He stepped closer, reaching me just as Alexander tugged the last button free. I let him kiss me for a few seconds, pulling back enough to look into his dark eyes. "Kiss Alexander."

They both paused, breathing hard, the only noise in the room. I recaptured Theo's mouth again, mimicking what he did earlier. He sighed into the kiss, shoulders relaxing, and I pulled back gently. "It's okay if you want to. Do you want to?"

He blinked and held his head back from me. "Yes."

Then do it.

He turned to Alexander, whose chest reddened at the intensity of Theo's gaze. Our bond hummed between us like it too was eager and waiting. I couldn't hear Theo's thoughts – not because he was shielding them but because his mind was racing too fast for me to follow. He stepped close enough to Alexander to touch and hesitated. "Do you—"

"You're so dumb," Alexander said, moving close so their bare chests brushed. Theo's mind hesitated enough for me to read his fear of rejection, but Alexander smiled. "Of course. Yes. Please. Always—"

Theo interrupted him with a deep kiss and Alexander's reaction seemed pure instinct, taking Theo's arms and wrapping them around him. The kiss lasted a minute, their tongues meeting and breathing combining. Through Theo, snippets of their thoughts bounced around in my head. *How hard do I have to kiss you for you to stay mine?* Theo wondered, gasping into Alexander's mouth, kissing him harder. *Warm*, Alexander thought in response, pressing closer, leaving no space between. *Finally warm.*

They fell into each other's gravity and I had to hold back a sigh.

"Bed?" Theo asked on a heavy exhale, turning from the kiss to ask me the question. Alexander's mouth didn't leave his skin, just migrated to the curve of his jaw, the soft skin under his ear. Theo's grip tightened, eyes rolling up into the back of his head and I gasped, echoing the sound of him in my head. When his eyes fluttered open again they held mine, the pathway between our minds clear and humming.

"Which one?" Alexander returned, tilting his head toward the options, his words muffled into Theo's neck.

"Both," I answered. "We can push them together."

We spent the next few minutes stripping off the rest of our clothes, taking time to stop and kiss newly exposed skin before pushing the beds together. When the mattresses touched, Alexander lifted me with his more-than-human strength and tossed me onto them. I laughed as I landed and watched as they both crawled toward me. Anticipation welled up, excitement and burning expectation dancing on every nerve ending.

Alexander settled on my right and Theo on my left, balancing on his elbow. He kissed me once, hand on my jaw, and then Alexander did the same. Oranges and black coffee. Alexander pulled away, resting his forehead against mine as Theo leaned down, placing one kiss on the constellation of freckles on my shoulder.

"You told me," Theo whispered, "after our first kiss that you imagined it your entire life."

I knew what he was asking even if he couldn't put it into words. My eyes closed and Alexander pressed a kiss to my cheek, my nose, my forehead. Theo's hands were calloused but still so soft against the curve of my hip as he held his breath and waited for my answer.

Growing up, whenever I'd thought about my soulmate, whenever I conjured in daydreams the kind of life we'd have together, whenever I imagined my back against silk sheets and another's hands on my body, my partner was a faceless perfection. A block of marble chiseled by insecurity into everything I thought I should want.

It was a tempting place to rest your head, the galaxy of romantic perfection. It wrapped you in blankets of poetry and stroked your hair from your face with fairytales, tucking you in with the tantalizing impossibility of it all. You missed the terrifying and scary and genuine and settled for made-up images dancing on the back of your eyelids.

This wasn't that. This was Alexander and Theo. Real, complicated, and imperfect.

"This is better than anything I ever imagined."

Alexander kissed me again and I felt it down to my bones. He traced my bottom lip with his tongue and the curve of my jaw with his thumb. He kissed the opposite way to Theo and it was obvious where he'd learned his best techniques. My body leaned into him, unable to help myself from wanting more.

"You are more than I could have ever wished for," Alexander said, forehead against mine and hard against my hip. "You have to tell me if I do something wrong—"

Though desire was gripping my insides, I shook my head, laughing with embarrassment. "I don't know what I'm doing either."

We both looked to Theo and Alexander said, "Show us?"

Theo closed his eyes, murmuring a prayer and pushing himself to his knees. "Of course. C'mere."

Getting to his knees as well, Alexander leaned over my body and let himself be kissed. Gold skin brushed against dark bronze and Alexander made this little sound – a moan or a whine – and I had to bite my lip to keep from echoing it.

Theo kissed Alexander relentlessly. He was sure, thorough, and holy Hades, Alexander's blush melted down from his face, painting his collarbones pink-red.

I needed more than to just watch though. I was more curious than I'd ever been. I had two marble statues in front of me, my hands trembled with the possibility of touching them. Slowly, I pressed my hands to their stomachs, dragging my nails lightly over defined muscles. Alexander, who could hold his breath indefinitely, broke the kiss momentarily to breathe heavily.

"Can I touch?" I asked, dragging my hands lower.

Alexander tilted his head back and groaned while Theo pressed his forehead to his shoulder gasping out, "Fuck, yes—"

"Please," Alexander begged, running his hands through Theo's hair and burying them as my fingers moved lower. "Vanessa—"

I palmed both of their erections over the fabric of their boxer-briefs, eagerly taking in the way they reacted. Alexander's hips flexed against the gentle pressure, almost involuntarily. Theo copied the movement but more controlled, practiced. Smooth, even as he licked into Alexander's mouth. I touched more firmly, attempting something of a rhythm, pleased when Theo groaned and Alexander tugged his hair harder.

I attempted to diffuse some of the heat pooling in response to how gorgeous they looked together by wiggling my hips, but I forced myself to wait before trying anything further.

They were hotter and harder by the time I eased my fingers under one waistband and then the other. Three sounds of pleasure burst at the first contact and, still curious, I cataloged the way they felt in my hands. Theo was thicker around and Alexander seemed longer, but they were both silk-soft and strikingly hot against my palms and fingertips.

"Gods," Theo flexed his hips again and pulled away from Alexander. The blond slumped back, resting on his heels. His full lips were red and looked downright sinful, kissed so completely. I pulled my hands away from their bodies, a little embarrassed by how forward I'd been.

Theo kissed me, shaking his head as he heard the thought. "No, you're perfect. Can I show you?"

One of his hands trailed from where he held my jaw in a kiss, down to my neck and then just a little lower. His intent was clear, and I swallowed and nodded, still nervous.

He kissed me again, but pulled back, saying, "Gotta say it out loud, sweetheart."

"Yes," I told him, loving him all the more for the words. "I want you to."

"Alexander," he said, dark eyes flickering to our soulmate, who was watching us with a spellbound expression of desire and amazement. "Why don't you get comfortable, baby? And hold her?"

His pupils dilated at the pet name. "How?"

There was an awkward few seconds where we all repositioned ourselves and I giggled as we struggled to untangle our limbs from where we sat. Theo snorted, grinning at me. Eventually, I settled back into Alexander's chest where he sat behind me, long legs bracketing me and arms wrapped around my waist, hands tangled in mine. He squirmed, getting comfortable with the way we were pressed against each other.

Theo spread my thighs and I exhaled sharply, turning red. He kissed me quickly, asking, "Still okay?" and I nodded. He knelt between my legs, leaning to kiss me again just a little deeper. "You can tell me to stop at any moment, alright? If you need—"

"I know," I said, letting go of one of Alexander's hands to hold Theo's face in mine. He smiled at me. That soft, small smile that made me go all fuzzy in my brain and turning his face into my hand, he pressed a kiss into my palm. "I trust you."

Alexander moved half of my hair to the side and pressed a soft kiss to that spot where my neck and shoulder met. "We both do."

Theo leaned forward to kiss me again, short and sweet, and then Alexander the same way. "Thank you." From there, his mouth kissed down my neck and without the permission of my mind, my hips canted up. He huffed a laugh, moving his hands over me and following them with his mouth. They trailed down my chest, through the space between my breasts, down the softness of my stomach, resting on my hip bone. Gentle, willing to stop if I'd asked.

I didn't and he pressed a groan into my skin, mind trembling with the force of it. *Ready?*

I was too caught up in the sensations to do anything but nod.

MADLY WORSHIPPED

Theo moved lower, no longer kneeling but on his stomach between our legs. He looked perfect. Like he belonged there and that filled me with an emotion too strong – too sad – for this moment. So, I focussed on the angle of his cheekbone in the lowlight, the curve of his brow, the shine in his eyes and that helped. My nails carved half-moons into the muscle of his arm where I held onto him.

His nose, one that I had often admired, nudged against the inside of my thigh softly before he moved back up my body. "I've wanted to do this for so long—" He cut himself off with a deep kiss to my lips and I let out a little moan as his tongue drew languid circles against mine. The steady weight of his body settled against mine completely, pushing me back on the bed, my back pressing closer to Alexander's sculpted body. Theo finally broke the kiss, his lips finding my jaw, then my neck, painting kisses up and down it as his hand teased the sensitive skin of my inner thigh. "I'm gonna take these off. Is that okay?"

Alexander groaned, hips flexing. I could feel him against the small of my back and his reaction had me nodding before I thought too hard about it.

Theo hooked one finger into the waistband of my underwear and started to pull them off one hip. "Vanessa, do you want Alexander to take your bra off?"

I blinked, tilting my head up so I could look at Alexander. He was pink as rose petals, licking his lips.

"Do you want…?" I asked, letting the full question trail off.

"Gods above," he answered, nodding too many times. A wave of blond hair fell into his eyes and I brushed it back without thinking, not wanting anything to obstruct my view of him. "Of course… if you're comfortable—"

I nodded. "The clasp is in the back."

It took him a few attempts to undo it but he managed and, with the utmost care, helped me pull the straps off my arms and then threw it off the bed with relish. I giggled at his triumphant grin and eyebrow wiggle, hardly noticing when Theo did the same with my underwear. Just when my brain started panicking at how exposed I was between them Theo said, "Why don't you tell her what you're thinking, baby?"

Alexander swallowed. "You're – you're so beautiful. We are – I am so lucky to – gods, Vanessa, what do you want me to do? How can I make you feel good?"

Theo stroked his thigh in approval and I blushed at them, shaking my head. "I'm not – I don't know. Just… touch me?"

Alexander nodded very seriously, lowering his mouth to my neck and kissing. One hand stayed intertwined with mine as the other turned my body so I was curved more into his side. With this angle, he could better see what he was doing and – gently, so gently that even I worried I might shatter – stroked his thumb over one of my nipples sending the smallest tingling, warm and vibrant sensation through me.

Alexander frowned, just a little. But before he could say anything, I gasped, "Keep going."

His jaw snapped shut and his eyes narrowed with the challenge. His next pass was more sure, the pad of his thumb rubbed a soft circle around my areola and my hips moved with it, the heat starting to simmer. He must have noticed because he kept going, working my nipple until I was gasping and arching my back.

"Try your mouth," Theo suggested, voice lower. "No teeth. Yet."

Alexander looked to me and I nodded in rapid succession. He pulled my nipple into his mouth and sucked and I cursed, the sound bounced off the walls and filled the room. I took my hand off Theo to clutch at Alexander's head as he kept going and just when the sensation dulled he switched to the other until my stomach hurt from the pleasure building.

"Sweetheart," Theo said, making my eyes snap open. He moved slowly as if not to startle me and lifted one of my legs so my knee hooked over his shoulder. "Can I?"

Nerves bubbled up my throat, imagining the overload of sensation. "I don't know what to do with my hands," I blurted and felt a warm rush of comfort from both sides of the bond.

Theo placed a quick kiss against my pout, soothing me. The little kiss felt like one of those adoring *I can't help but kiss you right now* kind of kisses and I accepted it easily. One side of his mouth lifted up into a pleased smile. "Here, you can put one in my hair. This way, you can tell me what you like and what you don't." He kissed the inside of my thigh again, once, twice. "And keep holding onto Alexander but don't touch."

Alexander went red. "Hey—"

"Trust me," Theo said, eyes going slightly unfocussed for a moment. "I was tempted. But you'll thank me, I promise."

Swallowing once, Alexander said, "Okay. Besides, I could do this all night—"

He punctuated his words with another lick to my already sensitive nipple and I moaned his name, throwing my head back until it rested on his shoulder and squeezed his hand again. I must have pulled Theo's hair as well because he groaned and finally pressed his mouth against my folds.

I would be lying if I said that I hadn't thought about Theo's mouth an inordinate amount since I'd met him. His full lips, wicked tongue, soft facial hair – it had definitely been the star of a few mildly-guilty self-love sessions in the last few months. The fact that Alexander, my beautiful, loving, amazing Alexander, was a solid, steady presence behind me, hard as he watched us, fingers and mouth creating their own trails of pleasure across my skin, was also way more of a turn on than I could have imagined.

Whatever Theo did with his mouth wasn't quite as powerful, yet. It was soft and hot and wet though and his eyes blew wide, eyes flicking up to my face to see my reaction. He pulled away from me just far enough to ask, "More?"

I managed, "Yes."

This is really happening. My hand clutched Alexander's, sometimes squeezing it, sometimes drawing delicate lines over his fingers. My other hand reached up and my fingertips ran through his hair, fingers dragging on his scalp before ghosting through the golden waves.

"Gods, you're so beautiful, Vanessa. Alexander," Theo said before he buried his head between my thighs completely, kissing along the seam of my thigh, wet, lingering kisses that were slowly moving closer and closer to where I was desperately beginning to want him. "Tell her what you're thinking."

Theo's mouth descended again, a little more purposefully, his teasing kisses stopped and his tongue drew a line along my lips, causing my hips to jerk upwards and a gasp to leave my mouth. Any teasing or pretense was gone as his tongue laved against me repeatedly, his hands holding my hips as I continued to squirm. He looked up at me through his eyelashes and groaned at the sight.

"*Gods*," Alexander rasped, lowering his mouth to my breast again and the pleasure was so intense, I was worried about passing out. "Gods, you're both so beautiful. I've never seen anything so beautiful as the two of you together in all my life."

Theo took my clit between his lips and sucked gently before licking against the sensitive flesh, then sucked again, longer. He repeated it, all the while looking up at me as my head began to thrash back and forth, my chest heaving as my breathing became erratic.

"Oh gods," I whined, "oh gods, oh *gods*."

My back arched. I squeezed them both harder and though my eyes were tempted to close, I kept them open. Theo's expression was worth it. When he pulled away, he was breathing hard and his eyes were slightly unfocussed. He looked... debauched, though he was the one doing the debauching. His eyes burned and there was moisture in the scruff on his chin. With deliberate slowness he brought one of his hands to my center and I caught a fragment of a thought *so wet...*

Because of you, I thought back automatically, honestly.

His throat bobbed, but his only answer was the slow slide of a finger into me.

I stiffened, adjusting to the intrusion. Alexander must've noticed my tension because he kissed me again and it was shockingly intimate, kissing Alexander with a foggy mind and Theo's finger inside me.

His thumb found my clit, circled it, massaging the front of my inner wall at the same time.

It was unfamiliar and disorienting and incredible.

When his finger curled, I bit down on Alexander's plump lower lip, relishing in the little groan I got out of him. He hummed and smiled that thousand-watt grin against my mouth, words coming out as easy as breathing. "Wish you could see how amazing you look. You always look so fucking sexy, but this is beyond… You two are going to be the death of me. Gods, I could watch this forever—"

He always babbled when his emotions were at their greatest pitch, but now the soft endearments and words of adoration only grew in sweetness the more I kissed him. As I did, Theo worked me over with his mouth and ground into me, a steady pressure now. Alexander's cock was hot and hard against my back, the head of it smooth and wet where it lay against his belly half out of his underwear. It drove me even closer to the edge, knowing how much he was enjoying this without either of us touching him. Yet.

The pleasure built and built with Theo's mouth sucking stronger. A second finger curled into me, hitting spots inside of me that had my eyes rolling back. All the while, Alexander rolled my nipples in his fingers and murmured things in my ear that made me hold onto him for dear life: how beautiful we were, how much he wanted us, how I looked, wet and ready for him—

"*Please*, Theo, please, I'm so close—" I panted and Theo sucked hard against my flesh one last time, groaning as I yanked on his hair and ground myself against his face. I called out for him as my orgasm rolled over my body like a tidal wave and felt his satisfaction thrumming through me alongside my own. My entire body trembled and I grasped onto them both with all my strength, wanting them closer than ever before. Alexander waited a moment, eyes fluttering closed at the noises I was making, but I yanked him into a rough, dirty kiss that had him groaning and licking into my mouth.

Theo, patient and steady, licked me through the crashing of the wave and only stopped when the initial sensation was over and I tugged his hair. He looked up again, a purely masculine, proud twist to his wet mouth.

"Come up here," I said, tugging again and he listened, lowering my leg back down to the mattress and kissing me. I could taste myself on his tongue but I didn't mind. We kissed for a few minutes, until my breathing slowed and my brain started functioning reasonably again.

"How are you feeling, sweetheart?" he asked, pulling away to kiss my nose.

I actually laughed at that. "Amazing. And you, handsome?"

His grin was wild, free. He looked years younger. "Never better."

"Gods above," Alexander panted, his arms wrapping around us both, binding us together and pulling us against him. He kissed my shoulder before pulling Theo into a deep kiss. I wondered if he could taste me and the thought made Theo groan. He pulled away from Alexander, peppering his face with kisses – his cheeks, jaw, nose – every bit of him he could reach.

"My beautiful, lovely soulmates, gods." Disbelief tinged Alexander's voice, along with a stunned sort of joy. His hands shook where they held us, and I pushed the sadness of "one night" down. "Gods, I could fuck you both forever—"

Theo cut the thought off with a rough kiss. "Vanessa first."

It took a few more moments of rearranging our bodies, but eventually I was laying against the pillows and Alexander let Theo move him between my legs. Theo knelt next to him, distracting himself with long, languid kisses every now and then. At some point, he helped Alexander get his blue boxer-briefs off before they removed Theo's dark gray pair, thrown with my underwear into the void.

I'd known they were beautiful since I'd met them, but seeing them completely naked before me was something like a religious experience. My first guess about their sizes was right, but now that I could see them, I realized that they were both much bigger than average. I thanked every god in existence while Theo smirked and Alexander blushed.

Theo reached to touch Alexander but the blond shook his

head, intertwining their fingers together, cheeks turning red as he admitted, "If you touch me, I will not last."

Theo's grin was pleased. "Good to know."

"Shut up," Alexander bit out, reaching out to touch him instead. When he got his free hand around Theo's cock he groaned aloud and Alexander grinned smugly. "See? Not so easy, huh?"

Theo laughed, bringing him in for a kiss that lasted three seconds too long, so I said, "Boys?"

Alexander pulled away with an embarrassed smile. "Sorry, honey."

"S'okay," I said, grabbing his free hand and intertwining us together. "Just excited."

"Are you sure you—" Alexander began to ask and Theo smiled.

"Yes," I said, eyes softer than silk. "I am completely sure."

"Let's make sure she's ready," Theo said, leading Alexander's hand to my center. My breath was coming hard and I was still sensitive from before, but his two fingers didn't cause me anything but pleasure. Theo reached over to the bedside table, and with an amused expression thrown in Alexander's direction, pulled out a small bottle of lube.

Alexander reddened even more. "The son of Aphrodite books a hotel room with soulmates."

"Cocky," Theo said, knowing it'd piss him off.

"It's not like I thought this—"

"Well, you certainly knew it was there—"

"It was an educated guess, asshole—"

"Boys," I sighed again, adjusting my position on the mattress. They snapped to look in my direction. "Can we maybe stop arguing about the lube and start using it?"

"Sorry, sweetheart," Theo said and did as I commanded. Alexander, obedient as always, got back to it, too. I must've made a noise Theo could translate because with a rough voice he told Alexander, "Try three now."

There was the smallest stretch when Alexander sucked in a breath and did as he was told, but if anything, it made me feel even better. Alexander had beautiful hands, big and a little cool, but they warmed quickly as he found a rhythm that had me humming appreciatively and begging, "Please, more. Alexander—"

Alexander swallowed, hand trembling a little as he lined himself up. Theo shifted behind him, holding onto his hips and guiding him until the head of his cock was at my entrance, and I shivered from the feeling alone. "Slowly, baby. Ness, how you feeling?"

I nodded a few times and ran my hand up Alexander's stomach and then up to his face. I pulled him forward into a kiss and then took a deep breath. "I'm ready."

Alexander bit his lip and closed his eyes as he pressed inside me for the first time. It looked like ecstasy, his face beautifully broken by the pleasure, but I squirmed, unused to the sensation of having something so deep inside me. It was slow going, just like Theo said, and Alexander's muscles were shaking from the effort.

"There, sweetheart," Theo whispered, gently slowing Alexander's hips and easing his entry, letting me stretch and adjust around him, rubbing my thigh at each thin, sharp sound I made at the unfamiliar invasion of my body. "How do you feel?"

I considered the question. It definitely wasn't painful, which was a good thing, but Alexander felt even bigger than he looked. "Full. Definitely full. Alexander?"

Alexander only groaned, sweat darkening his hairline.

Huh. Alexander speechless. Heat spread over me at the thought and I clenched around him.

He groaned again, deeper, his head thrown backward. His

hips twitched and I made another noise, more surprised than anything.

"Easy, baby, gotta give her time to adjust," Theo said, rubbing over just the right spot to make me tremble, to drown the pinch of Alexander's cock in pleasure. "Here, see how I was touching her? Yeah, just copy – perfect."

I was more than sensitive now and just their fingers on my clit had me close to orgasm again. I knew I must have been tightening as the pleasure surged because Alexander was breathing like he had just swum across the sea.

At Alexander's rough sound, Theo kissed his shoulder blade. Alexander's restraint showed in his every muscle, tendons standing out at his neck and elbows and wrists. I knew he wanted nothing more than to bury himself inside me again and again, but he held himself so rigidly still for me that he could be made of stone.

"Gods, Alexander, you're doing so good, baby," Theo told him, his voice laced with enough filthy suggestion that he swallowed hard. Alexander dropped his head to Theo's shoulder behind him, his hands holding Theo so tightly I thought he might color his tattoos with bruises. Where his hands touched me it was as if he was touching a delicate treasure.

The thought made me sure of my words as I said, "You can move."

"Oh, thank gods," Alexander sighed, hands tightening on my hips almost imperceptibly.

"Slowly," Theo warned again and Alexander nodded with another bob of his Adam's apple as he continued to let Theo guide his hips. I whined again as he pulled out, the drag of his cock sending little shocks of pleasure up my spine. He went slow enough that I knew he was feeling it every time I tightened around him and when he was all the way out he paused, closing his eyes and taking deep breaths.

"You okay?" I asked, concerned, lifting one hand to his cheek.

He nodded. "Yeah, just concentrating very hard so as to not embarrass myself."

I couldn't help the way my nose scrunched in laughter. "Your correct grammar is very cute."

"Vanessa," he said very seriously as he lined himself back up. His shoulders rose and fell with each of his breaths and his eyes were the color of the sky during a hurricane. "You can't compliment me right now, because I'm already like a gust of wind away from—"

Theo snorted a laugh, interrupting Alexander, who turned his head just enough to glare in his general direction. It just made Theo laugh more, and then I was giggling at the way Alexander's face went, somehow, even redder.

"This is supposed to be a romantic moment," he chastised us, even as the corner of his mouth ticked upward. My hand traveled down his chest and stomach again, stopping purpose-fully on the trail of darker hair of his happy trail. "And you two are making a mockery—"

"Alexander," I said sweetly, blinking up at him with big, innocent eyes in a way that had his mouth snapping shut immediately. "Can you please fuck me?"

His cock twitched where he was still pressed against me and he sucked in a breath.

"Holy fuck," he said, eyes wide.

"Fuck, Ness," Theo groaned, pressing his forehead into Alexander's shoulder. "You can't just—"

"Please?" I asked again, sticking my bottom lip out in a pout.

"Literally whatever you want," Alexander blabbed as he lined up again and pushed forward just a little. It still burned a little with the stretch, but it was definitely nothing worth stop-ping over. "I would give you the fucking moon, if you wanted. Gods above, holy shit, Vanessa, you feel absolutely amazing."

He pushed further and, this time, it didn't take nearly as much time or effort for him to be sheathed inside. Theo added more lube, just in case, thumb still heavy on my clit. Alexander paused like he was gonna ask if I was still okay, so I just nodded and said, "I'm good. Keep going."

He did. Slowly but more surely every second, he moved hips back and forth until he built a more confident rhythm. His eyes closed again, his hands trembling where they touched me, but Theo held him up and kissed the side of his neck, murmuring soft things in his ear.

At first it just felt strange but then he brushed something inside me that had me gasping and readjusting my hands so I was digging my nails into his sides. "Oh!"

"There?" he asked, angling his hips the same way and doing it again.

"Oh, fuck, yeah," I breathed as it took my breath away again. "Just like that – oh!"

The last part of my sentence cut off with a louder moan and he leaned down, no longer letting Theo hold him up, but adjusting so that he was holding himself up with his elbows. He pushed deeper with the movement and lowered his mouth to suck my nipple into his mouth again. Gasping, I threaded one hand through his hair. "Gods, Alexander, please—"

No longer needed to slow our soulmate down, Theo moved. He scooted up the bed to kiss me sweetly and wetly. As much as I could, I tried to concentrate on kissing him back, tangling my hand in his hair too. But with every thrust Alexander managed to pull a moan out of me until I couldn't do anything but close my eyes and pant into Theo's mouth.

"You're so fucking hot, do you know that?" he whispered to me, scruff of his beard reddening my skin. "Your mind is so blank with pleasure right now but I can tell you're feeling so much. Why don't you tell Alexander exactly how he feels?"

My next breath came out as a sob as Theo's hand found my

center again. But I couldn't manage any words, so he prompted again, "Ness, come on, sweetheart, tell him how good you feel—"

"So fucking good," I managed, gasping it out. Alexander's shoulders shook with the effort to keep the pace of his thrusts, if it felt half as good as it did for me it must have been a titanic effort. "You're doing so good. *Gratias di*, Alexander. So good—"

His hand pulled my hip up so that it was resting on his own hip, changing the angle just enough that I had to suck in my breaths purposefully or risk suffocating on the pleasure surging up my spine. It settled in my gut, heavy and pounding and growing with every thrust, every circle Theo drew around my clit.

Alexander's thrusts became more erratic and he moaned low, voice vibrating with the tone. "Are you close? Fuck, Vanessa, I don't know how much longer—"

"I'm so close," I told him, tilting his head up to look at me. "Please, please, don't stop."

His eyes focussed a little bit and, swallowing heavily, he thrust harder, deeper, getting some semblance of control back. "Whatever you need."

"Touch me," I begged him, though he couldn't be closer if he tried. Still, he attempted to listen to me, wrapping his big hands around my legs and shifting them even further up, so that my feet were pressed to the front of his shoulders and I was forced further onto my back.

I scrambled to touch him as much as possible, scrapping my hand through his hair. "Please!"

One of his hands joined Theo's and my spine bent and my throat croaked out a half-choked sound – their names? A prayer? – the pleasure blinding me for a moment and even my fingertips tingled with the sensation as I came, toes curling and head thrown back.

A PAGAN IDEA

There was a weight on my collarbone, Alexander's forehead pressed to my sweaty skin as his hips stuttered and then finally stopped. Without thinking about it, my hand carved through his damp hair.

Theo pressed a kiss to my temple, stroking my hair. His breath blew across the sweat covering my skin and I shivered with the lolling waves of pleasure and the cooling temperature.

Alexander's heart was pounding against my own. It was hard to tell the difference, really.

I stared up at the ceiling and tried not to let the prickle of tears in the corner of my eyes lead to anything more. Because I wanted this for the rest of my life and it was the one thing I could never have.

"Alexander," I tried, my voice breaking. "That was—"

"I know," he said and I believed him. "I know. Thank you."

That wasn't really what he meant, but neither of us were ready to hear the real words yet.

"Thank you."

With a groan of effort, he pushed himself back up and pulled out of me. My face went red at the sensation, even as he flopped next to me with his arm over his eyes. "I'm not sure I can move. I think my legs are still shaking."

They were. I could feel them. Mine were, too. Theo laughed, the smallest exhale of air, but I tilted my head to look at him. His eyes were still dark with lust, but there was this softness to his expression, and I knew he was feeling the same things I was and also refusing to say them.

I touched his cheek and his eyes fluttered shut for half a second. "Thank you too."

He snorted another laugh. "It was my pleasure."

I laughed, too, then. "Bad joke."

Alexander curled into my other side, throwing his arm around my waist. My skin tingled with his touch. "Inaccurate, too."

It took me a minute to realize what he meant and when I did, my eyes flickered down to Theo's body and saw that he was still hard. But Theo was already shaking his head. "It is true. I loved every second of this, regardless of whether I—"

"Oh," I said, frowning. "Do you not want to…?"

The sentence trailed off and, surprisingly, Theo's cheeks went red and his shield went up. Alexander's eyebrows raised in response and I frowned at our soulmate. He let out a stuttering breath and shook his head.

"It's not that I don't want—" Theo started before trying again. "This was for you two. And I was happy to just be included in tonight—"

"Hey," Alexander interrupted, frowning now, too. His hand moved across my stomach to intertwine his fingers with Theo's. It was shockingly intimate, to see their hands together on my own skin. Even after what we had just done, it felt... like the start of something. "We said together, right? That's all three of us."

Theo's eyes softened even more as he looked at Alexander, squeezing their hands together. I mustered all the energy I had left to sit completely up, both of them too curious to stop me. Even with my unsure limbs, I managed to sit myself between Theo's thighs, kneeling and taking in the absolutely baffled expression on his face.

"I'm not sure what I'm doing," I reminded him. They both were just looking at me. "So, you might have to give me some direction."

Theo's voice was tight, muscles tensed and cheeks bright red. "Direction for what?"

"Well," I said, scooting closer so he had to widen his legs more. I scraped my nails gently down to his knees and then back up. His cock twitched with my touch and that gave me the confidence to push my nerves down. "Well, if it's okay with you, I'd like to suck you off, Theodore."

He looked too surprised to react for a minute and then his eyes shut tightly. His hands clenched into fists. Alexander, still leaning against the pillows with space between them, groaned and covered his face again.

"Holy gods," he said with a prayer. "Vanessa, your mouth—"

"You don't have to do this," Theo ground out, taking deliberate deep breaths as he put his hands over my own to stop their movements. "This isn't... transactional, Vanessa, okay? You don't owe me—"

"I want to," I told him, the honesty sitting heavy in the room. "I promise. Please?"

I do not deserve this.

The thought bubbled through his shield and I started to frown. "Theo, you deserve good things. Things that make you feel good. Even if I suck at this." I paused, grinning when the double-entendre registered in my brain. Theo caught it too and let out a little huff of laughter. "What I'm saying is – I would really like to do this for you, even if it's not very good."

"Trust me, I don't mind," he said, swallowing heavily. He bit back the rush of words that was probably just him preparing to beg me, and tilted my chin up with a finger, bringing my eyes to his. "You've been incredible," he murmured. "Why would this be any different?"

"Okay," I said, leaning forward to hover over his face. "Then kiss me."

He caught me in a kiss, and pulled me back into his arms, big hands holding my jaw and throat with quivering strength. When the kiss ended, I glanced down, and my hesitancy disappeared in an instant. Alexander scooted closer and wrapped his arms around Theo, too, kissing down his neck as he had with me earlier.

"Oh. You're uh…" I paused and wrapped a small hand – fuck my hands looked so small like this around the base of his cock. I caressed him and then worked my hand up and down experimentally. Of course, I'd touched him earlier when they were kissing, but he was bigger now. And who could blame him?

His eyes rolled back into his skull. "Hard?"

I laughed a little at the way his voice cracked. "I was going to say big. But yeah, that, too."

"Gods above," he answered, swallowing hard as Alexander kissed down his neck, and I figured out the most comfortable way to hold him in my hands. "With the way you two look? Of fucking course I am."

"Plus," Alexander said, laughing into Theo's skin. "She's so small, anything would look big—"

"Yeah, that's true—"

"Hey!" I protested, pausing my hands. The muscles in Theo's arms relaxed at the pause, so I tightened my grip just a little. "Be nice to me."

Theo's eyes softened. "Of course, sweetheart."

Alexander laughed again, tangling his fingers with Theo's. "Wow, you figured out how to get your way fast."

Theo snorted, playfully glaring at him. "Oh, like you're any better. I'd give you the moon—"

"Boys," I said, trying to hide my smile.

"Hey!" Alexander interrupted, pinching Theo's side. "That's not fair! You can't hold the things I say during sex against me!"

"You were literally just doing that…"

Sighing, I lowered my mouth and took the head of his cock between my lips and tried to stop myself from grinning when he cut his petty comment off with a groan. The taste was different, similar to how he'd tasted after going down on me, but a little muskier. Definitely not bad, though.

"I think I'm going to die," Theo said, barely managing to get the words out. His hand tightened where it was holding my hair and his head tipped back against the pillows. "Fucking hell, Ness, that feels incredible."

"Looks incredible, too," Alexander added, swallowing and moving to press closer to Theo, eyes trained on my mouth. "Your lips wrapped around—"

"Fuck, Alexander, baby," Theo managed, taking a deep breath. "If you keep talking, this isn't gonna last long."

I pulled off of him, using my spit as lube to stroke him up and down again. "That's okay. Take however long you need."

"How is it?" Alexander asked, eyes focussed in the same way they do when we do homework or he's concentrating on swimming. "What's it like?"

Before I answered I took Theo back into my mouth, taking more than just the tip this time. I gagged when he hit the back of my throat and retreated just a little. Experimenting, I flicked my tongue along the underside of him and he groaned again.

"Honestly?" I answered Alexander, pulling off again and stroking him faster. He nodded, eyes sparking with the desire for an answer. "It's kinda fun. Do you wanna try?"

Both of my boys blinked at me. Alexander licked his lips, looking at Theo. "Is that okay?"

Theo breathed once, a prayer. "I think I'm already dead, actually. Yes, it's okay, fuck."

Alexander gracefully moved from his spot at Theo's side to join me between his legs. Theo watched him intently, almost in disbelief, as he left a trail of wet kisses down the length of him, licking up in a single, slow streak once he'd kissed down to his base.

I reached for Theo's hand when his leg started to shake, frowning. "Are you okay?"

Alexander repeated that motion over and over – slow, wet kisses on the way down, slow, single strokes up.

Theo's voice cracked as he answered, "Y-yeah, just fine, sweetheart."

But I could tell Theo was about to lose his mind. It felt like it had been minutes since he'd blinked, because he just... couldn't take his eyes off Alexander's mouth wrapped around him and, fuck, if I looked anywhere near as sexy doing the same thing, I understood why.

But Alexander seemed a little unsure about taking him completely in his mouth, so minutes passed and Theo's grip was strong enough to turn my fingers white. "Vanessa," he breathed, trying but failing to keep it together. "Please—"

"Here," I told Alexander, touching his shoulder so he let me take more control. "Like this."

I took Theo's cock as far as I could manage, swallowing around him when I started to feel the urge to choke, like I'd seen in porn. His groan bounced off the walls and his hand moved to my head, gently holding it as I bobbed up and down.

"Holy—"

"Can I try?" Alexander asked, interrupting with a determined frown. "I think I can do it."

I pulled off, a line of spit extending from my lips. I wiped it away with the back of my hand and Theo took the second to catch his breath. I rubbed his thigh, trying to comfort him. "Absolutely."

Alexander tried it once, going a little too fast and gagging. Theo choked on his words as his lips wrapped around the head of his cock. He sucked him into his mouth again and slid down slower, grasping his base with both hands.

"Fuck, baby—"

Theo's thoughts were all sensation: *Everything is warm and soft and wet and—*

Alexander pulled off, looking up at me. "Your turn?"

I smiled at him, leaning over to kiss him, quick but deep, the taste of Theo on both of our tongues. It left him breathless even as I leaned down to take Theo into my mouth again. I sucked and flicked my tongue over him, swirling it, and everything sent jolts of pleasure up his spine that had him gasping my name. It rippled through him into me, my bond practically sizzling with the attention. His head hit the headboard behind him when I started humming and trying to take him further.

"Fuck, Vanessa! Yes... keep going, please—" he begged, words interrupted by a groan.

Alexander's eyes fluttered shut. "You two look so hot together."

My hand tightened around Theo in response. I liked the way Alexander talked about us. Without jealousy, without possessiveness. Just honest-to-goodness desire. *Tell him to keep talking.*

"Fuck, Alexander, keep talking, please, holy gods above."

There was a sort of stunned silence from Alexander – who was certainly not used to being told to talk more – and then he started talking again. "Um, okay, uh, you're both so fucking sexy like this. Theo, do you like Vanessa being in control? I know I do. You'd do anything she wanted, huh?"

I made a humming, approving noise that vibrated around Theo's cock. Whatever response he had only made it out in a gibbering string of only partly sensible phrases. "Good. Fuck, please don't stop, Vanessa. Good girl, so good—"

I bobbed my head up and down on him and the noises coming from where we were connected were so wet and hot that I could feel myself blush. Theo's mind was spinning, absolutely unable to control the desire pounding through his veins. Every muscle was tensed, his thighs bunched under my hands where I was leaning over him.

"Gods," Alexander said, moving so that he was closer to me. "Vanessa, can I—"

I pulled off. "Of course."

Theo was squeezing his eyes shut, but he couldn't not look down and when he did Alexander was moving to suck him into his mouth again. Once he did, Theo cursed and Alexander stared up at him, a flush building on his face. His cheeks were hollowed out from sucking him. Not for the first time, I thought about him being a fucking dream come true. Literally. I'd had dreams about this, but none of them compared to the real thing.

Theo shuddered with the thought, feeling the pressure and tension building up, and he reached down to tangle his fingers in Alexander's hair. It didn't seem like he had any intention of stopping despite Theo blurting, "I – Alexander, I'm going to—"

But he did pull away and Theo nearly screamed with the teasing. Alexander looked a little sheepish and admitted, "I'm not sure about... the ending, I guess. Sorry."

"It's okay," I told him, cupping his cheek and kissing him again. He kissed back, slow and sleepy, and I realized how exhausting this must've been. I was pretty sure you guys were supposed to roll over and go to sleep after. Theo panted from his place on the bed. "I can do that part, okay?"

Alexander smiled and his beauty never ceased to amaze me. "Thank you."

"Of course, love."

He blinked at the pet name, but I refused to acknowledge it even as my cheeks darkened further. Instead, I focussed back on Theo's cock. With one soft smile at Theo's debauched face, my tongue lapped and swirled, my lips tightening around him and Theo's whole body tensed. Someone moaned – really, it could've been any of us – his head fell back. All of him fell back, his mind went completely blank with pleasure as he spilled in my mouth.

It was honestly not that bad. Not much different than the general taste of him throughout, just stronger. And more. But instinct did kick in and I swallowed it quickly, even though I was pretty sure I made a face when the taste had first hit my tongue.

I left him with a few more licks that made him let out these cute, little whines and he opened his eyes in time to see me pull off him with a wet *pop*. We were all breathing heavily, the only sound in the room.

Theo blinked at me in a daze as I wiped my mouth again, and grinned at him. "Was that okay?"

He couldn't respond right away, though I could tell that he was trying to formulate a thought. Instead, he sucked in a dozen deep breaths until his hands stopped gripping the sheets and his heart rate went down.

"Yeah, sweetheart," he managed, eventually. "It was really good."

Then, surprisingly, he yanked me down next to him. I yelped, and he swallowed the sound with a kiss as he crushed me to his chest, one hand in my hair, the other between my shoulder blades. He devoured me, his mouth slotting over mine, tongue working past my lips until he could taste himself on my tongue, and there was nothing in his mind – no plan or thought in sight – beyond the feeling of my body against his.

At the same time, we both grabbed for Alexander and pulled him down next to us. He, too, yelped in surprise, going stiff with shock even as Theo switched to kissing him with the same amount of hunger he had me.

Through Theo's mind, I could feel the moment he melted, just absolutely melted, under Alexander's touch. He threaded his fingers into Alexander's sweat-darkened hair, sighing into him, pulling him closer. Theo could barely think as he moved back to kiss me, biting at my lips, sucking them and licking into my mouth – lost himself in us as his mind began to settle.

Eventually our bodies slowed with the falling adrenaline and exhaustion. Theo tucked me into one side and Alexander found his place on the other. Theo had bite marks on his neck and thighs and Alexander had scratches down his back, his abs and his arms. I had half a dozen hickies on my body, their origins indistinguishable.

Theo said, "Together was a good choice."

I closed my eyes, breathing in the coffee-strong smell of him and relishing the way his hand felt on my waist as they drummed out a slow beat. The way his curls tickled my ear. The way he kept his voice soft as if not to break the delicate peace.

Alexander, blond waves falling over his eyes, reached a hand to caress my cheek. But he said nothing as his chest began to move up and down in a steady breathing pattern and I could tell he'd be asleep soon. I kissed his palm and closed my eyes, too, nudging Theo's shoulder with my nose before following him into our dreams.

"Yes," I agreed. "It was."

ΙΣΤΟΡΊΑ - ΣΎΝΟΔΟΣ

A MEETING

T he sea was loud tonight. Every drop seemed to be giggling, cheering with ecstasy as they bore the Goddess of Love and Lust and Sea to the shore. Eagles and hawks and chattering sparrows spoke in cawed voices to each other. They rested so heavily on the Mediterranean pines that they dipped low and the bottommost branches brushed the earth.

The beetles, slugs, and lizards all hissed, "She's never been here before."

Indeed, the goddess had never stepped foot on this particular island before. She'd never had a reason to. It was too far from the major cities to be convenient and not nearly as beautiful as Samos or Naxos or even little Andros. There was only one kingdom here and a smattering of small villages around the mountain. It had had nothing to offer to someone like her, but tonight there was nowhere she'd rather be.

The moment her soft-soled feet touched the sand, the sky cracked with lightning and the earth shuddered below. Aphrodite smiled as she felt a very particular divinity appear behind her. It was both light and heavy, dark and unbearably sunny.

The sea and the earth stared at each other, only the heavens allowing them to meet.

"Persephone," she greeted, her smile most charming.

"Aphrodite," the goddess responded, raising a dark brow. "What are you doing here?"

"You will not offer me any hospitality?" Aphrodite asked, batting her lashes.

"You are trespassing," Persephone said, pulling a glass throne up from the sand. The earth nearly tripped over itself to obey her every wish. "You and all the Olympians know Zeus tasked me with the protection of this useless place."

"Why?" Aphrodite wondered. She snapped her fingers and the animals around her jumped into action, collecting sticks and rocks and soft grass to make a similar throne. "Your husband's kingdom reaches beyond even our home in Greece. Why this island?"

"The river contains an entrance to my kingdom," Persephone answered, taking her throne. "The people born here have an instinctual attraction to it. The women worship me, dancing in the moonlight. They burn incense and meat for me, but I cannot allow them to find their way to me before the Fates summon them."

"Vanessa?" Alexander asked, standing beside me. "What is this?"

I blinked, turning to look at him. He looked just as he did when we were awake, naked and painted in shadows. We stood on a hill, overlooking the scene below of the goddesses speaking. "Shh," I told him. "Just watch."

"Are the people in danger?" Aphrodite asked, frowning her pretty mouth.

Persephone grinned at her, smug and confident. "And why would you care?"

"There's a man on this island," Aphrodite admitted. "We met in Athens when he came to discuss something with the Assembly. We fell in love. I wanted your permission to visit him."

"Just have him move," Persephone said with a dismissive hand.

"I cannot," Aphrodite said through gritted teeth. "He is the King."

Persephone's gaze narrowed. "Philipos."

"My father?" Alexander asked, with a frown. "Vanessa, what is this?"

"A memory," I answered, nodding at them. "An explanation."

"How do you know that?" he asked. "Do you have these often?"

"Constantly," I answered. "My life is a memory."

Theo was in my head, *Do you remember how I shared those memories of Margot with you? This is like that, but so much more. I can see it in Alexander's head, too.* A pause. *Does this have anything to do with what you said at the tattoo shop?*

"It has everything to do with my death."

"I have come to ask your permission to visit him," Aphrodite said and the animals dove back into their homes. "You and I have had no reason to interact in all our immortal lives. We hold no animosity towards each other. Please, daughter of Demeter, grant me this."

"You may," Persephone dismissed. "Once every ten years."

The goddess shook her dark hair. "That is not enough."

"Why not?" Persephone asked.

"I am with child," the Olympian responded, a hand coming to rest on the slightest curve of her stomach. "A demi-god. A beautiful boy. He will be – he will be everything good in me. You, of all the children of the gods, understand what it means to see a loved one for a brief time. Grant me more time to spend with him."

"That's me," Alexander continued. "How are we seeing this? Why is this in your head?"

"I lied," I admitted. "I wasn't saved by hikers when I fell into the river."

"Then how did you survive?" Alexander asked.

"I didn't," I answered. "I died. And Persephone allowed me to return with my memories."

Theo thought, *Why?*

"Because I needed to," I told them, "to be intiated into her Cult."

"Once a year," Persephone countered, sighing. Where she rested her feet on the sand, it became rich soil. "On the anniversary of his birth. On his wedding day. His ascension. For the birth of his children. His funeral. I will not give any more."

"Thank you," Aphrodite agreed. "I accept."

"You will owe me a favor in the future," Persephone continued and the Olympian goddess swallowed. "Anything I wish. Or, perhaps, anyone." A slow smile, a curving of dark red lips. "Do not worry, you will only benefit in the end. I know that is your only concern, Goddess of the Trojan War."

"Anything for my son," Aphrodite agreed. "Anything."

"Mother—" Alexander said, reaching his hand toward the goddess.

Persephone nodded her head.

The world trembled.

The memory ended.

WITH FEET TIED DOWN

W e woke up together. For a moment, the smallest glimpse of a second, I allowed myself to fall down the rabbit hole of imagining this forever. A forever of their limbs intertwined with mine, of our syncopated breathing, of exchanging morning-breath kisses with nothing between us but love.

But reality cared nothing for that forever.

Alexander's phone buzzed from under a pile of clothes, the sound just annoying enough to startle us into heavy blinking and slow breathing. Alexander, unashamed in his nudity, rolled out from under the blanket and turned the alarm off before pulling on a pair of sweatpants. I sat up, tucking the corner of the blanket into my armpits. Theo stayed laying down, eyes closed again, and lips pursed around his deep breath.

Once the ringing stopped, Alexander sat back on the edge of the bed, resting his head in his hands and rubbing the sleep away from his eyes. No one spoke for a few minutes and the weight of last night pressed down until it felt like a rock on my chest. I waited for the regret to come, but it didn't.

The muscles of Alexander's back rippled as he stretched. Theo's hair stained the pillowcases like ink.

I could never regret this. But I couldn't want it anymore, either.

A few minutes passed and Alexander said, "That wasn't just a dream, was it?"

I sighed. "No."

"Why didn't you tell us you were initiated?" Theo asked, refusing to open his eyes.

"I wasn't sure if I was allowed to," I admitted, thinking of my conversation with Rose. "Mystery Cult, you know? I planned on mentioning it last night, but—" I swallowed, looking away from their exposed skin. "We didn't have time."

Theo sat up, sighing too. Alexander stood, still facing away from us. More silence.

I continued, "The important thing is that I did initiate and that I have an open line to a goddess, even if she isn't an Olympian. It explains why we had the Chthonic god at the Ceremonial Building."

No response. I swung my legs off the bed. "I'm taking a shower."

Neither of them stopped me. By the time I came back out, they'd both shrugged on t-shirts. Theo ducked into the bathroom after me, already combing through his hair with his fingers and trying to get his curls to lay right. I tried to do the same, but it was a mostly unsuccessful operation. He brushed by, not touching me, and closed the door behind himself.

Alexander lingered for a few seconds, watching Theo leave without a word. His sigh was barely an exhale, but I recognized it anyway. I suppressed my urge to ask him about it, to comfort him. There was nothing that could make this better for any of us.

Instead, I made my way across the room, back to my phone and a distraction from the sad slope of Alexander's shoulders.

But as I passed by him, our arms brushed and, like the first time all over again, my skin burst into a million pinpricks. It was too much and I wanted infinitely more.

One of Alexander's hands wrapped around my waist, pulling me to him. My back to his bare chest, my jaw trembled with the attention. With the power of the *want* inside me. Brushing my hair from my neck to press a kiss at the junction, he murmured my name. I shivered. His other hand snaked down to my waist and I pressed my hand over his.

"We shouldn't," I whispered. "We said one night."

"I know," he agreed, pressing another kiss below my ear, "but I was right. I don't think it was enough."

I sighed, leaning back into him. I gave myself five seconds, maybe ten, and then pulled away. Turning around, I fiddled with his tie. He looked good, his clothes wrinkle-free and expensive. His hair was naturally laying to the right and there were no dark circles under his eyes. Even if being awake was hard, at least he'd slept well. "You look nice."

"So do you," he responded, looking down at me. "You always do."

Without my permission, my hand moved from his tie to the side of his neck as I breathed out his name. This, I thought, was the torture of Tantalus. To have tasted something, to be able to touch and know it cannot be yours.

The bathroom door opened and Theo stepped out, smoothing down his shirt. It was the same one he'd worn to the gallery event. But his beard had been trimmed back into soft stubble and the sleeves of his shirt were rolled up to reveal his gold bracelets, maybe for the last time.

Alexander and I stepped away from each other. Theo noticed, dark brows furrowing, but only said, "We should go downstairs soon. We don't want to be in line forever."

Alexander nodded. "Do we have everything?"

I lifted my backpack onto my shoulders. "I have the project papers. Do you have the cure?"

He only nodded again, pressing his hand to his own backpack to prove it to us. We left the room and the elevator ride was just as quiet as before. As we walked to the lobby, we passed by windows. Snow and ice covered the trees and ground, and our final assignment rested heavily on my shoulders. With every step, we came closer to the end of our group project.

A line snaked through the library, extending even out of the front doors. It led down through the middle of the fake Acropolis structure, passing the Parthenon and taking a left at the Karyatid porch. We all hesitated, unsure if we should make our way towards the front or try to get in line in the back.

"Mr. Crest!" someone called from behind the line. On the other side of the wall of people, the same receptionist from yesterday was waving her hands at us. As Alexander led us to her, I nearly slipped on the smooth marble and Theo gave me an arm to support myself with.

When we made it through the line, she continued, "One of your half-brothers called this morning. Your mother upgraded your seats and doesn't want you to wait in line."

"My mother knows I'm here?" Alexander shook his head. "How do we get in?"

"Follow me."

I ducked my head as we bypassed the people in line, who all looked eager for a long, impressive talk given by a being whose existence was older than even the titans. As we walked to the end of the Acropolis, the walls became marble too and the floor sloped downward like we were heading underground.

Someone's delicate hand had carved images into the marble, each with their own details – the birth of the universe, Zeus defeating his father, the creation of humans and the return of soulmates. The last one caused the power in my chest to thump, a reminder. I rushed past that carving.

At the doors to the auditorium, Cupids ushered in the crowd with their shrill voices. The line was split towards the two at the entrance, a velvet rope separating one queue from the other. The receptionist undid the rope leading to the emptier side and let us in. "You're in the front row. Should be seats one, two, and three. Have a great time!"

Then she left before Alexander could even offer her a tip. We entered the auditorium and the sheer size of it was a surprise. There was no way to tell from the outside that the hotel was capable of holding this many people in its basement.

People were shuffling into their seats around us but we were the first to arrive in our row. We were right by the stage, almost too close, but that was probably a good thing. This way, Aphrodite couldn't avoid talking to us after seeing Alexander.

I sat between them. Alexander stretched his legs as much as he could. Theo squirmed next to me and his mind buzzed with thoughts of discomfort. I grabbed his hand in mine and asked, "Are you okay?"

"Lots of people," he answered. "Not great with crowds."

"Once it starts," I answered. "I bet you won't even notice."

He smiled without confidence. "I'm sure you're right."

Alexander's leg bounced next to me and with my other hand, I pressed it down. He sighed and stopped bouncing it, intertwining his hand with mine. "Sorry. Nervous, I guess. I don't see her very often and it's always a big thing when I do."

"You don't need to apologize," I said. "Can I help?"

He shook his head. "No, I don't think so. I can feel Theo's anxiety in my head and my own is making it worse." He paused and I frowned, watching his face flicker between emotions. He squeezed my hand. "Can you just... not let go? Not yet."

I should have let go. But this could well have been my last chance to hold his hand.

441

"Okay," I said. "I won't let go."

We didn't say anything as the rest of the audience filed in. It took a lot of time, but I spent it listening to Theo's thoughts and trying to comfort them both. For the first time, I felt no envy about their shared physical collaboration. My own worry was eating away my brain. I would have hated to have theirs as well.

Looking over my shoulder, I saw almost everyone was seated and whispering with anticipation. The lights above us flickered, a signal that the talk was about to begin, and their whispers grew louder before dying off.

Then someone stepped on stage, but it wasn't the goddess. A man in an expensive suit tapped the microphone in the center of the stage. When he did, the screen at the back of the stage turned on. It announced the name of the speech: A NEW PARADIGM IN SOULMATES.

"Hello and welcome to the first speech in the New Paradigm tour," he said, coughing into the mic when it gave a little feedback. "I'll keep my introduction short, because I'm sure you all know why you're here. I'm honored to announce our magnificent guest speaker, the Goddess of Love and Beauty, Daughter of the Sea and Mother of Rome. Let's give a round of applause for Aphrodite!"

The crowd went wild, some Cult of Aphrodite members stood up and cheered loudly as the goddess stepped out from the right wing of the stage. Her beauty burned my eyes, and in the span of less than a moment, I thought, *She is the entire cosmos in one creature. Why can't I look like that? Is this what heaven feels like? Is love supposed to hurt?* And, then, when my mind came back to itself, *Alexander doesn't look like her.*

She had long, dark waves of hair and skin the color of the deepest depths of the sea. Her eyes, however, were the same blue as my soulmate's. Her teeth were startling white and just sharp enough that none of us could forget that the gods were, in their original form, the most powerful monsters.

She had a microphone taped to her jaw and her voice sounded like a giggle as she greeted the audience. "Hello, everyone! It pleases me so much to see you here. Thank you for your lovely introduction." This last part was said to the man in the suit, who seemed like the owner of the hotel. She pressed a kiss to his cheek, leaving a red lipstick stain. He touched it, his eyes growing glassy as he stepped off the stage.

To the audience, she asked, "Are you pleased to be here?"

The crowd cheered again. This time Alexander joined them and I smiled at him. The goddess had many abilities, but one of her major ones was the ability to change the mood of entire groups. She planted excitement and pleasure in all our brains as the scent of roses, violets and caramel swirled in the air.

"I'm so glad to hear it," she continued, her voice low like she had a little secret and it was just between us. "I'm sure you're curious about the topic of my talk today. I've been so very hush-hush about the subject, and a few of you have written to me, absolutely begging for me to spill the beans. But I've been so good!"

I raised my eyebrows, looking to Alexander. "Any idea what it is?"

He shook his head, but his gaze was focussed on his mother. "None at all."

Theo shifted next to me, still uncomfortable. "Do you feel that?"

I blinked at him. "What?"

He shook his head. "I'm not sure. It feels like our bond is... breathing."

I focussed on the forked bond in my chest, and he was right. It seemed to be expanding and contracting in the presence of the goddess, almost as if sensing her power. I wondered if anyone else felt it, but we were too close to the stage to ask anyone else without being noticed.

Aphrodite continued, "I've had a lot of help from two gods in particular with this little project. The first will come as no surprise. Of course, I'm talking about Great Zeus. But the second may come as a surprise to you and that's because, until this lifetime, all of us immortals have kept the origins of soulmates a secret."

A girl behind me whispered to her soulmate, "What is she talking about?"

My stomach dropped.

"Even from the lovely friezes that line the walls of this very hotel, we have stuck by a certain version of the story," the goddess said and pictures of the friezes flashed up on the screen. "That, because of our own benevolence, we the gods returned your soulmates. That, seeing the beginnings of rebellion and anger against the heavens, Zeus reunited your souls in exchange for your eternal worship and scheduled sacrifices. But this, my darlings, is only half the story. The other half is a story about a girl, a river and a choice."

Oh no, I thought. The downfall of knowing yourself.

"Vanessa?" Theo asked. "What's wrong?"

Aphrodite continued, "She died, drowning in the sea, and upon that short-lived death, she met the other god who helped me with the New Paradigm project." A dramatic pause. "Though we have publically interacted very little, there has been a thousand lifetimes of collaboration for this project with this goddess – the Dread Queen, Persephone."

The crowd erupted with gasps and whispers. Aphrodite had always distanced herself from the Gods of the Underworld. Love, she had said once in a daytime television interview, should never be hidden in the dark.

I was frozen in my seat, wide-eyed and terrified. Theo

looked confused, realization slowly clouding his features. Alexander hadn't made the connection yet, but he would.

The goddess continued, "Persephone offered this girl a gift. Anything in the world. Her dying wish was to reunite everyone with their soulmates. After she painted a picture of a godless world, one with corrupt politicians leading and Olympians fading into nothing but ancient myths, Zeus granted this wish."

"But such a gift came with a cost," Aphrodite said, her words almost an echo of the memory. The image of Persephone's face, illuminated by her necklace, flashed in my head. Theo must have seen it too, because his head snapped towards me, turning pale. "And she died before her soul could be matched with another. It damaged her soul and because of this, she was not brought back to live another life until her current one."

Awareness seemed to bloom across Alexander's face as he turned to me. "Is she talking about—"

"Me?" I interrupted, staring at the goddess, who refused to look at us. "Yeah."

"Why?" Alexander asked.

"I think," Theo said, "we're about to find out."

The crowd surged with excitement again. There was fear in my chest now, because the goddess was revealing information to the world about my soul that not even I knew. Alexander's hand went slack in mine as he closed his eyes, almost as if he was trying to pretend this wasn't happening. Unlike him, I couldn't take my eyes off the goddess.

"Yes, that's right," she continued. "Persephone and I have done everything in our wealth of power to ensure she's repaid for her wish." A dramatic pause. The screen above her changed, flashing to a screen split into three pictures of me, Alexander, and Theo. "Which is why, as of three months ago, she became the first soul to ever receive two soulmates instead of one!"

Everyone, including myself, leaned forward, eager to hear

her next words. She said, "And I say the first because, after the wild success of their three-person bond, we'll be rolling out a new generation of soulmates that include three people instead of the usual two. Every child born from this moment onward will have a fifty percent chance of being placed in one of these bonds. Now, you might be asking, how does this bond work? How is the process different? Well, who better to ask than the girl who started it all!"

48

THE GLORY

The crowd was deafening with their screams and I sank into my seat, looking around the edges of the auditorium for an easy escape. There wasn't one. News crews were set up in front of the doors, the green lights of their live cameras blinking mockingly in the distance.

"I brought her here today!" the goddess said over the noise. A spotlight of gold burnt my eyes. Two more, blue this time, shone down on the men next to me. "As well as her two soulmates! They're ready to answer any questions you have about this new paradigm of soulmates. Come up on stage, my darlings."

For the first time, the goddess looked down at us, smiling in that sharp way. Alexander, at this moment, looked more mortal than I would've believed possible. He was too soft for immortality. She offered us a wink and two of the security guards from the hotel stood at either end of the row as if expecting us to bolt. We didn't.

We did the opposite, as if our feet were nailed to the ground like a statue of a chaotic goddess. The people around us murmured, unsure what was happening. The guards pushed past the first people seated on our row and we all squished together, as if huddling would protect us from what lay ahead.

"Aw," Alexander's mother said. "They're shy. Let's give them a round of applause to inspire them. After all, if I have to answer all the questions myself, I won't be able to meet any of you afterward. And I know you'll have so many burning questions!"

The threat was clear. If we didn't go on stage, she would leave before we could get any clarity on our own situation. The power in my chest charged and I pushed myself to my feet. Alexander and Theo looked up at me as the crowd roared again.

"What are you doing?" Alexander asked, his voice drowned out by the screams.

"Going up there," I answered, grabbing his hand and tugging him to his feet. "We need answers. Come on, Theo," I added, grabbing his hand too. But he didn't come up easily. "We have to—"

"I can't—" he said, hands gripping the armrests of his chair like he was afraid they'd fly off. He looked up at me and the blue light made him look even paler than he was. I could see every bead of sweat running from his hairline to his cheeks. "Crowds. Remember? I can't. So many people."

"We have to," I insisted, grabbing his arm and yanking as much as I could. He lifted off of the seat but just barely. Alexander turned around to take everything in and the crowd roared. The guards came closer and my words rushed out, "All you have to do is walk and stand there. We'll answer every-thing. Please, Theo, we need you."

He looked up at us and blinked. "Vanessa—"

"Now, Theodore," I said. When I yanked, he stood up completely. I kept hold of his hand and pressed Alexander forward. I smiled at the crowd, but I tried to make it look like I was baring my teeth, too. Theo followed behind me, his long legs nearly causing him to run into me, but I kept pushing and dragging until we got to the side of the stage with stairs.

The guards directed us up the stairs and as we climbed them Aphrodite introduced us again, "Welcome to the stage, Vanessa Reyes, Theodore Patras, and my own son, Alexander Crest. Let's give them a warm welcome."

People from the wings pushed three chairs out onto the stage, all soft and comfortable looking. Aphrodite waved towards them and I pushed Theo down on the closest one. He refused to release my hand.

"Now," the goddess said. Theo looked terrified and my knuckles hurt from his grip. Alexander still looked blank and confused. "If you could line up in the aisles, we'd love to take your questions." People scrambled to join the lines in front of the microphones that the guards had set up. There was pushing and shoving and my heart beat fast.

Someone must have given a signal, because one of the people in front of a microphone cleared their throat, and bouncing on their toes, asked, "I guess my question – the first question! Thank you! – is for Vanessa. What made you choose soulmates as your one gift?"

An easy one. "I don't know."

The person frowned. Aphrodite pulled her mic away from her mouth and said, "Rushing through the questions won't make me help you. Answer well or don't bother."

Through gritted teeth, I continued, "I couldn't decide between the two men in my original life and when Persephone offered me anything in the world, I asked to stop feeling split." I let out a laugh, something mean and bitter. "I guess that's dumb to say now. Next."

A girl asked, "What abilities do you have?"

Alexander, voice flat and without any of his usual emotion, answered, "Theo and Vanessa have telepathy and memory sharing. Vanessa and I have dreamsharing. Theo can hear my thoughts, but I can't hear his. We also have physical collaboration."

The last part made the audience murmur in excitement. They, too, knew the significance of such a strong ability. The girl asked a follow up question, "Do you think these abilities are because your bond is old or because of the three-person aspect?"

It was Aphrodite who answered, "It's a mix of both. As you may not know, The Department of Soulmates doesn't keep track of abilities as they manifest randomly for each group of soulmates. However, the age of the bond and the compatibility factor into how the ability manifests. Because all three of them were specifically chosen for this threeway bond, we made sure they were compatible. But the original bond between Alexander and Theo formed pre-Bronze Age, so that could be it as well. Only the Fates could answer."

A guy in a suit stepped forward next. "To add to that, why were each of these people chosen for this? What qualities do they have to suggest they could handle such an unusual bond?"

Aphrodite nodded, as if she had been expecting the question. "My Alexander is one of the most loving souls in the world. Of course, as my son, he has an infinite capacity for love, which makes him an ideal candidate. Theo, after having his soulmate die just a year ago, has experience with relationships and abilities."

Theo, next to me, flinched as she brought up Margot in front of everyone.

Aphrodite continued without pause, "And, well, Vanessa here, is one of the few souls in existence that doesn't have a soulmate of her own. They both fell in love with her in their original lives, though in reality they were each other's soulmates. Using a term from the study of split souls, she would be referred to as the Extra."

My heart paused in my chest. Alexander and Theo whipped

their heads to look at me. I threw up my mental shield before Theo could say anything. I wasn't surprised. Not after I'd seen them together. But hearing it was confirmation of everything I was afraid of. I was glad we were sitting because I was pretty sure my knees wouldn't have held me up.

"Mother—" Alexander snapped, lip curling.

"How did the process for creating the bond work?" a man in glasses asked the goddess.

She nodded. "Persephone and I used a model already in existence, specifically that of the Split Soul Syndrome. A disorder that manifests as a result of unpurified familial miasma. It requires three souls and three conditions to be met. Someone with ancestral pollution, someone with a connection to a god or goddess and someone with a damaged soul.

"Vanessa's immortal soul was the anchor for the pollution, though it took much convincing to get the Fates to see it as such. Obviously, Alexander is the connection to me. Theo was the difficult part – this person in a typical SSS group is usually the result of the death of a plat or a romantic soulmate. Getting a temporary bond to form between him and his first romantic soulmate, Margot Simon, was one of the most difficult aspects on our side." Theo went still next to me, even more blood draining from his face. "It faded faster than we predicted, however. Her death came about six months too soon. The good news is that, because of the success of this new bond, we can create these new three-person bonds organically."

I wanted to say something and I could tell Alexander was about to, but a guy stepped up to the mic in the next aisle. He sent the stage a bright smile and he was beautiful in that Cult of Aphrodite way. He asked, "This one is for Alexander. How does it feel to have your mom be the one to give you such a gift?"

Alexander, snapping his head away from Theo, just stared out into the crowd, frowning. "A gift?"

The guy cleared his throat and continued, "I mean, having two people who love you—"

"This gift," Alexander said, face darkening as he stood and threw down his mic. His voice echoed anyway, and the air around him began to smell like ozone and chlorine. Even Aphrodite, armed with divine power, blinked in surprise at the anger coming off him. "Has made an absolute mess of all our lives and is nothing more than my mother using us as guinea pigs for her own power. I never believed what people said about you, Mom. About how you were mean and selfish and manipulative, but I see it now. I see exactly how they could think that, after you've pretended our souls were nothing more than your playthings."

He stormed off stage. Theo looked at me and I knew what he was asking. Swallowing, I nodded and he followed Alexander, throwing his own microphone down. It screeched with feedback and everyone winced. Aphrodite was looking after her son and she actually seemed surprised. She opened her mouth, but I shook my head. If she confronted him – or even pitied him – in front of everyone, she'd only make it worse. He'd forgive her, but not before he said something he'd regret later.

Before she could say anything, I said, "Next ."

Under the smell of a sea storm brewing, the sharp scent of pomegranates burned.

The crowd spat questions at me for another thirty-five minutes. Theo counted for me, letting me know the end must be coming soon. When he hit forty, Aphrodite stood up, clapped her hands, and declared the end of the event.

Four guards bracketed us as we were escorted from the stage to a hallway behind it. The lights were bright yellow, illuminating the faces of my soulmates, who were waiting for us there. Alexander was sitting on the ground, head in his hands between his knees. Theo was kneeling in front of him, hands on his shoulders.

Aphrodite dismissed the guards with a wave of her hands. They left us. She took a step towards Alexander, but Theo stood up and blocked her from him. Her eyes grew gray like storm clouds over the sea. "I know you're more powerful than I can even imagine and you could probably strike me down without even moving a finger, but he doesn't want to talk to you right now, so I can't let you."

Her mouth curled with distaste before it twitched up, smug. "What a powerful bond you share." She sighed heavily, turning to me. "I don't understand his complaints. You've obviously cemented the bond last night. Why are you unhappy?"

I couldn't stop the way my cheeks burned, but really, it was no different than things Tori had said to me. Clenching my jaw, I asked, "Are you seriously so out of touch with human emotions that you think anything you just did would make him happy?"

She raised one eyebrow. "My son doesn't get stage fright."

"But I do," Theo snapped at the goddess, before backing away when her gaze landed on him. "You just admitted to giving me Margot and then killing her for your own project. How do you think that made me feel? And he feels everything I feel. Not to mention, he cares more about Vanessa than anything and you broke her heart out there."

"Theo—" I started.

"I'm in your head," he interrupted, frowning back at me. "You can't lie to me."

"You're all so short-sighted," the goddess said, her voice lovely and cruel. "As is to be expected with mortals, but your care for each other is only proof that my 'meddling,'" she said the word with an eye roll, "worked in your favor."

"What do you mean?" I asked.

"You love each other," she explained slowly, as if I was a child. "And, seeing those hickies on your neck, you're obviously attracted to each other too. You have amazing abilities that manifested on their own. You—"

"Mother," Alexander interrupted, voice flat and hard, "bless the cure."

She pulled back as if his voice hurt her. I imagined she'd never had him speak to her with anything but the most religious loyalty. "What cure?" When Alexander pulled out the bottle of gold, frothing liquid, her gaze narrowed, her teeth looking sharper. "Alexander, what are you doing with such a thing?"

"We – I want you to break the bond," Alexander said, and I understood why he was saying it. This request, coming from anyone else, would have been nothing to a goddess. But from her son? A son that she would do anything for in this life or an ancient one? "Will it work?"

"Work?" she repeated, snorting. "If your intention is to break your bond and ensure you'll never have another soulmate, sure. It's like bringing in a bulldozer for the job of a hammer. And your bond is my own craftsmanship. Delicate, lovely, and precious—"

"Will. It. Work?" he demanded, shaking the bottle until more foam formed.

"Yes, I suppose, but why would you want to get rid of it?" She seemed curious. She sighed again. "Fine, I'll admit that you have a point about my manipulation, but does it matter if the end result brings you pleasure?"

My chest burned. I thought of my own goddess and her own manipulation of my memories. "That," I said to them, and to the ground below my feet, "is a slippery slope. We never asked for this."

She rolled her perfect eyes. "No one asks for their soulmates. You made that choice."

"And now I'm making another one," I said and stood up straighter, saying the words that I had dreaded to even think about for weeks. Since we had learnt about the cure. "Listen to your son. Bless the cure so we can take it and get rid of this broken bond."

"You're not broken," she said immediately, blinking at me like the word was confusing to her. "You're split, certainly, but that doesn't mean you're broken. A pomegranate isn't broken when you slice it open. On the contrary, it's only when you split it that you get the best part of the fruit. And, of course, that's not the only example—"

"Mother," Alexander interrupted again, pushing himself from the floor and stretching to his full height. He reached out, hand shaking but eyes steady, and took his mother's hands in his. "I've never asked you for anything. I endured a childhood of occasional visits and impersonal gifts."

"You loved your boats," she murmured.

"I loved you more," he responded, squeezing her hands. "But you weren't there. You didn't come to my swim meets. You didn't come to parent-teacher conferences. You weren't there for prom or my first time driving. I've never asked you for anything." He let out a breath which turned into a sob. "But I am asking you for this. Please. Bless the cure."

She looked up at him as he towered over her. For the smallest second, she looked vulnerable, unsure. "Even if I was willing to undo thousands of years of work, it's not as easy as you want it to be. There are stipulations, Alexander."

"There always is with you," he said, his smile bittersweet.

"It could be excruciating," she tried one last time.

His smile trembled. "It already is."

"It'll take a few weeks," she continued, a tear welled in her eyes, but she clenched her jaw and it dissipated. "I'll have one of your brothers deliver it. I'll have to get Persephone to agree, too. Alexander, are you absolutely certain? Not even I could reverse this."

"Bless the cure, Mom," he said, letting go of her hand. He grabbed the cure from where he had left it on the floor and pushed it into her hands. "And let us know when it's ready to be taken."

She nodded. He moved, grabbing his bag and slinging it over his shoulder. We didn't touch as we made our way to the end of the hall, toward the exit. We were at the end, nearly turning out of sight, when the goddess called, "You know I love you, darling?"

Alexander paused midstride. I could see the debate happening in his head. He was so angry to have been involved in that whole charade, but she had agreed to his one demand. She was doing us a favor by blessing a cure to something she had spent thousands of years creating.

Over his shoulder, he called, "I know, Mom. I love you, too."

He didn't wait for her to say anything else. I led us from the hallway and away from the goddess.

We had gotten what we wanted, but we'd never been farther from happy.

ΆΛΉΘΕΙΑ

THE VERY IDEA OF TRUTH

I stood in the middle of a field of white flowers. The sky was dark overhead, a sheet thrown over the world with only the pinpricks of stars coming through. The stems and petals swayed in the gentle breeze, tickling against the skin of my legs. I took a deep breath and though I'd never been to the sea, I recognized its smell.

If I concentrated, I could hear the sound of the waves just beyond a row of Mediterranean pines, the leaves budding with blooms, the bark strangely colored from the wildfires that had torn through the islands in the area just a few summers ago. The very tips of their petals peeked out from the green outer leaf, like lizard tongues seconds from catching a fly. They were a mark of springtime. Of change.

I took another breath and closed my eyes.

"Beautiful, isn't it?" A voice asked next to me.

I didn't jump. The voice was familiar and I had come to expect divine intervention. Opening my eyes, I saw the Goddess of the Dead resting next to me. She was sat on the ground, hands buried in the dirt.

"It is," I agreed, looking down at the goddess. "Home."

"More of a home than Michigan?" Persephone asked, raising an eyebrow.

I shook my head. "They both feel like home."

She gave me half of a smile. "Can't decide?"

I shrugged. "I don't want to."

She laughed and the flowers bent their backs, bowing to the sound. "No," she agreed, nodding. She lifted a hand to me, palm up. There was dirt under her fingernails and in the curves of her fingerprints. "I suppose you don't. Give me a hand."

I took her hand and she pulled herself to her feet, brushing the dirt from her hands onto her white dress. Green and brown stained the pure fabric, but it didn't look wrong on her. Once up, she held both my hands in hers. We were standing in the middle of a meadow, the moonlight making the faces of the narcissus flowers glow as they stared up at us.

"Why did you summon me here?" I asked her.

She laughed again. "I should be asking you that. You're in charge of all this, not me. I assume it has something to do with the announcement Aphrodite made today." Her eyes were assessing as they ran over me. "She tells me that you still asked for the cure to be blessed, even after she explained that this was your reward."

"Reward?" I repeated back just as I had wanted to do on the stage. "Persephone, surely, you of all people understand the problem with making someone choose a Fate they don't want and then trying to convince them it's a good one."

She swallowed. "I do understand. I do. I promise. That's why, if you decide to take the cure, I will not be angry with you. You can still run my Cult on your campus. You won't know any consequences from this. Not even from Aphrodite. You give me your worship, Vanessa, and in return, I shall give you protection."

"The choice is mine?" I asked her.

"Always," she breathed, letting go of one of my hands to touch my cheek. Her hands were cold. Like marble. "But the thing about choices is that they're never as easy as you want them to be. Just because you spent a lot of time making one choice doesn't mean it's the right one...

and if neither choice sounds good, it's up to you to find another option."

"What do you mean?" I asked.

"Come," she said, pulling me towards the edge of the meadow where the soil met the gray stone on the beach. The first lizards of the season blinked their diamond eyes at us as we passed. There were no flowers growing here, the soil contained too much sand, but the lizards smiled at the goddess, happily half-buried in the earth. An image of the goddess pressing kisses to each of their heads flashed in my mind. She led me to a wall of rocks, all a mix of strange stones and crushed seashells. Remnants of the ancient past, dating from before even the memory of my soul.

"I was raised as the child of two of the most important gods on Olympus," she told me. "Zeus, my father, loves his children and, somehow, Hera never minded me as a bastard. I believe she loves my mother, the way any sister does. But there was always pressure on me to be like the other immortals. To be beautiful like Hebe. To be wise like Athena. My mother, especially, pushed me to live on Olympus. To make the name Kore just as golden and perfect as the others. I tried. But I was miserable there. I was drawn to the earth."

"Because of Hades?" I asked. The wind grew colder with his name.

She shook her head. "No, because I've always loved every plant, every creature that scuttles and bird that soars. I am my mother's daughter, but I could never be just her daughter. And then he came for me. Took me from a field like this one. I became a part of the earth, but I was miserable without the sun speckled lizards and the yellow-pollened flowers. I put all my energy into being a good queen for him, for the souls below. I tried to be the Persephone the world needed me to be, but I could never get rid of Kore completely either."

She sighed, and where she rested her hand on the rock beside her, the moss grew to meet her fingers, soft and green even in the darkness. "I had the worst of both worlds, and no choice in either. So I did what I'm advising you to do now, Vanessa. I didn't choose between heaven and Hades. I didn't do what Hebe would do. I didn't do what Athena would do. I did what made me happy."

"You ate the pomegranate," I finished, nodding. I stared at the sea, how the waves rolled, uneven but comforting. I no longer feared the water. I didn't know if the river had washed away all the residual fear in my heart or if I just trusted the goddess enough to protect me. But, for the first time, I had the sudden urge to plunge into the waves. Well, the first time since my first life.

"I ate the pomegranate."

"So you stayed willingly?" I asked.

"I didn't choose," she corrected. "I am still Kore and I am still Persephone."

"Are you happy?"

"I am me," she answered. "And that is infinitely more important."

"Aphrodite says I don't have a soulmate," I changed the subject. "I want to be upset, to scream and cry and curse all the gods on Olympus and below, but I think I always knew it was true. There's no other half out there for me."

"Darling girl," the goddess said, "you are complete on your own. As I am half-Kore, half-Persephone, you are both Wanaxa and Vanessa. Half-ancient and half-modern. The best of both. Everything you crave in love you can provide for yourself."

"So I don't decide?" I asked.

"To decide is, in itself, a decision," she said, shrugging in the moonlight.

"That's confusing," I said, "and difficult."

"As the most rewarding things often are."

49

TO KNOW THYSELF

A s the winter night ate the sky as early as late afternoon, I stared down at the brown napkin with a date and time written on it – this Friday. My deadline. Rose had served it to me at the library cafe this morning under a pomegranate oolong tea, which I had actually asked for this time.

In the two weeks that had passed, the news had gone national. Our faces were on screens and newspapers, announcing to everyone our role in the new paradigm of soul-mates. My phone hadn't stopped ringing. Each call was a new station begging for a quote about the situation. About the deepest parts of my broken soul. On campus, people stared in class, whispering about me during exam review. My professors excused all my absences. Lux had even sent us an email to submit our project via email instead of as a class presentation.

We submitted the project the night before it was due, all of us online but not speaking. It was all business between the three of us. We only talked about the event at the hotel like it was a learning experience for the project. We used the words outlined in the syllabus and in the end, it was more impersonal than was recognizable to me. It could've been written by anyone. I didn't know if that was a good thing or bad.

There was radio silence on all parts. If it were possible, the group chat would be covered in dust. I didn't run into anyone on campus, which could only be a gift from the gods. I made sure not to be at the Laurel Leaf or Golden Rings.

Ronan moved out of our apartment when I wasn't home. He left a note, but I'd shoved it into my desk drawer and hadn't read it. Theo's mind was shut off from mine. Alexander wasn't in my dreams. Our bond threatened to snap, burning like a hole inside my chest. I told myself that I was okay. That my days and nights in the library were enough to fill the hole. That the aches in the gaps between my fingers were just in my head.

But I knew myself too well now to be convinced.

And now I had to make another decision. The brown napkin looked innocuous, almost flirtatious, but it was a reminder of everything. It reminded me of first life memories, certainly, but also of my first meeting with Theo outside of class when he asked for my number in the tattoo shop. What would have happened if I had said yes? If, before the start of all this soulmate bullshit, we'd found we loved each other? What would've happened to Alexander? What would—

My phone rang. My mother.

I answered the phone, and she said, "Why do I have the strangest feeling that you need to talk to your mother about something?" In the background, I could hear something musical, like maybe the old record player in our house. My dad's voice rumbled just below it. "Your father says to not overthink it, whatever it is."

"I'm not sure if that's possible," I told her. "It's pretty big."

She hummed. "Most things feel big while you're staring at them through a microscope." She paused and her voice lowered. "Have you talked to Ronan about any of this?"

I shook my head, though I knew she couldn't see me. "I haven't talked to him at all. He moved out."

"Do you think he could help?" she asked. "If he knew?"

I sighed and the edges of my napkin fluttered with it. "Probably."

"Then talk to him," I heard my dad say. "Easy."

"He's right," my mom agreed. "He's Ronan. He wants you to be happy."

I wasn't sure about that. We were both assholes the last time we'd talked, and I threw my death in his face like I'd wanted to hurt him. And I guess I had. Still on the phone, I walked over to my desk and the drawer where I'd stashed his note and pulled out the envelope.

"Okay," I told them. "I'll talk to him."

"You know you're not alone, right?" I heard my mother say, voice much closer than before. "I hear what those damn reporters are saying about this new paradigm stuff. About how you didn't have a soulmate in the beginning, but that doesn't mean you're alone. You always have us."

"I know, Mom," I said, my words echoing Alexander's at the event.

I read the letter.

The doorbell rang out as I stepped into the Laurel Leaf the next day. Ronan stood at the coffee machine, his back toward me, and called over his shoulder, "Welcome! I'll be with you in just a minute."

"That's okay," I told him. He turned, surprised to hear my voice. I'd almost surprised myself with it, too. Looking at the clock behind the desk, I said, "You have lunch soon, don't you? Meet me at the Golden Rings when you're off. Lunch and coffee on me."

"Vanessa," he said, but I shook my head and called back as I left.

"I'll see you, then."

I sat in the furthest booth from the door, shrugged off my backpack and let it plop to the floor. The semester was winding down and there was no homework left. Just a few last readings and studying for finals. The semester was ending, but there were so many things I had left to do.

Hands shaking but determined, I called Melissa, the president of the Society for Ethical Sacrifice while I waited for Ronan. "Hi, Melissa. This is Vanessa. You and Olympia are graduating next semester, and I want to put my bid in for president. It's early but I'm serious about this and think I'll be a great leader."

"Vanessa," she said, but I interrupted, staring at the cup of tea in front of me. Steam rose.

"I ran the event this year," I said to her. "I got useful volunteers and gave us the idea to split the speakers and intervened when the Cult of Demeter talked for too long."

"The election isn't until the end of the next semester."

"That's fine," I told her, nodding. Time would move fast, just as it always did. "But I know I'm ready."

The call ended after that and I slipped the phone away with a sense of relief. Another thing off my list. I was just pulling out a book, my head under the table, when someone slid into the booth opposite of me.

Not expecting Ronan to be done yet, I sat up and nearly hit my head, blinking at the person across from me. Tamara had her elbows on the table as she stared at me, taking in my presence at her cafe. She didn't say anything for a while, just stared at my wrists before finally reaching over and placing a plate of cookies next to me. I hadn't taken my bracelets off, I couldn't bear how naked I felt without them despite all the stares they attracted.

"Do you want me to leave?" I asked, swallowing, but hoping the cookies indicated the opposite.

She rolled her eyes, but stayed quiet for an extended moment. She reminded me of Theo so much that I couldn't look at her eyes without wanting to cry. I looked away, focusing on the line of people at the register.

"I don't blame you, you know."

My gaze snapped back to her face. "What?"

"Tori keeps going on about how you're the one who started all this," she explained, waving a hand around. "With Theo. Who isn't here by the way. But she seems to think it's your fault for not having a soulmate of your own."

I frowned. "Is she wrong?"

"I don't know. Is she?" she said with raised eyebrows. "Would you have asked for this?"

My answer was a snort.

She continued, "Of course not. So I don't blame you even if he's done nothing but mope and paint sad pictures for that group of billionaire hyenas." She paused. "Have you seen your portrait? It's gorgeous."

"Portrait?" I asked, blinking at her.

She looked surprised. "He said he was going to tell you during your little roadtrip thing, but I guess he was distracted. You would have to be blind as Homer to miss the hickies you were sporting on that stage."

I knew I was blushing. "Go back to the portrait."

"Right," she said, nodding. "He sold the one of Margot, but then they wanted something else, too, for his back-and-forth and the waiting period. He painted another one of you a few days ago, standing on a Greek island or something. It's cool. They suggested he submit it to some contests. But, of course, he's dragging his feet with that."

Something inside caught fire with the knowledge he painted me even after all that had happened. It was a strange

465

kind of fire, both warming and painful. "Thanks for letting me know. That you don't blame me."

She dismissed that with a wave of her hand. "My brother is dramatic – in a less obvious way than Tori. He won't scream and shout about how he's feeling. You just have to learn the language of his brooding. A tortured, artistic soul, I guess. But that's not why I wanted to talk to you."

"Oh?" I asked.

"You're graduating next year, right?" she asked. I nodded. She grinned and I saw the family resemblance all over again. It's strange, looking back, that I'd somehow lost count of Theo's smiles. "With a degree in Communications? Great. Then, I'm offering you a job."

I choked on nothing. "What?"

"My back-of-house girl quit a few weeks ago," she said, tilting her head back toward the kitchen. "I have my barista making cookies and sweets and I'm out here. Everything is chaos, you know?"

"What does that have to do with me?" I asked.

"Theo mentioned once that you helped out on your family's orchard," she explained, tapping her fingers on the table. "And, curious, I looked it up. It's not a small business. There are a few locations up in Traverse City, right?" I nodded. "And I assume you have some experience with running it? Not to mention, you've helped Sam with the Laurel Leaf for years now."

"Not that part of it," I objected.

"But your plat does that, right?" she asked like she already knew the answer. "So you have a year to ask him how to do it and then, when you graduate, you can come work for me."

I thought of Sam's offer to Theo. "Did Theo ask you to do this?"

"He may have mentioned something," she said with a shrug. "But you've helped us out a few times, like when Theo needed to take it easy after the tattoo. And, if you worked here, Theo could take the job Sam offered, which we both know is a better fit for him than making tea and coffee."

I opened my mouth to refute that, but I couldn't. She was right and she knew it. But there were a few problems with her plan. "Ronan and I aren't speaking. I doubt he wants to teach me how to balance a budget or buy supplies when we haven't seen each other in weeks." I paused and then continued, voice lower, "And I'm sure Theo mentioned how our road trip ended. We're taking the cure. Don't put yourself in the middle of this mess."

The door rang. I didn't look up, listening to Tamara's response, "About the second, we'll cross that bridge when we get to it. But the first," she said, sliding out of the booth. I followed the movement with my eyes and saw Ronan walking over. "Well, try not to burn it."

"Hi, Tamara," Ronan greeted, holding the strap to his bag in a tight grip.

She nodded at him. "Ronan. Can I get you anything?"

"Whatever sandwich you think is best," he answered, sliding into the booth across from me and taking off his bag. He looked vulnerable without it. "And coffee. Black."

She nodded, heading back to the counter and the kitchen. "Will do. Say hi to Sam for me."

"Will do," he echoed back.

I grabbed the tea in front of me, which was hardly steaming now. "Thank you for meeting me."

He raised his eyebrows. "You didn't really leave room for argument."

Shrugging, I agreed, "That's true. But we needed to talk. I read your letter."

He snorted. "Yeah, that's why I wrote it. A week ago."

"I'm sorry I didn't read it," I said, taking a drink of the tea and a bite of cookie. It was, of course, perfect. "I wasn't interested in hearing an apology, but thank you for giving one." A pause. "I'm sorry I was an asshole that day, too."

He sighed. Tamara brought his coffee over. He took a drink of it before continuing, "It just threw me for a loop. I didn't even feel anything when you... died. And you used it to hurt me. It was shitty."

"I know," I said, nodding. "And I won't do it again. I mean, I don't plan on dying any time soon, but I won't use my soulmate situation to make you feel worse." A pause. "You said in your letter that you felt like I stopped talking to you about anything but this. That I stopped asking about you. I'm sorry for that too."

He nodded. "I don't think you were doing it on purpose. I know you weren't, actually, but it just sucked to have to stop my entire life every time something happened with your bond." He paused. "I sound like a dick, now. I just mean—" He raked a hand through his hair. "I guess I was used to being the center of your world and included in everything, and then, suddenly, I wasn't. It sucked. Sucks."

I reached my hand across the table, palm open, and he took it. I swallowed the emotion it brought up. "I understand. That's how I felt during our freshman year. You were so close with all your Cult of Hermes friends and I just... didn't mesh with them. Not in a bad way. I just didn't. I spent a lot of nights alone in our prison cell of a dorm."

He blinked at me like I was crazy. "I didn't know that."

"I know," I told him. "I didn't want you to. You weren't doing anything wrong by making new friends, but you had just met Sam and then you had a bunch of new friends who were interested in the same things you were. I felt like I was getting left behind."

"That's what I've been feeling during all this," he admitted, and his eyes got a little watery. "Lord Apollo, Vanessa, why didn't you ever say anything? Actually, nevermind. I did the same thing. At least you didn't get petty and aggressive in front of other people at your workplace. I was a dick. I'm so sorry."

"We both fucked up," I said. "It's okay."

"No, it's not," he said, and I could feel his frustration at himself. "And I won't do it again. I promise you." He took a deep breath. "I've seen the news. About the event in Detroit. I mean, I think everyone has." I winced and he squeezed my hand. "I'm not bringing it up to be mean, I just wanted to say Aphrodite was wrong."

That surprised me and I was taken aback by the bold words. "What do you mean?"

"She said you didn't have a soulmate," he clarified. "And she's wrong. I'm your soulmate and you're mine. I know it's a mouthful and that's why we use the word plat, but we're platonic *soulmates*."

It was a sweet thought, but I shook my head. "I don't remember you in my original life—"

"Frankly, Vanessa," he interrupted, leaning forward. "I don't give a shit."

"What?" I asked with a laugh.

"I'm your platonic soulmate in this life," he said, taking his hand off his coffee to grab my other one. "And I don't have memories of my original life, so I can't say anything about that, but I don't care. All that is in the past."

"The past is important—"

"Again, let me be frank," he said. "The past only matters if you can use what it teaches you to make your present or future better. I'm your soulmate. Forget Alexander and Theo. Forget Sam. You and I are the real love story, here. Just because it's platonic doesn't make it any less important."

"I love you," I said because I felt it needed to be said.

"I love you too," he replied with just as much feeling. "And you know you're welcome to come back to the Laurel Leaf whenever you want. Sam's been on my ass for the last two weeks about talking to you. He misses you. I miss you."

I smiled but shook my head. "Thank you, but I don't think it would be right. I've missed you too, but I think I was using you as a crutch. It's time for me to do things that make me happy." I paused. "But that doesn't mean I don't want you involved. I just—"

"Want to be yourself," he finished for me. "I get it. Where do you think you want to go? What will make you happy?"

I looked to the counter, where Tamara was swirling whipped cream on someone's drink. She looked up and caught my eye. She winked.

"I'm not sure," I said to Ronan. "But I think I'm getting ready to cross that bridge."

I was tucking myself into bed that night, warm from the emotions bouncing between Ronan and I, when my phone buzzed alerting me to a new email. My stomach dropped when I found Lux's name on my screen.

Dear Alexander, Theo, and Vanessa,

With the end of the semester approaching, I've taken a look at your group project and have some concerns over the final result. Please meet me in the classroom at our usual time tomorrow to discuss your grade.

Yours, Professor Lux

For the first time in weeks, the groupchat buzzed with a new message.
Theo: You guys get the email?
Alexander: I'll be there.
Me: So will I.

Three blinking dots appeared by their names, both typing out a new response.

Theo: Do you think we failed?

Alexander: My mother called today.

The cure is ready.

50

DEPENDS ON US

My last final had ended an hour ago. The lights were off in the classrooms and the hallways were empty. My snow boots made the only noise as I walked, for the last time, into our Soulmates 101 classroom. A storm swelled outside but the first wave of snow barely touched the ground before melting.

It wasn't until I saw Alexander that the reality of the situation hit me. His back was towards me as he leaned over the podium where I expected Lux to be. I took him in for a moment, the curve of his spine and the exact color of his hair. I wanted to fall to my knees with the ecstasy of being close to him, but I was a tourist and I could only think of how hard it would be to remember this moment once I left.

I shook the thought off and said, "Where's Lux?"

He startled, jumping and turning to look at me. He waved the white paper in the air like he was surrendering. "According to this," he said with another more forceful swish of the paper. "She's not coming. We got an A."

I frowned and I was about to say something, but Theo walked in, his backpack on his shoulder and snowflakes in his dark hair. "Who's not coming?" he asked, setting his stuff on the first desk by the door.

"Lux," we both answered. Alexander clarified, "She says we did exceptional work, especially given the circumstances of this semester. She hopes to see us around campus in January."

"Well, that's annoying," Theo muttered. "I came from downtown for this. I thought we failed."

"What's it say on the back?" I asked him, seeing our professor's neat letters.

He frowned and flipped it over, apparently having missed the words the first time. "It says, *On a different note, I encourage you to use this time to discuss the cure and when you plan on taking it.* 'Discuss' is underlined three times."

"Did you bring it with you?" I asked Alexander. "We could take it now."

Theo dropped something that clattered. Alexander and I looked over as he scrambled to pick up his phone from the floor. "Sorry," he said, covering up the pain in his expression with blankness. A layer of black paint over the Mona Lisa. "I didn't expect to do it today. Do we know the, uh, side effects?"

I shook my head, but Alexander nodded, pulling the blue bottle from his own backpack. "My mother explained it to me. It'll hurt, like she said, but only for about a minute. She suggests no strenuous work for the first day after ingestion, but physically, we'll be fine."

"Fine," Theo snorted to himself. "Right. Sure."

I ignored it. "So, theoretically—"

"We could walk into this room with two soulmates and walk out with none," Alexander finished, setting the cure on the front desk. It was the desk he had sat at during the first weeks of the semester, before the group project started.

I shook my head. "I'm not your soulmate."

They both flinched. Alexander started, "Vanessa—"

"If you really think that," Theo said with an icy anger, "then let's get this the fuck over with."

He stood resolute, unmoving. Like Croesus on the banks of the River Hermus, he too was doomed to a fate he could avoid by just running from it. But he wouldn't. He was done running from things that scared him. Gone was the boy who ran when Alexander apologized, who kept his hands on doorknobs and eyes on the exits.

Alexander stayed too, less surprisingly. He stood with tears glistening in his eyes, but he held himself back from saying anything. He pushed back his grief, his pain, his disappointment for us. He, without even thinking about it, dismissed his own happiness because this was what we wanted. Gone was the self-absorbed boy from September, too caught up in his own desires to see how they were affecting the people around him.

And maybe we hadn't asked for this, didn't want it, didn't expect it. But we'd grown from it, found joy in it and each other. It hadn't been easy and we'd hurt each other when we'd been confused or angry or jealous. But we apologized and did better. We had figured shit out when real life came at us, unexpected and dangerous. Maybe we'd done things wrong and maybe there was more to learn but the bond buzzed happily in my chest and I didn't want to break it. We were better because of it and wasn't that the point of love?

They both looked at me, shoulders and chests tense. Alexander blew out a breath and nodded, moving to open the cure. He had his fingers wrapped around the cap of the container, about to twist, when I spoke.

"I don't want to take it."

Alexander nearly dropped the cure. "What?"

"I don't want to take it," I repeated through a clenched jaw and gritted teeth. The decision cut through my pride like a knife, but it didn't feel like murder. It felt like surgery. Like a cure. "I know we said we would, that we went through all the trouble of making it and getting it blessed. Hell, I literally died for it, but I don't *want* to drink it."

Alexander looked at Theo, confused. His words were slow. "So, just you and I take it—"

"I don't want you to take it either," I snapped.

Theo flinched. "I get it. I can take it by myself—"

"I'm so fucking sick," I said, anger inspiring tears, "of how often we all try to martyr ourselves for each other. It doesn't help. At what point are we all going to realize that this" – a quick, nearly violent gesture between the three of us – "doesn't work with only two of us? You and Alexander would rip each other apart. You and I would get so caught up in our thoughts, we'd never talk. Alexander and I would never escape our perfect, little dream world. It needs to be all three of us."

They both stared at me for a second. I cleared my throat and took a step back. The room seemed to close in on us. It felt like we were climbing up another cliff. But I'd dived off cliffs and I'd fallen too, and I would rather drown and die a million times before I tasted a single drop of that damned cure.

"I'm not sure what you're saying, Vanessa," Alexander said, jaw trembling. "If you don't want to take it, what do you want?"

I didn't want to decide.

Because there had to be a reason for all this. There had to be some greater truth to be learned from every fall, from every drowning, from every moment of pain lived and remembered. If I were to stand on that cliff with that other version of myself, the one with the long hair and golden skin and Greek accent. If I were to ask her what she wanted, what she'd chosen – well, she'd smile at me and shake her head.

She could never choose between the two of them.

My options weren't Theo or Alexander, anymore. It was Theo and Alexander or nothing.

Persephone's words echoed in my head. To decide was, in itself, a decision.

If I decided not to decide...

"Do you think you guys could get along?" I asked them, hands on my hips. Their heads snapped up from where they were concentrating on the floor. Alexander still looked confused, but there was something burning in Theo's eyes. Something like hope. "Because, I swear to Persephone, I'm not going to do this if you two are going to be at each other's throats constantly."

"Do what?" Alexander asked, frowning now.

"I think we could," Theo answered, taking a step closer to me. I was wary, looking him up and down, taking in his words and the way he reached to hold my hand. "Vanessa, are you considering—"

"Do what? Considering what?" Alexander asked again, and there was a little bit of divine demand tacked onto it. "I'm not sure what you're talking about, but there's a pretty good chance it involves me and you both know I can't do the mind reading thing—"

"We're not using the telepathy," I assured him. Theo looked at me with a kind of desperation. Like he needed me, at this moment, to take control. Like he'd said what he was able to say and the rest was up to me. "I think we're just on the same page for once."

"About what?" Alexander asked.

"I wasn't ready to talk about it that night," I said to them both. Theo nodded once. "But I am ready now. Alexander, do you love me?"

Alexander took a step back, like the question was a physical blow. Theo made a small noise, feeling that reaction, too, through their own abilities. "Vanessa, don't. Not when we're about to—"

"Do you?" I asked, taking a step closer. Theo stepped with me. "Be honest."

"Of course I do," he said, swallowing. "I have. For a while."

I wouldn't have asked if I wasn't sure. But hearing it was like a balm on an open wound. It felt a little bit like the weather outside. Building to something more. I hoped the snow would stick.

"Theo," I asked, turning to him. "Do you love me?"

He nodded, no hesitation as he answered, "I do."

"Do you love each other?" I asked, and this was the part that mattered the most. Because, as much as Theo would hate for me to think it, it was the truth. I was the Extra. They were the Originals. Though somehow, whether it was because of godly intervention or just pure luck between us, they loved me anyway. But none of this was even worth discussing if they didn't feel the same way for each other.

They were both quiet. It stretched into the hallway, into the storm outside. We all waited.

Alexander shook his head. "Not – not the way I love you."

The snow melted away, and I had to hide the disappointment freezing in my chest. Theo kept his face empty of any emotion, but he couldn't help the way he tensed at the words. He nodded, letting go of my hand and opening his mouth to admit defeat.

"But," Alexander continued, "I think I could learn to. I want to."

Theo licked his lips. "Yeah?"

"Yeah," Alexander answered. Theo's face changed, a glimpse into something much deeper than anything else he'd shown us today, and I wondered what Alexander was thinking to make him react like that. I'd ask at some point. "Do you?"

Theo shook his head, but he was smiling that half-smile and reaching to place a hand on his shoulder, solid and comforting as he spoke with such hope. "Not yet. But I want to, too."

"We've been an experiment this entire time," I answered, looking at my bracelets. "Aphrodite and Persephone's. Even Lux's, when she gave us those case studies and drew the comparisons. But let's start an experiment of our own."

"A trial run," Alexander finished, nodding. He let go of the cure.

"To see if it works for us," I agreed.

"Sounds smart enough to me," Theo said with a shrug. "How long?"

"A semester," I answered. "It took us that long to get to this point. We'll know if this is a success or a massive failure by the beginning of spring. When the first flowers blossom, maybe. Or the first baby birds—"

Theo grinned, bumping his shoulder into mine. "How about graduation?"

"Yeah," I said with a laugh. "That works, too."

"Wait," Alexander said, stepping away from his desk and closer to both of us. I offered him my other hand. He took it. Theo didn't offer his, not yet, but I could picture it happening soon and a different kind of burning erupted in my chest. It was a little like the burning of a bloody piece of paper. "Does that mean – we're really doing this?"

"Only if you want to," Theo murmured. "Only if we do it together."

"Together," Alexander breathed out like we had offered him the world. "Yeah, that sounds – well, it sounds perfect, if I'm telling the truth."

"I've never been able to make myself choose between the two of you," I told them, and I saw the same conclusion reflected in their eyes. "So, I'm done trying. I'm not choosing one of you. I'm choosing both, together."

Theo's mouth quirked up. "Together is a good idea."

"Yes," I agreed. "It is."

51

IT FALLS HERE

The snow crunched under my feet. I was leaving for the holidays in just a few hours and the December wind whipped at me as I made my way through the ravines for the last time this semester. But I wasn't cold. The cloak was thick and warm, protecting me from my head to the toes of my boots.

As I walked into the small campsite set up by the banks of the icy river, hooded heads turned in my direction. My own face was hidden in the shadows and I smiled at them. White teeth grinned back.

One figure stood and I recognized her posture. Strong, ready. Seven red stones glowed across her chest and it was the only burst of color in the brown and white of the forest. She pushed her hood back. Everyone followed the movement. A dozen faces were revealed, forming a circle around their leader. They were all smiling at me.

"Wanaxa," Rose greeted. "We're happy you made it."

"I'm happy to be here," I answered.

"Four weeks have passed," she said, taking three steps

towards me. She stood in the middle of the Cult of Persephone. I took three steps to meet her. "Do you have an answer for us?"

"I do."

"To join us," she said to everyone, her voice carrying into the emptiness, "you were forced to remember your past, to remember yourself in your first life. How was that?"

I grinned. "Difficult."

Her own grin widened. "As it should be."

She placed her fingers on the stone in the middle of the necklace, the largest one, and it hummed under her touch. Taking a final breath, seemingly to brace herself, she pulled the chain over her head. With an unshaking hand, she offered it to me, holding it between us. "Do you accept the offer of the goddess?"

My answer was thousands of years in the making. Life and death, drowning and undrowning, indecision and desperate wanting – all coming together for a simple response. The words were like a balm in my mind, in my throat, on my tongue.

Finally, I answered, "I accept."

Power burned like love in my chest.

I knew both, now.

Almost as well as I knew myself.

A GRADUATION

The April sun was warmer than the weathermen had predicted on the news this morning and thousands of Golden Valley students gathered at the largest, and now hottest, venue downtown. It was humid – we were in Michigan, after all – and the sheer number of people brought the temperature of the auditorium up a few degrees.

I sat next to Alexander, whose leg was bouncing with excitement. I pressed my hand down on his thigh and the jittering relaxed a little. He was wearing his nicest clothes, still feeling the pressure to impress the family members around us. Tamara was sitting on my other side, an old camera around her neck. Theo's mother was on Alexander's other side, the source of his anxiety.

The ceremony itself took too long. The president of the university read the names slowly and the keynote speaker was kind of redundant, but nothing could stop the immense joy I'd felt when I saw Theo crossing the stage in his blue and gold gown and mortarboard hat.

Unable to restrain himself, Alexander let out a cheer. It must have resounded in Theo's head because he grinned out at the crowd while he shook the president's hand. Tamara's camera flashed a thousand times and Alexander's phone was out too.

You look so good! I thought, watching him step down the stairs and sit in the section with the other graduating studio art majors. His Cult of Apollo sash blended in with the rest, but he still stood out. He always did.

I'm just glad I didn't trip.

Through Theo, I heard Alexander add, *I think your mother is crying and I'm sitting here, not knowing how to help. Please send help. For her or me. Either is acceptable.* The words were laced with a sense of panic, but Theo just sent me some comforting thoughts to relay as the president instructed the graduates to move their tassels to the other side of their caps.

They did, hollering their victory to the rafters.

I lost track of the next few minutes until Theo somehow found us in the crowd. He scooped me into his arms, spinning me around. Shrieking with laughter, I threw my arms around his neck and pulled him in for a kiss the moment he set me down. We were both smiling too much for it to be graceful.

We pulled apart and I moved my hands down to hold him around the waist. He pulled Alexander to him, cupped his sharp jaw with a calloused hand before he kissed him with just as much excitement as he had me. I pressed my cheek into Theo's arm, grinning into the slippery fabric of the gown.

Alexander pulled away and rested his forehead against Theo's. "I'm so proud of you."

"I know they're lovely, Theodore," Theo's mother said, laughing and crying as she moved closer, "but, please, it's our turn now." She opened her arms and Theo stepped into them, tucking her into his broad chest and kissing her forehead. Tamara hugged them both and her eyes were a little misty too.

Alexander sighed, grabbing me and then pulling Theo into him. "It's a good day."

And, Theo added in our heads, *it's about to get better.*

The ravines looked different in the spring but it'd been a slow transition for me. Since taking the necklace, I'd ventured into the local wilderness at least once a week with the Cult of Persephone girls. But each new green sprout, under the skeleton veins of dead leaves, was still a surprise to me and it made me smile.

Theo cursed as he collided with a spider's web ahead of me and Alexander laughed. The sound didn't travel far, with the river just on the other side of the wall of trees. But the first birds to return from the South peered down at us from their perches, glittering eyes annoyed. "The spot is coming up," I told them, raising my voice for the first time since we had set out and left concrete behind for packed dirt. "Just beyond these trees."

They didn't respond, but I could feel their relief in the bond. This wasn't an easy walk if you didn't know the right steps to take. I had made plenty of mistakes the first few times I had traveled on the hidden paths. It got easier every day.

In just a few minutes, we were wading through the branches and the river became visible. Something about it must've struck them as dangerous, because they both turned to me as if ready to protect.

"It's okay," I told them, moving past them to the edge of the water. They tensed further, but I put my hand in the water where it brushed against the bank. "I'm not afraid. Alexander, you have the cure?"

He nodded, taking his arms from his backpack to pull the cure out. It was unopened. In fact, I was surprised it wasn't covered with dust. When things had started looking good for the three of us, Alexander had handed it off to Eliza with the instruction to put it somewhere dark and cold and out-of-sight. Where it belonged.

"I can't believe we had to come back here to do this," Theo huffed, shrugging his own pack off and throwing it on the ground. He pushed his hair back from his eyes and the strands were wet with sweat. Much hotter than the weatherman had predicted.

"Back to the source," I reminded him, tilting my head toward the river. "Take nothing you don't intend to put back. Besides," I said, grinning as I took my jacket off, "I have fond memories of the memories the fall gave me."

"You'd be the only one," Theo said with a scowl, but there's a lightness about him that didn't seem to dim. I knew he was happy, with his graduation and our progress. He didn't realize how often he thought about getting rid of the cure, how frequently he daydreamed about flushing it down the toilet or throwing it off the pier at Alexander's house.

I held my hand out and Alexander placed the bottle in my hands. It tingled where the glass touched me. The power it contained and and thought of how close we came to drinking the vile stuff made me shiver. "Shoes and socks off, boys."

"You're in charge," Alexander said, immediately hopping on one foot to take off his right shoe. Theo used a nearby tree for balance. I sat on the ground, not uncomfortable with the cold or the dirt. In fact, almost the opposite, I stuck the tips of my fingers in the earth and a sense of calm came over me.

When we were all barefoot and our pants were rolled up beyond our ankles, I led them into the water. Theo, who was always so warm, surrounded by coffee and the energetic buzzing of a tattoo machine and Alexander's thoughts, flinched and almost jumped back out.

"Stay," Alexander said to him, tugging him further in.

Something melted in Theo's dark eyes and he relaxed again. "Okay."

I popped the cap off the cure, it fizzled like a can of pop and the white bubbles expanded. We made a promise to the gods, to each other. Then I poured the cure into the river. When it touched the water, there was a second where the gold remained, but then the color dissolved and there was nothing left to its power.

"Well," Alexander said as we watched it wash away. His hand found mine. "That was easy."

This wasn't the happily ever after I had imagined as a kid. The air was too humid and the water was too cold. The setting was all wrong and there was no perfect fairytale prince and no white stallion to ride us into the sunset.

"If you say so," Theo snorted, pulling him into his side and dragging him out of the water. "You guys ready to head back? We have a lot of shit to get done before I have to pretend to be surprised by the party everyone put together."

But that was because it wasn't an ending in the first place. It was a once upon a time.

"I'm ready."

ACKNOWLEDGMENTS

The Promise of Lightning is, first and foremost, a story about love. It's fitting, then, that this story reflects all the love I've received while writing it. Every bit of it led to this moment, this crazy accomplishment, and I couldn't have done it without each and every one of you.

First, I want to thank my friends, who've offered so much input and support for this little story. There's no particular order to this, I promise. Thank you to Sarah, the first ever fan of these characters and their messiness. Thank you to Jake, for all the coffee shops and adventures. Thank you to Kyle, for an always appreciated critical look and endless encouragement while this story was in the trenches. Thank you to Brianne, my first editor, and Michele, my first cover designer. To Ronan, my own platonic soulmate. To Joe, my big brother. To Allyson, Amy, Alex, Emmy, Emily K., Jocelyn, Katie and all my study abroad friends. I love you all. Thank you.

Thank you to my professors in the Classics Department, for teaching me and inspiring me, and to all my colleagues at Grand Valley for your excitement. Thank you to Zola and my wonderful team at SmashBear, who really believed in this story.

And thank you, Mom. I've dedicated every book I've ever written to you and it's been an easy choice, every time. You're my best friend. Thank you for everything. I love you so muches.

And, finally, thank you, O Muse, who inspired me on that train from Rome to Florence. Whatever you struck me with on that ride through the Italian countryside was the good stuff. This story has been one of the most special parts of my life for years and I'm grateful to have written it for everyone, but also just for myself. Let's do it again sometime, yeah?

And thank you, readers, for giving this story a chance. I appreciate you.

# #
DECLARE
YOUR
CULT

Thank you for supporting SmashBear Publishing and our authors.

For more information about our authors, upcoming releases and what we publish, you can check out our website

www.smashbearpublishing.com

Or find us on:

Dare you face the abyss within?

A SmashBear anthology in support of Women's Aid

Let me ask you a question. It's a pretty straight forward question, but one that you shouldn't rush to answer. Do you believe in magic?

Printed in Great Britain
by Amazon